EMBRACE THE POWER

EMBRACE THE POWER, Book #9 of the Blood Rose Series, a Paranormal Romance Series

By Caris Roane

THE BLOOD ROSE SERIES
BOOK NINE

EMBRACE THE POWER

CARIS ROANE

Do You Enjoy E-Books?

I love giving them away, especially as a benefit to my newsletter subscribers. To claim your e-Book today, and to be eligible for subscriber-only giveaways, subscribe to my newsletter on my home page at www.carisroane.com

Hugs,
C. R.
June, 2016

Dear Reader

Welcome to the final installment of the Blood Rose Series called EMBRACE THE POWER! Here's a brief look at the story:

Mastyr Vampire Stone wants to bond with Aralynn, his battle partner, until he learns she lives a double life as a woman he despises...

For hundreds of years, Stone has lived a solitary life, serving Tannisford Realm as he battles the deadly Invictus wraith-pairs with his Vampire Guard. In recent weeks, he's run missions with a beautiful wolf named Aralynn. Mortally wounded by the Ancient Fae, Aralynn saves Stone's life and one taste of her healing blood confirms she's a blood rose. He's all set to bond with her when he learns she lives a double life as a woman he despises. But how can he cut Aralynn off when her blood calls to him like nothing he's ever known before?

Rosamunde experienced the first real freedom of her thousand years of life when Davido the Wise taught her how to transform into Aralynn, a perfect battle partner for Mastyr Stone. But how was she to know that fighting wraith-pairs beside the Mastyr would incite every suppressed desire she's ever had? Worse, she carries three secrets, each one of which has the power to sever her relationship with him forever. How can she earn his trust, when she's lied to him and deceived him the whole time she's served beside him?

~ ~ ~

I hope you've enjoyed the Blood Rose Series. I had a wonderful time, though very emotional, as I wrote the last book of the series.

Enjoy!
And now, have a Wonderful Day and an Even Better Night!

Caris Roane

Chapter One

"Thinking about kissing that wolf of yours?"

Stone pulled his focus away from the large central monitor in his Communication Center. From his command station, he turned in a slow pivot to stare down his personal assistant, Delia.

"You've officially lost the last card in your deck. And she's not 'my' wolf. Aralynn and I run missions together. That's all." He tried to sound both innocent and slightly offended, despite the fact he'd been thinking about the exact shape of the woman's lips for the past half hour. Aralynn would be checking in soon.

But had he been thinking about kissing her? Hell yeah, about every other minute for the past seven weeks.

Delia's right brow rose as she lifted her head from her laptop and stared back. She wasn't intimidated by him, something he loved about her. "Hah," she whispered. "The minute she appears at the door, you light up like you've just discovered air."

Busted.

Despite the accuracy of her observation, he lifted his chin. "You don't know anything about it."

Delia ignored this comment. "She's pretty, I'll give her that.

Hey, I've got an idea. You should take her as your date to the gala. I'd like to see the two of you do one of those levitating waltzes you mastyrs are famous for."

"Not gonna happen."

He'd thought about it, though. But taking a date to a formal event would give rise to all kinds of gossip. The gala was Delia's idea and would be held in celebration of the Federation of the Nine Realms, a new organization to which all the ruling mastyrs now belonged.

It was an amazing time in his world. No one thought that a federation of the realms was possible, the mastyrs being supremely independent types. But the Ancient Fae had made it clear she wouldn't quit trying to take over their world until the last realm-person was buried six feet under.

Stone had pushed for the Federation as well as the Combined Forces of the Vampire Guards, and Shifter and Troll Brigades of all the realms. Over the past several months, since Ian and Regan had almost captured Margetta in the mountains of Camberlaune, Stone had worked hard to build a buttress against Margetta. He and Ian together had organized hundreds of training sessions for the Combined Forces, running drills and shaping a real army to battle against Margetta when the time came.

As for the gala, all the movers and shakers of each realm would be there, hundreds of elected officials. The ruling mastyrs would also attend, each with his bonded blood rose. If Stone took Aralynn as his date, the question would be raised: Was she his blood rose?

Like hell he was ready for that kind of question. The blood rose phenomenon had swept through the Nine Realms, assaulting one mastyr vampire after another. He'd escaped so far, but there'd been no indication Aralynn had blood rose ability. He didn't exactly crave her. Okay, maybe he did, but he'd been without a girlfriend for a while. It was time he hooked up with someone for a few months. He just wasn't sure how wise it was to get involved with his battle partner.

Delia, who seemed to be full of all kinds of ideas about Aralynn, pressed on. "And all these unattached Guardsmen, they try not to look at her, but they do. You might want to put a wolf-mark on her. Just sayin'." Because she was a wolf, sex and a good bite at the back of the neck would help keep unwanted suitors away, if temporarily.

Yup, he'd thought about biting her as well, and in more than one way. He had to take a couple of deep breaths, because the thought of his fangs tapping into the woman—

Still, he had no intention of talking this over with his executive assistant. "How about you keep your troll nose out of my affairs."

He wished especially that she hadn't spoken of the other men in his Communication Center. This place was alive with some of the most eligible bachelors in all the Nine Realms. A couple of the Guardsmen were even approaching mastyr status and all the warriors were built as hell.

Worse, he'd seen Aralynn checking them out.

He leaned close to Delia and growled. "And if you know what's good for you, I suggest you don't bring up these men again."

"Jealous?"

"No," he snapped. Like hell he would admit to anything so absurd, especially when what he really felt went way beyond jealousy. To put it simply, he was ready to kill if anyone so much as touched Aralynn, even if by accident.

Her lips quirked. "Ease-down, Mastyr. You've got your battle power ramped up and it's throwing off the monitors."

He shifted his gaze to the battery of flat screens that encompassed the main north wall of his center. Half the monitors were flickering and several of his men had turned to stare at him.

He took a deep breath and calmed himself down. The Nine Realms was a world of frequencies not unlike the way electricity and light moved. Lately, this had been happening a lot, that his emotions would charge his battle energy and afflict the screens.

He took a couple more deep breaths until the flickers and sparks began to subside.

Once he had his battle energy under control, the monitors resumed their placid response to the usual input. He saw the main streets of a number of his villages, rolling surveillance that watched for any sign of the Invictus enemy throughout Tannisford Realm.

Delia leaned close. "Apologies, Mastyr. I only meant to tease you, not destroy the electronics." She chuckled.

Delia was like a sister to him. He'd been raised by adoptive troll parents, so he understood troll-ness really well. They loved to gossip, that much was true, so he forgave Delia most of her indiscreet comments and questions.

She was a troll of some power with flowing blond hair and beautifully shaped hands. Her species was short and she ranged on the short side of squat. But she sat on a really tall stool in front of her workstation, in order to meet him eye-to-eye, which she reached through levitation.

"Yeah, well, no harm, no foul." He was way too on edge about

Aralynn. He wished he could get the wolf out of his mind, but he'd been running missions with her from the night she showed up ready to serve almost seven weeks ago. For a powerful wolf, she also carried an unusual secondary fae ability of prescience.

She'd come out of nowhere, which at first had made her suspect. But when she'd told him that Davido had sent her, he'd contacted a man he considered to be the wisest realm-person in their world. Davido had vouched for Aralynn and had informed him that she had special abilities that would help to predict Invictus intrusions in Tannisford.

Davido, had been right. From the first, damn if Aralynn hadn't matched Stone in power as well as in her love for doing battle. More than once, she said she was glad to be 'doing' after all this time. When he'd asked her what she meant, she'd talked about not liking her previous job as a castle guard very much. She preferred to be active and the Ferrenden Peace castle staff just didn't have a lot to do.

He'd never known someone who'd lived in Ferrenden Peace most of her life, so he'd learned a lot about the place that Queen Rosamunde had kept secret from the Nine Realms for the past thousand years. Everyone had thought the place a myth until Mastyr Quinlan and his woman, Batya, had somehow found their way to her kingdom.

Surprise. Queen Rosamunde was real.

He'd paid her a state visit, of course, as all the mastyrs had. But he didn't like her very much. She'd kept her secret by sustaining a veil of mist around Ferrenden Peace, a veil that Aralynn insisted had but one purpose: To keep Margetta, the Ancient Fae, away from Rosamunde's kingdom. Apparently, if

Margetta ever found her way inside, she'd gain some kind of additional power that would make it possible for her to take over the Nine Realms.

He thought it sounded like a lot of plain-old horseshit. From his perspective, he considered Rosamunde a coward, pure and simple. She'd lived an indolent, secluded life, safe in her stone castle, claiming that her protective mist had somehow served to keep the Nine Realms safe.

Hogwash.

But Aralynn was cut from a different cloth. She had a warrior's heart, one more reason he kept thinking about putting his lips on her mouth and all other kinds of places.

Sweet Goddess, Aralynn. She was tall, which he loved because he topped out at six-seven these days, having added another half-inch during the past few months. She was also pretty, with soulful brown eyes, full lips, pronounced cheekbones and an unusual perfume, like an herb found deep in the woods that worked him up. When he was around her, he had a hard time keeping his cock in a respectful position.

Delia was right, though. He'd been thinking about kissing her. A lot. And like the hot-blooded vampire he was, he'd almost taken her in his arms only last night when they'd been on patrol. It had been just before dawn and as usual, they'd battled at least a half dozen wraith-pairs and saved a whole lot of realm-folk.

By the time dawn had started sending warning signals down his spine, he'd returned Arralyn to the gates of Ferrenden Peace. He'd leaned in to kiss her, but she'd pulled back, then vanished before he could get his arms around her. The woman had power.

He was taking it slow because he could sense her resistance

like a steel rod running through her. Maybe she'd been badly hurt in the past, he didn't know. Yet he didn't know her well enough to ask.

He knew she wanted him, though. Her woodsy, herbal scent was laced with so many come-and-get-me pheromones, he'd almost jumped her then and there.

The trouble was, the woman could teleport so he'd have about as much chance of holding onto her as flying to the moon.

The last thing he wanted to do, however, was to share any of this with Delia.

He changed the subject. "How's that husband of yours?"

"Mm. As stubborn as ever—"

Something in the tone of her voice caused Stone to glance at her once more. He watched her shake her head, her three forehead ridges compressed together, her lips forming a tight line. The words were right, but they didn't match the concern he saw. He knew something was wrong.

He leaned in her direction. His Communication Center had doubled the staff from a year ago and there were so many ears listening to anything either of them said that he switched to telepathy. *What gives and you'd better tell me now.*

In all the decades she'd been with him, he'd never seen Delia shed a tear, not even when her favorite dog got slain by a wraith-pair. But she had tears in her eyes now. *Elias is missing, Mastyr.*

How long has he been gone?

I shouldn't be bothering you with this.

He reached over and took her arm gently in hand and repeated the question. *How long? Please, tell me. And don't think I'll let this go. You're important to me.*

Delia's lips turned down, but she squared her shoulders. *Two days and a night.*

That length of time during the war against the Invictus wraith-pairs might as well have been a week.

Any word from him during that time? A text? Anything?

No.

Sweet Goddess, why didn't you tell me sooner?

At that, she turned to glare at him then swept her hand from one side of the room to the other, encompassing the battery of images that each monitor displayed constantly. Forty realm-folk, half of them Guardsmen, manned the various stations. *You have something far more important on your mind than whatever might have happened to my husband. Maybe the Invictus got him, hauled him off to force him into a wraith-pair bond or maybe they slaughtered him. That makes me one of how many tens of thousands this has happened to? So why should I get any special treatment?*

Stone knew she was right. She shouldn't get special treatment. But she'd been the best assistant he'd ever had, she never let him get away with his usual bullshit, and dammit, she was family.

He looked around and seeing that one of his lieutenants had just come in, he called to him. "Harris, I need you on this."

Delia shook her head at him. "But Mastyr—"

He turned to her. "This is my call. Don't worry. All we're going to do right now is gather more information. I promise, I won't jeopardize any part of the war effort. Okay?"

She put a hand to her chest, her soft blue eyes stricken. "I couldn't live with the guilt if you did."

"Understood." One more reason he valued Delia. She knew the meaning of sacrifice.

Harris levitated swiftly to Stone's station. He was a full six-five and muscled and had long blond hair that he wore pulled tight into the woven Guardsman clip so that his cheekbones stood out like blades. He wasn't a mastyr yet, but damn near close.

When Harris reached Delia's workstation, Stone told him the gist then added. "We need more information."

Harris frowned slightly and glanced at Delia. "You and your husband live on a farm, out by Rutland, right?"

"We do. But Elias left there day before yesterday. He and a friend heard about this old gold mine southwest of Charborne. He'd gone there to see if the claim was worth re-opening."

The mention of Charborne set Stone back on his heels. Though it had been a long time since he'd lived in the area, the memories rushed forward as though having a life of their own. His chest tightened painfully. His parents had died near the village in one of the worst Invictus attacks of the Nine Realms during which half the villagers had perished.

He still owned his family's property on the outskirts of Charborne, some three-hundred acres, in the southwest quadrant. But for a long time now, he'd leased it out to a fae-troll couple who had lived on the land for the past two hundred years. He should have sold it to them long ago, but every time he got the process started, something stopped him. The past would always rise up to haunt him, tearing his peace down bit by bit, until he had to let the sale go.

Delia's strong voice brought him back sharply. "Stone? You okay?"

"It's Charborne."

"Oh, right. I forgot," she said. "Sorry."

He ground his teeth. "Can't be helped." He turned toward the monitors and called to the man in charge. "Alex, I need the current feed from Charborne. We may have a problem out there."

"Got it," Alex called back.

Stone crossed his arms over his chest, his gaze glued to the monitor directly above Alex. He'd built the center that now linked to thousands of cameras around his realm. Every main thoroughfare of every village had three cameras, more if the lane curved. The cities had hundreds and his crew checked the feeds constantly.

Behind him, he could hear operators talking softly to realm-folk who called the Invictus-sighting hotline he'd set up. Sure, they got more crank calls than he'd like, but his people had become one of his best weapons in alerting the Tannisford Vampire Guard and the Shifter Brigade to Invictus activity across the realm.

He waited as Alex's keyboard clacked softly. More than once the feed of Charborne came up then flickered away. "What's the problem, Alex?"

"Not sure. Could be the cameras."

Stone didn't like it. He had a missing troll and a wonky feed.

He turned slightly in Harris's direction. "Let's get a team out there to see if anything's going on." He could feel Delia's sudden tension beside him.

"Will do," Harris said. "But there's something else. I got a call from Merhaine that the Vampire Guard hasn't been able to locate Mastyr Gerrod for the past couple of hours. It's probably nothing, but about five minutes ago, I got a similar call from one of Mastyr Ethan's lieutenants."

"And you tried reaching them both?"

"I tried my cell and telepathy. Couldn't make contact with either of them. Of course, there could be lots of reasons, but it seemed odd."

"It does seem odd. Stay on that situation, would you? And if in the next hour or so, you still can't firm up a connection, let me know."

Harris nodded. "Also, did you see the latest analysis sheet on several of the western villages? Charborne was one of them."

"It was next on my list." For the past several months, the ruling mastyrs had hired several data analysts to compile numbers from as far back as each realm had written information on hand. Some of the realms had records from eight centuries ago.

Harris added, "In Tannisford, Charborne is one of the places that's had higher-than-usual Invictus sightings century after century."

Delia set her hands on her keyboard. "Let me pull it up." She tapped on her computer and quickly scrolled through her files. It wasn't lost on Stone that her fingers trembled. Yet, she kept on working.

When she found the document, she levitated to Stone's shoulder height and passed her laptop to him.

He scanned the list and there it was. Charborne had one of the highest recurrence rates in Tannisford and ranked tenth in all Nine Realms. He handed her laptop back. "That settles it. We need to get out there. Harris, take several squads. As soon as you have confirmation of even one wraith-pair, let me know."

Harris nodded, then headed toward the door. Stone could hear him talking quietly into his shoulder com and issuing orders.

So much had changed throughout the Nine Realms over the

past few years. All the mastyrs had upgraded to more efficient methods of communication. Not every realm-person could communicate through telepathy and even those that could were often limited by distance.

As for the gold mine, he remembered a small operation that started up about two-hundred-and-fifty-years ago.

Delia said, "Sorry that it had to be Charborne."

He avoided meeting Delia's gaze. "It's okay. All that matters is that we get this sorted, the sooner the better, and bring Elias home."

"So, do you know where the mine is?" She settled her laptop back on her desk.

Stone frowned at the screen. "Pull up a topographical map of the area and I can show you exactly what we're looking at. The good news here is that I think the mine is at the edge of a densely wooded area. If there was an attack in the vicinity, Elias was in the right location to secure a hiding place."

Delia did her magic and a few seconds later, Stone had the laptop once more in hand. He scrolled again, then put his finger on the spot. There was even a pick-axe graphic, typical of maps showing mine locations. "The mine is about five hundred yards north of Charbeetle Creek. I'll let Harris know."

"Thank you." Delia buried her face in her hands. He could see by the movements of her shoulders she'd lost it. But he'd been with her a long time. She was a woman with grit and would come around soon enough. In the meantime, he settled his hand on her shoulder and kept it there.

There was nothing to do now except wait.

His thoughts, as usual, turned to Aralynn. If a heavy

Invictus attack was going on out at Charborne, he suspected it wouldn't be long before Aralynn contacted him. Though she was predominantly wolf-shifter, her powerful fae abilities had more than once clued him in on a dangerous situation in Tannisford, things that his Guard patrols or village-mounted cameras weren't catching. But why her fae visions hadn't picked up on this situation before, he didn't know.

Unless, of course, Margetta herself had her hands in it. She had enough power to render the camera feeds useless and to disguise the area from outsiders. The more he thought about it, his own vampire instincts began to curl and writhe inside him.

The Ancient Fae had to be involved.

But where was Aralynn?

~ ~ ~

Rosamunde paced her private living room situated at the less formal west end of the castle. She could feel the sacred elf-lord power rumbling at a distance, which meant something was afoot in Tannisford and Stone would need her soon. She'd learned from experience to let the visions come when they wanted, not to force them.

But she was in deep trouble with Stone because if he ever learned the truth about her, that she was both Rosamunde and Aralynn, he'd never forgive her. The man had a hard head and a stubborn streak a mile wide.

A moan left her throat and she actually wrung her hands. Somewhere in the middle of partnering with Stone, the worst had happened: She was pretty sure she'd fallen in love with the intractable mastyr of Tannisford.

Goddess help her!

She had more secrets locked away as well, each of which could set an impenetrable block wall between herself and Stone. Because of it, she'd become a ridiculous tangle of nerves.

She'd tried to tell Stone the truth more than once, especially when he'd almost kissed her the night before while she'd been in her Aralynn form. But the words had gotten stuck in her throat as though they'd grown claws and held on for good.

She was in so much trouble especially because Stone didn't respect her as Rosamunde. He thought her lazy, uncaring and cowardly.

"Did you summon me?"

The woman's voice startled her. She whirled around and there was Vojalie, the tall elegant fae who had served as her counselor for centuries.

She threw her hands wide. "Yes. Vojalie, I can't do this anymore."

"Can't do what?"

"Keep being Aralynn when I'm with Stone when he doesn't know that I'm Rosamunde as well. I want to quit."

"But I thought you were enjoying your missions with Stone. You begged for years to be allowed to participate in the war in a substantial way and now you are." There was an amused light in Vojalie's eye.

"Are you laughing at me?"

"A little, but what did you expect? You've always had a thing for Stone, even at a distance."

Rosamunde dropped onto an ottoman, shoulders slumped. "You're right and I've become this ridiculous, weak-kneed female that I hardly recognize." She shifted her gaze to Vojalie's. "He only has to look at me with those beautiful mossy-green eyes of his and I swear I starting melting into a puddle. Have you ever experienced anything like that in your life?"

Rosamunde didn't miss the soft light that entered Vojalie's eyes. "Oh, yes. With Davido. All the time. Still."

Rosamunde found it very hard to believe. Davido was the ugliest troll she'd ever seen. How could Vojalie have what was obviously a full-on lust for the man?

On the other hand, Davido's charisma was pretty much off the charts, so perhaps that was the reason he'd wooed and won the most beautiful fae in the Nine Realms.

Vojalie gave herself a shake and drew close. She even settled her hand on Rosamunde's shoulder. "Stone has a severe bark and a quick temper. We both know that. Tell him the truth, tell him who you are. He'll understand. Eventually."

"He'll take my head off. You know how much he despises *this woman*." She waved a hand to encompass her long silk gown and the intricate braids she wore.

Vojalie's lips quirked once more and her eyes danced. "That he does. But I must say, it's only because you've done a very poor job at helping him to understand that you've single-handedly protected the entire Nine Realms against Margetta all these years."

"He scoffed when I told him, I mean when 'Aralynn' told him. He basically said that 'Rosamunde' was indolent. Maybe I was … am … I don't know. I'm very confused."

"You're halfway in love with him, is all. And sometimes it makes it hard to find the right words."

At that, Rosamunde grew very still. "I've tried to tell him that

'Rosamunde' found it difficult to leave Ferrenden Peace because supporting the mist was that important. And it is, I know it is. I remember when I went to heal Lorelei in Walvashorr, I was so afraid Margetta would realize Ferrenden Peace was unguarded. I'm still afraid, even now, when I leave my kingdom to run missions with Stone."

"You're afraid, even though Davido and I are helping to support the mist?"

"Yes. Even then. But only because I know what Margetta is capable of." She rose slowly to her feet and met Vojalie eye-to-eye. They were both tall women. "I love our land so much and our people. I haven't begrudged the sacrifice of service I've had to endure, not even a little."

"Or the loneliness?" Vojalie brushed her fingers over Rosamunde's cheek. "Davido and I both have felt for your plight and we value so much what you've done for our world. Would you like me to talk to Stone? Ease the way?"

"Oh, no, please, no never. I must figure this out. I just don't have your confidence that he'll understand."

Vojalie moved to sit down on the sofa. "So, did he kiss you last night?"

Rosamunde gasped, a long, odd sound. She even squeezed her eyes shut at the memory. "He wanted to and I wanted him to. We came so close, but I couldn't go through with it."

Vojalie giggled. "I feel very guilty about this because I'm enjoying your experience like a schoolgirl sharing secrets. So, do you think you'll let him tonight?"

"No. I can't. It would be very bad. He needs to know that Aralynn is Rosamunde." She put a hand to her chest.

"Well, if you want my advice—"

"Always."

Vojalie's lips curved. "Personally, I think you're being overly fastidious. Why not let the relationship with Stone, as Aralynn, take its course. I believe somewhere in there the situation will resolve itself in a very natural way. He'll come to see you as the brave wolf with whom he runs dangerous missions and the woman who has for centuries kept Margetta away from the elf-lord power that resides in Ferrenden Peace."

Rosamunde forced herself to relax and to consider Vojalie's counsel. The truth was, she craved a physical relationship with Stone. At times, when she was near him in her wild wolf form, she didn't know how she kept from jumping him.

What she really feared was that if he ever did kiss her, she wouldn't be able to hold back, which was why, last night, she'd panicked. She was still embarrassed that she'd teleported away from him just before his lips touched hers.

Once again, the familiar power of her kingdom, built on elf-lord power, began to rumble. It was a sacred vibration she'd known for the past thousand years. This power, which Davido had once explained to her as the same source that gave rise to the infamous elf-lords, was what helped all three of them sustain the mist veil around Ferrenden Peace.

While both Davido and Vojalie seemed unaffected by using the power, the moment it touched Rosamunde, searing pain drove through her body. She simply didn't have enough natural ability to bear the vibrations easily, not like her mother, Evelyn, when she'd been the queen.

Rosamunde had lived with this pain every night of her

thousand years and there was nothing she could do about it, but let it flow. Until recent weeks, the elf-lord power had served a sole purpose in renewing her strength nightly to sustain the mist. Now, however, that she ran missions with Stone, the pulsing energy also delivered up the visions that allowed her to see where the Invictus wraith-pairs were harming realm-folk.

As she opened herself up, the power surged and every muscle in both legs cramped until the only way she could remain upright was to levitate. She focused her energy in her arms and shoulders in order to remain in a standing position.

She breathed through the pain until she could let the power flow. As soon as it did, she began quickly to rebuild the veil of mist, a process she repeated every night.

What she couldn't get Stone to understand or perhaps to believe was that Vojalie was right; Rosamunde had been the sole reason Margetta had so far failed to conquer the Nine Realms. If the Ancient Fae, as Margetta was known, had once accessed the elf-lord power that originated in Ferrenden Peace and which caused Rosamunde so much nightly pain, Margetta would have funneled that power into her war machine. A thousand years of her savage rule would have come to every citizen of the Nine Realms.

She felt the veil of mist grow stronger and as it did, the pain dissipated.

She'd never told anyone about her suffering except Vojalie and Davido. The powerful fae had tried to work with her to help her channel the power better but it had come down to something very simple: Rosamunde did not have the proper physical structure for the process.

As the stream of energy receded, Rosamunde dropped from her levitating state to the woven carpet on her stone living room floor.

Vojalie was with her immediately. "I'm so sorry you've had to endure this."

"Actually, I'm not." And she wasn't. If she'd obeyed her mother as a child, Evelyn would still be alive. A thousand years of pain seemed like a small punishment for being the cause of her own mother's death.

She took a couple of deep breaths, grateful the pain was gone. "Thank you for coming to me tonight and lending your counsel. I don't easily go-with-the-flow, but I will try to where Stone is concerned. As for the mist, I've repaired it fully so you and Davido shouldn't have any problems. Will you both be at Joseph's for the evening?"

Vojalie snickered. "That forest gremlin should be shot. Have you seen his lair lately? I vow he has enough stolen goods in there to support a small nation."

"He's hopeless, yet somehow I adore him." She'd met Joseph a few decades ago when he'd been trying to steal a birdbath from her private castle garden. She'd never met a forest gremlin before. In fact, realm-folk rarely ever saw them. Yet, Joseph had stood there, then commented that she was as pretty as a sunset, what with her red hair and violet eyes.

He'd become an occasional confidante, though she reminded herself that self-interest would always define a forest gremlin and Joseph no less so. He'd left the garden without taking the birdbath, but by the next evening, the small stone edifice was gone. She hadn't been able to figure out how he'd managed it until he invited her to take tea in his underground dwelling. When she saw his intricate system of pulleys and rolling carts, she understood how the eighteen-inch tall creature had managed the theft.

Rosamunde shrugged. "He's a good man, he loves his wife, and he does everything he can to keep impressing her with his thieving abilities. The truth is, I hold him in great affection, though there are times I want to kill him."

"Same here." When Vojalie laughed, Rosamunde joined her. After a moment, Vojalie continued, "Davido is with him now and will be there through the night."

"But not you?"

"Not this time. Bernice has been cutting molars and is miserable without me, so I'll be returning to Merhaine to care for her. Don't worry, though. Davido can support the mist by himself."

"I'm sure he can." The old troll had more power than any realm-person she knew.

But there was a sudden odd light in Vojalie's eye, one of serious concern. Yet, she remained silent.

Rosamunde watched her for a moment. "What are you not telling me?"

Vojalie caught both her hands and squeezed them hard. "You'll need to be strong tonight, Rosamunde, stronger than you've ever been. And for the next few nights, as well. My instincts tell me we're fast reaching a crisis with the Ancient Fae. But that's all I can tell you. I can't even give you a direction for my concern."

Rosamunde squeezed her hands back. "Thank you for

the warning and please don't worry about it. I've been feeling something similar." Looking into the future was a difficult and not always advisable undertaking. Sometimes it was better not to know too much.

Rosamunde felt a new soft vibration in the air, very fae. She also felt the elf-lord power ramping up again.

Vojalie looked around and lifted her arms. "I can feel that Stone needs you, or rather Aralynn. I'm getting something about Charborne, the village where Stone grew up."

"Me, too. And a vision is coming."

"I'll stay with you."

"Thank you."

Rosamunde closed her eyes and accepted the terrible pain all over again. Because it was the second wave of the evening, she bore it better than the first.

This time, it was the vision she'd been waiting for and it came swiftly, as often happened after she'd channeled the elf-lord power for mist-rebuilding. She wasn't surprised that Vojalie felt it as well. These were fae attributes.

In the vision, she saw Stone's Vampire Guard battling a number of wraith-pairs in the village of Charborne. At what was twenty minutes in the future, she saw herself in the woods approaching what looked like an abandoned mine. She had the sense that Stone was on his way as well and would meet her there. At that point, the vision ended.

As the elf-lord power eased away, she shook out her legs. She also let a degree of healing flow through her body, which helped to ease the troublesome elf-lord power.

Despite the discomfort, there was one other thing that the

elf-lord frequency had given her, which made transportation a non-issue for her: She could teleport. She only knew of four other realm-persons who could do that: Vojalie, Davido, a powerful elf named Kaden, and of course, Margetta.

She shared the vision with Vojalie, who took it as her cue to take her leave. She kissed Rosamunde's cheeks in turn, then wished her a successful night batting the Invictus. Rosamunde thanked her again for coming to her and for sharing her troubles.

One last lovely smile, and Vojalie vanished.

Rosamunde informed her staff that she would be in meditation through the night and that she wasn't to be disturbed for anything. It was a ruse, of course, the best she'd been able to concoct while she went out as Aralynn. She didn't want any of her people knowing that she was living a dangerous double life.

Locking her door from the inside, she focused on 'Aralynn's' forest cottage. She'd taken many precautions to keep her dual identity a secret. Stone, for instance, believed that Aralynn had once served with the Castle Guard. She'd also told him that she was obedient always to the queen's wishes.

Arriving in her cottage bedroom, she transformed quickly into Aralynn. She no longer felt like Rosamunde, but took on Aralynn's experiences, her thoughts, and her wolfish love of battling. She wasn't sure how she'd achieved such a strong separation of personas, but for the sake of her work with Mastyr Stone, it had been necessary.

She opened her closet and pulled out her battle leathers, donning a dark green leather vest with fringe at the bottom, black leather pants and matching boots that zipped up the sides. She tore at her braids, the careful work of three maids. She caught the upper mass of her curly red hair in a woven clasp similar to the ones that Stone and his Vampire Guardsmen wore. But she let the lower half float free. She adored the sensation.

Freedom was what she felt as Aralynn, freedom from responsibility, from the drudgery of castle life, from a sense of invisibility. She'd never felt like a real person as the queen.

Once she had her long, silver dagger strapped to her hip, she prepared to contact Stone and let him know about the vision of Charborne.

She loved this moment every evening because now that she was Aralynn, she could let herself feel everything she felt about her battle partner.

She blew the air from her cheeks as pure desire raged through her. She wanted Stone bad, but had been holding back because he didn't approve of 'Rosamunde'. Yet, given the situation, she wondered if she should take Vojalie's advice, to accept Stone as her lover as Aralynn, then let the chips fall where they may.

A week ago, Vojalie had said something else, encouraging Rosamunde to reach out with both hands and take the life she wanted.

Both hands.

She'd definitely wanted to grab Stone that way, starting with his massive shoulders, squeezing hard, then moving down his chest, his abs, and lower still.

Her vision blurred and one of her brows drifted upward until all she saw was the image in her mind of Stone without anything on. How many times had she imagined him this way, every warrior muscle on display?

She gave herself a shake. Time to contact Stone and let him

know about Charborne, though her fae instincts told her he already did.

Stone?

Aralynn, we've got a situation near Charborne.

Stone's voice, even telepathically, hit her at the back of her knees and she levitated to keep herself from falling on her face.

I've had a vision about the village, that your Guard will soon be battling a large number of wraith-pairs. Any news at your end? What's going on? Over the past year, Stone had built an extensive surveillance system to watch for Invictus.

Delia's husband was out at Charborne checking out a gold mine. He's been missing two days and a night.

Oh, no. Delia was Stone's assistant and Rosamunde adored her for the way she challenged Stone, especially when he was being stubborn and at times overbearing. How surprised she'd been the first time she'd seen Delia in action. She'd learned a lot from the lovely troll.

However, it disturbed her terribly to learn that Delia's husband might have been caught in the Invictus attack.

Stone continued. *Elias's disappearance is what alerted us to the situation. We've since learned all the feeds are down in the village, or maybe blocked. I've sent Harris in with several squads to check it out. I should be hearing from him any minute now. I'm in the air. Where can you meet me?*

Her fae senses told her to consider the area carefully. She knew Tannisford's geography like the back of her hand. She'd studied all of the realms in depth, over and over through the centuries, maybe instinctively preparing for this moment in time. *Let me access Charborne.*

Good idea.

She and Stone had worked together long enough for him to know she could gain a strong sense of places, people and the immediate future if she had a focal point. She settled her thoughts on the village where Stone had grown up.

She felt remnants of the elf-lord power inside her, humming through her mind and her psyche. She brought the part of her that was Rosamunde and fae to the forefront. This was Rosamunde's forte. The fae part of her could feel the future like a mist, not very different from the one that protected Ferrenden Peace.

She mentally focused on Charborne. Images of the lovely forested foothills near the village sped through her mind. Yet right on the heels of these images came a vision of a lot of Invictus.

She wanted to know more, to see how many wraith-pairs and where they were focusing their attack. She let the vision unfold and saw at least thirty wraith-pairs.

She shared the details with Stone.

I'll let Harris know.

Okay. Now let me see if I can find Elias because my initial vision included the mine.

Do it.

Rosamunde took one side-trip and focused on Delia's husband. Images arrived of the mine, and the surrounding woods. The troll was within the mine, his back pressed up against the rocky wall. Rosamunde could hear wraiths shrieking in the distance.

Elias is in the mine and he's unharmed. You can let Delia know if you want. But we've got to get to him soon. Is the mine at the northwest end of the property, near the woods?

That's the one. Meet me there?

Will do. And Stone, it might be best if you brought someone else along who could fly Elias home. He can't levitate very well and I have the sense he's injured. The trip would be impossible for him to make by himself

Understood. I've got two Guardsmen with me.

She nodded, even though he couldn't see her. *I'll go to Elias now. We'll be inside the cave, waiting for you.*

Perfect. See you in a few.

Aralynn continued to focus her attention on Elias until his location was fixed in her mind. She panned back within the vision and found a covered area in the shrubbery near the massive rocks where she could teleport and still remain hidden in case wraith-pairs were scouring the area.

She checked her dagger on her left hip, then moved in a quick zip to the old mine. She arrived after barely a second of travel and on instinct hunkered down then looked up to check the night sky. The wraith shrieks were still far away, which she considered a good sign.

When she didn't see or hear anything suspicious either above or near her, she eased her way around the rocks, careful to watch for the smallest sign of Invictus.

She levitated just above the earth to keep her boots from making noise on the leaf-strewn ground. Moving swiftly, she entered the mine and called out softly. "Elias? It's Aralynn. Mastyr Stone and his Guardsmen are on the way. Are you here? Are you okay?" She knew what she'd seen in the brief vision, but she was still so new to the process she wasn't entirely confident she'd caught all the details.

But Elias's voice streamed toward her. "In here."

She slipped past the initial large cavern and found Elias

exactly where she'd envisioned him, his back to the wall of a shaft entrance.

She moved toward him, surprised at his looks. Davido might be ugly, but it was possible Elias was the most beautiful man she'd ever seen, with dark brown hair that flowed from his uppermost forehead ridge in sculpted waves. It was no wonder Delia had fallen hard for him. His complexion, however, was very pale, no doubt at least in part from dehydration.

"How did you know I was here?" He kept his voice to a whisper. "I've been trapped for the past two days. Wraith-pairs have been all over this area."

"I had a vision."

"About me?" His eyes widened.

"Charborne, actually, then you."

"Is it bad? The village, I mean?"

"Not sure. But Stone's on his way as well as Harris and they're bringing the troops in. So, you were smart to hide out here."

He shook his head. "That's not it. I'd been deep in the mine when I took a fall. Cracked my head. I was unconscious for I don't know how long. My friend went to get help." He then gestured with his free hand to what she now realized was a broken arm, held in a makeshift sling. Not all realm-folk had self-healing power sufficient for serious breaks. "But he never came back and my phone had no reception in here. I'd just made my way to the entrance when I heard the distant shrieks, though that wasn't very long ago."

"All right. We're safe for now." Even as the words left her mouth, however, she knew they weren't. She could feel Invictus moving in their direction. "Let me contact Stone."

His head drooped with fatigue and he nodded. She wished she'd brought some water with her. But there was one thing she could do. She might not have the healing powers of some of the more powerful fae, but she could offer Elias some relief.

She put her hand on his head. "This should help."

He sighed heavily as she let her power flow. She then contacted Stone. *I'm with Elias. He's severely dehydrated and has a broken arm.*

We're almost there and we're coming in from the east. Can you leave the mine?

Maybe. The woods give excellent cover. I'll try to get us both out there, but I think we've got wraith-pairs moving in.

Do what you can, but stay safe.

She loved that about Stone. They might have run over fifty missions together throughout the last few weeks, but he never took chances with her safety.

She told Elias the plan then moved toward the mine opening. But the moment she stepped into the larger, cavernous entrance, a wraith-pair dropped into view just outside.

"Well, lookee what we have here, Imogen."

The duo, wearing rags but carrying sharp, honed weapons, hovered right in front of the mine's opening. The female wraith, in a shredded, red gauze dress flew in a circle above her vampire mate's head. The vampire's fangs made an appearance, and saliva dripped down his chin.

The wraith was as vile in appearance as any Rosamunde had ever seen. Her lips were almost black and it wasn't just lipstick. The whites of her eyes looked jaundiced and her irises were similar to the violet of Rosamunde's.

The wraith shrieked so loud, Rosamunde had to cover her

ears, as did Elias. Her mate was a powerful vampire, just shy of what Stone would call mastyr status.

Imogen added, "And listen to how my voice echoes into the mine."

Rosamunde covered her ears once more, protecting herself from the shrill barrage. Suddenly, another wraith-pair showed up behind the original couple.

As the second wraith let loose, Rosamunde contacted Stone. *We've got two wraith-pairs in front of the mine entrance.*

I see them. Stone's voice was very quiet within her head. *Stay put, but this will probably get messy.*

I'll try to distract them.

After telling Elias to stay well behind her, she drew her dagger. "You call that loud?" she shouted, waving her weapon. Her heart thumped in her chest. The wolf part of her was loving every second of it, but the fae part kept wanting to put the brakes on.

This was Aralynn's show, however, so she let her wolf be.

"Come on, wraith. Let's hear a couple more."

The wraiths took the bait and Rosamunde covered her ears once more.

Chapter Two

Levitating just inside the tree-line, Stone heard Aralynn taunting the wraiths. He waved his Guardsmen up and forward. One of them was another of his lieutenants, Cole, whom he relied on as much as Harris.

Both Guards rose high in the air, then dove swiftly at the four levitating Invictus blocking the entrance to the mine. Each released blue battle energy from their palms as they flew by.

At the same moment, the wraiths turned and fired off red killing vibrations from their hands, wrists and arms. The quick reactions caught the Guardsmen's battle energy midair. Red and blue parks flew into the air as the disparate energies collided.

Cole, swing back around but fire at the vampire. I'll take down the wraith closest to me.

Got it.

Stone watched Cole and the other Guardsman, now high in the air, turn back toward the mine, the wraiths' attention fixed on them.

Stone moved swiftly, just a foot above the woodland path then at the last moment, put on his vampire speed.

The wraith didn't see him coming. Flying straight for her, he took her down, an arm around her thin neck. He jerked hard and heard the crack. He let her body fall to the ground, ready to face the vampire.

However, because of the bond, once the wraith was dead, the vampire fell hard to earth, his life-force depleted. He might have been able to recover, but took a blue streak of Guardsman fire-power straight to the head as Cole dove in for the kill.

Both Invictus were dead.

The second wraith rose in the air, facing the two Guardsmen, firing her battle energy and shrieking. But her vampire bond-mate came at Stone, throwing his axe with skill. Stone dove to the right away from the mine entrance and felt the axe just graze his bare shoulder. He'd have a metal burn but the blade didn't break skin.

Stone fired his battle energy, hitting the vampire square in the chest. He flew backward several feet, landed on his back and didn't move.

The second Guardsman had come in low from the west, exchanging fire with the wraith. But she'd dropped from the air at the same moment Stone's battle energy struck her mate.

Both pairs were dead.

Cole and the other Guard flew down to Stone's position. He ordered them to stand watch outside the mine and to only engage the Invictus enemy if necessary. He wanted to get Delia's husband to safety first.

Aralynn, I'm coming in. Is the situation secure?

It is. Tell Cole that was some awesome shooting and you didn't look so bad yourself wrestling that first wraith to the next life.

Stone smiled as he walked inside the mine opening. It was

clear it had been a cave at one time well before gold fever had struck.

He found Aralynn blocking Elias protectively, though she stepped out of the way as soon as she saw he was alone.

He addressed the troll who looked weak from stress, hunger and thirst. "My men will get you back to Rutland. Delia's waiting for you there. First, though, what happened? What can you tell me?"

Elias rubbed his forehead. His hands and nails were dirty from being in the mine. "I didn't see anything. I was with a friend who wanted me to have a look at the mine. We'd been exploring for a couple of hours when a wooden plank gave way and I fell maybe eight feet. I hit my head. When I woke up, my arm hurt like hell and my friend was gone. Hearing some wraiths shriek, I stayed put until I knew it was daylight, then I made my way back up here."

"So, there were wraith-pairs here last night?"

"Yes. I don't know if they got my friend, or not."

He shook his head. "Sweet Goddess, they've had free range of the village for a full night and now a second."

But Elias cut in. "I remember a warning siren. Mastyr, you've trained your citizens well. I'll wager a lot of the villagers took shelter before the attack."

"I'm going to hold to that thought." He glanced behind him. "Cole, have you got some water?"

"I do."

Cole moved forward and handed a small flask to Elias. He drank too fast and came up sputtering.

Stone took the metal flask. "Take it easy or you'll lose it all. Been there."

Elias laughed, then tears filled his eyes. "Thank you for finding me, Mastyr. Is Delia okay?"

"She's fine. Cole, let her know that we have her husband."

"I'm on it." Cole turned away and spoke quietly into his com.

"I felt sure there'd be fighting in the village," Elias said, his gaze stricken. "But I hid out here like a damn coward."

Aralynn touched him on the shoulder. "But you had a broken arm and no weapons. What could you have done?"

"Something. Anything."

Stone could see his suffering and he knew the feeling well. "Elias, every man worth his salt has felt the kind of guilt you're experiencing when he holds back from battle. In this situation, I would have done the same thing you did. In fact, over the course of my years of service, I've done exactly that, probably hundreds of times. You did the right thing staying put."

Elias stared at him, his eyes taking on a hard look. "That's bullshit. You've never run from anything in your life. You're the Mastyr of Tannisford."

"Wish that were true. But it's not. I've chosen plenty of times to live to fight another day. There's no shame in it. A couple of months ago, I watched one of my Guardsmen hauled into the sky by a powerful wraith-pair, while I battled three on the ground. I could have gone after him and part of me still wishes I had. But I would have been slaughtered in the air.

"Yes, I fought off the three that were coming at me. Even then, I quit the field as more wraith-pairs moved in. I would have been killed by not retreating or by trying to save the one I lost. We make hard choices in war and I'm telling you right now, you did the right thing. You survived."

Elias nodded.

"How about we get you home."

Cole pivoted slightly in Stone's direction. "Delia will be waiting for Elias at the farm and the second wave of Guardsmen have just hit Charborne. I have good news: The Invictus are retreating."

"That's wonderful," Aralynn said.

Stone issued orders to have the men fly the troll home.

Elias straightened his shoulders and since Stone knew he was going to offer to remain and help with the clean-up, Stone shook his head. "You're leaving. Delia's expecting you and if I don't have you home within the hour, she'll quit my employ. And I don't have to remind you she's the only woman who can manage me."

At that, Elias cracked a smile. "As to that, my woman's never been happier than serving at your side."

"She's been a blessing to me." Stone then nodded to Cole.

Cole had brown eyes and long dark hair and offered Elias a smile. "Let's get you in the air."

Elias thanked Stone and Aralynn, then moved outside with the two powerful Guardsmen. He accepted Cole's extended hand.

Because trolls were short and Vampire Guardsmen on the massive, muscled size, Cole swung Elias in a practiced move up to his shoulder where the troll perched, one hand hooked into the opposite shoulder strap of Cole's coat. The vampire immediately took to the air. The remaining Guardsman followed on his heels, rising swiftly as well, but watching the skies while they headed southeast toward Rutland where Elias and Delia lived.

Once they disappeared from sight, Stone opened up his pathing frequency and contacted Harris. *Tell me what's going on?*

We've got Charborne contained. The electronics were jammed, as we'd suspected, but the Com Center says the feed is now back online. What we don't understand is that there aren't any dead, except the wraith-pairs we battled.

Stone was mystified. *You mean realm-folk? You haven't found any deceased among the villagers?*

That's right.

Then they must be in hiding.

That's what we hope, but we're not sure. I know the mayor of Charborne had taken great precautions against an attack, ordering the construction of secret hiding places inside dwellings and out in the farmlands and the forest. And he had a large number of the villagers on constant patrol each with the ability to sound the alarm. Stone, I think it's possible the mayor saved his people. Wait, here is he now. Give me a sec and I'll get his report.

Stone stood very still. Was it possible that no villagers were lost?

After a moment, Harris pathed, *Yup. It happened just like I told you. The mayor said that they've been running drills every single night for months, with the full participation of the residents. No matter where everyone is or what they might be doing at the time, they have to know where the nearest hiding place is and get there. Anyone left wandering around is fined. He's calling his people in now. I'll have more information over the next hour, but I think we have reason to celebrate.*

It sure sounds like it. By the way, we have four dead Invictus out by the mine that will need to be processed.

I'll take care of it. And what about Elias?

Stone heard the sudden tension in Harris's voice. *Cole and one of his team are taking him home as we speak.*

Thank the Goddess. Harris sounded relieved. *The last thing any of us wanted was for Delia to lose her man.*

I think it would have killed us all. Okay, so bring in the troll clean-up crews to process the Invictus bodies. Aralynn and I will be heading back to the Com Center.

Will do. But one last thing. No word yet on either Gerrod or Ethan. I wasn't able to raise Quinlan either.

Stone had an uneasy feeling about the mastyrs. Were they missing? He sure hoped not. *Stay on top of it, Harris. And let me know the moment you get definitive word.*

You got it.

When he ended the telepathic conversation, he turned to Aralynn and shared the news with her about the villagers. She lifted her fist and gave a shout. "That's the best news you could have told me."

The brief battle, however, still had his blood pumping and he became acutely aware he hadn't been with his *doneuses* yet this evening. He should have made a stop before he went to the Communication Center. But his thoughts had been full of Aralynn and how he'd almost kissed her the night before, so that he'd forgotten about his chronic blood starvation.

Until now.

And unfortunately, he could smell Aralynn's blood which made his mouth water. He couldn't believe the layers he could detect, a rich wine and something again very herbal with a woodland aroma. She was definitely a woman of power, which he believed must have also given her blood the same scent that came off her skin. Initially, he'd thought it was her perfume, now he realized it was just Aralynn. And he loved it.

There was only one problem. Aralynn was in no way prepared to take on the duties that belonged to his harem of *doneuses*. To ask her to donate was impossible. She'd become his battle partner and taking from her vein was definitely crossing the line.

"I'm so glad Elias is safe."

"Me, too." Brilliant response.

She glanced at him quickly, a brief fluttering of her eyelashes in his direction then away as she stared out into the night. Something was on her mind.

He flared his nostrils and drew in a slow deep breath, taking in every subtle scent of her. Besides the heightened quality of her blood, he could now smell her growing desire for him. The wolf wanted him … bad.

He salivated. Aralynn was athletic and strong. She'd make a perfect lover for him. He'd wanted her all this time, craved her in ways he'd never before experienced.

Her red hair was wild around her shoulders. But the upper half was pulled back and revealed her strong cheekbones. She was a beautiful woman with large brown eyes and arched brows.

Something about her reminded him of Rosamunde in a way he couldn't explain. But Aralynn hadn't just served in the Castle Guard, she'd studied under the queen. Apparently, Rosamunde had served as her mentor, which he considered an unfortunate circumstance. Yet he saw little of the queen's influence in Aralynn. She was an excellent warrior-partner, had all the courage he could ever want in a woman, and she was game for about anything.

Above all, Stone trusted Aralynn. She'd proven herself over and over from the time she first showed up at the Com Center ready to serve.

And yup, he wanted her bad, too.

As though understanding the trend of his thoughts, she slowly turned to face him. Last night, she'd disappeared before his lips had touched hers. But right now he knew something had changed with her. This time, she would stick. He could feel it in his bones. Her brown eyes glittered and her desire became a beautiful resonance moving over his skin.

It would seem she'd finally come around, that they could enjoy each other for a time, while the terrible war against Margetta and her wraith-pairs played out.

She didn't say anything, but waited, her breaths high in her chest.

Her lips called to him, luscious and full. He was barely a foot away from her now, standing like a massive shadow over her. He was taller than most Guardsmen, and heavily muscled, a perfect counterpoint to her lean female wolf's body. He didn't fully understand the hold she had over him, because even the scent of her blood had him rock hard.

His heart pounded in his chest. He'd wanted this from the same night they'd worked together for the first time. She'd had a vision about a busload of troll kids and he'd gone with her to see if her vision was accurate and it had been, down to the last detail.

At the time, a small river had flooded and the bus had tried to cross the bridge. But part of the supports had been damaged and threatened to collapse. The driver had started backing up, but one of the supports had given way and the right front wheel had lost traction. He'd basically kept the bus from plunging off the bridge and she'd somehow added a burst of power that had helped him get the bus back on solid ground.

He'd been hooked since.

He doubted Queen Rosamunde would be happy if he established a liaison with Aralynn, yet somehow he didn't care.

This time, when he drew close, she didn't pull away or vanish as she had in the past.

Instead, he could feel her surrender like falling into a warm pool of water. He dipped his head ready to take the kiss he'd wanted for so long.

~ ~ ~

Rosamunde stood so close to Stone her whole body vibrated with need. Her heart felt heavy yet excited. She knew what she was doing was very wrong, but she couldn't help herself. She was a wolf in this moment, Aralynn, who ran missions with Stone, who'd learned to anticipate his thoughts and moves, who'd wanted the vampire like she was a dry desert plant and he was rain.

She could also sense the depth of his blood starvation, a chronic condition that afflicted all mastyrs. Each lived with tremendous pain and she wanted to ease his suffering. Maybe because she knew what it was to endure pain every night, she felt as compassionate as she did.

But it was the thought of his vampire fangs breaching her vein that caused her gaze to fall to his lips.

Sweet Goddess, those lips that she'd dreamed about so many times, dozens in fact since she'd first shown up at his Com Center. But Vojalie was right about one thing. She'd had a thing for Stone since he'd made his first formal visit to Ferrenden Peace.

He leaned in, ready to kiss her, but she put a hand on his chest and met his gaze.

He frowned. "You're stopping me? Again?"

"No. I wouldn't be so cruel. I wanted to tell you something. It's important to me."

His expression softened. "You can tell me anything."

For a moment, his words made her pause. Could she tell him anything? Could she tell him she was Rosamunde? The part of her that understood him knew she couldn't, not if she wanted a kiss. So she let it go. Guilt hit her, but she ignored that, too.

Instead, she told him what was on her mind. "Do you remember the first mission we ran together?"

He narrowed his eyes. "Of course. I was just thinking about it, too. The troll kids on the school bus."

She nodded. "You were so reassuring with those kids as well as the driver, then you pulled the bus back with the sheer strength of your arms."

A smiled played over his lips and he slid his hand beneath the mass of her curly hair and caught the nape of her neck. "You've forgotten."

"What?"

"I didn't do it on my own. You joined your power to mine, remember? I couldn't have pulled that bus back on my strength alone."

She chuckled and even grinned. "You're right. I forgot I'd helped out. All I know is you were absolutely magnificent and that's the reason I want you to kiss me."

"I don't think you could have said anything better to me. Thank you, Aralynn."

He tilted his head slightly, and the thing she'd been craving was suddenly hers. She closed her eyes and centered every thought, every sensation on the press of his moist, warm lips against hers. She wanted to remember it forever, that despite what might happen in the future because of her subterfuge, she would always have this moment with him.

He used the pressure on the back of her neck to move her just so, to pull her closer and deepen the kiss. When she parted her lips, his tongue slid inside, a penetration that felt as sensual as if he'd entered her body with all that was male.

She moaned heavily, not for his sake but because she couldn't help it. It felt like heaven, especially to her wolf. She loved his hand on her neck and would like even more being controlled from behind.

She melted against him. He tightened his hold on her because he must have sensed what she felt, that she'd fall to the mine floor if he let her go. *Stone, I've wanted this night after night for so long.*

He groaned, a gravelly sound that forced her arms to snake around his neck. He pressed his body fully against hers. She felt the brute strength of his muscled arms and heavy powerful thighs. She could feel as well that he was hard for her.

Something like a sob caught in her throat. So this was what she'd been missing for so many centuries. She tried to be reasonable, to pull back and let the kiss just be a kiss, maybe a sedate beginning of sorts. But she couldn't. Her own hunger demanded she keep going, keep feeling the pulse of his tongue and the way he ground his hips against hers.

She wanted him to the point of desperation.

But the part of her that was more fae than wild wolf, began to come to the fore. This was Stone, the man who disliked

'Rosamunde' with a passion. To keep kissing him was a lie and her conscience could hardly bear it.

She began to ease back until her hands were on his chest.

"What's wrong?"

She couldn't meet his gaze so she leaned her head against his chest. "There's something else I need to tell you, I just don't know how."

He chuckled softly. "I'm guessing you've been with other men."

He'd given her an out. "When I was much younger."

She felt him grow still. "It's been awhile, then?"

"Yes."

"You want to slow this down?"

"I do. I think it would be wise."

He rubbed her back and she could feel his chest rise and fall as he took a series of slow, deep breaths.

She had to tell him the truth, but it was so hard.

A memory flew back at her, biting her with sharp teeth. When it had become widely known that Ferrenden Peace really did exist and was ruled by a queen, Stone had requested an audience with her. She'd received him formally, sitting on her throne, feeling like an imposter, but holding her head high. This was months before she'd learned she could transform into 'Aralynn'.

Even then, she could recall how she'd responded to the sight of him, to his muscled body and the tattoos that she could see rising on his neck. She wondered how many his Guardsman outfit concealed.

He'd begged her to become more engaged in the war effort against Margetta. In vague terms, she'd told him that the mist she sustained required her constant vigilance and that the same mist kept Margetta from gaining access to a kind of power in Ferrenden Peace that would enable the Ancient Fae to take over the Nine Realms.

He'd stared at her with lips that turned down and such terrible disdain that color had risen on her cheeks. "I don't believe you. What power?"

"I'm not at liberty to say." And she hadn't been. Davido had forbidden her to ever discuss the true, elf-lord nature of the power that resided in her kingdom. The elf-lords that had once conquered the Nine Realms had created a terrible stretch of realm history, something horrendous in the ancient documents. To even use the term 'elf-lord' was to strike fear into the heart of all Realm-folk.

He'd lowered his chin and flared his nostrils. He'd looked like a powerful bull ready to tear into her. But he'd held his temper in check. "Here's the deal, my Queen, I can sense the innate power that you possess and I know in my gut that if you'd made a push, we'd have had Margetta on her heels by now. That's what I know." He'd hit his chest with his fist. "I know it here. You've held back and thousands of Realm-folk have died because of it."

When he'd left, she'd wept for nights. He'd been wrong, but she'd found no words to persuade him otherwise.

Now he was holding her in his arms, only it wasn't really 'Rosamunde', but Aralynn whom he trusted and valued.

When she drew back, he looked at her, frowning. "Why the tears?"

"I was remembering something, but it doesn't matter."

He caught her chin. "It always matters. Have I hurt you?"

The warm compassion on his face made her chest ache all

over again. "You couldn't hurt me, Stone. You always act from a place of truth and honesty, from your devotion to Tannisford. There's nothing you could do that could harm me in any way."

He tilted his head slightly, mossy-green eyes narrowed. "That's the way you see me?"

"It is." But as the words left her mouth, a new frequency hit her, striking deep in her brain, one that felt horribly familiar.

Margetta.

"Stone, we've got to get out of here. The Ancient Fae is coming toward the mine. Sweet Goddess, how fast can you fly?"

He gripped her arms, staring into her eyes. "You should leave. Teleport now. I'll escape somehow."

"I'm not leaving you. No. Way. Stone, she's gunning for you. I can feel it."

"Okay, then." He didn't ask permission or give her the smallest warning. Instead, he caught her up in his arms, levitated, then flew straight out of the mouth of the mine and headed into the air.

But a terrible gold wind already filled the dark, starry sky. Margetta's signature.

Rosamunde had seen it once before, the night her mother had died.

Her first instinct was to teleport, but she couldn't leave Stone. Though she'd learned a lot over the past few weeks while serving beside him, she didn't know what to do or even what she could do.

Stone spun them in a circle. "She's surrounded us."

Margetta's gold wind tossed them in the air. If she caught them, Rosamunde knew she would die. But she knew something else as well: Margetta didn't want Stone dead, she wanted him for herself. But why?

Rosamunde had to act quickly. She had only seconds to get herself and Stone away from Margetta.

The Ancient Fae appeared, beautiful in a long purple velvet gown and blond ringlets dangling past her shoulders. She had a softly-pointed fae chin, arched brows and looked like a princess.

"Mastyr Stone, what do we have here? A wolf?"

"What do you want?" Stone's voice reverberated through the air.

"Why, you of course, but I must say you could do better than a wolf." She snorted and wrinkled up her nose.

Rosamunde closed her eyes and focused on the elf-lord power. She wasn't in Ferrenden Peace, but she remembered that her mother had accessed the power outside of the kingdom's boundaries. Maybe she could as well.

Just like that, the elf-lord power began to stream into her, causing the muscles of her legs to seize.

"What's this?" Margetta shouted.

"What's happening?" Stone asked.

Aralynn switched to telepathy. *Hold onto me, Stone. You're feeling the power of Ferrenden Peace. I might be able to get us away from Margetta.*

Margetta clucked her tongue. "Sorry, Stone, but I can't let you keep your wolf. But don't worry, after you're mine you won't care one whit for the wench."

She raised her hands and black-and-gold power began to swirl around them. Her large violet eyes glittered with what Rosamunde knew was a sense of victory.

"Get behind me!" Stone shouted. He even turned and pulled her in that direction just as Margetta released her battle power.

"Stone, no!" Rosamunde shouted, but it was too late.

Stone's body arched hard in the air as Margetta's red battle energy struck him. Rosamunde tried to reach for him, but he began to fall and there was nothing she could do about it. Yet, if he hit the earth from such a height, he would die.

And Stone couldn't die.

Something happened to Rosamunde in that moment, something inexplicable and profound. She dove after him and caught him easily, not with her arms, but with the elf-lord energy that surrounded her. At the same time, she created a wind similar to Margetta's but which was violet in color and provided a protective shield as well. She headed swiftly in the direction of her kingdom.

She felt Margetta in pursuit. She could hear her shouting in distant streams of unintelligible words. She experienced a buffeting against her shield and knew Margetta was firing at her. Yet, her protection remained intact.

As Rosamunde flew toward Ferrenden Peace, she knew Stone was mortally wounded and needed a powerful healer badly. She had some ability, but not enough to bring him back from the edge of death.

There was one man in Ferrenden Peace who had that power, a warrior elf named Kaden. He was a friend of Joseph's and Davido's. If she could get Stone to Joseph's lair, she felt certain Joseph could contact Kaden and maybe then she'd be able to save Stone.

She flew faster than ever, the wind propelling her and sustaining Stone. She stayed near him, her arm around his waist for balance, though she could tell she didn't even need to touch him to keep him safe. As she neared her kingdom, the gold wind disappeared entirely and she knew she'd outstripped her aunt.

Margetta was gone.

As Ferrenden Peace's veil of mist appeared, Rosamunde moved through it easily and felt it seal up behind her.

They were safe now from the Ancient Fae.

But Stone was near death.

Joseph's home was hidden deep in the woods, a good mile from 'Aralynn's' cottage, and protected behind a dozen shielding layers.

Rosamunde had never quite known where Joseph, a mere gremlin, had gotten so much power. Though she'd long suspected he'd purchased the illegal security system on the black market from a powerful fae. Right now, however, she didn't care.

Joseph would be able to help Stone.

As she drew near, she could hear Joseph shrieking through his shields. He must have sensed her, which meant the gremlin had more power than she could have ever supposed.

She pounded on the low, arched wooden door. "Joseph, let me in right now and none of your shenanigans. I have Mastyr Stone of Tannisford here in dire need of healing. I need you to contact Kaden."

"I'm not at home." The gremlin's voice carried a rough edge as though he gargled with sawdust.

"Let me speak with Davido then, right now!"

"He's on a walk, surveying the mist. He'll be back in an hour."

Oh, sweet Goddess. She'd been counting on Davido being able to knock some sense into Joseph. She opened up her telepathy and contacted Vojalie.

The powerful fae returned quickly. *I'm here.*

Vojalie, I need a healer for Mastyr Stone. Now. I need Kaden but Davido isn't at Joseph's and I have no idea how to reach the elf. And the gremlin, as usual, is being difficult. Her telepathic voice broke. *Stone will die if I don't have a healer here in the next few minutes.*

I'll contact Davido. Someone will be there. Just get him inside Joseph's home.

Rosamunde grabbed a deep breath and shouted. "Joseph, I just spoke with Vojalie. She wants Stone in your house now."

When she heard the sound of locks turning, hope rose.

A moment later, the door opened a crack, then wider so Joseph could see both her and Stone.

With his forehead wrinkled like an old man, the gremlin wore a severe expression. The color of his skin was paper white except for a few yellowing spots. He had a long narrow nose and stood a foot-and-a-half tall. Even so, he wore hip boots to fit his diminutive size, leather pants, and a woven shirt in the Guardsman style. His hair stuck out in long reddish-brown tufts. His fingers were his best feature, however, long and shapely. They moved constantly. Gremlin's loved to work with their hands.

Mostly, they pilfered.

Stole.

Burgled.

Schemed.

And were a wretchedly secretive bunch.

Joseph lowered his gaze to Stone. Rosamunde followed his widening eyes, and for the first time she saw the wound Margetta had inflicted.

Her stomach turned.

Blood seeped from a messy through-wound in his abdomen

where Margetta's battle energy had blown straight through Stone.

Joseph made a disgusted snorting sound, rolled his eyes and threw the door wide.

With her wind still swirling behind her, she tried to levitate Stone straight in, but nothing happened.

"This area out here is a magical dead-zone, stupid fae-wolf. I'll have to get my sling." He flung a hand toward the ceiling. She saw an overhead track running from the doorframe that held a series of pulleys and hooks.

She didn't understand how a simple forest gremlin could be in possession of so much power that he could block some of her abilities. Had to be a black market spell of some kind.

He came back with a wheelbarrow piled high with canvas. She levitated Stone forward to the point where the magic stopped her. Joseph intervened and used his own considerable kinetic levitating abilities to unfurl the canvas beneath Stone.

With Joseph's directions, Stone was soon secure in the sling. Tears were in her eyes with this terrible, useless delay in getting him safely inside.

But the moment Joseph moved the sling, the wheels on the rails whipped forward like lightning. The well-oiled apparatus shot into the house and Rosamunde had to fly quickly to keep up.

The house was entirely underground with dozens, maybe hundreds of small rooms jutting off either side of the main hallway. Each room was well-lit and full of so much polished junk, it looked like a hoarder's paradise. If there'd been any doubt about Joseph's essential nature, the gaudy showrooms confirmed him as a gremlin thief.

Joseph stopped the sling abruptly near a long slab of beautiful gray marble. He guided the sling directly overhead, then lowered Stone until he lay flat.

"He's bleeding." Joseph made another raspberry-like sound from the side of his mouth.

"Really? I hadn't noticed." She resisted the urge to scream her frustration.

She thought Joseph would either begin the healing process himself or summon Kaden. Instead, his gaze roved the metal clasp at the shoulder of Stone's Guard uniform, then down to the dozen antique silver studs lining the outer seams of both boots.

"Would you stop weighing the value of Mastyr Stone's silver embellishments and start healing him?" Her voice had moved into a screech that sounded more owl-like than wolf. But she was desperate.

Joseph, levitating across the slab from Rosamunde, made another disgusted snorting sound with the usual accompanying eye-roll. "I don't have the power to manage a battle wound like this one. Besides," he sniffed the air, "it carries Margetta's taint which means a poison is working in him. This man is dead."

Rosamunde lifted both hands in the air. "But I thought you could do something."

"You thought wrongly. Goddess save me from idiots."

Rosamunde had never known such distress as in this moment. Tears rolled down her face. "Dear Goddess, what have I done? What I have done?"

Joseph held one well-groomed hand out for inspection. "I would be willing to summon Kaden for you … for a price, that is." He met her gaze, his tiny cat-like, almond-shaped eyes boring into hers. "Kaden, as you know, is very gifted and would no doubt have Stone fixed up in the twitch of a mustache."

She stared at him for a quick moment as the fine hairs all down her spine rose in protest. She thought for a moment she might actually shift into her wolf and tear his throat out. "You're asking for payment when a man's life hangs by the width of one of your cheap-ass nose hairs?" Though still in her Aralynn form with no fur showing, she leaped at him like a wolf, straight across the table and levitating just enough to make sure she cleared Stone's massive body.

She extended her hands reaching for Joseph's throat when suddenly she was grabbed around her waist and held suspended in the air.

Kaden had arrived.

He'd caught her midair and with a smooth motion set her on her feet. With his other hand, he grabbed Joseph by his suspenders and held him at face level. Their noses were separated by maybe two full inches.

"How many times have we discussed the importance of compassion over avarice, my friend? Will you never learn?"

Aralynn slowly backed away from the beautiful elf with long flowing brown hair, a face like a god, and eyes the color of the daytime sky.

"Hello, Kaden. We're in trouble here."

"Vojalie summoned me a few minutes earlier. She'd had one of her visions. And ... apologies for Joseph's extortion efforts."

Rosamunde felt something from Kaden that she couldn't comprehend. A pair of hyphenated words kept forming in her head – elf-lord – but it was far too absurd. Kaden couldn't be an elf-lord. They were all extinct. They'd been hunted down and destroyed millennia ago. Yet the power that still hummed in her because of the violet wind she'd so recently made, prompted her again: *Elf-lord.*

As Kaden moved to the head of the marble slab, she felt his power like a warm flow of water moving through the tunnel.

Joseph drew close to Kaden then climbed monkey-like to sit on his shoulder apparently intent on observing the healing process. Joseph had known Kaden a long time.

Kaden glanced at her, and as he did a large pair of scissors appeared in his hands. "I need you to get these clothes off Mastyr Stone. All of them. They'll cause him pain because of the poison Margetta has used."

Poison? Oh, no.

She moved close and took the scissors. As she began quickly cutting Stone's Guard coat away, the shimmering light of Kaden moved like a thin mist around him as he put his hands on Stone's abdomen. Stone's body arched once then fell immobile as it had been before.

She could feel the healing flow and the breath she drew shuddered with a few suppressed sobs.

She got his boots off without cutting them, but couldn't help but notice that the muscles of his thighs had seized. Had to be the poison. She would have asked Kaden, but she didn't want to disturb him.

She worked quickly to get his leathers off.

Kaden spoke quietly to Joseph, who in turn left his perch, then returned with a towel which he handed to Rosamunde. He resumed his post on Kaden's shoulder.

Rosamunde placed the towel over Stone's groin. His abdomen had started cramping as well, the defined muscles rising and falling in what would have been painful waves if he'd been conscious.

Her throat was unbearably tight as she watched the healing process. Kaden explained things along the way, specifically how the poison was slowly infecting Stone's blood.

When Stone began to writhe and moan, Kaden met her gaze. "He's beginning to return to consciousness and his abdomen is almost completely healed, but the poison is the problem now and he needs blood. You should feed him soon. That will help more than anything else could at this point to clear the taint from his system."

Thinking about their earlier kiss, she pressed a hand to her chest. "I-I really shouldn't do that. He has a number of *doneuses* he calls on to service his blood needs. I can bring one of them in."

"I'm sorry, my Queen, but it won't do. We don't have time and I have reason to believe your blood carries more power than his *doneuses*. Without your offering in the next few minutes, he'll fall into a lethargy and die. And afterward, I promise you, Margetta will have possession of the Nine Realms. Mastyr Stone is the key to saving our world. And you're the key to keeping him alive."

Rosamunde stared at Kaden for a long moment. She felt his sincerity and knew in her heart she'd reached a critical crossroads. Her faeness, despite the fact that she was still in 'Aralynn's' form, told her he was right. And calling her 'my Queen' meant he knew exactly who she really was.

She'd sensed it as well from the moment he'd pulled that bus out of harm's way: If Stone perished, the Nine Realms would be lost. Besides, from the time she'd first arrived at his Communication

Center all those weeks ago, she'd known that part of her job was to protect him.

"Is there no other way?"

"No. And you must prepare yourself. Once you share your blood with Mastyr Stone, there will be no going back. Not now. Not ever. And there's a good chance the vampire will break your heart."

Chapter Three

Stone's eyes hurt. A strange light pressed on his eyelids making him wonder if he'd been caught outside during the day.

He tried to lift his arm to block the glow, but couldn't move any part of his body. He examined his limbs as best he could, but there was so much pain moving through every muscle he possessed, he could barely breathe. Was he chained up or something? Had Margetta captured him after all and now held him prisoner?

He felt nauseous and a second, very specific pain ran through his stomach and into his back. He writhed.

Help me, he called out. He tried to open his mouth, but couldn't even manage that. Was anyone nearby?

Be at ease, Stone. I'm here.

His mind began giving shape to new images. He saw Queen Rosamunde, a beauty with long red hair, bending over him and caressing his face. Goddess, she was beautiful. For months now, he'd been attracted to her, even craved her at times. He'd never told anyone how drawn he was to the Queen of Ferrenden Peace. Yet he despised her for her arrogance and her unwillingness to use her considerable power against the Ancient Fae.

He met Rosamunde's gaze or thought he did. Was he hallucinating? *Why won't you help the Nine Realms? You have the power necessary to defeat Margetta, but you won't lift a finger. Why?*

You're wrong. I wish you weren't, but you are. I don't have my mother's ability and I know you've never understood. But I truly don't have enough power to defeat Margetta, not on my own.

He shook his head. *The war will be lost because you must face her. I know it in my bones.* He didn't know why he was so intractable on the subject, except that he'd felt it from the beginning that she would be the one to vanquish the Ancient Fae.

She moved backward and vanished from sight. He realized he'd only imagined the encounter. Great. Hallucinations it was.

"I'm sorry, Aralynn. You must feed him." Stone heard the man's voice, but he didn't recognize him. Whoever he was, he was right. Stone needed blood from his donors.

He forced his lips apart and finally managed, "Get my *doneuses.*"

"There you see, Aralynn? He's confirmed what must be done. Feed the mastyr or all is lost." The man sounded stern now. Even adamant. But why should Aralynn be forced to donate?

A rough, high-pitched voice, though very male, broke in, "She's selfish, that one."

"Hush, Joseph. You're not helping our cause, not when you had every intention of charging Aralynn for my healing powers. Pot and kettle, my good man."

He blew a raspberry. "Just thinking of my future, is all."

"You have more money than I do, than even the Queen."

"But the wench I love, my dearest wife, wants more and more

and more. You think I'm greedy? Try dealing with a female forest gremlin. Grabby, that lot."

"Then why not divorce her?"

Another raspberry. "Like most men, I'm a slave to the needs of my cock. And Little Joseph needs *her*. No other woman will do."

Stone heard the other man laugh. "I know the feeling well."

Stone had an impression of size in the one man and a massive amount of power, more than even Stone. But Joseph, by the pitch of his voice, appeared to be the forest gremlin Aralynn had told him about. If only Stone could open his eyes.

Had he imagined Rosamunde?

More things returned to him. Of being at the mine near Charborne with Aralynn, then Margetta's sudden appearance and her gold wind swirling everywhere. The Ancient Fae aimed her battle energy not at Stone, but at Aralynn. That's what had happened. He'd moved like lightning to protect Aralynn and had gotten hit in the stomach. He remembered falling and thinking he would die. Then, nothing.

Now here he was. Aralynn must have saved him, though he had no idea how.

But where the hell had she taken him anyway? And who was the powerful man healing his wounds?

"Aralynn, you have to open a vein. The poison is in Mastyr Stone and only your blood can heal him."

Stone understood. Margetta had delivered a terrible fae potion with her battle energy that now afflicted his entire body. Whatever the nature of the poison, it sent a wave of fire through his bones. He couldn't prevent the groan that erupted from him.

"Blood...now...."

~ ~ ~

Rosamunde couldn't put off the inevitable a moment longer, not when Stone was in so much pain. "Fine, but I'll need some privacy." She'd heard many stories over the centuries about the seductive nature of blood donation. Given her current desire for Stone and his clear craving for her, she suspected that a lot more than a mere kiss would follow.

Kaden nodded and with Joseph still sitting on his shoulder, she expected the pair to leave together. Instead, when Kaden moved away from the stone slab, Joseph remained levitating right where he was, a wicked glint in his eye.

But Kaden, called to him, "What am I going to do with you? Sweet Goddess!" When Joseph stayed put and even crossed his arms over his chest as though getting ready to watch the show, Kaden added, "Get your butt over here, little man, or I will wring your neck."

"Fine." Joseph, who could make more rude noises with his mouth than any realm-person Rosamunde had ever known, let loose with a wet rubbery sound somewhere between a raspberry and a cheek pop. "Have fun."

Once Joseph reached Kaden, the pair vanished, another sign of Kaden's essential power. Rosamunde kept wondering if what she suspected was true. Yet the last of the evil elf-lords had died at least two thousand years ago, maybe three.

Turning her attention back to Stone, she saw that his face was pinched in a painful grimace. His legs were now locked in painful cramps, a condition she understood very well. The poison appeared to be working in his body the way the elf-lord power always afflicted her lower limbs.

She wasn't sure exactly what to do, but she held her wrist to his mouth. "I'm here, Stone. Take what you need."

She thought she might have to encourage him, rub her skin against his lips or something. Instead, he must have smelled her blood because he grabbed her arm and opened his mouth. In a flash, his fangs appeared and he bit down on her.

A small cry left her throat before she could stop it. The nip didn't really hurt and was over before it had begun, but the quick bite had taken her by surprise.

He had his lips around the wounds and was sucking hard.

Maybe too hard.

He could collapse the veins if he wasn't careful. "Easy, Mastyr."

His eyes shifted to her. He squinted and she saw that the whites were a dark red. Even the irises were discolored from the poison. Instead of the beautiful mossy-green she'd come to know they were almost amber. He barely looked like himself.

She pressed her free hand to his shoulder and let some of her own healing power flow into him. "You're sucking too hard. Please, ease back a little."

He breathed hard through his nose as though struggling, then finally gentled the pulls on her wrist.

She glanced at his legs and saw that the painful cramping of his muscles had begun to subside. Her blood must be working fast. She kept her healing power flowing as well.

Stone's skin was the color of a golden tan. He had a lot of tattoos especially over his broad chest, mostly swirls of knife points. A wavy row of black leaves and thorns went from his right thigh to his ankle.

She let her gaze move all the way to his feet, then took her time on the return trip back up his legs. He had warrior limbs, sculpted with muscle and without hair of any kind. He was beautiful.

Her heart started to pound in her chest and she felt suddenly light-headed. At first, she wondered just how much blood Stone had taken. But she knew from long study that wrist-draws were fairly weak in terms of delivering a large amount of blood, especially for a mastyr vampire.

So, a loss of blood wasn't what was causing her to feel a little faint.

Had to be Stone, himself.

As her gaze reached the well-defined muscles of his thighs, her breathing grew rough and out of nowhere a ripple of pleasure ran deep between her legs.

Sweet Goddess.

She couldn't catch her breath. The response was so purely sexual, she couldn't have mistaken it for anything else. She was grateful his private bits were covered up by the towel, though the lump of them had begun to expand. Again, a donor's blood on a male vampire had very specific affects. His erect cock was lifting the towel.

Her rational mind had stalled out. She should look away, but she couldn't help herself.

What was wolf and very physical took over. She could even feel the beginnings of a shift, that delicious sensation of energy racing through her muscles and bones. Her nostrils flared and her lips pulled back.

Aralynn, his mind called to her.

She met his gaze and growled softly, a low throaty sound that even to her own ears had the quality of an invitation.

His eyes were no longer pinched and their beautiful mossy color had returned. The whites were as they should be.

He stopped suckling and swiped his tongue over the wounds. Her forearm tingled with pleasure as the small cuts healed instantly.

She had a moment's awareness that her heart felt lighter.

He slowly sat up. His complexion still hadn't fully recovered. "I need more."

"I can tell you do." She could feel his requirements like a vibration in her chest informing her exactly how much she needed to deliver in order to take care of him. She wondered if this was true for his *doneuses* as well. Could they sense his need as she did right now? "Do you want to take from my neck?"

His eyes darkened and his gaze dropped to her throat. "Yes."

She flipped her hair back so he could get a good look. She could feel her vein pulsing, ready to give him all that he desired.

The problem was, her own needs had formed a demanding symphony in her body and it went a lot farther than just his fangs in her throat. His scent teased her, though she could hardly define it. But it was sensual and smelled fresh, like a quick stream moving over rocks. There were undercurrents of gritty sand and moss and flowing water.

She slowly unbuttoned her green leather vest. "If we're going to do this, Stone, to get you fully healed, I need something as well, something I've wanted for weeks now. And I'm not holding back."

He lowered his chin and stared at her hard. He dropped his hand to his lap and pulled the towel away, setting it on the slab. Her gaze fell to his arousal. He slid his fist around his cock and began to pump slowly.

A shiver chased over her body and she ached so deep within her well that she could hardly breathe.

She took her time removing her vest. She wore no bra so that his eyes flared the moment her stiff nipples came into view. His fist went faster.

Getting out of her boots and pants was a much less elegant process so she made quick work of it. Having gone commando, she now stood naked in front of him.

He wore a dazed expression and he held his hand very still.

They'd barely done anything and he was on the verge.

She drew close and caressed the hand that held his cock. "You're a beautiful man in every way."

He searched her eyes and a pained expression crossed his face. "You don't have to do any of this, Aralynn. I need you to know that. You're my battle partner and I want to do right by you. A blood donation would be enough."

At that, she shook her head. "I need to be with you, Stone. This isn't pity-sex. Trust me."

"Are you sure?"

She leaned in to kiss him, then drew back holding his gaze. "I'm doing this because I've wanted you from the time you saved those troll kids. It's as simple as that." The fae part of her kept sending sharp warnings that she should tell him the truth about who she really was. But right now, her wolf had command and, as Aralynn, she was not letting the moment pass without being with him fully.

He nodded. "I've wanted you as well. I've had dreams about you. I've craved you." His eyes fell to half-mast and seated as he was now on the side of the marble slab, his hands landed on her hips. He spread his legs wider and drew her close.

She slid her arms around his neck and his lips met hers, but not gently. Instead, it was a strong pressure that had her making warbles and coos in her throat. She wiggled her hips until she was smashed up against him and could feel the solid line of his cock against her abdomen.

Her coos turned to a series of moans.

He drew back and searched her eyes. "One last chance."

Her lips curved. "What are you waiting for, Mastyr. I've already said yes."

In a sudden whirl of motion, Stone levitated, picked her up with both arms then laid her out on her back on the slab of marble. At about the same time, he pulled her beneath him.

She was a very physical woman, this shifter part of her, and she loved that he was strong enough to make the aerial move. This was all Stone, his ability, his muscles, his strong warrior physique.

She felt him, the size of him, what she'd seen him hold in his fist. He settled his palms beside her shoulders and kept himself suspended above her. He held her gaze with the ferocity of his green eyes, his mossy irises with shards of gold.

This was her time with Mastyr Stone, no matter what happened in the future.

His gaze fell to her neck and the moment it did, she once more tilted her head in response, exposing the long line of her waiting throat.

~ ~ ~

Stone's fangs throbbed in his gums all over again and he let them descend once more. His nostrils worked like bellows now because her scent was really getting to him.

The wound in his abdomen was completely healed and the blood he'd taken from her wrist had eradicated Margetta's poison. But he still needed more blood to return to his usual Guardsman self.

Within his chest, he felt his mating frequency light up.

What the hell? His mating frequency had been dormant for a long time. So long, in fact, he'd thought it dead. But here was a fae-shifter, with red hair, and blood that smelled like the woods around the castle of Ferrenden Peace and his heart was on fire.

Her eyes popped wide. "What is that? What am I feeling?"

His gaze fell to her lips. "My mating frequency just came alive. Maybe you're feeling yours as well?" He leaned down and settled his lips on hers.

He felt an electrical current that had him moaning. What was it about this woman?

When he drew back, she put her fingers on his lips. "Can you feel that, Mastyr?"

"The soft vibrations? Yes, and call me Stone."

Her gaze slipped back to his eyes. "Stone. I've known who you were for a long time, I know your reputation, I've read every blog written about you. And here you are on top of me."

"So, you really do want me." His lips curved.

She slid her hands down to his waist and pulled him against her. She rocked her hips into his, then rubbed to feel him. "I want this, Stone. I want you. Buried between my legs. I can't explain it, but I need this. You almost died out there tonight and getting you back here where you could be healed, well it's done something to me. Take from my vein, and use my body. Now."

Something about the force of her voice, put him in motion.

He stopped questioning whether or not this was the right thing to do. For now, he would slake his thirst on Aralynn's blood.

When she drew her knees up, he reached low, took his cock in hand, and pushed inside. The fae-wolf was wet and so ready that despite his girth he slid straight in. He groaned heavily and kissed her first on the mouth, then all down her throat.

Her hands were wild on him, grabbing at his arms, his shoulders, his back. She cooed, cried out then gripped his ass hard.

He drove into her a few times, letting her get used to him, while he licked a solid line up her throat. *I'm going to bite you again.*

Do it. How easily she pathed with him. The woman had power.

He paused the movement of his hips, then angled as she tilted her neck.

He heard her sharp intake of breath. *Stone, this is going to feel so good. Sweet Goddess!*

When his fangs descended, he bit quickly to the right depth. Blood, tasting woodsy and full of herbs, once more flowed into his mouth. His cock twitched and bucked inside her then he began to drive once more.

He formed a careful seal around the punctures as his fangs retreated. He began to suck and with such a bountiful flow within his mouth, his whole body went haywire.

As fire flooded his chest and his heart, his mating frequency spun so fast, he got dizzy. Though he'd only stroked her sex a few times, he was ready to come.

Aralynn, I won't last long. Your blood has wound me up like nothing I've ever experienced.

I won't last either. Go for it. Give me all you've got.

Rosamunde was already rising toward a strong wave of ecstasy, only a lot more was involved than just the sweet spot between her legs. Pleasure flowed hard and fast around her chest and her mating frequency sparked and sizzled as though summoning Stone's.

Suddenly, his frequency broke through her chest, covering her own, swirling over hers and intensifying the pleasure as it crested. She shouted as he suckled her neck and drove in hard thrusts into her sex. He lifted off her neck shortly after then shouted as he came as well, his hips moving fast.

Her own ecstasy tore through her once more, taking her sharply to the peak again. Her back arched and her hips rose to meet his as he released into her. She screamed, the pleasure was so intense.

"Aralynn." His deep vampire voice called to her. "Open your eyes."

She hadn't even known they were closed as she blinked then met his fiery green gaze. His mating frequency was still swirling around and over her own, stroking her in a way she would never have believed possible.

She moaned. "Sweet Goddess, that feels good. But you'd better stop. We really don't know each other well enough, right? I mean, a bond would follow." Bonds like this one would be permanent.

He stared at her, then peered into her eyes as though he didn't understand. "Aralynn, I would swear for a moment your eyes were violet, like the queen's. Is there a chance you're related?"

Rosamunde had to think fast. "I don't know. Maybe." Great, now she was telling lies.

Her heart pounded all over again, but for a different reason.

She needed to own the truth. But how in the world was she supposed to tell him she was Rosamunde?

He stroked her cheek, then her throat where he'd fed from her. "Hey, I didn't mean to upset you. I was surprised, that's all. And I know you have immense power and I also know that you're fae. It sort of makes sense that your eyes might change color. They definitely do when you shift into your wolf form."

"That's true."

He relaxed against her while still holding most of his weight off her body. "A beautiful amber brown when you're a wolf." He caressed her hair. "Damn, I feel better. Healed. Your blood is amazing, just like the rest of you."

Rosamunde finally took a decent breath. She slid her fingers into his long black hair. "This was wonderful, Stone. I mean not Margetta attacking us. But being with you. I can't explain it, but it feels so right."

He kissed her. "Very right. And I love your mating frequency."

Rosamunde focused inwardly for a moment, on how their frequencies flowed over each other, back and forth almost with affection but certainly with a sense of belonging. She'd meant it when she'd said this felt right. It felt perfect.

She blinked and focused again on Stone. "I think we'd better disengage our frequencies, don't you?"

"Probably a good idea because I'm having all sorts of visions about keeping this going." He rocked his hips so that she could feel him. He was firming up again.

Her whole body did a rolling arch and she squeezed her eyes shut once more. "You feel too damn good."

He chuckled.

She smiled up at him. "All right. We've got to be sensible and I'm going to do this." She gripped his arms suddenly and lowered her chin. "I'm going to send your frequency packing, but you'd best hold on."

His lips quirked once more. She was pretty sure he thought she was offering a challenge. "I'm ready. Show me what you've got."

She revved up her internal skills and with a sudden jolt that passed through her chest, she pushed his mating frequency out of her body."

His brows rose. "That was something."

She caught his face in both hands. "I'm missing you already. But I think we might have work yet to do tonight and I promised Rosamunde I'd check in with her." How easily the lies rolled off her tongue now.

"You're right." He sounded reluctant as he eased out of her and made his way off the table using levitation. Even so, he took care not to jam either of his knees into her thighs or any other part of her body. She took it as a sign of his general consideration as well as his agility. There was so much to like about Stone.

He picked up the towel from the end of the table and handed it to her. She slid it between her legs, yet didn't mind at all that she lay so exposed and vulnerable on the marble. She trusted Stone that much and of course the wolf part of her felt very natural without anything on.

Keeping the towel in place, she sat up and let her legs dangle over the edge of the slab. He'd turned away from her and was checking the room out, so she took the opportunity to do the same to him.

Somewhere in Margetta's attack, his hair had come loose from the woven clap and was wild around his face and shoulders. He looked like the warrior vampire he was and desire for him spilled over her entire body once more. His tattoos called to her as well. If ever there was an invitation for exploration.

He was phenomenally well-muscled, a stallion in every respect. She wanted more and her mating frequency still hadn't settled down even though she'd kicked him out.

When he'd made a full circuit of the table, he finally said, "Aralynn, I remember getting hit then falling. I was sure I was a dead man. How did you get me here?"

She told him about the violet wind she'd created similar to Margetta's. He frowned. "How did you do that?"

She shrugged, but for a moment she had to think exactly what to tell him. Davido wouldn't want him knowing about the elf-lord power in her kingdom. "Honestly, I'm not sure. But I think it's the same stream of energy that provides the prescient visions for our missions. All I know is that I couldn't let you die. As I focused on somehow saving you, I experienced an unusual surge, I created a violet-colored wind which allowed me to outrun Margetta and get you safely to Ferrenden Peace."

He nodded slowly, his brow furrowed as he digested what she'd told him. He glanced around once more. "So, where are we exactly?"

"I brought you to Joseph's lair. The forest gremlin I told you about."

"Oh, right. Given the short height of the usual gremlin, this place is much bigger than I would have expected. I don't even have to duck."

"Apparently, Kaden is one of his good friends and he's very tall."

He turned to look at her. "Who's Kaden?"

"The powerful elf who healed you."

"Right. But *who* is he? Does he live in Ferrenden Peace?"

She slid off the table and grabbed her leathers and vest. "I'm really not sure. I think so, but I've only met him a couple of times and we've never talked at length. He's a friend of Davido and Vojalie."

Dispensing with the towel, she stepped into her pants and pulled them up quickly. Now that she was off the marble slab she suddenly felt self-conscious. It also didn't help that Stone was still completely naked. Desire for him was always a quick thought away as it was, but all his beautiful flesh kept hounding her.

Stone grew very still. "Now that I think about it, I've felt Kaden's power before. I know I have." He turned to stare at her. "Actually, it reminds me of yours, what I sense when you teleport to me. It's very different from anything else in the Nine Realms."

"I think you're right. I think the power is very much the same." He was getting way too close to the truth for comfort. She buttoned up her vest, but avoided meeting his gaze. At some point, she'd have to tell him about her true identity and that the power she made use of was essentially what was called elf-lord power. But she couldn't, not right now.

"So you don't know Kaden very well?"

She shook her head. "As I said, not really. But Joseph seems to like him and trust him."

Stone chuckled. "From what I remember of Kaden's exchange with Joseph, the latter is a real piece of work."

Rosamunde laughed. "He actually would have stayed and watched us if Kaden hadn't called him away."

Stone called out. "Master Joseph, where are my clothes?"

Rosamunde remembered the scissors. "Kaden had me cut them off because of the poison, though the Guard coat and pants were already ruined because of the direct hit."

Joseph's high, somewhat whiney voice called back. "Your duds were bloody ruined, Mastyr, but I have some you can buy. Hey, Ow. Knock it off, Kaden." More muttering, then Joseph continued with. "I've got your boots. They're fine. And I'll see if I have some other Guard pieces that might fit."

"Anything will do."

"Look sharp!" Joseph called out.

Rosamunde watched as in the next split-second, a large, pink bath towel hit Stone in the face. She chuckled.

He glanced at her, grinning. "Yup, a real piece of work." He wrapped the towel around his waist.

Rosamunde was relieved that finally at least part of his body was covered up. But those arms. Those shoulders.

She had to look away. Had she really just had sex with the Mastyr of Tannisford, one of the biggest hunks in all the Nine Realms?

She stood up a little straighter. Yes, she had. She'd bagged a big one, maybe the biggest one of all.

And it felt good.

If her conscience prickled, she set aside those concerns. She had no doubt there'd be a reckoning for her lies, but it wouldn't be this moment.

~ ~ ~

Stone moved to the marble slab and leaned his ass against the edge. He wasn't even sure what Joseph generally used the marble for. Although that was true of most everything Stone had seen in the lair so far. He'd never been in a forest gremlin's home before. Or maybe this was a place of business, Stone wasn't sure.

Though he was underground, and there were no windows to give him a sense of distance, his vampire abilities allowed him to assess that he was at least a hundred feet or more from the front rooms but only fifteen feet below ground.

Aralynn now stood by the far doorway behind him. "I'm seeing more small rooms. Though I've been here before, I haven't been this far in. Joseph's place seems to go on forever."

"Maybe it does."

"I wouldn't be surprised. For a thieving bunch, forest gremlins are incredibly industrious."

Absently, Stone touched his abdomen where he'd gotten hit. Nothing remained of the original injury, no scar of any kind. He was fully healed.

In fact, it dawned on him that he had no pain, as in *no pain,* not even a single stomach cramp.

He frowned and pressed his hand higher to encompass where he normally would have experienced intense cramping. Even after being fed by Aralynn, he should have been hurting. Apparently, he'd received some miraculous healing from Kaden.

He knew the man wasn't a typical realm-person. While being healed, Stone had felt the quality of the man's power. Whoever Kaden was, he was extraordinary.

Yet even Kaden hadn't leached Margetta's poison from his system. Only Aralynn's blood had been able to perform that service.

He turned slowly in Aralynn's direction. She was attempting

to reorder the mass of her frizzy red hair, her arms raised as she worked the errant curls into the woven Guardsman clip.

His mind suddenly felt full of static.

Her blood had cleansed his body of Margetta's poison. What kind of blood could even do that?

What had he been thinking about?

Right. He needed clothes.

He pushed away from the edge of the marble slab, then tightened the towel once more around his hips.

Yet, he returned his hand to his stomach and actually looked down as though trying to comprehend. He felt as though he knew something that his mind refused to take in.

He waited for the pain to return, for that slicing ache that had dogged him since he'd become a mastyr vampire.

But there was nothing there.

Nothing.

Not even a faint warning twinge.

That's when the truth dawned.

Aralynn drew close, her eyes pinched. She grabbed his arm. "Stone, what's wrong? You look really upset. Are you in pain? Did the poison return? Do you need more of my blood?"

He met her gaze. "More of *your* blood?"

"Yes, do you need me to donate again?"

He shook his head.

"Then, why so distressed?"

"Aralynn, I think you might be a blood rose."

She laughed outright. "No, that's not possible." When he didn't respond with an answering form of amusement, her cheeks took on a sudden drawn look. "You're serious?"

"I am." He leaned close and sniffed her. "From the time I met you, I could smell you, your skin and your blood. You have a profound scent that I'd say is somewhere between the richness of these woodlands and an herb I can't place. I've never known another woman to smell as you do, to give up such a rich erotic scent. Every time I smell it, my groin heats up and there's only one experience in the Nine Realms that corresponds to all of this: to my lack of pain after feeding from you, my craving to be near you, my intense dislike when you look at other men, and the way you smell. You're a Goddess-be-damned blood rose."

Aralynn's lips parted and her eyes widened. She shook her head repeatedly. "No. That's not possible, Stone. It would be the worst joke on me and on you. I can't be a blood rose and especially not to you. Oh, no wonder our mating frequencies played against each other the way they did and the ecstasy that followed was unreal. Oh, no." She put a hand on her cheek.

To Stone's horror, Aralynn, the tough wolf warrior that she was, burst into tears.

Like any man, he had no idea what to do. He wanted to pat her shoulder but was afraid she'd freak out if he touched her.

She moved in a circle, both hands swiping at her face, her eyes pinched. She was murmuring something unintelligible.

He still couldn't believe it himself. Yet even beyond how her blood had magically dispelled the residual poison in his system, he simply had no more pain.

From the time he'd become a mastyr so long ago, he'd lived with a terrible agony in his gut, unceasing and unending. The blood he received from his *doneuses* did little to allay the problem. He required a nightly supply, without which he would have died.

But the pain in his abdomen had been with him from the time he'd risen to mastyr status.

Like most mastyrs, he'd trained himself to function as though nothing was the matter. Ever. Yet, sometimes the pain was so bad, it was like knives cutting him from within.

But right now, he had no cramps, no sharp slicing sensations, just … nothing.

And it felt like heaven.

He took a series of strong deep breaths, pulling his shoulders back and lifting his chest at the same time to further test what had happened to him. It took him a moment to realize that what he felt was what he remembered as normal before he'd risen to mastyr level.

He might be stunned that the Goddess had sent him a blood rose, just as she'd provided a like woman for each of the eight ruling mastyrs. But he wasn't horrified, which Aralynn seemed to be. He couldn't understand the strength of her reaction or why she would consider being a blood rose and servicing him some kind of 'cruel joke.'

She wasn't making sense.

"I can see this is upsetting for you." He didn't know what else to say.

She nodded in stiff jerks of her chin. "It is, though I think I should leave. I need time to think."

He drew close and caught her arm gently in hand. Of course this simple touch alerted his mating frequency and he had to release her almost as quickly.

But he stayed close and held her gaze. "You don't have to be my blood rose, Aralynn. You're not obligated to me. This is an amazing feeling, to be free of pain after so long. But your life is your own."

She shook her head. "I've read the blogs and the newspaper accounts. I've talked to Lorelei at length. I just can't believe it. And I apologize for losing it."

"But why did you call it a 'cruel joke'? I don't get that."

Her brows rose. "Is that what I said? I think I was just so shocked. That's all. Please just ignore it."

He nodded. "Of course. We both need time to figure this out."

"And...and I'd like to talk this over with Queen Rosamunde. She was the one who encouraged me to follow my first mission vision and help you with the troll children on the bus. But I'm sure she had no idea I was a blood rose."

He couldn't help but snort. "Of course." He bit his tongue.

Despite the fact that he'd kept his opinion to himself, fire flashed in Aralynn's brown eyes. "She's a good woman, Stone, no matter what you say. She's beloved here in Ferrenden Peace and others actually admire her for her commitment to protecting the Nine Realms from Margetta."

He lifted his chin. "We'd better not engage in a discussion about your protector. My opinion of her will never change."

A sad light entered her eye and her shoulders slumped. "Of that I'm certain."

Chapter Four

Rosamunde reached the living room where Kaden had just taken a sip of brandy. "I thought Davido would be here. I was hoping to speak with him." She'd known the old troll her entire life, Davido being the oldest person in the Nine Realms.

Joseph's eyes widened oddly and Kaden turned to look at her with a funny expression. He choked on the brandy and begged pardon.

When Kaden wiped his mouth, he said, "Davido had to return home for a bit, something about Bernice. But don't worry. He, uh, taught me how to support the mist."

She looked away from him, chewing on her lower lip. "Fine. That's fine." She sensed Kaden was as good as his word. "When Davido returns, please tell him I must speak with him."

"I will." Kaden frowned. "Can I help?"

At that, her brows rose. She hardly knew the powerful elf. "No. I don't think so. But thank you anyway. And now, I have to go."

She thanked Kaden for his help in healing Stone and bid good-bye to her diminutive host. The pair watched her curiously, but said nothing more except that each hoped to see her again soon.

When she was in the woods once more, she breathed in the sweet, rich air which helped ease her sadness. She could have teleported back to the castle, but she thought a walk would answer much better.

She couldn't believe her new reality. She was a blood rose. Sweet Goddess, could this get more difficult?

The moment Stone had spoken the words, Rosamunde had known it was true. It explained so much, just as he'd said, point-by-point.

But being a blood rose complicated her situation about a hundred-fold. She'd always envisioned that she'd continue to serve beside Stone, as Aralynn, until Margetta was defeated. Then, she'd return to Ferrenden Peace for good and never see him again.

Worse, however, was that she couldn't just walk away, otherwise she'd do it right now, without the smallest hesitation. He'd never accept her as Rosamunde.

But her powerful fae senses told her that the safety of the Nine Realms depended almost exclusively on Stone staying alive and leading the way to victory. He was the commander of the newly created Combined Forces. He'd spent the past several months, since Mastyr Ian had found his blood rose in Regan, training the troops in all the realms. He'd also worked on improving communications realm-to-realm and keeping the war against Margetta focused on one night facing her in battle.

Even if her fae senses hadn't told her how critical Stone was to the war effort, his leadership over the past few months had made it obvious.

Right now, though, she needed time to think, to prepare herself for the trials of being with him and being a blood rose, yet restraining the cravings to go to bed with him again.

When she thought back at how their mating frequencies had been so thoroughly in tune with each other, she knew they'd come dangerously close to forging a bond that would have quickly become a nightmare. She bore too many secrets to ever be that close to Stone.

No. Her relationship with him had a beginning and it must have an end. She must help him stay alive until the defeat of the Ancient Fae, then she would break with him permanently.

Until then, she needed some kind of guidance on how to manage this latest fiasco.

When she didn't hear from Davido, she decided to contact him directly. Opening her pathing frequency, she focused on him and let the vibration fly.

And how may I serve you this fine night, my lovely queen.

She heard the ever-present amusement in his voice and something inside her chest eased in quick stages. *To be honest, I'm frightened out of my wits right now. But I don't want to bother you if you need to be with Vojalie and Bernice right now. Kaden said you were called away because of your daughter.*

Don't be troubled. I spoke with Kaden and I was just about to reach out to you myself. I'm perfectly able to have a conversation with you.

Oh, good. She told him everything beginning with the attack at Charborne.

And so you actually created a violet wind more powerful than Margetta's gold cyclone?

Yes, but it wasn't me alone. It was the elf-lord power and I think Mastyr Stone might have had something to do with it as well.

Ah. I think you may be right.

Davido, I'm overwhelmed with all these new powers of mine and all because you showed me I could transform into Aralynn. And … there's something else.

What, my child?

She had a sense he already knew, but it came pouring out of her perhaps as a result of his troll charisma. Davido truly could get blood from a stone.

She told him about Joseph and Kaden, the latter's healing ability, and about the poison Margetta used. *But Stone was desperate for my blood and when I fed him it turns out all his pain disappeared.*

You mean his stomach ailments.

Yes. They were all gone.

Then you must be a blood rose.

That's what we both think. And when we were engaged, so to speak, our mating frequencies lit up like you wouldn't believe. We could have bonded so easily.

She heard Davido sigh. *Yet, he doesn't know who you are.*

Exactly. Or the other terrible secrets I keep, one of them belonging to you.

I know, he said quickly. *And in due course, I promise I will relieve you of that particular burden.*

But what am I supposed to do in the meantime? Stone speaks of 'Rosamunde' in the harshest terms. He will despise me when he learns the truth.

Davido was quiet for a long moment. She suspected he'd

reached inward for the right words. *My dear, just try to be brave. Vojalie has told me that you will face many challenges in the very near future. Try, if you can, to trust in this process. It's not an accident that you've been given the blood rose gift or that you, as Aralynn, are so compatible with Stone. But sometimes life must unfold in ways that disturb and mystify us. But if you have courage, and stay the course, all will be well. Can you lean on that for the time being, even if you can't see the future?*

For a moment, she felt as though everything about her life was veiled; her identity, what she knew about others, and about the guilt she bore. Only Davido and Vojalie knew everything. They were loving and kind and completely non-judgmental. They'd both, at different times helped her to make peace with her jumbled life.

Yes, I can lean on that.

Just remember, you must protect Stone at all costs. Watch your visions carefully over the next two nights and if you feel the smallest call to be by his side, ignore his anger, and stick close. I can't impress this upon you enough. The entire future of the Nine Realms depends on Stone fulfilling his destiny and he won't be able to do that without you, as both the queen and as Aralynn. Do you understand?

I do and I won't let you down.

And now, my lovely wife is calling to me.

Davido? She had one more thing she needed to say.

Yes, sweetest queen?

I want you to know that as hard as the past several weeks have been and despite how frightening the immediate future seems, I'm so grateful you taught me how to become Aralynn. These changes have helped me to experience a kind of freedom I've never known before.

I am gratified that you've found pleasure, my dear. You've deserved it for a long, long time. And now, I must go.

Good-bye.

Though nothing in particular had been resolved, Rosamunde felt infinitely better after speaking with Davido. Essentially, she must ride out this storm. But how to do it without losing her heart completely to Stone, was not something she could yet see.

~ ~ ~

Stone had been sorry to see Aralynn leave. He felt the need to talk this out with her, but she'd been profoundly overcome, something he still wasn't sure he understood.

For himself, he was beyond grateful to be free of his chronic blood starvation. Yet, he couldn't see how he could take any extra time to be focused on a blood rose. He had an Ancient Fae to put in the ground.

Joseph appeared in the doorway, levitating so that he was eye-level to Stone. "So, you ready to bargain for some Guardsman apparel? I've got a couple of coats and leathers you can take a look at."

"I appreciate it."

He pursed his lips. "Follow me."

Joseph levitated and led the way up the tunnel in a direction Stone intuited was fairly west with slight jogs to the north. Before long he flew in front of what proved to be a host of small rooms full of junk. As Stone moved, he had to keep his head lowered several inches and in some places lower still. Gremlins being as small as they were didn't need ceilings of any particular height.

When he reached the space Joseph gestured to, Stone drew to

a stop, turned to survey the available garments, then dropped his jaw. "Sweet Goddess, what the hell is this?"

"Exactly what you need, right Mastyr?" A gravelly, high-pitched chortle left Joseph's throat.

Stone planted his fists on hips. Hanging on what had to be dozens of racks, in a very large space, were the traditional black leather, calf-length sleeveless coats the Guardsmen wore.

He snorted. "You think you have something in my size?" As in half the coats he was looking at.

Joseph levitated to Stone's shoulder height. He stroked his chin. "For the right price, I'm sure we can find something that fits."

Stone glared at the gremlin. "You are aware that these uniforms are stolen property and I could turn you over to the queen and have you jailed for this."

"But why would you do that to the one who saved your life? As in me? I was the one who brought Kaden here to heal you. My good man, you'd be tits-up except for what I did for you."

Forest gremlins lived a reclusive life apart from all other realm-folk and stole anything they could. In the past, if Stone caught sight of one, by long habit he usually fired off a blast of battle energy hoping to be rid of what he'd always thought of as a useless, thieving race.

To his knowledge, however, he'd never hit even one of the quick bastards. "Fine," Stone said. "I owe you and I need to get out of here. What's your price?"

Kaden called from a distant cavern room. "Give him what he wants, Joseph, or you'll have Margetta tearing through your dwelling the moment she takes over Ferrenden Peace. This man is all that stands between you, your people, and the evil golden one. I have it on good authority she makes footstools out of your kind."

"Kaden," Joseph shouted in his shrill yet gravelly voice, "You're cramping my style, which is to say if I don't meet my nightly quota, my cock will not be happy." He nudged Stone's shoulder with his small elbow. "The little woman has the heart of a miser." Maybe he meant it as a dig, but his eyes shone with pride.

Goddess, save him from gremlins.

But Stone waited quietly for the gremlin to acquiesce or not. Kaden was not exactly someone any realm-person could challenge, at least not without serious consequences. Even separated by a few walls, Stone could feel the man's energy vibrating along the tunnel.

"J-o-s-e-p-h." Kaden's voice carried a resonant warning. "I mean now."

Joseph finally huffed a sigh and blew the air from his cheeks. "Oh, very well. You'll find your size there at the east end of the racks."

Stone went to the right of the doorway, in the direction of Joseph's waving hand and could see at a glance that the Guard coats were suited to the breadth of his shoulders. He'd pushed three aside when he came across one with special silver studs that looked remarkably familiar. "What the hell! Joseph, this is my coat and I know exactly when it disappeared. I went swimming in my lake one night and got out of the water to find my clothes gone. And how the hell did you even get past my security shields?"

He turned, intending to glare at his forest gremlin host, but Joseph was nowhere to be seen. Stone's turn to puff out his cheeks, then sigh.

He grabbed the coat and it didn't take him long to find the

matching leathers and black boots with star studs down both sides. After foraging among stacks of woven shirts, he also discovered a cache of several with his name stitched along the inside neckline. One of his *doneuses* had been making these shirts for him for decades. Not that he always wore them, but dammit, these shirts were his.

He muttered under his breath as he dropped his towel and got into his uniform.

When he'd pulled up his boots then ran his fingers down the familiar studs on his leathers, he started to call out for Joseph. But his sensitive vampire hearing detected two voices toward the west end of Joseph's home: Kaden and Joseph were squabbling.

Stone heard Kaden snort. "I'm not using 'keylap' because that's not a word. You made it up."

"I did not. And it fits. See? Six letters. All right. I see you still don't believe me, so let me explain. I was at a gremlin strip club near the Vermed Sea and that's what the dancer called it, but you had to be in a private room and pay extra: Keylap. Now do you see?"

"Did you get one?"

Stone heard the shudder in Joseph's voice. "I was tempted. That woman had breasts the size of plums. Now that may not seem big to you but for a woman only a foot and half tall, they were hefty honkers." Another shuddering sound ensued.

"I'm telling your wife where you went."

Joseph blew another fatty sound from between his lips. "You do and you won't be welcome back here anytime soon, then where would you be? And I'd like to see another realm-person anxious to open his dwelling to a Goddess-be-damned elf-lord."

Stone fell very still and a terrible chill went through him.

Elf-lord?

Holy fuck.

Several questions ran through his head. Was it true? If so, how had an elf-lord survived all this time without detection? And what was he doing in Ferrenden Peace? Did Aralynn know what Kaden was?

In ancient Realm history, the elf-lords had subjugated the entire population of the Nine Realms and a reign of terror ensued. Over the centuries, a resistance movement arose that eventually wiped them out.

If Kaden really was an elf-lord, then Stone had an obligation to turn him over to the Sidhe Council, but that hardly seemed like a just recompense for a man who had healed him of an otherwise mortal wound. Stone would have died without Kaden's healing touch.

He turned the issue over in his head several times eventually deciding that he'd keep his mouth shut for the time being. Joseph was so full of horseshit, Stone thought it possible Kaden was no such thing. For now, Stone had a war to win against someone clearly more dangerous than this particular elf.

Putting his feet in motion, he arrived at the doorway and finally understood the nature of the discussion about the word 'keylap'.

Kaden sat in a large comfortable leather chair, a lamp lighting up his right shoulder with Joseph perched on his left. Kaden had one leg balanced on the other at the ankle and he held a crossword puzzle book on his knee, a pencil in hand.

Both men glanced at him, their eyes dipping to take in his uniform.

"I see it still fits." Joseph lifted a brow. His lips turned down at the same time. "I could get a couple hundred at least, on the black market."

"Give it a rest." Kaden snorted.

Stone stepped into the room, dipping below the arched doorway. Because Kaden was a tall man and clearly a frequent guest, Joseph must have shaped a few of his rooms for him.

Stone frowned as he met Kaden's gaze. Now that he'd heard the words 'elf-lord', he was tuned into the man. He was definitely of elf origin. He had a strongly pointed chin and with both ears exposed, the curled points were dotted with small diamond piercings. Many of the elves he knew liked to adorn their ears. His wavy brown hair was loose to his shoulders, yet styled. He had a rich, immaculate look. If he was an elf-lord, he definitely looked the part.

The elven and fae species were cousins, though with enough differences to be separate lineages. Fae had softer elf-like features and a gift for seeing the future. Elves were highly industrious and enjoyed the physical world, as opposed to exploring other more mystical aspects of life.

Whatever his suspicions, however, Stone owed Kaden a debt. "I want to thank you again for the healing. Much appreciated."

"You're welcome. But I only got you halfway. Aralynn took you the distance."

"Yes, I know."

Kaden shifted his gaze to the side of the room, his right ear twitching. He then angled his head toward Joseph. "We've got company and I'm liking it a lot. Go let her in."

Stone hoped to hell it wasn't the queen.

Joseph levitated off Kaden's shoulder, frowning. "I didn't

invite anyone here and my wife knows not to disturb me in my place of business. But if Rosamunde has come back—" He let the words hang as he rubbed his hands together. "She's always good for a few gold pieces or sometimes she brings me rubies. But Kaden, don't interfere this time. Think of my cock."

Kaden grimaced. "This may come as a shock to you, but I try not to."

Joseph chortled. "Good joke."

So, Rosamunde knew this odd forest gremlin as well. Of course, she did. She was the queen. But if Rosamunde was here, Stone wouldn't be staying long. With Margetta's latest attack in which she'd intended to kill Aralynn, Stone didn't want to be anywhere near a woman who could have made a difference in the war a long time ago.

Then again, maybe Aralynn had returned.

Joseph whipped out of the room. For a forest gremlin, he had a lot of power and moved like lightning. Stone was impressed.

Kaden said nothing more but rose to his feet.

Stone turned to extend his hearing. He recognized the woman's voice right away, then met Kaden's gaze. "Vojalie's here?"

Kaden nodded and licked his lips. "Yes, she is."

He hadn't seen the powerful fae in a while, not since he'd started running missions with Aralynn. She was on the Sidhe Council so Stone had a few questions for her like did she or any of the other gifted fae have an inkling that Margetta had meant to attack Aralynn at Charborne? The Council had been remarkably unhelpful over the past several months.

He realized it was likely Margetta had somehow blocked their ability to see the future, but it pissed him off that except for

Aralynn, he had no real access to the future. He moved farther into the parlor, off to the right side of the room. The air felt suddenly itchy to him and that's when he realized the elf was glowing, that white, misty light of his. He seemed revved up.

As he stared at Kaden, Stone knew that the light he emitted was what Stone had perceived when he'd started coming back to consciousness. Damn, Kaden had power. Maybe he was an elf-lord.

When Vojalie appeared in the doorway, she let out a soft slow gasp at the sight of Kaden.

Stone immediately sensed her interest in the tall elf. Sweet Goddess, where was Davido? Stone felt a profound need to warn the ugly old troll that he had competition for his woman.

"I didn't know you'd be here," Vojalie said, her gaze glued to Kaden.

"It was the only way to get Stone the healing he needed. It's good to see you, Vojalie." Kaden's lips curved as though his words carried a hidden meaning. Had Vojalie been involved with Kaden prior to wedding Davido?

The most powerful fae in all of the Nine Realms continued to levitate. She floated across the room and extended her hand to Kaden, barely noticing Stone's presence.

Kaden took her hand and while holding her gaze pressed his lips to her fingers.

Stone kept his amazement to himself. If Vojalie's husband, Davido, had been here, the ugly troll would have attacked Kaden for this piece of seductive insolence.

"It's been such a long time, Lord Kaden."

'Lord' Kaden?

So, Joseph hadn't been kidding: Kaden was definitely an elf-lord.

Stone decided to address the issue. Now that he knew what Kaden was, he had obligations to protect the Nine Realms. What he couldn't know was exactly how much of a threat Kaden posed.

He took a step forward. "There aren't supposed to be any of your kind left. I felt your power, Kaden, and I heard Joseph use the term 'elf-lord', but it seems Vojalie's has just confirmed your true identity."

Vojalie turned to him then glanced quickly at Kaden. "Have I said too much?"

But Kaden shook his head. "No. The truth was bound to come out over the next few nights. Might as well be right now. Stone should know. And yes, I'm an elf-lord. Or rather, I was at one time. I've since renounced the power that corrupted so many. "

Stone shook his head. "But I thought your kind was extinct. Our ancestors killed the last of you thousands of years ago."

For a moment, Kaden looked both serious and despondent. "If it's any consolation, Mastyr Stone, I am the last of my kind."

"Good to know." Stone could feel the pinch of his own brows. This was a terrible conundrum for him. "I should turn you over to the Sidhe Council."

Kaden's lips twisted into a wry smile. He inclined his head to Vojalie. "The Council knows of my existence. Vojalie runs interference for me and so long as I remain in Ferrenden Peace, I'm allowed to exist. But I keep a very low profile.

"With that said, Mastyr Stone, I wish to assure you that I am a friend to the Nine Realms. Long ago, I supplied power to the resistance movement that allowed the ruling lords to be brought down. I've lived quietly and respectfully for thousands of years."

Stone was relieved to learn that the Sidhe Council already knew about Kaden. Historically, elf-lords were half-gods in terms of power, probably at the level Margetta had achieved in recent decades.

Kaden added, "There's one more thing. If I'd had the power to counter Margetta, I would have done so. I want you to know that. Also, I have assisted Vojalie and Davido in supporting the mist that has kept Margetta out of Queen Rosamunde's kingdom, thereby preventing her from gaining access to the elf-lord power."

Stone thought this through. "So, the power of Ferrenden Peace is also known as elf-lord power."

"It is. It's the same power each of us has utilized to sustain the veil of mist around the kingdom."

"I don't understand why, if you're an actual elf-lord, you don't have sufficient power to battle Margetta. That makes no sense."

He shook his head. "I am forbidden to access the elf-lord power in that way. It's a degree of engagement with the power that would turn me into a monster as it does everyone who gives in to its seductive call. But there's more. If I ever do fully engage, I'll be executed. I'm bound by very strict rules lest I become a worse threat than the Ancient Fae." He glanced at Vojalie, holding her gaze. "And I've worked hard to fulfill my vows to the Council. Nothing else is more important to me."

Vojalie smiled, a look of affection on every feature. "I know you have." She lifted her hand and for a moment, Stone thought she intended to run her fingers through Kaden's hair.

What the hell?

Kaden was a good looking man and taller by an inch than Stone. He could be a real threat to an ugly, small troll like Davido.

Though Stone knew Vojalie quite well, Davido was like a father to him. He'd been Stone's mentor from the time he was a boy. So like hell he was going to let Kaden, and all his extraordinary abilities, become a wedge between Davido and his woman.

Stone crossed the space in two long strides and gripped Kaden's arm. "You need to step away from Vojalie right now. You might have saved my life, but Vojalie's husband is a man I admire and trust and I won't have you interfering with their bond."

Kaden's lips curved for a moment. He looked supremely amused which only made Stone tighten his grip around Kaden's arm. "Let her be."

Vojalie quickly moved away from the elf-lord. Kaden in turn, lost his not-taking-this-seriously expression and nodded. "I accept your rebuke, Mastyr. I'll mind my manners better. And you're right." His gaze shifted to Vojalie. "Davido doesn't deserve to have any man disrupt his domestic harmony."

"No," Vojalie added sincerely. "That he does not." But even Vojalie's eyes danced as though sharing a joke with the elf-lord.

No doubt Vojalie had known Kaden a long time, but Stone wasn't about to condone this kind of familiarity, not in his presence.

Stone released Kaden's arm aware that his hand was vibrating from the man's energy.

Vojalie crossed to him suddenly, a warm smile on her lips. Though she was a tall woman, she had to lift up on her tip-toes in order to kiss Stone's cheek. "How grateful I am that Davido has a friend like you. But you don't need to worry about Lord Kaden. He will not cross the line. I promise you."

Stone still cast a hard look at Kaden. "He'd better not." Of course, Stone had no idea how he'd go about fulfilling a threat to an elf-lord. "Well, that's settled then. Good. And now, I have a war to get back to."

But Vojalie caught his arm. "Don't leave yet, Stone. Actually, I'm here for you."

"For me? Why?"

She moved away from him and huffed a sigh. "I need you to consider doing something you won't want to do."

Stone frowned once more. "What do you have in mind?"

"I need you to align yourself with Queen Rosamunde. Actually, I need you to bond with her."

He couldn't help it, he laughed outright. "You're kidding. But you and every other realm person in our world knows how I feel about our reluctant queen."

"She needs you right now. Badly. All I'm asking is that you give her a chance."

"In what way does she need me and why the hell should I care? She's the only realm-person I've known who has enough raw power to stand up to Margetta. Instead, she's holed herself up in her castle, enjoying her safe life, while so many of our people have died."

The expression on Vojalie's face bewildered Stone. For a long moment, she appeared as though she was staring straight through him. "There's so much I want to say to you, but I can't."

"About Rosamunde?"

"Yes."

He snorted. "I'll happily run missions with Aralynn who I know to be a friend to the queen, but Rosamunde is out of the question. Are we done here?"

Vojalie's lips parted as though she wanted to say something more. She closed them as quickly, then nodded.

Stone bid all three farewell, then headed to the front door. He had to dip low since Joseph's front entry catered more to his short-statured clientele.

Joseph had followed him and as Stone moved up the path, the gremlin called out from the open doorway. "You're wrong about the queen."

A wet, fat raspberry followed.

Stone ignored the diminutive man as he set his feet toward Aralynn's cottage, hoping he'd find her there. More than anything, he needed to talk over their difficult situation.

~ ~ ~

After leaving Joseph's, Rosamunde had walked in the woods for a few minutes then finally headed back to Aralynn's cottage. Once there, instead of remaining in her Aralynn form, she transformed back to her fae body, with her dominant fae thoughts. Aralynn, as a lusty wolf, wasn't giving her very much peace.

And Rosamunde needed to think things through.

She still wore her bloodied battle clothes and she was more distressed than she could remember being in a long time.

Making love with Stone had been extraordinary and that alone had left her feeling as though her whole life had been turned upside down. But the other reality had sent her peace-of-mind to hell and beyond.

For the past several minutes, she'd done little more than pace the small three-room dwelling and every once in a while touch her throat where Stone had so recently broken her skin.

And taken her blood.

And made her feel as though being connected to his body in every possible way was heaven, and nothing less.

A blood rose.

Nothing could have complicated her life more completely than learning she was the very thing Stone needed most in his painful mastyr's existence.

She'd meant it when she said it was a cruel joke because Stone despised her as the queen. Stone was a man of tremendous power and her fae instincts told her he had potential way beyond what he possessed right now. She thought it possible his opinion of her was based on his own self-knowledge rather than on an accurate assessment of her own essential power. She just didn't know.

Or maybe he'd long since sensed that she was a blood rose without knowing it. After all, the women who experienced this phenomenon often increased in power and ability. Would she? Was this what Stone had intuited about her without knowing the real source? And was it possible she now approached a place where she could actually do battle with Margetta?

She took a moment to access her inner self-knowledge, but what returned was still a profound sense that the veil of mist surrounding Ferrenden Peace must still be her priority, that at all costs Margetta must be kept out.

These thoughts and perceptions began returning some of her peace to her.

As for the blood rose bond, Stone would never accept her as Rosamunde. Whatever affection and respect he felt for Aralynn would disappear the moment he learned the truth. Stone was a forthright man incapable of deceiving anyone. He'd never forgive her for playing the wolf when she was equally the Queen of Ferrenden Peace.

She heard a rapping on the wooden door and whirled to face it, but remained silent.

"Aralynn, are you there?" Stone had come to her cottage. "I can see the light on and I'd like to talk things over with you. Would you oblige me? Please?"

Rosamunde was about to answer in the affirmative when she realized she was still in her fae form. She also wasn't exactly ready to tell him the truth and until she was, she didn't want to be with him right now. But she could hardly turn him away. They were battle partners and he might need her.

Transforming back into Aralynn, she called out, "Hold on." She still needed distance, though, and sought about in her mind for it. "I'm just hopping in the shower." It wasn't much, but at least for a few minutes, she wouldn't have to be in the same room with him. "Give me a sec?"

"Sure."

She quickly gathered up a fresh set of clothes and as she headed into the bathroom, she called out. "Come in. I won't be long."

She closed the bathroom door and forced some air into her lungs. How much she wished he wasn't here, but it couldn't be helped.

So many emotions whirled around inside her that she made quick work of her leathers, vest and boots and hopped into the shower.

She turned on the water without thinking and yelped at its freezing temperature. She backed into a corner to avoid most of the spray as the water warmed up.

When it finally did, she slid under the steaming flow and sighed with pleasure. Sometimes there was nothing better than a hot shower.

She heard Stone's voice nearer than she wanted. "Can I come in so we can talk?" He must have opened the door.

Oh, well. So much for distance.

"Of course." She got her hair wet, then lathered up with her favorite herbal shampoo. Stone's wound had created a spatter that had gone everywhere when she'd flown him back to Ferrenden Peace, including into her hair.

"I want to complete the blood rose bond with you."

Her fingers froze and soapy water poured over her face and into her eyes. The burn was instantaneous.

She flipped around to lift her face to the warm stream. "You can't be serious." She carefully wiped at her eyes to work the soap out.

"I'd be a fool not to bond with you, which means I'm thinking mostly of myself here."

She knew him better than that. "You're thinking about your people. I know you, Stone. And I understand your motivation. You'll increase in strength and ability if we bond and those qualities alone could really help with the war. I get it." She turned around once more and started rinsing the soap out of her hair.

She heard him chuckle. "How well you know me."

"Your drive to see the war come to an end matches my own. So, yeah, I know you. We both want the same thing." As soon as the soap was out, she worked crème rinse through to the ends. Without it, whether Aralynn or Rosamunde, her hair would be uncontrollable.

"Then why not bond with me? I admire you, Aralynn, and I trust you with my life. And with what happened back there at Joseph's, it's clear to me we're physically compatible."

She couldn't argue with the last part and in other circumstances, she might have felt the same way, as in why not bond? But she held three secrets from Stone. How could she bond with him when any one of them would be enough to destroy his willingness to even be near her?

"It's all so sudden, though." She thought the argument reasonable enough. "There might be things about me that you would find intolerable once you got to know me better." She stepped under the flow of the water once more and worked the rinse from her hair.

He didn't answer for a moment, then finally said, "And I could say the same thing. I'm pretty impatient. Even impulsive."

She chuckled. This much she knew to be *very* true. "Yes, you are."

She heard him laugh as well. "Hey, you didn't have to agree so readily."

With the crème rinse out of her hair, she shut the water off then slid the green curtain back a little, just enough to see him. "Toss me a towel?"

He pivoted, grabbed one off the rack and handed it to her. But he remained turned away from her, something she appreciated since they had a serious issue to resolve. She didn't want the situation to become electrified with sex, which it so easily could.

As she dried off safely behind the shower curtain, she addressed her biggest concern. "I believe the bond is permanent. We'd be tied to each other for life and I'm not sure that's what I want. Are you really convinced you could live with that? I think we've gotten to know each other pretty well over the past seven weeks and you know I admire you tremendously, but a blood rose bond?"

She heard a deep intake of air as though he would need every molecule of oxygen to make his next statement. "I'm willing to take the chance, to make the sacrifice. I feel I owe it to my people."

She wasn't at all offended.

Wrapping the towel around herself, she tucked it in tight, then stepped from the small shower. Of course, Stone was so big he pretty much filled the space with little left over for her. Everything in the cottage was undersized, since the original owner had been a troll. Improvements had been made later to expand the ceiling height. The roof had even been raised two feet. But the proportions were still on the small side.

"Sorry. I need to dry my hair."

But he stared at her for a long moment as though caught. "You're beautiful, Aralynn, though sometimes I swear your eyes turn violet then shift back."

She had to think fast. "I have fae blood and some of my people have violet eyes."

He nodded as though this made sense. She then gestured with quick flips of her hands for him to retreat.

He got the message and backed toward the doorway. As tall as he was, he clunked his head on the upper frame.

He chuckled as he ducked, then moved the rest of the way into her combination living room-bedroom.

She pulled out her hair dryer and went to work. It was never an easy thing to deal with her mass of red hair. "I'll be a while. There's beer in the fridge."

"That sounds great. Thanks."

She was relieved he disappeared toward the front of the small cottage. She took the opportunity to close the door again. Her fingers shook. She felt as though she was dancing around a bonfire, getting closer and closer to the flames. At some point, she was going to get burned. Badly.

Once her hair was dry, she pulled the upper half back and secured it with a woven Guardsman clasp. All the Guardsmen had long hair, usually very thick, so the clasps were made for them. Given the mass of her hair, the clasp fit perfectly.

Dressed at last in a fresh set of battle leathers, including another sleeveless green vest, she left the bathroom. Stone wasn't near the bed, thank goodness.

She hadn't exactly figured out what to do about his suggestion. They weren't all that different in basic philosophies. Each believed in self-sacrifice and doing what they could to end Margetta's assault on the Nine Realms.

But did that mean they had to bond? And if they did form what she knew to be a powerful blood rose bond, would it really make a difference? Or would coming together in that way only complicate her situation even more?

Before she could give Stone an answer, however, he had to know the truth. The moment had come and part of her was relieved that she would finally be telling him that the queen and Aralynn were one in the same. Even so, her heart sank about two feet into the earth.

Of course, she strongly suspected this would end any interest he had in the bond.

But so be it.

"Stone?" She could feel a draught of cool air coming from the direction of the front door.

"I'm over here." He had the front door open and was standing in the doorway. "I was just looking at the moon through the beech trees. I like your cottage."

"I do, too."

She drew up behind him and rose up on tip-toes to peer over his shoulder. The front doorway was a few inches over seven feet, though fairly narrow so he pretty much filled the space. He leaned his shoulder against the side frame and lifted his bottle of beer to his lips.

He took a deep swig, then said, "I checked in with Harris. The Invictus dead at Charborne have been taken care of and the villagers are returning to their homes and farms. I've put the mayor in for a commendation. Even Elias's friend has been found. He'd been hiding out with one of the local farmers."

"That's amazing, on every front. And the Com Center? Is Tannisford quiet?"

"Yeah."

"Hey, you don't sound pleased."

He turned toward her and the moment his gaze touched hers, desire flowed like a fast-moving river. She had it bad for the Mastyr of Tannisford.

The left side of his lips curved. "You like me, don't you?"

"More than I should, given that we have a war on."

He caught her arm suddenly with his free hand, his eyes glittering. "Bond with me. I know it's the right thing to do."

The moment, however, that his fingers wrapped around her bare arm, the earth began to rumble beneath her feet once more.

She glanced down. "Do you feel that?"

He nodded. "Kaden says this is elf-lord power."

She blinked, lifting her gaze to stare at him. "You talked to him, then?"

"He admitted he was a reformed elf-lord. Did you know that's what he was?"

"I did."

The rumbling grew stronger. "He said you use the same power to sustain the mist."

"That's true and it also provides the visions, the ones we've used on our missions. And a vision is definitely coming right now, but you've never been with me before when I channel the elf-lord power. Stone, it always hurts, so be prepared. In fact, maybe you should let go of me."

He released her arm, but he didn't move away from her. His eyes were wide as she braced herself for the power to hit.

When it struck, her back arched and the muscles of her legs seized as though there was just too much power for her to handle. She clenched her teeth and squeezed her eyes shut. She levitated a couple of inches off the floor to keep from falling.

"Aralynn, this is too much. I can feel your agony."

She bit the words out, her eyes still closed. "It'll be okay. You'll see."

"No, I don't see." Suddenly, his hand was on her arm once more and at the exact moment he made contact, skin-to-skin, the elf-lord power left her body and flowed straight into Stone.

And just like that, there was no more pain. She levitated in a descent until her booted feet touched the floor.

She gasped as she opened her eyes. "What did you do?"

But Stone merely stared at her, an expression on his face she couldn't read. Was he in shock? Was the elf-lord power hurting him?

She didn't know.

When the earth quieted down, he released her arm. "I sense a vision coming, about the three mastyrs."

"What do you mean?" she asked.

"Earlier this evening, Harris mentioned no one could raise Gerrod, Ethan or Quinlan on their coms, but I know now that each was taken by Margetta against his will. That's what the vision will be about when it comes. Aralynn, how do I know this? I'm not fae."

"I don't know." She was thoroughly confused about what was happening. "It must be the elf-lord power."

"When I spoke to Harris just a few minutes ago while waiting for you, he said he was going to try to track the mastyrs down. Now he won't have to."

He turned and set his half-empty bottle of beer on the nearby kitchen counter then met her gaze once more. His whole body was vibrating with the power that flowed through him. "I don't know how this is happening. Vampires don't have visions. And this power. Sweet Goddess, it's as though I've been born to it."

"Did it hurt you?" she asked. "I mean when you first channeled it?"

He shook his head. "Not even a little."

Rosamunde didn't understand what was going on.

His lips parted. "The vision is almost on me. Sweet Goddess!"

Chapter Five

Stone felt the elf-lord power vibrating through every part of his body. It was different than any frequency he'd ever experienced, as though it enhanced each ability he possessed while at the same time elevating his power levels.

The vision played at the edges of his mind. He felt the need to do something, but he didn't know what. This was fae territory, not vampire.

He focused inward and worked at opening his thoughts and inviting the vision forward. He already had a sense of it, that he'd soon learn where to find the three, now missing mastyrs.

His heart pounded, sending a sluicing noise through his ears. He was as devoted to the other eight ruling mastyrs as he was to all of Tannisford. They were a brotherhood now, fully united through the Federation against Margetta.

He closed his eyes and embraced the elf-lord power. He could feel its seductiveness like a warm call to every ambition he'd ever had. He could rescue the three mastyrs and be a hero. He wanted that more than anything.

When the elf-lord frequency had engulfed him completely,

the vision began to flow. He knew that what he was seeing would take place within the next few minutes.

Gerrod, Ethan and Quinlan were chained to the damp wall of a dark cave. Nearby, a portable fire pit, glowing with bright red coals, held several branding irons. The skin of each warrior was pitted with deep burns.

For hours now, they'd been tortured, with several bulked up male vampires ready to deliver another round of red-hot pain. Their bonded female wraiths flew around the cave shrieking.

On instinct, Stone began panning back so that he could see the entire cave. As soon as he did, he recognized the system. He'd spent years early on in his Tannisford life exploring the hundreds of miles of caves in the mountainous region behind Dracut Falls near the Sterling River.

He had a small window to get to the men. But he had the elf-lord power in him. He'd be able to fly faster than ever and to fight better.

He shifted his gaze to Aralynn. "I have to go."

"Stone, what did you see?"

"The three mastyrs. Margetta somehow took them. She's holding them in a cave."

She put her hand on his shoulder. "Stone, this doesn't feel right to me. Something's off."

He shook his head. "The vision was perfectly clear and I know exactly where to go and what to do."

When he turned to leave, she caught his arm. "I should go with you."

At that, Stone smiled. "Why? When I have this?" He lifted his arm and a silvery glow of elf-lord power shone from his hands.

He didn't wait to explain anything to her. He had elf-lord power now and he knew he could take on a dozen lesser vampires, all at the same time, if necessary.

He left the doorway and flung himself high into the air. Just as he'd thought, he could fly faster than ever.

With that, he headed southwest toward Dracut Falls. Within a minute, he'd reached his destination, having covered an immense distance of three hundred miles.

He was at least five hundred feet in the air and had an excellent view of the land, the river, and the waterfall. His vampire vision warmed up the landscape so that it was as though a late afternoon sun shone on the green pines and frothy white water.

The river ran at full-bore most of the year, having its source high in the northern, snow-laden Dauphaire Mountains of Tannisford. Several springs and a hundred creeks made their way into the single artery that ran through the western part of his realm.

He was a lot like Quinlan, one of the mastyrs chained in the cave. They'd both spent a lot of time combing every square foot of their respective realms.

In this particular cavern system, that had an entrance behind the fall of water, the caves were cold and wet. Water seeped through the stone walls constantly. He knew what the three captive ruling mastyrs were enduring. Even if Margetta wasn't torturing them, just being tied up in the caves would be hard to bear.

Slowly, he levitated toward the falls. He knew there was an entrance to the caves directly behind the water, which had the easiest access and the men weren't far from the falls. But he was also aware of a couple more entrances within the forest itself on the upper plain. Each was at least two miles past the falls, but his instincts told him Margetta might not know about them.

He passed over the loud rush of water and was surprised by the sudden quiet as he began to fly above the pine forest directly west. The terrain was full of rocks and hillocks along with the pine trees, but it was as though every contour of the land had been burned into his mind.

Love was what he felt for Tannisford and he wasn't alone in that passion. All the ruling mastyrs had developed powerful attachments to their realms. The rise and fall of the land itself was part of that love.

But as he drew close to the land, he suddenly became aware that the elf-lord power he'd been experiencing had dwindled significantly. He slowed his levitation and took a moment to explore the phenomenon. But there was no denying, he was back to his usual self. Whatever it was he'd experienced at Aralynn's cottage had been temporary, perhaps even connected to Ferrenden Peace or to Aralynn or both.

Fine.

Great.

Whatever.

It seemed typical of his experiences tonight that he wouldn't be able to count on what he'd hoped was a war game-changer. Though he had to concede that Aralynn's blood continued to strengthen him and he still had no pain whatsoever.

His thoughts turned immediately to his battle-partner, Aralynn. If he'd been able to sustain the elf-lord power, he wouldn't have hesitated heading straight in. As it was, he had only one goal: To get his men out safely.

That meant, he needed support. He opened up his telepathy. *Aralynn, you there?*

He could feel the wolf's pathing frequency respond immediately. He could also sense her relief. *Where are you? Can I help?*

His heart swelled up like a damn balloon. She'd said exactly what he'd hoped to hear. *I'm at Dracut Falls and yes, you can definitely help. The elf-lord power I'd been channeling … is gone.*

On my way.

He felt the vibrations in the air then Aralynn was right there, her wild red hair flying around her shoulders. She met his gaze then glanced at the terrain below. They levitated about forty feet above the land.

He gripped her shoulder. *I don't know if this will work.*

What?

He didn't try to explain, but he brought the vision forward then sent it along what he hoped was her pathing lane.

"Oh." Her large brown eyes widened and she blinked several times in quick succession.

When the vision played out, she met his gaze and nodded once. *Let's do it.*

Follow me.

He dropped closer to the earth, approaching the westernmost entrance to the cavern system then eased behind a hillock composed mostly of rock and a lot of grasses and forest weeds. The pine trees had encroached through the area but hadn't successfully planted a single sapling on the hill.

He extended his hearing to see if he could detect sounds of the enemy. But nothing returned except the wind in the pines, a very lonely sound in this part of his sparsely populated realm.

Embrace the Power

Keep levitating. We don't want the noise of our boots to alert the enemy.

I agree. Besides, isn't this system really wet?

It is. He was constantly amazed at how well Aralynn knew his realm. She'd said she'd made a thorough study of all the realms, but this was one of those times she'd proven her knowledge yet again.

He had to duck down in order to move inside, but as with the space behind the falls, the initial cavern was tall and quite deep. He knew each of the pathways by heart and skirted any avenue leading directly to the falls.

Circumventing the easy paths, he made his way slowly toward the cave rooms near the falls.

When he drew within fifty feet of the torture area, he heard voices first, and painful shouts that made him cringe and grit his teeth. The rough, agonized moan let him know he was hearing Quinlan at the vile end of a burning hot branding iron.

Rage flooded him and pumped up his arm and leg muscles, while tightening his abdomen. He fired up his battle energy. He had a couple more turns to make, then one short cavern tunnel and he'd be in the middle of it.

But just as he was about to surge forward, Aralynn's voice entered his head. *Slow down, dammit! I know you want to charge in, but the moment you do, Margetta will use one of her deadly fae nets to control you. Stone, she's seen you coming.*

Stone froze in his tracks and began to levitate backward, melting deeper into the caves. He turned to Aralynn. *You've had a vision?* Why was he surprised?

Yes. Use me. I think you're high on elf-lord power and you're not yourself yet.

He planted a hand against his forehead. *I think you're right. The power might be gone, but not a kind of driving ambition I'm having a hard time turning off.*

He planted his hands on his hips and while levitating stared at the pools of water on the stone floor. He was being more impulsive than usual.

She drew close and sniffed him like a wolf would, wrinkling her nose as she met his gaze. *You're right. I'm not smelling elf-lord power. So, what happened?*

It dissipated once I left Ferrenden Peace.

She didn't seem to question this statement but looked around. Another moan sounded. *I'm hearing Mastyr Quinlan, aren't I?*

You are. You know him?

She looked confused for a moment. *Well, not personally, of course. But I know what he looks like. I have a computer and access to the realm-web.*

Right. Okay. So, the vision you had?

Here it is. Margetta's told one of her henchmen you'd be barreling into the main cave. One of them is holding the net and I recognized it at once. It's treated with a fae potion and you'd never be able to escape it.

Sweet Goddess.

Yeah. She wrinkled her nose again but this time for a different reason. *The thing is, she abducted these mastyrs for one purpose: To draw you here and capture you. She's after you, Stone. I'm not sure why, but I have a strong feeling it has to do with your ability to channel the elf-lord power.*

Margetta's presence changed everything. And he agreed with

Aralynn. Earlier, at Charborne, Margetta had aimed for Aralynn, not for him. The Ancient fae had wanted his battle partner dead.

I think you're right.

She nodded. *And after the way you so easily channeled the elf-lord power, it all makes sense. If she'd killed me at Charborne, she would have had you.*

His turn to nod. *She just hadn't counted on a wolf from Ferrenden Peace possessing the kind of power you have.*

Her solemn expression blossomed into a smile and his heart once more felt swollen with affection. This was one of the reasons he hadn't hesitated suggesting they bond. He'd run missions beside her for seven weeks and he loved everything about her.

What? She asked, no doubt surprised by his expression.

He took both of her arms in hand and leaned in. He planted a quick, firm kiss on her lips and let her feel what he felt. *Just that.*

~ ~ ~

Rosamunde froze in her levitated state. She was in the middle of a rescue with Stone and he could make her feel so much with just a brief pressure of his lips on hers.

When he drew back, she couldn't quite close her mouth. *Oh, my.* She wanted to speak aloud, but she was afraid their voices would carry and alert the enemy.

Images flowed through her head of taking Stone back to Aralynn's cottage and keeping him in her bed for the entire day.

She drew close to him, and settled her hand on his face. *How about we go get your men then maybe we can do more of that. What do you say?*

It's a perfect plan.

She chuckled softly. *Except for one small thing. How are we going to rescue the mastyrs from a madwoman and a cave full of her minions?*

He narrowed his gaze at her. *You know that wind you created, the one that got me safely to Joseph's house? The one that evaded Margetta?*

Yup.

Can you use it in another context? I've felt your power level and I think it might be possible for you to create something similar that would hide our presence from the Ancient Fae?

You think so?

He tilted his head slightly. *You really don't know what you have, do you?*

I've never thought about it much. But I trust you, so let me investigate and see what can be done.

Stone's belief in her abilities, gave Rosamunde confidence. She pulled away from him just a little to give herself enough space to draw inward without the distraction of being so close to him.

She closed her eyes and thought about the veil of mist she created through the elf-lord power. Could she do something similar, a kind of mist that would allow her and Stone to enter the cave unseen?

She opened her eyes, meeting his gaze. She thought it best to warn him. *I'm going to try to access the elf-lord power from here. I don't know if I can, but it would be the means by which I could create a kind of shield for us.*

He frowned. *But the pain. I don't want you to hurt like that again. Should I try to channel the power?*

I honestly don't know. But I want to make the attempt and we can figure it out as we go along.

Sounds good.

She nodded once then closed her eyes again. She drew inside herself and focused solely on the elf-lord power. Only a couple of seconds passed before the earth began to rumble. She knew Margetta would sense the shift, so whatever she was going to do, she had to act quickly.

When the pain started, she knew she couldn't afford to wait for it to ease up. Stone would have to be involved.

She grabbed his arm and held on, then let the power flow into him. Only this time, she focused on bringing it back to herself.

When she felt it return, yet without the smallest discomfort, she began constructing something she'd never made before: A shield that would block their presence to outsiders.

I can feel what you're doing and there's no pain for you, is there? Stone's telepathic voice sounded excited within her mind.

She felt the same way. *No pain at all. But I'm sensing movement.* She opened her eyes and glanced up the tunnel. Stone followed her gaze.

In the distance, was a golden glow.

Margetta. Stone drew close, sliding his arm around her waist. *She must have felt the earth rumble when you accessed the elf-lord power.*

Rosamunde's heart slammed around in her chest until she felt sure it would burst. *What do we do now?*

Stone drew her tight against the miserably wet cave wall. *We wait to see if your shield holds.*

~ ~ ~

Stone watched Margetta's gold light grow increasingly intense until suddenly the Ancient Fae appeared around the corner. She was a striking woman whom he'd only ever seen in her long velvet gowns. She wore a dark blue one now as she levitated slowly in their direction. Her violet eyes were wide and searching. Her long blond hair, sculpted into large ringlets, floated around her shoulders all the way to her waist. Except for the hard line of her lips, she was a beautiful woman.

"I can feel your presence, Mastyr Stone, but I can't see you. What has your clever wolf done for you this time?"

Stone tightened his arm around Aralynn. She trembled beside him, but the elf-lord power kept her shield tight and he knew it would hold.

He held his breath as she breezed past them, flying even more swiftly back down the tunnel. She carried an evil stench, like rotting garbage.

He didn't move, however. Aralynn didn't either. Margetta wouldn't leave her captives for very long. Barely ten seconds later, the gold light returned and flew past them. He couldn't even see Margetta this time, just the brilliant light surrounding her as she raced back in the direction she'd come.

When she disappeared, Stone released a strained breath. Aralynn turned into him and slung her free arm around his waist.

He surrounded her with his arms and held her close. Her voice hit his telepathy. *That smell. I hate it more than anything.*

You've smelled it often?

Not really. Just once, when I was a little girl. Margetta killed my mother.

Stone grew very still. The revelation was not something Aralynn had told him before. *No wonder you're shaking.*

Slowly, she drew back and lifted her face to his. Her brown eyes were wet with tears. She offered a faltering smile. *But the shield held, so we're good.*

We're good.

She took a deep breath and her lips curved. *Let's go get your men.*

He loved her courage more than anything and without thinking, he kissed her again, another quick press of his lips to hers. She caressed his face and nodded.

Releasing her, he levitated away from the wall, yet he could feel the shield like a clinging drag of mist all around him. He was grateful for the physical sensation since he'd be able to detect any change if something went wrong.

I know these caves inside and out and I've seen exactly where Margetta has the mastyrs chained up. Stick close. The words sounded like a bark, even telepathically.

Her lips quirked. *Yes, Mastyr.*

He smiled. Aralynn, like Delia, never let his head get too big. He liked that about her as well.

He shifted his gaze to the tunnel and charted his course. Levitating slowly and once more extending his hearing, he could hear laughter, both male and female, coupled with jeers.

The Invictus bonds were permanent and eradicated a sense of morality from both the wraith and the victim. The worst characteristics of each individual came to the fore.

Wraith-pairs quickly became thieves and murderers. They developed an instant addiction to blood and killed their victims often by draining them to death. Those they attacked were all ages. Murdering rampages quickly became the preferred way of life.

The enemy was vicious and without conscience.

We're only a few yards away.

He felt Aralynn's battle vibration begin to beat at him. She also carried a dagger in her sheath that she knew how to use extremely well. *I'm ready.*

Her confident response urged him forward. *We'll be entering at the back of the cave well behind the Invictus and across from where the men are chained.*

Got it.

The back entrance area was to the west of what he knew to be a large cavern. He could hear Dracut Falls easily now, though the cave was set back about thirty yards from the waterfall.

As he levitated into the back of the cavern, he could smell the burning coals. A few feet more and the portable fire pit came into view. Branding irons stuck of the middle of the blazing coals, heated up and ready for use.

He stopped for a moment, needing to take it all in. Aralynn drew up beside him. The shield she'd created held tight. The men he'd served beside for centuries were manacled to the opposite wall: Gerrod, Ethan and Quinlan.

Though he had a strong impulse to charge in, he needed to be wise. *I want to get the layout,* he pathed to Aralynn.

Though there were natural stone pillars separating their side of the massive cavern from the rest of the space, he could see the ruling mastyrs easily. Each had been stripped down to their leathers, whipped and beaten.

Blood ran from several chest and abdominal wounds, and he could now smell burning flesh, inflicted by the branding irons. At the same time, self-healing energy boiled from the men. They weren't powerful vampires for nothing and each had bonded with a blood rose, adding to their abilities. That Margetta had overpowered them in some way was a testament to her essential power.

The wraiths flew slowly around the space, yet in an agitated, predatory manner. Their shrieks had died down for the moment.

Aralynn grabbed his wrist. She was trembling again.

He glanced at her, holding her gaze. He knew she'd seen a lot in the seven weeks they'd been battling together, but nothing as heinous and personal as this. *I know this is hard to take. Do you want to sit this one out?*

She shook her head. *I'm overcome with rage, not fear. I hate what's happening here with a passion.*

He could feel it now, the strength of her anger which matched his own.

The cavern curved toward the southeast, so that he couldn't actually see Margetta from where he and Aralynn hovered. But her golden glow spilled from the space nearest the east exiting tunnel.

Margetta called out. "Be ready, my servants. Mastyr Stone is here."

At the mention of his name, two of the wraiths shrieked and took to flying rapidly back and forth through the air near the two-story cavern ceiling.

The third and tallest wraith floated in the air and turned

slowly in a circle, hunting for them. Invictus wraiths were fierce-looking, and this one was no different. Her skin was white to the point of opaque and she had yellow fangs, dark lips, and small eyes. She wore the traditional wraith gown made up of gauzy red strips of fabric sewn loosely together to float around her thin legs.

She smiled, showing red gums. "We'll find him, Mistress Margetta."

Stone took Aralynn's hand. *Let's get higher in the air.* He rose as he spoke, Aralynn with him.

With no pillars to obstruct his view, Stone caught sight of the Ancient Fae. *I see Margetta now.*

She squeezed his wrist. *Me, too.*

"Take Gerrod again this time." Margetta's voice had a special ring of authority, something he knew to be manufactured. She used her voice to control her subjects.

"Yes, Mistress." All three vampires responded in unison.

One of the powerful male vampires, just shy of mastyr status, headed in Gerrod's direction. He moved slowly and bore bruises up and down his legs and across his abdomen.

Stone smiled. The ruling mastyrs had fought back and apparently Margetta didn't do anything to protect her minions. Typical.

Gerrod's head hung down and it seemed to Stone that though he appeared unconscious, his thigh muscles flexed.

Stone needed more information about the shield. *Aralynn, Can I cross the space and still be invisible?*

Let me explore this new creation of mine. He knew she'd focused her thoughts inward. After a moment, she released his wrist. *Yes. Absolutely. It won't dissipate until I want it to. The distances within* the cavern are not an issue. Though I have the sense any farther and the lack of close proximity would become a problem. So what's the plan? I'd like to have a sense of where you might need me.

I'll go to Gerrod first, Stone said. I think I can help him in a way that will appear as though he's the one battling the vampire when the captor draws close.

Got it. I'm going to rise to the ceiling and remain above you, out of the way but ready. Just call me into action at will.

Good. He glanced at her. He could see her easily, though a soft violet mist surrounded them both.

As the vampires drew close to Gerrod, his fists raised protectively, Stone sped in Gerrod's direction. He opened a path to the heavily muscled ruling vampire of Merhaine Realm. Gerrod, keep your eyes down. Try not to look surprised.

Stone? Is that you?

Yes. Stone saw how careful Gerrod was being. But then control was this mastyr's forte. Take a moment and let both Quinlan and Ethan know that I'm here. The wolf, Aralynn, is helping me to sustain this level of invisibility.

Gerrod's even, formal cadence entered his mind. Margetta is here, Stone. This is a trap. You should escape while you can.

Not gonna happen. Not on my watch. Let the other men know that a rescue is at hand, then return to path with me.

If that's what you want.

It is. He waited until he saw that Ethan's shoulders tensed and Quinlan eyes shifted slightly to the side as Gerrod pathed with the two mastyrs. But other than these reactions, Stone doubted anyone watching, including Margetta, would have a clue what was going on.

Seeing that one of the Invictus wraiths now pulled a hot branding iron from the coals, and the male vampires advanced on Gerrod, Stone pathed. *When the wraith gets close, I'm going to engage. Use your feet to hold off the vampires as I see you've been doing. I have to make this look like you're the only one battling.*

Understood.

The deep bruising on Gerrod's sides told Stone the mastyr probably had broken ribs.

As the smiling, evil wraith descended toward her prey, Gerrod's deep voice sounded through Stone's mind. *Ready when you are. Let's take these bastards down.*

Stone levitated swiftly and positioned himself next to Gerrod.

He let the mastyr feel the pressure of his hand on his shoulder. The advancing vampire held his body low to catch Gerrod's legs if he started to kick. The wraith with the iron moved around her mate's shoulder. *Lift your leg to kick at her.*

The moment Gerrod grunted heavily and swung the lower half of his body in the wraith's direction, Stone launched at the wraith, caught her on her stomach and flew her backward to land on the hard cave floor. The branding iron clattered away. The other wraiths shrieked.

The vampire minion caught one of Gerrod's legs. Stone grabbed the vampire's wrist and twisted hard. The bone cracked. The vampire fell sideways screaming in pain.

"The rest of you punish Mastyr Gerrod." Margetta's voice filled the space, but her words told Stone his ruse had worked. She didn't know he was there.

Stone watched as the two remaining vampires moved in from either side. He shifted pathing frequencies. *Aralynn, can you get the manacle keys and release the others while* Gerrod *and I engage the two vampires?*

Will do.

From high in the ceiling, he felt her move toward the rack to the left of the mastyrs that held the keys.

Stone once more took up his place next to Gerrod. *I'm beside you again. Aralynn is going to release the other two while we're engaged. So, I need you to battle viciously and make a lot of noise. Can you do that?*

With pleasure.

As the wary vampires got within a few feet, Stone saw that each pair of eyes had the crazed look of an Invictus maniac. Snarls formed on their lips and saliva dripped from each chin. The ferocity that accompanied their deranged minds would have intimidated Stone if he hadn't been fighting them from the time he could remember.

Aralynn's pathing voice intruded. *I've got the key, but I can tell Margetta senses something's going on. I think she's tapped into my presence. Try to keep her distracted, so I can get these manacles off Mastyrs Quinlan and Ethan.*

That's the plan. Stone then instructed all the ruling mastyrs to let loose with as much shouting and obscenities as each could muster.

The vampires made their move, intending to pulverize Gerrod with their fists. But Stone revved up his battle energy and gave each of them a good zap then began throwing punches. All three mastyrs started shouting as loud as they could, which further incited the Invictus vampires. Even so, they remained focused on Gerrod.

As each made a move to attack Gerrod, Stone intervened doing his best to make it look like Gerrod had so much power he was thrusting them away with his battle energy. And every time Stone's fist connected with one of the torturers, his spirit soared. He wanted to shout along with the others, but he worked instead to sustain the deception as long as he could.

The wraith-mates rose into the air and delivered even more noise to the chaos.

Because Quinlan and Ethan were shouting to the Invictus vampires, calling them every wretched name possible, one of the vampires soon shifted his attention to Ethan. Being next to Gerrod, he made the easier target. Ethan kicked wildly with his feet. Stone shifted some of his battle energy to Ethan's attacker, but the close quarters made doing anything tough.

Aralynn, how we doin'?

Almost got Quinlan's manacles off. One is gone, but he's holding it in place against the chain for effect.

I see it.

Suddenly, Quinlan's arms fell free of the shackles and he went after the nearest vampire that was attacking Ethan. He rained blows down on the bastard's head.

"What's going on here?" Margetta shouted.

In the next few seconds, Aralynn freed Ethan.

In the meantime, Stone continued helping Gerrod battle the remaining vampire, while still attempting to disguise his presence as best he could. The vampire with the broken wrist hung back as the wraiths continued to shriek, but he'd gained his feet.

Ethan launched onto the back of the nearest vampire and pounded on the man's ears. The vampire fell to his knees in agony but his wraith-mate soon attacked Ethan from the air, jumping on his back and biting his neck hard.

A wind suddenly filled the cavern and Margetta's golden glow flooded the space. "Stone, show yourself? I know you're here, but how are you remaining invisible to my practiced eye?"

Stone ignored the Ancient Fae. He used his battle energy and struck down one of the wraith-mates. She dropped dead near her companion vampire. Because the bond gave so much shared strength, once death intervened, the mate fell at the same time.

One pair down.

The vampire with the broken wrist launched in again.

Quinlan pinned him easily to the ground while Ethan battled a wraith and her bonded vampire with his blue battle energy. Blue and red sparks rose into the air.

Aralynn, I'll try to get this vampire under control then you can work on Gerrod's.

I'm trying to stay out of the way of battle fire and your fists almost got me twice. But, I'll see what I can do.

Stone leaped onto the back of the vampire attacking Gerrod, and got him in a head-lock. He drew him away and watched as Aralynn made quick work of Gerrod's manacles.

Gerrod wasted no time, but came at the same vampire and punched him hard in the stomach. When the vampire fell forward, Stone released him. Gerrod then brought the full force of both fists down on the back of his neck. Stone heard the crack.

The vampire was dead.

The bonded wraith fell from high in the air, struck her head on the side of the fire pit. Stone checked her pulse. She'd died instantly, her face half-submerged in a puddle of cave water.

Two pairs down.

Aralynn's voice pierced Stone's mind. *Margetta's winding up her power. I've got to lead her away or she'll kill the ruling mastyrs.*

He looked around for Aralynn and saw her high in the cavern, toward the ceiling. *Will you be safe?*

Yes. I already know I can outrun her.

Contact me as soon as you're free of her.

Will do.

With that, Aralynn whipped toward the eastern tunnel that led to the waterfall. She created her former and very powerful violet wind. She flew straight at Margetta then clipped her hard. Margetta fell to the stone floor, but rose almost as swiftly, cursing loudly.

She took the bait and went after Aralynn.

With Margetta gone, quiet filled the cavern. All six Invictus were now dead and the ruling mastyrs were breathing hard and working on self-healing. Because Aralynn had left, his shield dissipated quickly.

He didn't waste time, but contacted Harris for back-up. He briefed him quickly and ordered several squads dispatched to Dracut Falls immediately. Within minutes, any vampire Guardsman or Brigade shifter in the area would be rerouted to Stone's position. If Margetta returned, they'd be ready for her.

Harris would also call for a troll removal team to care for the dead Invictus.

Stone turned his attention to the mastyrs.

Gerrod drew close and planted his hand on Stone's shoulder. "Thank you, Brother."

"Of course." But his gaze shifted to the place where Margetta had followed Aralynn in pursuit. He couldn't help but worry. The woman he wanted to bond with was being pursued by the Ancient Fae.

Ethan moved to stand in front of Stone, Quinlan with him. "How the hell did you find us? We were dining in a private room in a restaurant in Grochaire Realm, Margetta showed up and suddenly we were here. We had no way to contact anyone."

Stone forced his attention back to the men. Each was sweating heavily besides being bruised, cut up, and branded. But they were already healing themselves.

"How did I find you?" He debated exactly how much to tell them since he didn't want to reveal that elf-lord power was involved. "Because of Aralynn. I know I've talked about her."

The men nodded. Quinlan said, "She's the one who gets the fae visions, though she's mostly wolf. That's a helluva lot of power."

"It is." He felt the need to twist events around a little. "But tonight, when she got the vision of the three of you, she touched me. The moment she did, I saw the vision as well, that you were here, behind Dracut Falls."

Gerrod's serious blue eyes pierced him. "The power of the Nine Realms is moving through Tannisford, isn't it?"

He'd said it exactly right. "Aralynn is a blood rose."

At that moment, he felt Aralynn tap on his pathing frequency. He lifted his hand toward the mastyrs. "Hold on. She's reporting in." He switched to telepathy. *Everything okay?*

I made it fine to Ferrenden Peace. Like last time, I was able to lose her pretty fast.

He released a heavy sigh. He hadn't even been aware he'd been holding his breath. *That's good news. I'm wrapping things up here with the mastyrs. Harris is sending troops in as we speak.*

I'll wait to hear from you.

Good deal.

He felt her end the communication and he reverted his attention to the men.

All three of them were smiling.

"Is everything okay?" Ethan asked, showing all his big teeth, the handsome bastard that he was.

"She's fine. She's back in Ferrenden Peace, safe and sound. She lost Margetta just a few miles out."

"Good to hear." Quinlan nodded. Though usually dour, his lips had an upward slant as well. "So, she's a blood rose."

Stone nodded. "That she is."

Gerrod once more clapped him in the shoulder. "I trust this is a good thing." His speech was as formal as ever.

"A very good thing. I admire the hell out of her. She was the one who kept us invisible from Margetta so that we could initiate a rescue."

Gerrod nodded solemnly. "But it's a difficult path at first."

Ethan clubbed Stone on the arm. "But worth it. Have you tasted her blood yet?"

Stone nodded and just like that the memory flooded him, of what it had been like. For a moment he couldn't speak, then finally said, "There's no more pain."

"It's damn overwhelming." Quinlan's deep voice brought Stone's attention back to the moment. Quinlan added, "I know it's only been a few hours, but has anything else changed in our world? Do you know if Batya has been harmed? Abigail? Samantha?"

Stone shook his head. "I haven't heard anything about your women. I'd only barely heard from Harris a couple of hours ago that there was some concern you couldn't be reached."

He felt it then, the profound need the men had to get back to their women, to their blood roses. And they each needed to be fed. Though they'd bonded with women who had freed them from their chronic blood starvation, they were still vampires that had been wounded badly and would need to be restored.

Quinlan continued, "Has anything new surfaced with Margetta? While she had us in chains, did she send her army to attack any of the realms?"

"No. Nothing like that, at least not that I've heard."

Ethan shoved at his wild curls. He frowned. "So, what's going on, then? She could have killed us all, at any time. Instead, this had to have been a trap of some kind. Was this about you? Or Aralynn?"

Stone shook his head. "We think it's about me." He then told them about Charborne and the Ancient Fae's attempt to kill Aralynn.

"She doesn't want you dead, then?" Gerrod narrowed his gaze. "If not, what does she want from you?"

Stone shrugged. "Hell if I know." Though in the back of his mind, he suspected it had to do with his ability to channel the elf-lord power. If Rosamunde was right, and Margetta had been trying to acquire the elf-lord power all this time, then Margetta might have learned through a fae vision of her own that Stone could channel this power. But he was so new to the phenomenon, he didn't know what to think and he didn't want his brothers-in-arms distressed by something called 'elf-lord' power. It would raise a dozen questions for which he had no answers, at least not yet.

Ethan said, "If she was aiming for Aralynn, it's possible she's just trying to get you off your game. We all know what an effective battle partner she's become for you."

"You got that right. She's saved my ass a number of times as it is."

Ethan glanced around. "So what did Aralynn do? I saw a purplish wind that disappeared down the east tunnel. Then Margetta's gold wind followed."

"She led Margetta away because the Ancient Fae was preparing to fire on the three of you. If she'd succeeded, you'd all be dead."

Gerrod nodded. "Sounds like you're an excellent team."

Stone agreed. "But right now, I want to get you men back home."

As the mastyrs each contacted their respective realms, Stone thought about just how long it would take for the men to fly back on their own power. He decided to give Davido a telepathic shout.

And how do you fare, my good man?

Stone's lips curves. Despite the terror of the last few minutes, the sound of Davido's almost quaint speech made him smile. He told Davido about Ethan, Quinlan and Gerrod. *So, I'm wondering if you could give them a lift home. Otherwise, it'll take hours to fly. Apparently, Margetta swept them all here with her teleporting ability.*

Davido said nothing, but the next moment, he stood beside Stone in the wet cave. He cursed on arriving because instead of levitating he'd landed in a puddle of water. "Damn the elf-lords to hell, these are my new Italian loafers."

All four mastyrs turned to look at him, smiling.

Davido levitated so that he could meet the men in the eye, then looked each of them up and down. As a group, they ranged from six-five to six-seven. If Davido topped out at five-three, Stone would be surprised.

"So the old bat took branding irons to the lot of you, did she?"

Stone shook his head. Ethan and Quinlan laughed outright. "The 'old bat' did," Quinlan said. He lifted his arm, then cringed. "Sweet Goddess, I need a bath."

Davido glanced at Stone and winked. "Let's get you boys home."

With that, the oldest realm-person alive vanished, with all three powerful vampires.

Stone let Harris know that the ruling mastyrs were headed back to their respective realms. A moment later, the first team of Guardsmen arrived as well as Harris.

Knowing that the situation was well in hand, Stone levitated to the falls, slid from behind the powerful curtain of water then took to the air. He desired nothing more than to sleep away the day in his private lake home.

While he flew, he pathed with Ian, the ruling mastyr of Camberlaune Realm. He filled him in on all that had happened, though even from him, a man he considered to be his closest friend, he withheld any information about the elf-lord power.

Ian served as his second-in-command of the Combined Realm Forces. *And all three are safe now? So it was a scheme of the Ancient Fae's to reel you in?*

Exactly. But I couldn't have freed them without Aralynn. He then shared about the wolf being a blood rose.

Ian congratulated him but offered a warning. *Remember, she'll be a beacon to all mastyrs. Best keep her close.*

I've asked her to bond with me, but she's hesitant. I like this wolf a lot. I admire her and she has a boatload of power. I see no reason not to get on with things.

He heard Ian laugh telepathically. *That is so like you. Always ready to jump in with both feet.*

But would Aralynn ever consent to the bond?

Chapter Six

Rosamunde hadn't gone to Aralynn's place. Instead, she'd headed straight to the castle. She wanted the security of the thick stone walls. Not that it would help one bit if Margetta ever got past the veil of mist, but she still felt safer than if she'd been in the small cottage.

She'd also transformed back into her fae form. She needed time to think and Aralynn's fiery wolf nature tended to keep her thoughts fixed on things she shouldn't be thinking about, like Stone's lips and his broad shoulders and what it had felt like to make love with him.

She sighed and went into the bathroom to fetch her brush. Her hair needed attending.

Shortly after she'd flown away from the cave with her violet wind whipping her high into the air, Margetta had revved up her battle energy. Sensing Margetta's intention to fire on her, Rosamunde had been forced to access the elf-lord power while in flight. Even though it hurt like hell without Stone nearby to channel the power away, the boost had made her fly like a rocket. She'd outstripped the Ancient Fae fairly quickly, not once getting hit or even singed.

Though she could have easily teleported, she feared her aunt would be able to follow her. In many respects, she simply didn't know the extent or limitations of Margetta's powers. Except, of course, that Margetta lacked Rosamunde's speed.

She'd also needed to keep Margetta focused on her. She didn't want the Ancient Fae going back to Dracut Falls and the longer she kept Margetta in pursuit, the safer Stone was.

It was still inconceivable to Rosamunde that her own aunt wanted her dead, but so she did.

By the time she'd passed through the veil of mist surrounding Ferrenden Peace, most of the cramping in her legs had begun to dissipate. Safely inside her kingdom, she'd teleported to her castle bedroom.

She was about to sit down in a chair near her ornate dresser, when a feminine voice called to her. "Don't be alarmed. It's just me."

Rosamunde whirled to find Vojalie standing near the long narrow windows that overlooked the east castle gardens. "Vojalie, what are you doing here?"

"We need to talk. I know it's been a long night so I'll keep this simple: It's imperative that you bond with Stone."

Rosamunde shook her head and set her brush on the dresser. She then pulled the Guardsman-style clip from her hair. It felt good to set her frizzy red mass free. "I can't and you know why."

"You need to tell him you're Aralynn."

She picked up her brush and started working it through her long tresses. "What happened to going with the flow?"

Vojalie clamped her hands together tightly. "I had a vision."

At that, a chill went through Rosamunde and she set the brush back on the dresser. This could not be good. She wasn't even sure she wanted to hear the details.

"Does Davido know about the situation at Dracut Falls?"

"He does. He pathed to tell me about it, but that's when I had the vision."

Slowly, Rosamunde crossed the room to stand near Vojalie. "What did you see?" Rosamunde had never seen Vojalie this upset. Usually she bore such a peaceful spirit that her mere presence was comforting.

Not right now. Vojalie blinked more than usual and held her hands in tight fists. Even her breathing was erratic.

"It's about Stone. He's in terrible danger, which means our world is as well. I don't know how to say this, but I've seen one version of the future in which he bonds with Margetta."

Rosamunde gasped, her hand flying to her chest, just over her heart. "What? No. That can't happen. I won't let it."

"I know you'll do everything you can but the surest way to avoid it is if you bond with him. And I don't think I need to tell you what happens if Stone falls to Margetta."

Dizziness assailed her as well as a fae certainty that Vojalie had translated her vision accurately. "I know. I feel it was well, that the Nine Realms will be lost for a thousand years."

"Exactly. And most everyone we know and love will die within the first decade of her reign."

Rosamunde turned slightly then sank into a tall wing-back chair to the right of the window. She closed her eyes. She was weary from the events of the night and all she wanted right now was a good day's sleep.

Now the pressure for her to bond with Stone was stronger than ever.

But after so many centuries of isolation and service as the queen, Rosamunde's temper spiked. She rose once more and faced the powerful fae. They were both tall women so she met her eye-to-eye. "How can you lay one more burden on me? Have I not done enough, sacrificed enough, suffered enough through the years? Must the fate of the entire Nine Realms also lay on my shoulders? Must I bond myself to a man who despises me?"

Vojalie shook her head. "Again, you need to talk this through with him, to help him understand that he's completely mistaken about your natural ability. And on what exactly does he base his summation of your powers?"

"Do you remember when I first met Mastyr Quinlan and Mastyr Seth? And that Quinlan had brought his woman, Batya, to the castle along with Margetta's daughter, Lorelei?"

"I remember. Was Stone there?"

"No. But he heard about how I'd put both mastyrs in stasis because they were about to kill each other over Batya. She hadn't yet bonded with Quinlan and Seth was drawn to her. I froze them in the air."

At that, Vojalie smiled. "Right. I taught you that trick."

"But I was only able to do it because of the elf-lord power and it hurt like anything though I made sure no one saw the pain I was in. Because of this, Stone seems to believe that I have so much ability that I could have taken on Margetta at any time over the past thousand years. And as I've said before, as Aralynn I tried to explain the truth to him, but you know how stubborn Stone can be."

Vojalie chuckled softly. "Men."

"And I have too many secrets. You know I do."

"I know. And it doesn't help that Davido has sworn you to secrecy about his own involvement in Stone's life. But the time for revelation on that front is coming soon. Never fear."

"But don't you see that when Stone knows that I've been party to the secret, he'll resent me for not telling him?"

Vojalie seemed to relax a little, though she suddenly appeared very sad. The light in her eyes had dimmed. She stepped forward and settled her hand on Rosamunde's shoulder. "I apologize for laying this on you because you're right. The fates have not been kind to you and I can see now how deeply complicated your relationship with Stone is because of these secrets. I know him as well. He will hate the restraint, the lies, the deceptions. All of it.

"I also think until this moment I didn't quite understand what you were up against. The worst, of course, has to be Margetta's visions and the terrible burden you've born because of them."

Rosamunde shuddered. The truth of what she'd endured because of Margetta was the hardest part of her life. Only Vojalie and Davido knew what she'd suffered over the centuries at the Ancient Fae's hands.

Margetta had a way of sending her very specific visions designed to cause Rosamunde tremendous distress. In each vision, Margetta would show her exactly what she intended to do within the next few minutes of the vision and it always involved death. The same words would accompany the vision: *Respond to anyone telepathically, dear Rosamunde, and these lives will be spared.*

The message had a specific meaning that Rosamunde understood very well. If Rosamunde so much as whispered to another individual with her pathing ability, Margetta would be able to get a fix on her position and teleport straight to Rosamunde. Once within Ferrenden Peace, Margetta would have complete access to the elf-lord power.

Yet each time Rosamunde held her ground, refusing to deliver the warnings of impending tragedy, Margetta would make good on the visions. Hundreds of realm-folk had died because Rosamunde had refused to give up her location and therefore access to the elf-lord power. She knew she'd saved tens of thousands of lives in the process, but the inevitable attacks slayed her soul every single time.

The catalog of these terrible events went as far back in Rosamunde's history as she could remember, so far back that Rosamunde knew of the slaughter of Stone's adopted parents before the event happened. She therefore could have warned Stone of the impending attack and he could have saved his mother and father from being killed. And that was one of dozens of terrible visions Margetta had laid out for Rosamunde over the centuries with the purpose of torturing her into giving up her location.

Vojalie and Davido knew of the visions and Vojalie would counsel Rosamunde whenever the ensuing tragedies became too great for Rosamunde to bear.

She turned to look out the window that overlooked the eastern part of her kingdom. The castle bedroom was at least three stories in the air and because the entire structure was perched on a higher elevation, she could see the town laid out before her to the south, lights twinkling, and troll laughter drifting along the air currents. She remembered vividly Quinlan, Batya's and Lorelei's visit and how much she'd envied the way Quinlan had already become devoted to Batya.

Now Stone was devoted to Aralynn. She put a hand to her chest again. She felt the new heaviness that indicated her heart had already increased its blood supply for him.

So this was what it was to be a blood rose.

She realized with a start that she couldn't carry this around with her forever. She'd have to donate.

Another reality of the blood rose phenomenon struck her suddenly. Other mastyrs would catch the scent of her blood, those unbonded, and they'd crave what she had to offer, just as Stone did.

Without warning, Stone's voice pierced her mind. *Just checking in. Everything okay? I'm heading to my lake house.*

I'm fine. I'm safe in Ferrenden Peace. I lost Margetta, though I had to access the elf-lord power to get a final burst of speed to escape her. Did everyone get away okay?

I had Davido come in and teleport the mastyrs home. So, yes, all is as it should be.

Stone's telepathic voice deepened. *So, I was wondering. I'd like to ask you something.*

Sure, but could you hold on for a sec?

Absolutely.

She turned to Vojalie and aloud, said, "I'll think about what you've said. I will. I'll weigh it all, including what I've suffered and my need to help Stone to understand my reality as the support for the veil of mist. But right now, I can't promise that I'll bond with him. Once he knows the truth, he won't want me."

Vojalie lifted her chin sighing deeply. "We've come to a point in realm history where the immediate future is little more than a boiling mass of chaos. But I trust you and I know you'll do what's best for the Nine Realms." With that, she vanished.

Aralynn, hey. You still there?

I am. Sorry. Vojalie was here and I had to finish our conversation. She just left.

Understood. But I've had an idea. We've got a couple of hours before dawn and I don't know about you, but I'm starved. A friend of mine owns a wonderful restaurant in Sandismare and she's holding a booth for us. That is, if you'd like to join me for a late supper.

Rosamunde pressed both hands to her cheeks. They were burning with so much pleasure tears started to her eyes. *I'd love to.* She didn't dare say anything else for fear she would betray just how much a simple dinner invitation meant to her. It was thoughtful and even romantic and just what she needed given Vojalie's horrendous vision.

But there's more, Stone pathed. *Will you join me at my lake house afterward? I'd like to be with you for the day. And yes, that means I'm asking if I can take you to bed.*

Rosamunde gasped. The invitation was bold, to the point, and very much Stone.

She put her hand to her chest again. Being with him would at least take care of her too-much-blood problem.

For a moment, she forgot all about Vojalie as well as Margetta's intention to subjugate the Nine Realms to her bidding. She set aside her need to tell him the truth about her identity and her fear that one day he would discover that she'd had foreknowledge about the deaths of his parents.

Instead, she chose for herself. No matter what happened in the future, she would have this date with Stone and a day spent in bed with him. Maybe somewhere in all of the intimacy, she'd be able to tell him the truth about herself in a way he could accept.

I'm with you, Stone. All the way.

Good. He gave her the address and they settled on forty-five minutes, which provided enough time for a shower.

When he disconnected his telepathy, she headed for the bathroom. At some point during the next few hours she would have to reveal the truth to Stone about who she really was even though she felt sure Stone would never forgive her for the deception.

Despite it all, she was going to have dinner with him and spend the day at his private lake house.

The chips could just fall wherever the hell they wanted to.

~ ~ ~

Stone stood beside the booth, waiting. He'd made arrangements with the club's owner, Marny, a fae woman whose troll husband kept her very pregnant. They had a brood like none he'd ever seen, but he wasn't sure he knew of a happier couple.

Marny had set him up in a private corner, slightly apart from the rest of the club so that he'd be able to talk with Aralynn while enjoying the live jazz music at a quiet distance.

Marny returned with a candle in a crystal bowl. "She still coming?"

"I hope so. We've only got an hour before dawn and it's been a long night."

Marny put her hand to the small of her back. "I hear that." Her belly looked exactly like she'd taped a basketball to her stomach. "I know I look ridiculous."

"Have you picked out a name yet?"

She grinned. "If it's a boy, we're thinking 'Stone.'"

"You're not serious?"

"I am. Can't quite persuade Bertie. He thinks I've got a crush on you."

At that, Stone glanced at the fae woman. Did she?

She fluttered her eyelashes up at him and rocked her head back and forth a few times, playing it up absurdly.

He rolled his eyes.

"Don't mean anything against you, Mastyr, but Bertie's got a kind of charisma that will have me dancing around his feet forever." Her face took on a faraway expression that confirmed what she was saying. When she came back to herself, she said, "All right. I'll keep an eye on you myself. Hope your girl makes it."

He'd already had Marny pour two dark beers into tall glasses. Aralynn preferred beer to wine and he wanted her to know that he was thinking of her. Marny, aware he was on a romantic hunt, had also provided him with a red rose in a small vase.

He had his hand on the back of the booth, gripping it tighter than he should. He even released a series of deep breaths to try to calm himself the hell down.

He shouldn't be this jumpy, but after he'd arrived at his private lake house, a place he wanted to share with Aralynn, he remembered her restraint. He'd jumped the gun, as he so often did, leaping in with his proverbial impulsive feet and hadn't considered what this must be like from her point-of-view.

He was a strong man and he'd been told he had a booming voice. When he'd been with Aralynn earlier and had *suggested* they bond, he now realized it had probably sounded more like a command than anything else.

For himself, he had no doubts that completing the blood rose bond was the route to take. But how to persuade a reluctant wolf?

Movement near the entrance shifted his gaze to the new arrivals. He was absurdly disappointed that a fae couple walked in, until he caught sight of dark red hair and creamy white skin just beyond them.

Aralynn.

He was heading in her direction before he'd ordered his feet to move.

As he drew close, her eyes widened. She looked him up and down. "You're wearing a suit. Is that silk?"

She'd asked a question, but he hadn't heard her. "You look beautiful." Understatement. She'd somehow tamed her hair into a braid she'd twisted and pinned to the back of her head, showing off her strong cheekbones. She'd added some make-up as well that enhanced her brown eyes.

He leaned close and could smell the rich scent of her blood. He kissed her cheek. *Aralynn,* slipped from his mind to hers.

She caught his arm. "We have to talk."

"We will. Whatever you want." He meant it, too.

But right now all he could think about was how beautiful her throat was. She wore a black dress with a neckline that plunged to a deep 'V' and really showed off her breasts. As he guided her to their booth, his gaze kept returning to the sight of her cleavage. His tongue vibrated with need. What they'd done earlier in Joseph's lair had been wild, incredible and very fast. This time, he wanted to slow things down.

She scooted into the booth and he joined her on the opposite side. "You ordered a beer for me. Thank you." Her wolf voice called to him. "But I think maybe you'd better kiss me before you explode."

His arm was already settled along the back of the booth, close to her shoulders. "Does it show?"

"Not 'show'. But your mating energy is pounding against mine so hard, I'm not sure how long I'll be able to keep my hands off you."

His gaze fell to half-mast. He leaned in and as she turned her head in his direction, he caught her lips with his own. He hadn't even noticed his mating drive, but she was right. He was already begging admittance.

He deepened the kiss and when she parted her lips he moved inside, plumbing the depths of her mouth with his tongue. She moaned softly and pressed herself against him.

He only stopped when he heard Marny clear her throat. He drew back. "Sorry to disturb, but here are the grilled artichokes you ordered." Though she spoke respectfully, her eyes were dancing.

He picked up his beer and let a few gulps slide down his throat. He needed to calm down, but he wasn't sure how.

Aralynn sipped her beer as well, her complexion high. "I'm so embarrassed," she whispered, once Marny left. But she was laughing.

"Why embarrassed? Don't worry about Marny. She's discreet."

"That's not it." She met his gaze. "Because kissing you isn't exactly a simple business." She switched to telepathy. *The whole time you were working your tongue in my mouth, I was thinking about your cock and having you inside me again.*

He sat back in his seat and gasped for air. Her words had stiffened him so fast, he was bent sideways at an uncomfortable angle. He had to move to adjust himself.

"This artichoke smells wonderful." She smiled at him as she drew the small white platter closer and began serving up portions.

He took a moment to look away from her and to focus on anything but his desire for her, like the new accounting staff he'd hired to maintain the business end of the Com Center. One of the recent invoices was at least five pages long. He'd been right to hire some accountants.

Okay.

Better.

For the next few minutes, he focused on his beer and the artichokes. He let her know he'd ordered filets, rare. Her eyes lit up. "I'm always surprised how hungry I am after a night of battling. Steak sounds perfect."

Pleasure filled his chest at knowing that he was taking care of something as basic as what she needed to eat. He was providing for his woman and he loved it. He hadn't expected to feel this way ever, but in the time they'd been together, and maybe especially since he'd made love to her on the marble slab, he'd come to really care about her.

When she picked up her beer, she put a hand to her chest and rubbed. "I keep forgetting that I'm a blood rose now and you're a mastyr vampire. I'm feeling very full here, having created a fresh supply for you."

He pressed his hand over hers. "What does it feel like?"

"A heaviness, as though my heart is pumping harder than normal."

"Are you in pain?"

Her brows rose. "No, not at all. It's not a discomfort. In fact it's pleasurable, even sensual."

Sometimes Aralynn surprised him as she did right now. She spoke straight and true. Not unlike Queen Rosamunde. Odd that he would think of the queen right now. But if he'd understood Aralynn, the queen had trained her from the time she was a child so of course there would be similarities.

She bit the end of the artichoke leaf. He followed suit. Food was a good thing for warrior-types who battled all night.

The steaks arrived soon after and he ordered a couple more beers, this time with a shot of whisky.

She grinned and tipped the shot glass back eagerly. She came up sputtering. "I've never done this before."

"Really?"

"The, er, Castle Guard post is a pretty tight leash. You have no idea."

"Drink your beer, then. Time to let go."

"I think you may be right."

~ ~ ~

Rosamunde leaned back in the booth and closed her eyes. The steaks had been heaven, very rare which her wolf loved. And the whisky had set her mind to spinning slowly. She was behaving badly and she knew it. She'd had two beers and a shot of whisky and she wanted more.

She didn't want to think about *that other thing*. She wanted to forget that she was the Queen of Ferrenden Peace and for just this moment in time pretend she was a simple realm-woman, a shifter wolf on a date with a handsome man for whom she felt a mountain of admiration and yes, affection. Hell, maybe she even loved the vampire.

"You okay?"

"Unh-huh. Sort of. Really good and yet, Stone there's something I've got to tell you. It's important."

He drew close and cupped her face, then kissed her. *You sure it can't wait?*

No, it can't.

He drew back. "All right. Let's have it."

But Marny returned at exactly that moment with two snifters of brandy. "I saved this for you guys. It's from my best stock."

Stone took one of the goblets and dipped his nose close. "Nice."

"From France," she added. "Extra-aged." She then got a very serious look on her face. "And it's on the house, the whole dinner. My treat, for everything you do for our world."

Rosamunde watched tears fill the woman's eyes. Stone grabbed Marny's hand and squeezed. "I say this with my whole heart: It's my pleasure. What I do, how I serve Tannisford, it's my pleasure."

"You're a good man, Stone."

She pulled her hand away and drew upright. She wiped her tears then patted her belly. "Sorry, I've been very emotional lately."

When she moved away, Stone handed Rosamunde the snifter then picked the other one up for himself. "To Tannisford." He held his goblet close to hers.

"To the Nine Realms."

When he nodded, she tapped the glass gently against his. She took a sip and saw that Stone's eyes were wet as he tilted his head back and took a drink.

Rosamunde didn't really taste the brandy even though she suspected the bottle cost a small fortune. Instead, all she could do was look at Stone and marvel at the man he was, at his goodness and the way he viewed centuries of sacrifice as *his pleasure.*

She made a decision then and there that she was done talking. She'd tried several times to bring up the difficult issue, and she would have seen it through if she hadn't witnessed the tender, powerful exchange between the restaurant owner and Stone.

She knew she was being selfish, but she wanted this time with him, to open her vein for him, to make love with him and to share his bed through the day. She knew something else as well, he'd have a hard time forgiving her once he learned the truth. But she couldn't help that and right now, after her own thousand years of sacrifice, she would have this one moment with the man she loved.

Yes. That was it. The man she loved.

She loved Stone.

She had since he'd first come to the castle to meet her as the queen.

"Stone?"

"Yes?" He settled his snifter on the table. "Right. You had something you wanted to discuss."

"I've kind of let that go for now. I have something else on my mind. You have a home here in the city, don't you?"

"I do." His lips curved. "You'd rather go there than my lake house?"

"I would. It's closer, right?"

His lips curved. "Hell, yeah, it is."

"Then I want you to take me there," she paused for effect. "Then I want you to take me to bed."

As he rose to his feet, he leaned close to her and growled softly at her words. "Let's go."

~ ~ ~

Stone thanked Marny for their meal, bid her a goodnight, then led Aralynn out onto the sidewalk. He held his arm out to her. "It's only a few miles from here."

He hadn't flown Aralynn often. He hadn't needed to. She usually either levitated by herself or if she knew the destination well enough, she teleported.

He lived in the hills northeast of the city in a house he'd built twenty years ago out of a lot of stone and wood. It was a sprawling modern home, single story with terraced landscaping front and back and lots of concrete.

He loved his city dwelling but spent an equal amount of time at his lake house. He also had an apartment downtown which he reserved to meet women or at other times his *doneuses* when he needed to feed.

He took her on a brief aerial tour of the property which spanned three acres with the house in the center. A powerful security system, similar to the one at the lake house, covered every inch of his home and gardens.

He'd made a woodland environment with tall pine trees around the entire perimeter. Holding Aralynn tight against his side, he pointed to the south. "The trees begin there and make a full circuit."

"I see you have a dedicated path."

"Yeah. I wanted that, too. A place to walk and think."

"I know this may sound odd, Stone, but suddenly I want to run."

He felt her strain against him as her wolfness rose to the fore. He felt an urgency to hold her close since his blood-hunger had risen once he had her in his arms. His fangs throbbed in his gums.

But he set aside his own need and dropped down to the edge of the long driveway where the walking path began. He was a little surprised when she leaped from his arms and shifted into her wolf form while midair, absorbing her clothes as she went.

She landed hard then rolled. She lay on her back for a moment, and yelped playfully a couple of times. *Stone, I'm tipsy. What with the beer, the whisky and the brandy.*

He smiled. "Maybe we should just go inside." Okay. He was totally thinking about himself.

Not a chance. I'll make one circuit, then I'm all yours. She flipped over and took off running at breakneck speed.

"I'm coming with."

He flew above her, careful to keep from slamming into any trailing branches. She ran hard, her paws barely visible as she weaved and lurched along the winding path.

You're loving this.

I am. I'm always cooped up in the castle.

What?

He heard her wolf voice, a sort of strangled yelp. Maybe that's how wolf's laughed. *I mean my cottage. Yup. I've been drinking.*

She rounded the back of the property and he continued to move with her. He could feel her joy like a wave of pleasure rising from her body. She was beautiful to watch as she ran. She had dark reddish brown fur with a darker strip down her spine. She had a narrow muzzle and elegant forelegs.

He had it bad for Aralynn which made him think they were

meant to be together even if she had concerns she needed to tell him about.

As they reached the far side of his property, a warning vibration went down his spine. *Dawn's close.*

I know. I'm feeling it, too.

Suddenly, she whirled through a shift, returning to her womanly form. She rose into the air at the same time and threw herself on him. He caught her and held them both steady in the air as he settled his lips on hers and kissed her hard.

She drew back. "We'd better get inside. I can hear your automatic steel shutters lowering all over the house."

He flew with her in his arms, cutting through the woods. He crossed the east collection of concrete pads, garden beds and the occasional massive landscaping boulder. He landed on the front walkway which was lined with large pots of evergreens.

He lowered her to her feet and walked her to the front door. He used a keypad and let them in.

Whisking her into his arms, he took her across the threshold.

Once in the foyer, and with the door closed securely behind him, he levitated to a stop. He held her cradled in his arms once more and realized there was something he wanted to say to her. "I've never had a woman here like this before. I never wanted to. I've had parties and meetings, but nothing of a personal nature. Not like this and I want you to know that. You're special to me, Aralynn."

She stared at him, a soft smile on her lips. "I love that you've brought me here, Stone. This means a lot to me, more than you can know."

He levitated slowly to the right of the large entry and passed by the library, then the closed doors of his massive office, and a billiard room. When he reached the small atrium that was normally open to the sky, Aralynn said, "I love the design of this home. And all night you could see the stars through there."

"Yes, you could." Now, however, the atrium was shuttered but soft lights throughout the space created a glow revealing an array of ferns and palms.

"This is such a beautiful home. I'm impressed."

"I've always loved it. I had a spectacular elven architect who took my less than well-formed ideas and turned them into this house." He moved past the atrium to a small sitting area that led into his large bedroom. The windows were shuttered as well. "You can see the pool from the window when we're not closed up for the day."

Setting her on her feet, she went straight for his large Guardsman-sized bed. Without hesitation, she flipped the covers back, throwing them all the way to the bench at the end of the bed. Very wolf.

She turned to him, laughing. "I've always wanted to do that."

"And I think it's brilliant."

Because of her wild shifting, her braid had come undone. He went to her and helped her pluck the pins out and free the rest of her hair. He set the collection on the nightstand, then slid his hand behind her neck. "I've wanted this so much, Aralynn, ever since we were at Joseph's. That must make me sound crazed. Hell, maybe I am."

He kissed her hard, driving his tongue in and out of her mouth. She groaned, but not politely like she had in the restaurant. This time, she let it out.

Her arms snaked around his neck and he held her tight against him. He was pressed the full length of her, enjoying how she writhed against him.

He released her, whirled her around to face away from him then unzipped her dress. He didn't waste time, but unhooked her bra, then fell to his knees. While she remained standing, he grabbed her hips and spent some time kissing her bottom. He bit at her playfully which caused her to cry out. "Yes! More of that. My wolf wants to feel those teeth."

He was careful not to use his fangs. They were meant only for opening a vein. But his incisors he used vigorously which had her reaching to pull off her panties.

"Bite me everywhere."

He removed her heels and her thong. "I want you face down on the bed."

She chuckled. "Yes, Mastyr."

He watched as she slowly and with several intentional rolls of her hips, obeyed him. He'd been with several shifter females and knew what they liked. He was glad of the experience because the only thing that mattered to him right now was making sure Aralynn loved every second of what he was about to do.

He stripped out of his suit in a blur of motion. It felt good to be naked, in his home and with the woman he intended to make his own.

He moved in behind her, slid his hands beneath her thighs, then pulled her backward to the edge of the bed until her feet were flat on the floor. He dropped to his knees again and took his time kissing the insides of her thighs. He nipped at her as well and used both hands to knead the flesh of her ass. She moaned often.

He began kissing her sex which made him as stiff as hell, especially because she tasted of her woodland-herbal scent. He used only his lips at first, but when her hips began to rock and she was groaning heavily, he dipped his tongue inside.

She arched and cried out. "Sweet Goddess, Stone! Do more of that."

Hell, yeah, he would. He licked her sex in long swipes then once more dove inside. He set up a rhythm that had her crying out again. But he wasn't about to make this simple for her.

He withdrew and kept up the external kissing and licking then added some serious bites. She growled and yipped in her wolf voice and hit the bed with her palms.

He tongue fucked her again only this time he added a vibration that had her shouting for more. He lifted up her hips to get the right angle then went vampire fast with his tongue, pummeling her until her whole body writhed and she jerked sideways several times, shouting the whole time.

He felt her release roll through her, which had his cock twitching some more.

When her body began to relax, he slowed the movements of his tongue and lowered her hips to the bed. He rose up and drifted his erect cock over her dripping sex.

He wanted to be inside her so bad. With all those juices flowing, he'd slip all the way in. But he wanted her to take a moment.

Stone, you okay?

You're beautiful from here and I loved what I just did to you.

I need more.

Tell me. I'll do anything.

To his tremendous relief, she rose up on her hands and knees then looked back at him. "I'm a wolf, remember? You need to bite the back of my neck to really bring me. I mean, to bring me hard."

He climbed up on the bed, his gaze fixed on her swollen sex. His cock straight as an arrow aimed right for her.

Settling in behind her, it was just as he'd thought, because the moment he pressed the head of his cock into her sex and pushed the smallest amount, he slid in.

He groaned heavily. "You can't imagine how good that feels."

She arched her hips which gave his cock a tug and dammit if he didn't almost come. "Oh, yes I can."

He grabbed her hips and held her steady. He squeezed his eyes shut. "I want to do this right, but I'm on the edge, woman. You've made me hard as a rock."

"Stone?"

"Yeah?"

"Can you feed from me after you bite me?"

"Is that what you want?"

"Yes. Please. I feel desperate for both things, a strong wolf bite then your vampire fangs."

He leaned over her and carefully pulled the mass of her hair off to the right side of her neck. He pumped into her in long, deep thrusts. She kept her head tilted as well so he could see her throat and the pulse of her waiting vein.

Despite the fact that his fangs wanted to descend, he needed to take care of her first. He leaned over her. He'd been taught where and how to give the dominance bite and that it released a hormone in the female that made her sex constrict.

He couldn't wait.

Slowly, he moved his cock in and out of her as he lowered his teeth onto her neck. He opened his mouth as wide as he could, stroking her deep the whole time.

He began moving his hips faster. He could hear that she was breathing hard in anticipation. When he knew he had his teeth in the right spot, he bit down, driving faster still. He held on as she bucked beneath him, then cried out and howled.

At the same time, he couldn't help what happened next. Her well began pulling on him like a fist and he started to come. He rose up and slammed into her as each pulse of his cock added to the lightning strike of pleasure that kept flowing.

He shouted over and over as the orgasm rolled, maybe the best he'd ever known. He kept pumping, her howls stroking his balls. Sweet Goddess!

When at last he'd emptied all that he had into her, he was breathing hard. It took him a moment to settle down. He followed her as she flattened herself onto the bed and ended up lying on top of her.

"Holy fuck," he whispered against her neck. "That was amazing."

"You didn't drink from me."

"How could I with your sex working me like nothing I've ever known before?"

He felt her chuckle. "I'm so glad. And it was amazing."

After a couple of minutes, she shifted enough to meet his gaze. "I caught a glimpse of your shower and I'd sure like to try it out. Care to join me?"

He growled softly. "Yes, I would."

Chapter Seven

As Rosamunde headed to the shower, she was still dizzy from her recent release. She swore she had enough feel-good shooting through her veins to last her a lifetime.

Right now, as she stepped into his shower with five awesome heads, she fired up the water not caring that she got her hair wet.

Stone wasn't far behind. But instead of joining her right away, he leaned against the frame of the shower for a moment, watching her.

He was smiling and looking her up and down. She turned to face him and was careful to give him a good show, lathering up her breasts and between her legs while keeping her gaze fixed on him. He stroked his cock at the same time.

Now it was her turn to watch as he grew erect again.

Mastyr vampires had stamina.

A marble bench ran along the entire side of the shower, which gave her an idea.

She crooked her finger at him. "Come, let me get you clean." She then leaned down and patted the bench.

She didn't have to ask twice. He moved in swiftly and sat down.

He sprawled for her, throwing his legs wide and giving her room. She left the shower for a moment and grabbed a towel which she threw down on the tiles for her knees. She wanted to take her time.

She sank down and made herself comfortable. Using the soap, she smoothed the foam up his cock and slowly massaged, rimming the crown, and using her palm all the way to the base. She did the same for his balls, exploring the heavily ribbed skin and the vulnerable jewels within.

His hips rocked more than once.

She told him to stay put as she rose up and directed one of the heads over his groin. With the water flowing, she cleaned away the soap. After she'd adjusted the water away from him, she once more dropped to her knees then lowered her lips to him.

She heard him hiss as she surrounded the head and sucked lightly then licked and played with him. Her fingers spread up and out, searching the muscles of his abdomen then falling along his hips and down his powerful thighs. She kept sucking and occasionally worked his cock with her hands as well. But mostly she felt him up all over, reaching as much of his amazing body as she could while still using her mouth to pleasure him.

His tattoos called to her. Especially the vine that travelled down his leg. She left his cock to kiss and lick her way to his ankle then all the way back up. His pecs were thick and as worthy of her lips as his cock. She sucked on one nipple then the other, using her hands to caress and massage.

He had swirling knife-point tattoos all across his chest that looked like a tangled mass of weaponry. It was sexy as hell. She licked each black-ink blade and ended up straddling him, her arms around his neck.

He grabbed her bottom and lifted her up. She could feel him reaching for her well so she took his cock and guided him in. She held his gaze as his tip found her wet opening and began to push inside.

"I'm going to ride you, Stone." Never in a million years would she have imagined saying something like this to the Mastyr of Tannisford. But it felt wonderful. As Aralynn, the wolf, she was much bolder than the queen would have been.

Once he was seated inside her, she rode him, up and down. He helped with his powerful arms and his hands still planted on her ass. "You're riding me, Aralynn."

"Yes, I am."

He slid his arms around her fully and drew her against his chest. "I'm loving this," he whispered against her ear.

"Me, too." More than she could say, more than she even understood. She felt as though all the loneliness of her life descended on her in this moment and she let the tears fall, let the emotions swell over her, through her, then out of her.

This was what Vojalie had with Davido, what Delia had with Elias, what all the happily married realm-folk of Ferrenden Peace had.

The water washed the evidence of her sadness away and she returned to the pleasure of feeling Stone inside her. She felt like a normal woman and it made her so happy.

He drew back and pushed her dripping hair away from her throat. "I want to feed from you, but not in the shower. Come back to bed?"

She nodded then lifted her hips up, easing off him.

He turned the wonderful warm spray of water off then led her from the shower. He took what turned out to be an oversized towel and started drying her off.

It was such a tender gesture that she leaned up and kissed him.

His lips curved as he finished his task then made short work of his own massive body.

While he hung up the towel, she took another one and wrapped up her ridiculous hair, then leaned over and towel-dried as best she could. Stone did the same for his own long black mane.

When she was done, he once more picked her up in his arms and carried her to the bed. She half expected him to toss her and let her bounce.

Instead, his expression grew solemn as he laid her down gently then climbed between her legs.

"You're beautiful, Aralynn, and I feel blessed to be with you. The whole time we've been here together, my mating frequency has been on fire. And there's only one way to say this: I'm in love with you." He smiled softly. "I love you."

She was stunned as she touched his face with the tips of her fingers. "You love me?"

"I do."

She saw the sincerity in his eyes and responded from her heart. "I love you, too, Stone. I have ever since you saved that busload of kids. And when we were in the restaurant and Marny got so teary-eyed, she fully expressed what each of us feels who knows you, how in awe we are at your dedication, your self-sacrifice and your love for your people. How could I not love you?"

He smiled suddenly. "Then bond with me."

She had to rein in the powerful impulse to say 'yes'. Instead, she smiled. "Maybe. Ask me again tonight, after our day-sleep, okay?"

"I will. But I'll never stop asking and that's a promise."

She lifted up and kissed him. He followed her back down, returning her kiss. It wasn't long before he was buried between her legs once more and pushing into her.

Only this time, he added a vibration to his cock that had her back arching. "I didn't know you could do that. But now let me offer you something in return."

She turned her head just so, exposing her neck and he groaned heavily. He continued thrusting into her as he licked several long lines up her throat. She could feel her vein rising. Her chest was heavy with the need to give him what she now made in abundance.

She could also feel his vampire drive to break her skin. "Do it." Her voice was raspy.

He paused his hips and in a flash bit her throat, striking to just the right depth. A sensation of euphoria rolled through her as he began to suck. He drove his cock into her again and the dual sensations sent flurries of pleasure up and down her body, through her and over her.

His mating frequency battered her now and she let him in, even though she knew she'd have to work to keep the bond from forming.

She was overwhelmed with everything she experienced.

He sucked harder and thrust faster, all the while sustaining the erotic vibration of his cock. His mating frequency covered her and stroked her so that she was crying out in brief bird-like cries.

Building.

Rising.

The wave caught her in a sudden explosion of ecstasy. Was she screaming? She couldn't tell. The sensation was like being caught at the very birth of the universe with all its magic and mysteries. Pleasure gripped her and flowed, then gripped her again.

Look at me!

Stone's commanding telepathic voice forced her to open her eyes. When had she closed them?

"Stone." Meeting his gaze sent another wave of pleasure flowing. She panted.

He'd lifted off her neck and now pummeled her well relentlessly, his gaze fixed to hers. He was hard as a rock and she felt his mating frequency. She understood then that he was asking again to bond.

"Not yet. But come for me. Come hard, Stone."

His body arched and his hips paused then he moved faster and faster. She could see ecstasy riding his face.

Another wave broke over her. She added her own vibration deep inside her well. He cried out then began pumping into her once more.

He shouted as he came for the third time, his long black hair wild around his shoulders. She used her internal wolf muscles to grip him and stroke him, teasing every last bit of his seed out of his cock.

His hips gyrated, his face twisted, he shouted over and over, until the moment finally passed.

Deep within her chest, she felt his mating frequency holding her own and loving on her.

She'd never been as satisfied as she was in this moment. She would remember this always as the finest dawn of her life.

She reached up and touched his cheek. "I love you, Stone. I say that with all my heart."

He kissed her. "I love you, too, Aralynn."

And there it was, her wolf name and the deception. Yet she still refused to give in to the grating fear of what he would do when he learned the truth.

Not yet.

Not yet.

His brows rose. "What do you mean, not yet? The bond?"

She'd accidentally slipped into telepathy. "Right. Not yet."

"But soon. Tell me you'll really think about it."

"I will. Of course, I will."

With that, he relaxed though he continued to kiss her, to nuzzle her throat, to thank her for feeding him. "You have no idea how wonderful I feel now, free from pain, satiated as I've never been before. I can't thank you enough."

"I'm glad I could do this for you. It seems like such a small thing."

"Sweet Goddess, it is so much more than you can imagine."

She wrapped her arms around him and held him close for a long time. It wasn't but a few minutes, however, before sleep began curling in her brain. The night had been full of stress and surprises. Having sex had eased her and all she wanted was to close her eyes.

He left her body just as she was drifting off. She felt him kiss her cheek then a minute later tuck a washcloth between her legs. She turned on her side and fell into the beautiful oblivion of sleep.

~ ~ ~

Stone showered up and when he returned to bed, Aralynn

was sound asleep. With her features relaxed and her eyes closed, with her dark red hair in a fan around her shoulders, she almost looked like the queen herself.

He'd never noticed it before, which made him wonder if Aralynn was perhaps related to Rosamunde, maybe even her daughter.

It hardly mattered who Aralynn's parents were, however, even if it meant that Rosamunde was somehow related to her. He'd come to love her, to value her deeply and to trust her in the short time he'd spent battling beside her. What the queen lacked in boldness, Aralynn had a thousand times over.

He slipped into bed, drew close and spooned her, sliding his arm over her waist. She caught his hand in hers and in her sleep held on tight. "I'm so sorry, Stone," she mumbled. "I'm so sorry."

He chuckled softly. What on earth did Aralynn have to be sorry about?

He fell asleep for the day to thoughts about how blessed he was to have her in his life.

~ ~ ~

Rosamunde awoke to the smell of coffee, but not just any coffee. What was that spice?

She rolled onto her back then the rest of the way to face the other direction. For a moment, she buried her face in Stone's pillow and drank in his vampire scent. Even his pillows had the rocky streamed scent that she'd grown to crave. Desire once more curled between her legs. Memories of all that they'd done together, the pleasure he'd given her and what she'd returned happily, danced in her mind.

She couldn't remember being this happy in her entire life.

The protective shutters had already retracted for the night, which meant she'd slept a long time. The back of the house faced west and there was just a hint of the setting sun, the faintest glow in the distant horizon.

Her wolf's hearing allowed her to detect Stone's bare feet on the slate floor and the smell of the coffee grew stronger.

She was about to flip over in bed when awareness dawned and she touched her face, her shoulders, her arms. She glanced at her hands. She wasn't looking at Aralynn's hands at all.

Somewhere in her sleep she'd become Rosamunde.

She drew in a deep breath and transformed back to her wolf-self.

A second later, Stone appeared in the doorway. "You're awake. Good."

She pushed herself up with her hands. "Good eventide, Mastyr Stone." She gasped. Aralynn wouldn't offer such a formal greeting, but Rosamunde would.

He frowned as he handed her a steaming mug of coffee.

She thought a hard shift of subject might help. "This smells heavenly. What's in it?"

"Cardamom."

"I love that spice. Very exotic." She brought the mug to her lips.

"Are you all right? Your cheeks are red."

She wasn't surprised. She'd almost been caught, which forced her to face the promise she'd made to herself, one that would end her time with Stone, probably for good.

She took another sip of the savory coffee then set her mug on the nightstand. Pulling up the sheet around her, she scooted to the side of the bed. She saw that Stone had picked up her black dress from the night before and had draped it over the back of a chair near the door.

She unwrapped the sheet, then rose to her feet, very naked.

She had to do this.

Her heart ached as she crossed the room to the chair. But what if she waited one more night? How much could that hurt?

No, the moment had come.

She sighed heavily as she picked up her dress.

She had to tell Stone the truth then beg him to forgive her for the deception. She couldn't do it, however, without a stitch on.

She heaved another sigh as she slid the dress over her head.

"Aralynn, what are you doing? I don't want you to go. At least not yet."

"I need to get back to the castle."

"Does the queen need you?"

"You could say that."

"But you no longer serve in the Castle Guard."

Now that the moment had come, the weight of both what she'd done and what she was about to lose crashed down on her. She turned around and crossed back to Stone, who stood by the bed, frowning deeply.

Damn. If only he didn't look like a move star. She drew close and ran her fingers over his strong cheekbones, one after the other.

He caught her hand. "What's going on, Aralynn? You look unbearably sad. I don't get it." He set his own mug down next to hers on the nightstand.

She withdrew her hand from his then straightened her

shoulders. Though she'd gone into battle with Stone dozens of times over the past few weeks, some in harrowing situations, she vowed this was the hardest thing she'd ever had to do.

"I've done you a terrible disservice, Mastyr, and I need to confess something to you. I've actually tried several times to tell you what's been going on with me, and one of them was last night at dinner, if you'll recall. Then Marny interrupted us with the brandy and made her speech which in turn made me do this horribly selfish thing."

He shook his head. "I have no idea what you're talking about. But I've known you for the past seven weeks and not once have you done something I would describe as selfish. Not once."

"Stone, you were right about something. I am related to the queen."

"Oh, is that it?" His features relaxed for a moment and he even smiled. "I sort of thought you might be. Are you her daughter? I mean these things happen. I promise you it's not a big deal." He took a step toward her and she could see he meant to take her in his arms again, but she couldn't let him.

Instead, she held her hands up in a blocking motion, until he drew to a stop. His frown returned.

"I'm not Rosamunde's daughter or niece or grandmother or anything. I'm not related in that way. Stone, *I am* Rosamunde."

Stone stared at her and cocked his head. "What?" Then he chuckled. "That's not even possible. You don't look like her. Your hair and coloring might be similar, but this," he waved his hand up and down to encompass her body, "this isn't Rosamunde."

"Maybe it's best if I show you."

"Well. Okay. But you're not making any sense."

For a moment, she couldn't do it. The tears had started and she couldn't stop them. "You'll hate me."

"I could never … I won't … I don't get this."

She closed her eyes and transformed. The dress sort of fit her though it was much tighter in the bodice. As Rosamunde, she had bigger breasts than Aralynn.

Stone's mouth fell agape. He looked her up, then down, then back up. He took a step away from her. "What does this mean?"

"I'm Queen Rosamunde and I'm Aralynn, the wolf-shifter. I'm both women. Davido came to me a year ago and showed me that I was capable of being both persons. He then taught me how to use my powers and become Aralynn. He said 'Aralynn' would have an important role to play in the war against my aunt. My cousin, Lorelei, has a similar ability."

"Fuck. Me." He took another step back, his hand to his gut. "But this isn't possible. Aralynn is nothing like Rosamunde …" No other words followed.

Rosamunde remained silent and very still, giving Stone time to adjust to this new reality. Her only movements involved swiping at the tears that wouldn't stop flowing down her cheeks.

Finally, he shifted to sit down on the side of the bed. "You're Rosamunde? All this time? But what the hell kind of trick was this to play on me? How? Why? What the holy fuck did you think you were doing? Sweet Goddess, all this time." His gaze fell to the rumpled sheets. "And I made love to you last night."

"That's the selfish part because I didn't want you to know. I knew how you felt about 'Rosamunde.'" Goddess help her, she did air quotes. "Then once you kissed me in the mine out at Charborne, I was lost. And if you remember, I was trying to tell you even then, but Margetta showed up. Then at Joseph's, you needed my blood and everything got out of hand so fast and, oh, Stone, I couldn't help myself. I've wanted you so badly, almost from the first time you came to the castle.

"And I've loved being Aralynn and battling beside you. For the first time in my life I was doing something, actually *doing something* real and tangible. I mean besides holding the veil of mist intact. I always knew how important that was, but when Vojalie and Davido came to the castle—"

"Wait. Then they both know who you are and what you've done? About this ruse?"

"You can't blame either of them. Keeping my identity a secret is on me alone. I knew your opinion all too well."

"Your aunt is Margetta."

"Yes. Lorelei, Mastyr Seth's woman, and I are cousins."

He shaded his face with his hands. "You left Ferrenden Peace to heal Lorelei. I remember."

"It's the only time in recent history I've left my kingdom. Even then, Davido took my place to support the mist as best he could. But she would have died without my healing efforts."

"If you healed Lorelei, why didn't you heal me? Why did Kaden have to do it?"

"Stone, your wound was beyond anything I could have treated. Your liver was destroyed and part of your intestines. I got you back to Ferrenden Peace, but Kaden saved your life, or at least he restored your body and apparently my blood cleansed you of the poison."

His mossy-green eyes appeared as though she'd crushed him. He'd never looked more hurt. "I just don't understand how you could have done this."

"It was utterly and completely selfish. I … I knew once you learned the truth you'd never forgive me for the deception, so I chose to have one night with you. And it was amazing and beautiful and everything I'd always wanted with you.

"But I know what you think of me." She couldn't continue.

She moved to sit down on the tall chair opposite the bed. She buried her face in her hands and sobbed.

~ ~ ~

Having learned of Rosamunde's existence in recent years, and knowing that she had sufficient power to create a veil of mist around Ferrenden Peace, Stone had believed from the outset she'd used the Nine Realms badly. Any person with that much power, could have fought Margetta with her own two hands. For the Goddess's sake, she'd put both Mastyr Seth and Mastyr Quinlan in stasis so the men didn't kill each other.

From the time he'd learned she had stasis ability, which to his knowledge no other realm-person did, he'd become convinced she was the one person who could have made a difference in the war against Margetta. And she could have done it a long, long time ago.

Despite that she sat across from him weeping into her hands, he still believed he was right about her, that she had the innate ability to defeat Margetta if only she'd put her mind to it. That she hadn't made the effort resulted in the deaths of tens of thousands of realm-folk who had died because of her indolence, including his own adopted troll parents.

Even now, with the undeniable proof that she could be both Aralynn and Rosamunde right in front of him, he was convinced more than ever that he was right about her.

Embrace the Power

"You should have been straight with me, Rosamunde, from the first. Why didn't you tell me you were Aralynn when you first came to the Com Center? Hell, I probably would have come around right away since you were finally doing something, just as you said. You'd gotten off your ass at long last."

At that, she rose from the chair and went into the bathroom. He heard her blowing her nose.

When she returned, she moved straight up to him. "You're wrong. That's all I can say. You're fucking wrong, Stone. I'm not indolent or uncaring. Every fae part of me knows that I don't have enough essential power to battle Margetta, not even when I access the elf-lord power. In fact, all I've really accomplished where she's concerned is that I can outfly her, thank the Goddess.

"I know you don't believe me, but don't you think if I'd had that kind of potential that I would have been able to bear the elf-lord power as well? Yet, I can't. Century after century, when it arrived, it always brought crippling pain."

Stone gained his feet, not caring that her violet eyes had filled with tears yet again. "Let's say you're right, which I'm not conceding, how could you have deceived me like this?"

She shrugged. "I've already explained the process. Even early on, I wanted to tell you, but I was too afraid of your opinion of 'Rosamunde'. I feared not being able to battle beside you as Aralynn. And yes, it was wrong. All of it. And I'm so very sorry, Stone."

She looked contrite. He'd give her that. She wasn't enjoying any of this. But she was right about one thing, he'd never forgive her for tricking him.

As she picked up her shoes and her underclothes, she added, "Again, I'm sorry for what I've done. I don't expect your forgiveness, but I hope we can continue working together to bring Margetta down. Beyond that, I have no expectations of you."

"But what I want to know—"

Just like that, she was gone, teleporting away, another sign of her genetics. Sweet Goddess, he'd made love to Margetta's fucking niece.

And Aralynn was Rosamunde.

He felt an urge to shower again, to cleanse himself from Rosamunde's deception.

Instead, he sat back down on the bed, picked up his coffee and sipped. It was lukewarm and not exactly appealing, but he didn't care.

He was pissed as hell. If Rosamunde really was Aralynn then she'd saved his life, more than once. He'd be dead if it weren't for her.

A disgusted sound came from the back of his throat. He'd despised Rosamunde for so long that he hated the idea of owing her anything.

He opened up his telepathic frequency and tapped on Davido's path.

I'm at your service, oh, wise Mastyr of Tannisford.

Cut the crap. Why didn't you tell me Aralynn was Rosamunde?

A stretch of silence followed, after which Davido lowered his telepathic voice, *Because you, my friend, are a pigheaded impulsive fool who rarely listens to my counsel.*

What? That's not true.

Yes, it is. And I never objected before, but I must now. You've been very wrong about the queen and I'm begging you to make peace with her. She doesn't possess the power you believe she does.

Then how did she create stasis?

Embrace the Power

Haven't you figured that out? The elf-lord power, with Vojalie's training, of course. But it's not innate with her, which is why she suffers when the power comes to her. Wake up, Stone. For reasons I don't understand you've had it in for her and that's something you might want to explore as well. Why have you been so intent on disliking Rosamunde?

Stone couldn't respond. Not yet. He had to think this through, especially that she'd deceived him for weeks now.

On the other hand, Davido's loyalty to Rosamunde meant something that Stone couldn't set aside. But he needed to understand the full picture. *Davido, why didn't you teach her sooner how to transform into her wolf-state and by the way, who in any of the realms can do that?*

Only a handful that I've known over the centuries. Her cousin, Lorelei can.

So she does have the power to defeat Margetta.

No, Stone, she doesn't. You've made yourself blind with these thoughts. Margetta has more power than you can fathom. And Rosamunde, well, I will tell you something no one else knows.

When the troll didn't finish his thought, Stone grew impatient. *What? Just say it.*

She was never meant to be Queen of Ferrenden Peace.

Stone had to laugh. *That makes no sense at all.*

Rosamunde was very young when she discovered she could manipulate the veil of mist that her mother, Queen Evelyn, had created to protect the kingdom. She was only a child of nine. She learned that she could create pathways through the mist and she would take her miniature goats out into what was then part of Grochaire Realm.

Margetta found her and enthralled her young mind, working to trick her to show her the path into Ferrenden Peace. Fortunately, Evelyn got wind of Margetta's doings and left the kingdom to battle Margetta and to save her daughter's life. In the process, Margetta killed a queen who was supposed to reign for a thousand years.

Stone frowned yet again. *Not Rosamunde.*

That's right. Ferrenden Peace never had hereditary queens. They were chosen by the Sidhe Council as a result of fae visions. Rosamunde has been a place holder all this time until Quinlan's daughter, Viola, is old enough to take her place.

Quinlan's daughter? The one who's just a few months old?

That's right.

This was all such new information that Stone didn't know what to think. He'd never understood Rosamunde, but from the few things she'd revealed and these new insights from Davido, it seemed her life had been one misadventure after another. *And this is why the elf-lord power has caused her such disabling pain?*

That's what I believe. She was never the right vessel to serve Ferrenden.

Yet she's done so for a thousand years.

Davido continued, *She laid down her life, Stone, just as you have. She deserves both your respect and your trust.*

So, you're saying I've misjudged her.

Badly.

A few expletives rolled through his head, to which Davido cried out. *Calm that damn battle energy of yours, Mastyr. You've practically destroyed my last working brain cell.*

Apologies. But he laughed. Davido, so far as Stone knew,

was the most power-laden realm-person in the Nine Realms. If he'd been a vampire or a shifter, he would have been a formidable Guardsman in their world and at the very least a ruling mastyr. Despite Davido's protests, a little pathed profanity wasn't going to harm his head.

Still, he didn't know what the hell to think except that it would be a long time before he could forgive Rosamunde's deception, even if he had misjudged the woman.

~ ~ ~

Rosamunde sat quietly as her maids bound her hair once more in the intricate arrangement she'd worn since she could remember. Tears kept flowing and she kept wiping them away. Her maids eyed one another in the mirror but said nothing to Rosamunde, for which she was grateful.

She finally offered, "I had an argument with Mastyr Stone. That's all."

The maids nodded but otherwise remained quiet.

Her chest felt caved in except for her heart which was swollen with an excess supply of blood. She'd need to donate at some point tonight or she was pretty sure the small organ would simply explode from having to work so hard.

Though thoughts of Stone kept intruding, she chose to focus on her most immediate problem: Finding a vampire to take the surplus. There were several lesser mastyr vampires in Tannisford Realm and one in particular came to mind.

His name was Rez and he was a tough, powerful man, which gave her pause. If she fed him, would he expect more? She'd heard that the drive to feed mastyrs was almost overwhelming and in response those she fed would feel a need to bond with her. And do other things.

She remembered all over again what had happened between Mastyr Seth and Mastyr Quinlan. Seth had come across Lorelei in the castle and because Lorelei had been unbonded at the time, Seth went berserk with his sudden need for her. In response, Lorelei had actually engaged with him. Quinlan found them before events got too far along, but the ensuing violent encounter between the men had reverberated through the entire castle.

Using the elf-lord power, she'd intervened, putting both mastyrs in stasis.

So, the question remained, if she sought out Rez in order to get relief from carrying too much blood, what would happen? Would she suddenly desire Rez the way she did Mastyr Stone?

Once her braids were intact, she sent her maids away in order to deal with her problem. She decided that to be on the safe side, she would offer herself first to Stone. She didn't hesitate to tap on his pathway.

His response was less than hopeful. *What do you want?* Even telepathically he sounded hostile.

Pacing her private parlor, Rosamunde pressed a hand to her chest. His curt attitude did not help her faltering peace of mind at all. *I won't keep you long. Probably because of the things we did last night, I've built a blood supply that needs ... sharing. Is there any way you can help me out here?*

A long silence returned. *I need you to leave me alone for a while until I sort this out. But you should know I doubt I'll ever be able to trust you again.*

I know. But Stone, I don't want to donate to another mastyr.
She let the words hang, hoping he would intuit the larger issue.

Instead, he shot back. *Hey, at this point that's your problem, not mine.*

He shut down his pathway and she had to let him go. She called down to the kitchen and ordered a glass of wine.

With the bottle.

Maybe wine would relax her heart and help her get through the night without donating.

But even by the time her butler brought her the tray, she was feeling very strange. She had to release the supply she'd built or she wouldn't live to see the morning.

As Aralynn, she and Stone had finished up more than one night in a bar, having a final beer before dawn.

She remembered one particular place where Rez had come up to them. He'd been interested in 'Aralynn' and had a real player's vibe. Now that she knew what she was, she wondered if he'd sensed on some level that she had blood rose potential.

Stone had given him a cold eye until he'd begged pardon and strolled, or maybe swaggered away.

As she recalled, the town was in the eastern part of the realm not far from the Dauphaire Mountains and Dark Gorge. The latter extended all the way into Mastyr Ian's Realm of Camberlaune. And because she could teleport, the trip would be easy enough to make.

Fine. So Mastyr Rez would be the one she would feed tonight.

Unwanted desire, however, began to curl everywhere as she thought about him. She'd seen him at least three times through the past several weeks and he'd always looked at her as though he liked what he saw. She'd liked looking at him, too. His wavy brown hair, complete with sexy blond highlights, was at shoulder length and he had gorgeous blue eyes, a dimple in his chin. He had a scruff, too, that made him look dangerous and he never lacked for female attention.

She summoned her maids again and had them tear the braids apart. She'd wear Aralynn's jeans. Maybe she'd go as Aralynn.

But she dismissed that idea right away. She was done hiding behind her wolf-self. She was Rosamunde, she was a blood rose and she could ease Rez's suffering tonight, as in right now. As a mastyr, Rez suffered from the crippling pain like the rest of his kind.

As soon as her hair was back in its loose, frizzy mass, she told her maids she'd be in seclusion for the night meditating. This had been her cover for weeks so not a single one of them expressed surprise.

As soon as she locked the door from within, she teleported straight to the interior of Aralynn's cottage. She rooted around in her dresser and found a sparkly, low-cut purple tank top that she knew Rez would like. Sliding it on, she could see that 'Rosamunde's' bigger breasts created an erotic four-inch line of cleavage. Sweet!

Next, she hunted for Aralynn's tightest jeans. Finding them, she loved the way they showed off her beautiful ass and her oh-so-long legs.

She was set to go, except for her hair and make-up. She wanted to do something different with her red frizz. She created two braids that ran down the sides of her face and tied them together in the back to weigh her hair down.

She then went to work on her make-up. As Aralynn, she enjoyed mixing it up.

But this time, as Rosamunde, she didn't hold back. She loaded her eyelids with dark purple shadow, deepened the red of her brows to a beautiful brown, and put on a dark shade of purplish-red lipstick.

She had only one thing to add. She climbed into a pair of black stilettos, with rhinestones down the back of each spike and damn if she didn't look good. She hardly even recognized herself. Maybe this is the woman she would have been if duty hadn't stuck her in a castle for a thousand years.

The world of a queen was highly overrated.

With her sights set, she teleported to the town of Millerell to an alley across the street from the Wild Boar, a bar catering to tough types. She stayed in the shadows gaining her bearings. Several Harleys were lined up outside. She was pretty sure Rez rode one. Stone did as well, that is, when he wasn't battling the Invictus.

She quickly set thoughts of Stone aside. She had a job to get done, so, Rez it was.

Desire once more curled around several inappropriate places.

She wanted a ride all right, but not on a motorcycle.

Was this really her?

Just as she was about to step out of the shadows, another Harley arrived with the signature tall handlebars.

She drew in a quick breath.

Rez.

As he backed in his bike, then straddled it standing up, he lifted his nose into the air. He wore a black t-shirt with the sleeves cut off to better display his guns. And what freaking hot guns they were. He might not be as tall or as built as Stone, but he looked damn good.

She watched him sniff the air more than once.

Was he catching her blood rose scent? Her heart pounded, clearly recognizing in Rez exactly what she needed.

She waited for him to go inside, but once he did, she set her stilettos straight for the propped-open door of the Wild Boar. Live music spilled into the street as well as a lot of raucous laughter.

The place was hopping.

And for the first time in her life, Rosamunde would be hopping, too.

Chapter Eight

Stone paced his Communication Center, a few feet behind his work station, and was pretty sure that if one more person asked him where Aralynn was, he'd throw a punch and not care who fell to the floor.

"You got a forest gremlin up your butt?"

He turned to glare at Delia. "What?" She could be damned insolent.

"I haven't seen you in this kind of temper since I don't know when. What gives?"

Stone ground his teeth. "And you're not even supposed to be here. You should be home with Elias, where you belong."

"Elias knows I need to be here. He's showing his patriotism right now." Delia then levitated, turning in the air in order to meet his gaze straight on.

No bullshit, she pathed. *What happened to Aralynn? You've been stuck to each other for weeks, battling happily together and suddenly she doesn't show. Worse, you're in a mood that's probably going to blow the local transmitter then where will we be?*

He was pretty sure that if he didn't unload, he'd kill someone. *She's a blood rose and she lied to me.*

Delia's jaw fell slack. *Say, what?*

Which part?

The first one. Aralynn's a blood rose?

Yup.

She drew in close and shifted to nudge him in the shoulder, which given his size and her lean troll frame felt more like a gentle pat. *But this is great news. Is your pain gone?*

He couldn't help that his hand went to his stomach. *Every last bit.*

Delia turned her back to the monitors to once more face him. *I've read up on these women. Three of them were interviewed in a blog. I think they were bonded to Mastyrs Seth, Jude and Malik. I can't remember their names—*

He helped her out because he knew each one well. *Lorelei, Hannah and Willow.*

Right. Well, anyway, each said the drive to be with their mastyrs was beyond overwhelming and one of them, I think it was Willow, said she had the hots for Mastyr Zane the moment she saw him and Mastyr Malik about split his own brain open keeping them apart. So, are you worried about another mastyr getting to her? I hear the bond can be forced on a blood rose.

Stone suddenly recalled what Davido had called him: Stubborn and pigheaded. He was levitating before he knew it.

Where are you going?

I've got to find her. She said she needed me.

Though Harris called to him, Stone sped out the door. He pathed with his lieutenant and explained his problem. *Take over for me?*

You got it. Hope you find her fast.

Once he was in the air, he stalled out. He had no idea where to go. Would she still be at the castle? Had she left to find someone to take her extra supply? Sweet Goddess, what if she ended up at the fang-end of the wrong kind of vampire?

He opened up his telepathy once more and focused on Rosamunde. *Hey, are you there?*

I am, but you don't need to worry about me. I've got my sights set on a Harley-riding mastyr with no sleeves. Oh, and he's got a swagger like he wouldn't turn me away if I suggested I wanted to open a vein for him.

She sounded pissed, something he would have addressed then and there, but damn if the woman didn't shut her pathway down. No matter how hard he tried to reach her again, he couldn't.

It would seem the very proper Queen of Ferrenden Peace was on the hunt and about to land a vampire.

He recalled visiting a certain bar in the east out at Millerell in the Dauphaires and that a good-looking mastyr had come over to her. What was the name of that bar?

The Wild Boar.

If she was there, she wasn't too far away, but could he get to her before she did anything foolish?

~ ~ ~

Rosamunde felt nothing but exhilarated as she stood in the doorway of the bar. The place was jumping. A three-piece band banged away in the corner, playing something that sounded like a bluesy country song. They weren't the best, but they were loud and loud was what she wanted right now.

And nothing complicated. Just the right man with the appropriate dental hardware, and maybe a private corner, and she'd be all set.

She'd always liked this place. Something very female in her responded to the look of the men. They were tough, a bunch of real fighters. When she was with Stone, she'd caught a few sidelong glances because no one was going to mess with the ruling Mastyr of Tannisford. But right now there was nothing but open gawking and glances that traveled up and down her body.

Truth? She loved it.

She felt like a desirable woman and it felt good.

Two shifters came up to her. "Buy you a drink?"

"I'd love it." She wasn't holding back, not tonight, maybe never again. She was done being formal and demure. Stone might not want her, he probably would never forgive her, but getting a pair of fangs into her was exactly what she needed.

The shifter was tall with shoulders that could have supported a boat. He had blond hair, blue eyes and called out over his shoulder, "Rachel, a beer for my friend, here. What's your name, Sweetheart?"

"Rosamunde."

"Just like the queen."

"Yup. Just like her." She even smiled

Rachel shouted back. "What's your pleasure, Hon?"

"Anything amber. And thanks."

"You got it. Pull up a stool and don't let any of these cretins give you a hard time."

"Don't worry, I won't." Hell, if she got in trouble, maybe she'd just call on the elf-lord power and put any troublesome man in stasis.

With her two swains flanking her, Rosamunde made her way toward the horseshoe bar, packed two-deep. A number of the men turned to stare at her. But when she was within a few feet, a stool moved as though magically reaching for her. A heavy boot was attached, one looped with three chains around the back.

Her gaze followed that boot and a leg encased in tight leather, until she was looking at the vampire she was after.

Rez.

He'd pushed the empty stool out for her and she could feel his chronic blood hunger like a fire on her skin.

She thanked the shifters for the warm welcome to the Wild Boar, then made a beeline for the tall metal stool.

Both of them complained as Rosamunde climbed up and seated her ass with a firm wiggle then grabbed the beer. She could smell the vampire next to her. And his salty, nutty scent mixed with a very fine aftershave sent shivers chasing down both shoulders.

Once more, her heart pounded.

The shifters tried to push in, but Rez lifted up on his stool. "Beat it. The woman's made her choice."

Both men opened their mouths to protest, but Rez growled, a loud resonant sound that had half the heads in the loud bar turning in their direction. The shifters each took a step back, lifted their hands then moved away. That's when Rosamunde realized Rez's fangs were sitting low.

And what a display.

In any other circumstance, she might have been scared out of her mind. But she was a blood rose and needed what he was offering.

She sipped her beer, but her gaze was fixed to the sharp pearly tips.

He tapped her pathway. *You ever been bitten, Sweetheart?*

Uh-huh. She couldn't look away and her heart was now slamming in her chest. *Loved it.*

He leaned closed. *Sweet Goddess, your blood smells like something straight from heaven.* He sniffed low on her neck and close to her vein. *What is that, Rosamunde? Pretty name, by the way.*

Maybe he felt obligated to make small talk.

She didn't. *I want to donate. Is that something you'd be interested in?*

The vampire didn't need much encouragement at all. He put one hand on her thigh and slid the other around the back of her neck. She tilted her head. She was so into it, she wanted the bite right now, in front of the Goddess and everyone. She just didn't care.

She felt his tongue on her neck then suddenly, he was airborne, but not in a good way. An enormous roar filled the entire bar, which stopped all talk as well as the sounds of the clunky band in the corner.

She shot around on her stool.

Stone was here.

And he was beating the shit out of Rez.

Holy crap. She honestly didn't think he'd come or even be able to find her.

Stone had Rez up against a wood-paneled wall near the door, pinned by the throat, and was pummeling him with his fist.

But it wasn't right. Rez hadn't done anything except respond to her invitation.

She levitated and leaped onto Stone's back. "Stop it!" she shrieked, almost sounding like a wraith.

But Stone kept hitting Rez.

With her arms wrapped tight around his neck, she shouted over and over, but he wouldn't listen.

She needed help. "Some of you get hold of Mastyr Stone's arms or he'll kill Rez!"

When no one came forward, she hopped off his back and tried to access the elf-lord power, but she knew she didn't have time for that.

She shouted, "Please help Rez! You don't understand. I'm a blood rose and Stone will kill him and Rez doesn't deserve to die."

When she leaped up on Stone's back again, the men in the room began to move in and before long, Stone was spinning in a circle, with several shifters weighing him down on both arms.

Rosamunde held on tight then pathed. *Steady yourself, Stone. Come on. That's it. I'm here. I'm with you and I need you. I've got a full supply and I want your fangs. Only yours.*

All of it was true. She had hold of the man she loved, even if he was completely out of control and breathing like a monster in heavy, full-throated rasps.

She kept talking him down as he spun the men in a circle. Finally, he started growing fatigued until he stood in one place.

The nearby tables and chairs had been turned into a junkyard with pieces heaped on each other. The room was empty, except for the half-dozen massive shifters who'd helped bring Stone to a stop.

Stone looked around. "Oh, shit. Did I do this?"

She dropped off his back and circled to stand in front of him. She put both hands on his face. "The next time I tell you I've got to donate, get your ass over to me. Understood?"

His eyes widened and he nodded in what appeared to be a dumb fashion.

His gaze shifted to Rez, who'd ended up in an unconscious heap at the base of the wall. He was coming to and holding his jaw with one hand.

When he caught sight of Stone, he pressed himself up against the wall. "I didn't know." He mumbled the words. Rosamunde was pretty sure Stone had broken his jaw. His face was a bloody mess.

"Sorry, Rez, but she's mine."

Rez mumbled his position again. "I fucking didn't know."

"Damn." He called to Rachel. "Get this man the best fae healer you can find and send me the bill."

"I'm on it," Rachel said. She had her cellphone to her ear.

Rosamunde kept her hands on Stone, but addressed Rez. "I'm sorry, too." Rosamunde felt it was the least she owed Rez. "I shouldn't have come here."

Stone glanced around at the broken furniture then turned toward Rachel again. "And send me the bill for the furniture."

"I'll do no such thing for either the healer or the furniture and you know why."

Rosamunde knew as well. Stone and his Guardsmen had rescued her from an Invictus onslaught about a year ago. She was being carted off and would have been paired with a wraith by now if the Guardsmen hadn't intervened.

Stone nodded. "As you wish." He then shifted his attention to Rosamunde and that's when everything took another quick, hard turn. He caught her up in his arms and she was airborne and flying out the open door before she could blink. She held tight to his body for fear any loose limb would get knocked off if it contacted something solid.

Stone was breathing rough again and sounded like a beast warming up to devour something. Maybe her. A girl could hope because the rock-laden, stream scent pouring off his body, sent pleasurable lightning strikes straight between her legs.

She wanted a taste and began wiggling upward in his arms. When she'd gone as far as she could go, she was inches away from his neck. She reached out with her tongue and swiped. He tasted like the way his eyes looked, yet with a flowing stream and rocks beneath: Rocks, moss and water.

She grabbed hold of his neck and sucked on him.

He lost control in the air and rocked wildly back and forth, which meant his grip lessened a little. Because of it, she was able to climb the last two inches and really latch onto his throat. She didn't exactly understand the impulse, but she began to suck harder still.

He groaned then roared.

She had no idea where they were as he began his descent. Though when he landed her in the middle of a pine forest, she had a sense he'd taken her deep into the forest of the Dauphaire Mountains.

He lifted her up and the next thing she knew she had a tree at her back and this time he was sucking at *her* neck.

His voice entered her mind. *Pants off.*

She wasn't about to argue since that was all she could think about as well.

The moment he drew back, she got rid of her stilettos and jeans as fast as she could, then levitated slightly to keep her bare feet out of the pine needles.

She knew exactly where this was headed and she was so on board. But she wanted to make sure he understood her willingness.

Take me. All the way. Now.

His tongue slathered her neck while down low she felt his hand between his body and hers as he took his stiff cock in hand. She released a strangled, hungry moan and arched her pelvis, then lifted her legs, wrapping them around his waist.

His whole body was writhing anxiously as he pressed his cock against her opening. The moment he began to push inside, she let out a long, low moan that echoed around the forest.

Her heart literally ached at this point. *Take from my vein, now, Stone. Please.*

He grunted his assent, licked her neck twice and struck with his sharp fangs. Another lightning strike of pleasure zapped her between her legs where he was already pistoning.

As the extra supply began leaving her body, euphoria rained down on her. She was lost in all the sensations, in her love for this man, in the feel of him working her body and in how hungrily he took her blood.

His mating vibration had already punched inside her and now surrounded hers, but not gently like before. This was a commanding flow of energy, a dominance move that the wolf in her loved. She felt herself flowing from one vibration to another, back and forth, then from Rosamunde to Aralynn. Each 'self' gave and took something different.

Rosamunde had more pure affection. Aralynn focused on his cock. Rosamunde savored that she was sustaining him with her life force. Aralynn kept feeling up the heavy muscles of his arms, shoulders and back.

Ecstasy built quickly and the harder he sucked, the closer she got to the final climb. *That's it, stone. Drink me the fuck down.* Aralynn's voice.

He didn't respond with words, just more grunting as he sucked on her neck and pistoned inside her.

Stone, you're magnificent. Rosamunde.

More grunting and his hips went faster.

He was hard as a rock and when he released a vibration from his cock, she fell right over the cliff of ecstasy.

She hoped they were in the middle of a very large forest because she couldn't hold back the cries of pleasure as her body pulsed inside. The feel of him, as he broke from her neck and roared his own release, took the orgasm to a new height that had her crying out in a high, shrill sound. Pleasure rolled up and up, through her abdomen and grabbed her heart.

A beautiful explosion followed until she was soaring into the heavens.

~ ~ ~

Stone came back to himself in slow, euphoric stages. His head felt light and almost blank. He wasn't even sure where he was, except that he had his cock inside Rosamunde, the Queen of Ferrenden Peace. Or was it Aralynn?

Sweet Goddess. How had this happened?

And how had he ended up so out of control? Had Rosamunde somehow done this to him?

He had to start back at the beginning. Delia had been pathing with him, rattling on about some blog that had interviewed three of the blood roses and how Willow, Malik's mate, wanted another mastyr the moment she saw him as though her blood rose drive had no discernment.

Panic had set in. That he could remember.

He'd pathed with Rosamunde and learned she was intent on delivering her blood somewhere, anywhere. The moment his brain made sense of her intentions, he'd plowed air faster than ever before. His heart had beat so hard he'd wondered why it hadn't exploded.

But all that was nothing to the sight of Rosamunde, in a do-me-now outfit, with a mastyr vampire at her throat.

The rest was a blur that involved beating Mastyr Rez senseless before he knew what hit him and then what felt like a monkey scrambling onto his back.

Rosamunde. Right.

Then it seemed like the whole room all but tackled him and he spun in circles until he couldn't move anymore. It had taken six shifters to stop him.

Rosamunde's voice had helped him come down from his rampage, but images of Rez at her throat had him flying her out of there and up into the Dauphaire Mountains. He needed to show the woman that she wouldn't be feeding anyone else so long as he was alive. And as for her body taking another cock, well, fuck that.

She belonged to him.

When his breathing had finally settled down, his rational mind returned in full. He was pressed up against Rosamunde and had her secured with his body to a pine tree. Her legs were still wrapped around him, his cock buried deep.

Rosamunde?

Hmm? She sounded so strange, not like herself or Aralynn.

He drew back slowly and looked at her face. Her eyes were closed and because his vampire vision lit up the night, he could see that she really had gotten dressed up for the occasion. She'd caked on some dark violet or maybe brown eye-shadow, maybe both.

She looked different, not like the queen at all. She wore a couple of braids, but these were meant only to hold her hair back a little.

Are you hurt? He had to know. He'd acted like a tornado and maybe she'd gotten injured in the process.

No. Even in his head her pathing voice sounded odd, not all there. And her eyes were still closed. She sighed. *I'm not hurt. I'm happy.*

She looked content beyond words and so beautiful, maybe even prettier than her wolf counterpart, Aralynn. He'd just never allowed himself to think of Rosamunde as a woman before.

Yet here he was, still buried inside her and half stiff because her blood had him pumped. Sweet Goddess, he'd just fucked the Queen of Ferrenden Peace and given a little encouragement, he would do it again.

The queen who wasn't supposed to be a queen. A woman who'd lived in isolation her entire life.

He still wasn't convinced she couldn't have battled Margetta. Davido might have a boatload of power, but he was fallible and Stone had always sensed that an infinite kind of capacity existed within Rosamunde. But what if that was the elf-lord power, and her painful connection to it, and not her own innate ability?

He had a lot to think about.

When he finally withdrew from her, he pulled up his leathers and tucked himself back inside.

Her eyes blinked open, a lethargic movement that told him volumes about how she was feeling. She even looked around then chuckled. "I saw stars. No, I mean, really. I was transported into another galaxy. I swear it."

So, this was Rosamunde, with a sexed up, satiated look on her face, her blood flowing with feel-good hormones, a smile on her lips. She'd always looked fairly stern the few times he'd been in her presence. Now she was here, his blood rose.

His.

For the first time, since he'd learned the truth about who she was, he felt torn.

She met his gaze. "Oh. Right. You're still mad at me." She glanced at the forest floor. "You know what. I'll be right back. I need to freshen up. But stay here."

He didn't want her to go.

When she reached for her clothes, he grabbed at her with both hands to keep her with him, but she'd already vanished.

Strange, how empty the space felt without her in it. Yet, with all that he had to think about, it helped to have some distance.

He walked in a slow circle, the pines towering above him. A light breeze blew and the forest made its soft shushing sound.

It took him a moment to gain his bearings. He'd made a smart move, taking her to the middle of the Dauphaire forest, miles away from the nearest village. She'd let loose with a series of cries that would have been heard otherwise. His own shouts, when he'd come, had split the night sky as well.

He wasn't sure, though, what to do with Rosamunde right

now. It was clear he had to keep her close, but he didn't relish the idea. She'd deceived him for weeks now, knowing exactly who she was and how he felt about her.

As Aralynn, early on she'd asked him not to disparage the queen too much. Now he knew why.

He heard sounds high in the air. He looked up, and saw a red wind. Holy fuck, Invictus, this far out, in the forest.

He thought about his battle partner and made a quick decision. Maybe he had to keep Rosamunde close for now, but it would help if he saw her in her other form, the one more wolf than fae.

Rosamunde. I need Aralynn. If you're game, I've got what looks like four Invictus pair and they're ready to fight. I'm moving into a larger clearing. The wraith-pairs are circling in the air.

Aralynn's voice came back strong. *On my way.*

~ ~ ~

Rosamunde heard the tone of Stone's voice and knew exactly what needed to be done. She could almost see the wraith-pairs.

She'd returned to the cottage to get cleaned up and had been debating whether she should put on a fresh pair of jeans, or something else.

Something else it was as she drew a new set of battle leathers from her closet: Green vest, black boots, matching pants. The latter had silver medallions down the sides to the knees, which the boots then picked up.

All set, she teleported to Stone's side, dagger in hand.

But he frowned at her. "You're not Aralynn. I think we need her here right now."

She glanced up at him. His stern, disapproving expression had returned. She lifted her chin. "I am Aralynn. If I need to transform, I will. And you need to get used to who and what am I. Now."

"Fine. This clearing that we're in won't leave much room for maneuvering. So, I want your back against mine."

As she moved to take up the position, however, she kept thinking about whether or not any of the wraith-pairs could be saved. Mastyr Ethan and Samantha had the ability to break the wraith-pair bond and a lot of realm-folk, bound unwillingly to Invictus wraiths, were now in recovery.

Yet, thinking this way didn't feel right to her. She realized that if she remained in her Rosamunde form, she would have difficulty doing battle the way her wolf could. "I've changed my mind. You were right. I need to be Aralynn to do this, otherwise I'll jeopardize both our lives."

He glanced at her, his eyes narrowing. She knew he wanted to watch. Without giving it too much thought, she transformed. At least her vest wasn't so snug when she was in Aralynn's skin.

He dipped his chin. "Good call."

"Just made sense. Aralynn has stronger battling instincts. She's more like my shifter father than my fae mother."

The wraith-pairs moved in suddenly and the wraiths shrieked until even the trees swayed as if in pain.

"Sweet Goddess that hurts my ears." Rosamunde side-stepped in a stealthy circle, matching Stone's stride and movements.

He pathed. *That wraith low, take out her heel with your wolf teeth and I've got her vampire mate.*

Rosamunde didn't hesitate. She shifted swiftly into her wolf form, leaping at the same time. She caught the wraith's bare foot in her maw, pulled her through the air and struck her against a tree. She hadn't killed her, but she fell to the forest floor unconscious.

She heard the sound of Stone's battle energy, then the smell of burning flesh. *One pair down. Three to go.*

Rosamunde pivoted and saw that the vampire had taken a hit to his chest. He was dead. His wraith-mate would soon follow as often happened with wraith-pairs. The bond made it almost impossible for the mate to survive.

She waited in the shadows for Stone's next orders. The wraiths had set up a terrible racket, flying in circles with their mates, well above the clearing. It was like listening to the frightened screech of monkeys, only dozens of them instead of just what was now three wraiths.

Still in her wolf form, Rosamunde remained very still. As was true of all predators, motion caught the eye. Wraith-pairs, being already in a more animal-like state, were particularly tuned-in to the smallest movement.

Stone whipped to his left, which was the western edge of the clearing. She understood why. He'd pegged the troll and his mate as the weakest link.

His strong voice hit her mind as he pathed, *Get the female wraith-mate.*

I'm on it.

Rosamunde shifted from wolf to her Aralynn form and with dagger in hand flew like a shot through the pine trees, singling out the wraith flying erratically around the canopy above her troll-mate. The troll levitated with a battle axe and now flew in a fast descent toward Stone. The other pairs remained in the air, but Rosamunde sensed they were winding up their battle power.

She darted behind the wraith and sliced at the backs of her legs, then slipped back among the pine trees, shifted into her wolf and held herself motionless once more.

The wraith screamed then fell into the tree-tops and became tangled up in the branches of the upper canopy. Her pained shrieks continued.

When she saw that the other pairs were focused on Stone, she transformed back into Aralynn. She moved closer to the clearing and could see the red Invictus flashes of battle power striking into the pine needles. Stone moved in quick darts to avoid getting hit while at the same time maneuvering closer to the troll.

He was short, but with the Invictus power, kept rising swiftly into the air, then finally threw his axe. Stone almost got nicked, though he kept firing his hand-based energy at his adversary. The troll was very fast and as the pairs above shot battle energy at Stone, he flew into the clearing to retrieve his weapon.

Again, Rosamunde remained very still and with her wolf coloring blended into the pines. From even a short distance, she doubted she looked like little more than a shrub. She waited for Stone's orders.

In a sudden blur of motion, while sidestepping twice to avoid battle energy strikes, Stone levitated and kicked the troll in the chest. He flew against a pine tree and fell hard to the ground.

Stone slid into the forest to avoid a final barrage of red battle strikes.

The shrieking of the wraiths had dimmed considerably, then stopped.

Stone's voice hit Rosamunde's mind. *We've only got four Invictus left, but they've descended into the forest. Both male vampires are coming for me. Take the southernmost one out at the back of the thigh.*

They'd worked out the best system since 'Aralynn' had never seen battle before the past few weeks. Stone always made sure she was in the least vulnerable attack position.

Rosamunde began to move, weaving among the trees once more and heading southeast. She could smell the vampires in the forest. She also had a sense of movement above her, which meant she had to pick up speed since one of the wraiths was tracking her.

She felt a brush of something against her tail. Crap, the wraith was right on her.

But she wasn't without a lot of power and added a burst of speed. She saw her target in front of her, who was almost on an already battling Stone. She leaped, bit hard into the vampire's fleshy thigh then melted back into the forest, heading away from where she'd felt the wraith's touch. The bite into her mate would also help keep the wraith somewhat incapacitated. The uninjured mate always suffered when the other was wounded.

The wraith made the mistake of shrieking her agony. Rosamunde shifted from her wolf back into Aralynn then flew at her from below. Using her knife, she cut her hamstrings, then flipped back into the forest, shifted to wolf, and once more remained still. She loved that shifting allowed her to keep her weapons and clothes.

She was breathing hard and felt exhilarated as she always did during battle. She was fighting the enemy, those who had kept the Nine Realms in a state of ongoing terror for centuries.

She knew better than to distract Stone by pathing. They were a team and he called out the orders. She had no trouble obeying a man who had fought the Invictus since he'd become a Guardsman over three-hundred-years ago.

Through the trees, she watched him battle hand-to-hand against the vampire. In a sudden, quick maneuver, he levitated, caught the vampire around the neck and snapped. The vampire dropped as did his wraith-mate.

The two that Rosamunde injured, rose together into the air and disappeared.

The last pair, however, had also taken to the air, circling the forest canopy slower and slower. After a full minute, they also took off. Rosamunde could sense they'd left for good.

Stone pathed. *That's it. They're gone. I'll make sure these four that we brought down are either dead or unable to do harm. Make a broad circuit of the battle area, both on the ground then in the air.*

Will do.

From experience, she knew he wanted her to hunt through the forest to make sure the enemy really was gone. Still in her wolf state, she began to run. *I'm heading south. I'll pace at a distance of fifty yards and lope the circumference around you.*

Good. I'm contacting Harris next to see where we're at and to arrange for clean-up. He'll get the process started.

She slowed her speed for a moment. She knew the tone of Stone's voice well. Something was troubling him. *What is it?*

I keep forgetting how well you know me. On this last vampire, I found a chain around his neck with all kinds of souvenirs. I've found a ring that belonged to one of my troll aunties. She was killed during the original attack at Charborne.

Stone, I'm so sorry.

Hey, at least I avenged her death. How does the forest feel to you?

Very quiet.

She made the fifty-yard circuit in good time, but the forest had a stillness that said the enemy had left. *Heading out to do a hundred-yards then I'll hit the skies.*

Let me know when we're clear so I can give the order for the trolls to come in.

Will do.

Her wolf loved this final part of Stone's procedure. She loped another fifty yards south to begin her second much wider circuit. As she weaved swiftly through the trees and her wolf senses kept her moving in a near-perfect one-hundred-yard orbit around Stone, she neither saw nor smelled anything that would indicate the Invictus were nearby.

She was just returning to her starting point, when the earth rumbled.

The elf-lord power!

She stopped where she was, her heart pounding, then transformed back to Aralynn. A vision so close on the heels of a battle was rare.

Stone. A vision.

I'm feeling the rumble. Should I come to you?

No. Stay where you are. Let me see what the vision means.

But you'll be in pain.

Nothing I haven't endured for a long time. Please, stay put til I know what's going on.

She could feel a terrible prescience coming toward her, though not from Margetta. For that piece of grace, she was grateful.

She took the power in and accepted the painful cramping of her legs for what it was: A warning. The vision followed and it was bad. Within seconds, Margetta would be on Stone in the forest. Apparently, the team of Invictus had relayed their location and Mastyr Stone was their target.

Though still cramped and hurting, she teleported swiftly to Stone but at the same time transformed to Rosamunde's form in order to create her powerful violet wind. She grabbed his arm and with the elf-lord power on her, she carried him high into the sky. She saw Margetta's gold light explode over the forest below and the wave of power it carried tumbled her and Stone though the air, but Rosamunde held steady and kept moving.

Stone fought her at first, probably unaware why she'd done what she'd done.

Margetta, was all she could think to path.

As soon as the word hit his mind, he stopped struggling against her power and settled down. He even added his levitation which forged with her own and smoothed the flight out. Together, they went faster than ever.

He drew closer to her and slid an arm around her waist. *Where are we going?*

I have no idea. Somewhere my aunt isn't.

Sweet Goddess. She was almost on me, wasn't she?

Yes. She would have been, but I could feel the vision moving hard. In it, I saw her coming for you.

Sorry I battled you, he said. *But I didn't know what was happening.*

There wasn't time to even speak the words.

I know. But are you okay? I mean, are you still hurting?

Rosamunde love that he remembered how much pain the power caused her. She even smiled. *I'll survive. Do you want to head back to the city? To your Com Center? I can return to Ferrenden Peace if you like.*

I'm not sure what the hell I want to do at this point, or what I should do. But every instinct tells me Margetta is after me and won't give up. We'd better stick together, at least for now.

Chapter Nine

Stone wasn't sure what he wanted to do or where he wanted to take Rosamunde. The night had already become as volatile as the night before when he'd first slaked his thirst at Aralynn's vein and learned she was a blood rose.

Only tonight, he'd discovered Rosamunde was Aralynn and that he'd made love to a woman he'd despised for months. Then of course, he'd lost his mind at the Wild Boar and practically killed another vampire because of his bone-deep belief that Rosamunde, as a blood rose, belonged only to him.

The sex.

Sweet Goddess, his mind still spun and she'd been so into him, so much unlike the woman he'd always thought Rosamunde to be.

But what really filled him with confusion was when she'd become Aralynn again and fought beside him.

Rosamunde.

Aralynn.

The same woman.

And she'd saved his life again when Margetta had made yet another appearance.

The whole thing was really fucked up and he found it hard to order his thoughts.

He needed some peace and quiet.

He needed his lake house.

Just like that, the decision was made.

We're going to my retreat.

He felt her slow down the rapid flow of her violet-colored wind and after a few seconds he was suspended in the air beside her. The temperature was cold since she'd taken them high into the atmosphere.

Still levitating and holding onto her, he spun them in a swift three-sixty to see where they were and to make sure Margetta was nowhere to be seen. The wind flowed around them like a cyclone and they were in the center.

"We're safe for the moment, Stone. I'd know if the Ancient Fae was nearby. So, where's your retreat? I mean you've mentioned it, but only in the vaguest terms."

He held her gaze, getting lost for a moment in her violet eyes. Rosamunde.

He knew he was scowling, but he couldn't help himself. "On a private lake I own and around which I set up a dense fae security system. I had Vojalie hire the contractors, then wipe their minds afterwards. No one knows about my place. But I can fly us in."

He was about to take off, but she held him back. "I'd like to try something, if you wouldn't mind, something I've never done before."

"And what's that?"

"I've never teleported someone with me. But my fae instincts now tell me it's possible, maybe because I've become a blood rose, I'm not sure. But are you game?"

Caris Roane

Her lips curved. Dammit, she knew him too well. 'Are you game' always spiked his competitive nature. "Hell, yeah."

"Let's try a short distance. What's the nearest landmark or village?"

He glanced down, then pointed. "There's a hill in the middle of the forest. Can you take us there?"

He watched Rosamunde draw a deep breath. She levitated away from Stone, then took his hands in hers.

It was one of those signature moments. He didn't know why, but holding her hand like this meant something, a connection to her that he'd been avoiding since she'd told him the truth.

It meant: *Not going back.*

He was in deep and despite his reluctance he had a profound, fae-like intuition he'd never be able to go back. But he'd sure as hell like a few minutes to at least think things through.

She closed her eyes and the next moment, he felt himself move but not through air. This time, it was a slip through space, an odd vibration. He hadn't even blinked and now he levitated above the hill. In the distance he saw members of the Tannisford Shifter Brigade patrolling the forest east of the village of Billeford.

Are they your wolves?

Yup. But I don't want to distract them.

Okay. What's the village closest to your lake?

Hawsdale.

Right. You took me there once, as Aralynn, to the bar. What was the name?

The Hungry Mule.

Her lips twitched. *I always liked that name. So, shall we go to Hawsdale?*

Embrace the Power

Yes. Let's do it.

Again, it wasn't like flying at all, just a soft vibration and the feel of a different kind of dimension, then he was levitating five feet above the roof of the Hungry Mule.

She still held his hand. *Want to get a drink?*

Stone shook his head. *I'd rather we went to the lake. It's time to regroup, to talk, maybe figure some things out.*

He looked around to gain his bearings then felt her give his hand a squeeze. He glanced back at her, surprised.

Stone, I'd love a chance to talk, really talk.

He nodded, but he felt grim. He didn't want Rosamunde thinking he'd forgive her easily for holding back her true identity.

We'll talk. We're not far, but you'd never find your way in on your own.

How about you form a picture in your mind and I'll see if I can take us there?

Well, we can give it a shot. He supposed part of the process for them moving forward would be to explore not just the nature of the elf-lord power that she could channel, but also in what ways their rose blood connection amplified each of their natural abilities.

He took a moment to settle his mind and focus exclusively on his retreat. The warrior vampire in him was always thinking two or three steps ahead, like his need to contact Harris and see how things were going. For now, he centered his thoughts on the lake house, then squeezed her hand as a signal.

Oh. The surprised sound of her voice, made him open his eyes and look at her.

What is it?

I … I can see everything. The lake, your beautiful home, the

*trees on a rim of hills surrounding a beautiful expanse of water. The
north side has reeds and the south a narrow beach. It's exquisite.*

He stared at her for a long moment. *You've described it exactly.*
Her violet eyes glowed as she looked inward at the image in his
head. He didn't get it. The woman beside him was so different from
the woman he'd known as the queen. Was Davido right? Had he
misjudged her? And had he done so on purpose? But this made
no sense. What would he possibly gain from thinking bad of her?

Let's go, he pathed.

The quiet slip through space happened again and much to his
amazement, she had no trouble teleporting through his security
system. Which meant if Margetta ever learned of the location,
she'd find it easy to break through as well.

But he wouldn't worry about the Ancient Fae right now.

He now levitated above the wood dock. Releasing her hand,
he descended to plant his boots on the seasoned, gray planks.

The gibbous moon cast a glow across the water.

Rosamunde landed beside him and made a complete circle.
"This lake has to be three hundred yards across and you say you
own it?"

"I do. I purchased it from a fae woman who'd lost her husband
to an Invictus attack in the area. She moved to the U.S. shortly after
with her five children. I didn't blame her for leaving. Her husband
was one of several extended family members who'd been recently
murdered."

She turned toward him slightly. "You're one helluva man. I
just want you to know that I know who you are and I admire you
fiercely." She smiled, if ruefully. "The truth is, I wanted to become
more like you and I hope I have."

He stared at her. Was this truly Rosamunde, the cold, authoritative royal living in a remote, stone castle?

Everything he'd believed about Rosamunde seemed to be falling away before his eyes. She wasn't the indifferent, cowardly person he'd believed her to be. Yet, how could he suddenly shift his opinions, when he'd held to them like a drowning man?

Maybe he should, as Davido suggested, take a hard look at *why* he'd been so quick to judge Rosamunde in the first place. Why had he refused to believe her about her lack of power to battle her aunt?

When he saw that she was looking toward the house with curiosity, he encouraged her to look around. He would welcome the time apart.

She glanced at him over her shoulder. "You don't mind?"

"No, of course not. Unless you're in league with Joseph. Should I start nailing everything down?" He didn't know why he was teasing her.

At that, she smiled and raised an arched, playful brow. "I've thought about going into business with him more than once. That gremlin has more money than the Goddess herself."

He stared at her as she turned and headed up the dock toward the small, single-story house. His heart ached in a strange way, something he didn't get. Except that, he actually *liked* Rosamunde and he'd never expected to, not in a million years. But it did help to see her out of her intricate braids and flowing gowns.

He recalled what Davido had told him, that Rosamunde was never intended to be queen, that she'd only been filling in for the past thousand years waiting for Quinlan's daughter to come into the world.

Her life had been no picnic. She'd been orphaned by Margetta at a young age. He couldn't imagine what that had been like for her. She'd also suffered every day of her life as she channeled the elf-lord power and experienced severe pain in order to support the veil of mist. She'd lived a life of sacrifice, something he valued.

As he watched Rosamunde open the sliding door that led into the living room, his gaze spanned the row of full-length plate glass windows that ran the length of the house. The kitchen was at one end and his master bedroom at the other with the living room in between.

In the space of a few hours, Rosamunde of Ferrenden Peace had become a complete mystery to him. He'd had her all figured out, to the last cell of her seemingly selfish body. Yet what he felt from her, and the level of her vulnerability, pummeled his heart. How had he ever believed her soulless?

As he moved in her direction, crossing the dock to join her in the living room, he realized the elf-lord power had remained with him, probably because of Rosamunde's proximity. Again, he sensed her vulnerability. "You're being very open with me right now, aren't you?"

"I don't think I can be anything else." She waved her hand between them, her wrist flowing elegantly. "Whatever this is, it's torn down the wall. You can ask me anything and I'll tell you whatever you want to know."

He saw the fear in her eyes almost a kind of dread and it surprised him. He drew close. The violet of her eyes seemed to have a strange glitter to them and for a moment they turned brown, like Aralynn's. Was it his imagination, or did her features seem to shift as well, her brows more arched, her lips fuller, her expression more challenging.

Sweet Goddess, there was so much more to Rosamunde than he'd ever suspected.

"Are you hungry?" he asked. "Would you like some homemade bread, maybe some soup? And I have beer or sweet German wine, if that's what you, as Rosamunde, prefers."

"Thank you. That's kind."

She looked at him with such surprise, that he had to laugh. "I never meant to be a monster, Rosamunde."

"I never thought you were. But I did know you were angry with me, all the time."

"I didn't understand you," he said. "And truthfully I'm still not sure I do."

"Maybe time will take care of that."

When his stomach rumbled, he put a hand to his abdomen. Thinking about food had reminded him he hadn't eaten since he'd risen for the night.

She smiled. "Hungry, huh?"

"I sure am. But I want to thank you for donating again. I've never felt better in my entire life and I owe you that."

"You're welcome and Stone, I wouldn't have gone to the Wild Boar at all except that with the surplus I'd created I knew I wouldn't have survived the night."

He drew close. "I was being, as Davido put it, pigheaded again. But this has all moved so fast, I haven't had time to absorb the implications. But when I saw Rez ready to use his fangs—" A powerful shudder went through him. "Yeah, we'd best stick close for the next few nights."

Rosamunde got a funny look on her face, an expression he couldn't read and her cheeks colored up.

He frowned. "Would that bother you, to be so close to me? Maybe you'd rather be back at your castle?"

"What? Holed up again like a criminal?"

He cocked his head, confused. "Is that what it's been like for you?" He was pretty sure he'd had the wrong take on everything all this time.

"It often felt that way, like I was imprisoned. But I hate complaining. It sounds so ungrateful and I've felt blessed to do my part." She turned toward the kitchen. "So what kind of soup have you got?"

His lake house was a simple home, made up of a lot of wood inside and out. He had slate on the floor, like his Sandismare home, and the windows were trimmed with black steel. The kitchen bar had been constructed of concrete.

He didn't have a dining table, just a couple of stools not far from the stove. His retreat wasn't a big place meant for entertaining, just a place where he could get some time away from the demands of Tannisford. He never brought women here. Like his home in the city, Rosamunde was the first.

She sat down on one of the tall stools and swiveled to look at the lake. He pulled out a container of vegetable beef soup from the fridge as well as a round loaf of French bread.

He put the latter in the oven to warm and dumped the soup in a pot. He lit up the gas flame and let the appliance do its job.

He had to keep reminding himself that Rosamunde was two different women, yet very much the same. He knew Seth's woman, Lorelei, was able to take on different physical forms. "So Lorelei is your cousin."

"Yes, well, a half-cousin. I tutored her for several months when she first arrived in Ferrenden Peace." She smiled at the memory. "Then I had a vision and sent her to serve as Mastyr Seth's bodyguard."

"I remember. Lorelei has made Seth very happy."

"And the other way around as well."

He glanced at her. If what Rosamunde had said was true, that her primary job all these centuries had been to keep her aunt away from the elf-lord power, then Margetta must have tried dozens of ways to invade Ferrenden Peace.

He also knew that both Lorelei and Margetta had wraith blood. "So, are you part wraith like Lorelei?"

"No. My mother had a different father than Margetta."

Stone breathed a sigh of relief. It was tough enough to deal with 'Aralynn', but if there was a third persona in there somewhere, he'd probably toss up his hands and back the hell out of there for good.

Rosamunde chuckled. "You look like you just escaped the hangman's noose."

"I'm not as flexible as Seth. I'll tell you that straight out. And Seth might be comfortable being bonded to a wraith, but if I knew you had wraith blood I'd call a halt right now."

"Well, I don't and honestly, I wouldn't blame you, not even a little."

He set out spoons and big bowls, plates for the bread. He slid a tray of fresh butter down the concrete counter. "Look sharp."

She turned in time to catch the ceramic dish then laughed. She squinched up her face. "Oh, that soup smells so good already. Where'd you get it?"

"There's a village nearby. And a troll has cooked for me for years."

"I take it you pick up the food then bring it here."

"I do. Once a week."

She looked around. "Do you do the cleaning and maintenance?"

At that, he smiled. "Nah. I use a service and have a fae wipe the memories afterward. I pay extra for everyone's trouble."

"So, there's at least one fae that knows about this place."

He shook his head and his lips curved. "Not exactly. She carries a potion with her to erase her own memories as well. And I watch her down the vial at the Com Center every time. I trust her, too. She's a friend of Delia's." He opened the fridge again. "Beer or wine?"

"A cold bottle of beer sounds like heaven."

He chuckled softly once more. Again, she'd surprised him. Aralynn had no problem guzzling from a bottle, but the much more formal queen?

As he pulled two amber ales from the door of his fridge, he wondered about her all over again. "Do you want a glass? I don't have any chilled." So how formal was she? Now that he had a better picture of her past, he knew that being queen had been thrust on her as a child, a duty she'd accepted. He'd always supposed she'd loved lording it over the realm-folk in her kingdom. He'd never thought for a moment she didn't adore her castle life, not until tonight.

"The bottle's fine, Stone."

"Slide it to you?"

"Sure, why not?"

He couldn't make her out. Though she was in her Rosamunde form, she seemed more like Aralynn right now. Her violet eyes were bright and almost enthusiastic as she held out her hand, curved her fingers in an arc, and waited for the brew.

He slid it as he had the butter.

She caught it easily and drew the bottle straight to her lips. She even tilted back her head as she drank. And no simple ladylike swallow. She guzzled half the contents, then pressed her hand to her mouth as she belched into her palm. "I'm so sorry. I think I'm a bit punchy from all that's happened. And I definitely didn't expect to see you again. At least, not so soon."

"Your blood rose qualities have complicated everything."

"They sure have." She frowned and shook her head. "This is as much your difficulty now as mine and I'm sorry for that, I really am. You didn't ask to have me as your blood rose."

"Well, you're right about that. And though the other mastyrs warned me it's a tough journey, I never imagined I'd be ready to kill to keep other men away from you." He frowned and sighed. "We both need time to adjust."

"Yes, we do."

He turned back to the stove and stirred the soup then swigged his beer. What was it about a cold one that so often hit the spot?

He opened the oven door and gave the bread a poke. "Almost warmed through."

"Good, because now my wolf stomach is grumbling."

He turned the heat up under the soup and kept stirring to keep the vegetables and chunks of beef from burning. Another minute and he was ladling the soup into bowls and slapping the bread onto a large board. He pulled it apart in a few big chunks.

After grabbing a pair of cloth napkins, he joined her at the counter, then tapped bottles with her. "Dig in, Rosamunde."

She flashed him a smile that grabbed something deep inside his chest all over again.

~ ~ ~

Rosamunde savored the soup, the warm bread with melted butter, and the beer. She'd had a chef at the castle for years, but she swore a meal had never tasted as good as this one.

As she glanced at Stone, she wondered if he was the cause, his company and being in his home.

She lifted her spoon to her lips once more, savored the fresh vegetables and flavorful beef and gave herself to a deep, contented sigh. Stone had grown quiet, though she suspected he wasn't thinking about much of anything. He kept tearing off chunks of bread, slathering each piece with butter, then using it as a soup-scoop.

She set her spoon down for a moment, aware suddenly that she'd never had a normal kind of life, like eating soup and savory French bread in a man's kitchen.

She'd had a life built on duty, doing what was required and expected of her. She really wasn't complaining. She'd long since accepted what she'd needed to do to save the Nine Realms. Despite Stone's prior disapproval of her, she'd been proud that she'd kept Margetta away from the elf-lord power all these centuries.

"Stone, I wish I'd been able to sit down with you long before this."

He picked up his beer and swigged. She glanced at his long

legs, noting that even the counter and bar stools had been built to accommodate his six-seven frame.

"I've misjudged you, Rosamunde. Davido told me you were never supposed to be queen."

The reality of how she'd become queen, that Margetta had killed her own sister, hit her all over again. "No, I wasn't and I was reminded of that fact every time the elf-lord power struck."

"I wish I'd understood. I was way too hard on you."

She leaned forward slightly. "I won't disagree, but I never really blamed you."

He set his bottle back on the counter, then continued eating, but his cheeks looked drawn and his eyes were narrowed. She could tell he was thinking hard.

She picked up her spoon as well and let the subject rest. She knew this situation was especially difficult for Stone. He was a straightforward, up front kind of guy. Her deception must have hurt him badly.

She sipped her beer and took another chunk of bread. She added the local butter and moaned softly as she took a bite, then followed up with another spoonful of soup. "This cook deserves to win awards."

"I think she has."

"Well, I'm not surprised."

Glancing at her empty bottle, he left his bar stool then returned with two more beers. She accepted hers readily and took a sip.

"I don't know if you'll want to talk about this, but how did it happen that Margetta killed your mother? Davido told me a couple of details, while at the same time calling me pig-headed."

"Why are you asking?"

"I want to know you better and I think you know a lot more about me than I do about you."

Rosamunde nodded. "You're probably right. After all, I've read every blog post ever written about you, but I know there's not much on the web about me."

"Exactly. You're something of a mystery."

Her throat grew tight. She debated whether to share the history with Stone, but it seemed pointless to not let him know the worst shame of her life. She'd long since forgiven herself, but it was still hard to talk about how and why her mother had died at the Ancient Fae's hands.

"When I was young, I had several miniature goats that I adored and tended. Though my mother was queen, I had chores around what was then a large though simple home with a thatched roof. I was a typical girl and dressed my small goats up in scraps of woven fabric. My mother insisted the goats wear bells around their necks. She told me it was so that if they got lost, I'd be able to find them. Now I realize her real purpose was to keep track of me.

"I was adventurous back then. I think my father's shifter genes were strong in me from the beginning.

"Anyway, I knew there was a mysterious veil of mist around the kingdom that kept Ferrenden Peace separated from the outside world. And I used to play near the mist barrier every day. I was so curious about how it was made and since I was forbidden to go into the mist, well, I had to go.

"The first time I passed into the veil, I was alone. But I could hear my goats, so I knew the way back."

She leaned her elbow on the counter. She wasn't looking at Stone, but staring way into the past. "The mist was an incredible experience and had an effect on me. Some of my powers came alive and soon I was manipulating the mist. I could create all kinds of pathways through it.

"Eventually, I started taking my goats with me and even justified my adventures because the goats loved the grass in the mist.

"I would take their bells off so that no one would know I was in the veil.

"After weeks of exploring, I eventually made it all the way through to the other side, to Quinlan's realm, Grochaire. And that's when a golden wind arrived and I met my Aunt Margetta for the first time.

"She was so beautiful to my young eyes. I can recall her words to me. 'Well aren't you pretty. Are you Evelyn's daughter? Rosamunde?'

"I remember how proud I was to proclaim myself as the daughter of the queen. 'Do you know who I am?' she asked. I couldn't believe this beautiful, angelic woman was talking to me. 'I'm your Auntie Margetta.' I can remember very clearly how she looked past me and said, 'And what a clever girl you are because I can see that you've created a little tunnel through the mist.'

"I was feeling very excited about the encounter and couldn't wait to return so I could tell my mother that I'd just met my aunt. But the next moment, Mama arrived in a cloud of teal-colored wind.

"I remember only two things, my mother shouting at me to get back through the mist, then a violent explosion that had me running as fast as my legs could carry me."

Her throat was tight again. "My mother died battling her

sister, while saving my life and keeping Margetta out of Ferrenden Peace.

"Afterwards, the Sidhe Council was brought in to figure out what to do. When it was discovered I could sustain the mist and keep Margetta from reaching the elf-lord power, even as a child, I was given the job." She realized a couple of tears had rolled down her cheeks.

She remembered how badly it had hurt, that first night when the elf-lord power came to her. She'd only been nine, but her fae instincts had told her what needed to be done, even if it took her years before she understood the whole picture.

"Even as a child you had to endure the elf-lord power?"

She nodded.

"Sweet Goddess." He took his napkin and drew close to dry her tears. It was such a tender gesture that she stared at him in wonder. "Stone, you have this big, masterful voice and you're as tall as sin. But I think you must be the kindest man I've ever known."

"Thank you. That's nice to hear. But I'm sorry you had to go through such a terrible thing, especially so young. Though I can relate to feeling responsible for the death of a parent. I shouldn't have become a Guardsman when I did, even though my adoptive parents insisted I join up."

She saw the glint of pain in his eyes. "What do you mean?"

"I haven't talked about this for decades. But when I was young and living in Charborne, I'd taken to fighting wraith-pairs, any that came near our farming community. That was a good decade before the then current ruling Mastyr of Tannisford invited me into his Vampire Guard. There were many times I was the sole reason a lot of villagers didn't get slaughtered. I knew that joining the Guard would put Charborne in some jeopardy, but the mastyr made sure squads went out often to patrol the village and surrounding farms.

"This was three-hundred-years ago, long before electricity and the resulting resources we have these days. So, basically, I knew I was taking a chance, but no one could have predicted the kind of attack that occurred."

Rosamunde knew what happened only too well. She'd seen the devastation in one of Margetta's heinous visions. Later, she'd read the reports in the newspapers.

He slid off his stool and took her bowl and plate, stacking them with his own. "The major assault on Charborne, that took the lives of my parents, and so many others, happened six months to the day after I'd become a Guardsman. I don't think I've ever gotten over the tragedy. There was so many lives lost that night. If only I'd been there—" He let the words hang.

"I know. I totally get it. If only I hadn't gone into the mist."

He moved to the sink, taking the dishes with him, then met her gaze. "I thought you'd understand."

When he started rinsing the dishes, she asked. "Do you want some help?"

At that, he smiled. "Do you do dishes, Your Majesty?"

She put both her hands on her cheeks. "Not once in my life, not even as Aralynn. I only kept beer in the fridge. If I got hungry, I'd head back to the castle. But I'd like to help."

His lips curved. "Come here, then."

She slid off her stool and picked up the breadboard. There was only one small piece left. She hardly thought it was worth saving, but she had an idea what to do with it.

She set the board next to the dirty dishes. Stone was leaning his hip against the concrete surface. She held up the piece of bread for him. "Want this last bit?"

She was surprised when he took her wrist in hand and drew the bread toward his lips. She watched him open his mouth, then guide the piece inside.

Except, he took more than just the bread.

His lips surrounded two of her fingers and her thumb. She felt a sucking pressure as he slowly took the bread from her.

Rosamunde froze where she stood. The cool air hit her now damp fingers. Stone held her gaze, his brows low, his green eyes glittering.

Deep within her abdomen, a vibration began, one that she recognized as her profound need to bond with him. She could hardly breathe as sudden desire began to spread from the point of that vibration throughout her entire body.

Her cheeks heated up. "Stone are you really suggesting what I think you are?"

Was it possible he'd started overcoming his anger? And so soon? She knew Stone had spoken with Davido. Maybe the wise old troll had offered Stone some advice.

~ ~ ~

The last thing Stone had expected was to see the complete vulnerability in Rosamunde's violet eyes. He couldn't believe how much he'd misjudged the woman. He'd always thought of her as cold and reserved, stuck in her royal life and indifferent to the plight of the Nine Realms.

Nor could he deny a need to embrace what his fellow ruling mastyrs had already experienced; a deep, overwhelming call not just on his body, but on his soul. He hadn't expected the latter, which worked to complicate everything.

The experience of the elf-lord power had not only ramped up his mating vibration, but also told him quite simply that Queen Rosamunde of Ferrenden Peace was in a similar state.

Slowly, he extended his hand in her direction. Was he really going to do this? Was he really going to make love to Rosamunde?

His palm touched the bare skin of her arm and an electrical current began to pulse, a very Nine Realms vibration. In response, she drew in a slow, halting breath punctuated with faint gasps. He held her gaze.

Whatever this was going to be, he wanted her with him all the way.

"Rosamunde, are you sure you want to do this, because I know once we begin this journey, there's no turning back."

Tears touched her eyes. He could see she was overwhelmed. He was no less so and felt as though if she refused him right now, if she said she couldn't continue, he'd break apart in a way that could never be restored.

He didn't get this. He didn't get any of it.

Then she did something he knew he'd never forget for the rest of his life. She lifted her hand and settled her palm on his cheek. She never once averted her gaze. He knew what this was costing her, how much courage she showed in just looking into his eyes. He could hear the quick, erratic beats of her heart.

"I'm scared half out of my mind right now." She swallowed hard. "But the elf-lord power tells me this is the right, maybe even the only possible path, not just for me but for you as well. Yet you and I have been enemies for so long. How can we come together like this now?"

"After all that we've been through just tonight, especially beginning with events at the Wild Boar, I want us to be together, as close as we can be, short of a true bond. We'll get to know each other and maybe the rest will follow."

"Then it's a matter of faith and of trust?" she asked.

"Rosamunde, tell me you trust me, that you believe in me at least that much." He knew he'd spoken stridently and her sensitive fae features startled then paled quickly.

She gasped again, but she never broke eye-contact with him. Damn, the woman had courage, more than he'd ever supposed. She was practically splintering in front of him, yet she held her course.

He felt her answer before she gave it. "I never disagreed with your character, Stone. Only with your attitudes toward me. With all my heart, I trust you. Sweet Goddess, I trust you with my life."

He slid his arm all the way around her, pulling her tight against him. He crashed his lips down on hers because he couldn't do anything else. Her words had lit a fire in his heart, his soul, his body that wouldn't be denied.

~ ~ ~

Rosamunde felt as though she was falling backward and just kept falling, even though she remained upright. The sensation was sublime. She also couldn't believe that in the space of a few hours, he'd changed his view of her. Davido must have helped, yet at the same time, she knew the battle for his forgiveness wasn't over.

For now, though, she focused only on him. He had his arms tight around her, so she felt safe, absurdly and ridiculously safe.

Until the past two nights, she hadn't been with a man in so long that she'd forgotten the thrill of experiencing the sheer physical strength a man possessed, especially Stone.

Her heart pounded. She'd already begun producing the extra portion for Stone and she was eager to have him feed from her again. But she didn't want to hurry the process. More was happening here than just sex. She knew that. She might not be able to quantify everything, but this was the beginning of a bonding process that had to take certain steps.

How odd that these thoughts went through her mind, yet they did.

His hips met hers in a slow grind. Very male.

As he kissed her, his tongue played inside her mouth, at times licking and at others, thrusting. She melted against him, which caused his arms to tighten a little more. Her breasts pushed against his chest as though searching for a way to get closer.

He must have read her mind. "I want your clothes off."

"Same here." He released her. But instead of letting him go, she planted her hands on his shoulders then smoothed her palms down his muscled chest. The leather of his Guardsman coat was soft beneath her fingers.

Without giving it much thought she began undressing him. If it crossed her mind that maybe he wanted to take her to his bedroom, she really didn't care. This time belonged to her, no matter what the future held.

The Guardsman coat was a simple matter. The garment had a heavy hook at the waist which she undid with a quick flip of her fingers. He wasn't wearing the traditional Guardsman shirt, either, so when she pushed the sleeveless coat over his shoulders, his chest was fully exposed.

He didn't try to catch the coat, but let it fall to the wood floor behind him.

Though he was breathing hard, he made no move to engage her. He must have understood what she needed. She'd been hungry for a man for so long that she had to take her time right now, had to savor, had to *feel*. She might have been with him as Aralynn and in a wild state after the Wild Boar, but not truly just as Rosamunde.

She ran her hands down his chest and let her fingers trace each of the unique tattoos. Most were designs without words, a lot of swirls that ended in knife-like points. But among these swirls were his thick, muscled pecs and tight nipples.

A growl formed in her throat, something more wolf than fae. But she let it roll as she surrounded his left pec with her mouth and sucked.

She heard him groan and his hands found the front of her vest. "I love that you're not wearing a bra."

"Unh," came out of her throat as she suckled.

Despite that she was sticking to her enjoyment of his pecs, he found a way to work free the few buttons of her vest until it fell open.

He bent over her as she suckled, in order to reach her breasts with his hands. The angle must have been awkward, but he made it work and her hips writhed as he fondled her, turning her nipples into firm beads.

Shivers chased down her neck and shoulders. Her hands kept moving over his corded arms. He had a warrior's lean physique and every muscle stood out as though a sculptor had personally crafted his body.

When she shifted to take his other nipple in her mouth and used both her hands to shape his pec, his body rolled beneath hers and heavy groans left his throat. He moved slightly to surround her with his arms.

As desire flowed more and more heavily, her knees weakened and she found herself sliding her lips down his body. His riverbed scent had her nostrils flaring, trying to take in as much as she could. She kissed along the ripples of his abdomen until she reached the waistband of his leathers. His hands were in her hair and on her shoulders, then back and forth.

"Sweet Goddess, Rosamunde."

She worked his zipper carefully, revealing the manliest part of him. Tugging his pants below his hips, she licked a slow line from the base of his cock all the way up.

She took the tip of him in her mouth and sucked. His breathing turned ragged as her lips pulled on his crown.

How her body ached. She needed him inside her yet she loved having him in her mouth. She wanted to keep him there.

But his movements became erratic so that she had to draw away. She leaned back on her knees, looking up at him.

With his boots still on, he pulled his pants back up. He lifted her to her feet then made his way to sit on an ottoman in front of the sofa.

He worked at his boots, but she saw that he was struggling since his gaze was fixed on her breasts. She thought she understood why. As Rosamunde, for whatever reason, her breasts were bigger than Aralynn's.

She smiled as she levitated in his direction. She dropped once more to her knees then went to his aid and got both his boots off. She would have taken care of his pants but he stood up and got rid of them like he was running on coals.

When he was completely naked, he reached down and caught her arms, pulling her to her feet. She chuckled softly, loving how anxious he was to get close to her. She'd never felt more like a woman than in this moment.

He smiled as well as he dragged her into his arms, slanting a kiss again over her lips once more.

He pummeled her mouth in the best way and only stopped when she grabbed his bottom with both hands and began to explore.

"Sweet Goddess." He'd said it again, but this time added, "You're killing me. Every touch sends a thrill straight to my cock."

When she bit his lip, he drew back and with his mossy-green eyes glittering, said in a deep hoarse voice, "Okay, that's it. I've got to take charge or I swear you'll vaporize me."

Without warning, he slid his arm behind her knees and lifted her into the air.

A long breath deserted her body as he swept her in a darting levitation, through the living room and into a short hallway.

The trip to the bedroom was brief then she was flying through the air. She landed on her back on his bed and laughed a little more. It was an extraordinary thing to be handled by such a strong man.

As he drew close and leaned over her, she tried to reach for him, but he put a hand between her breasts to keep her pinned down. "No. It's my turn. You need to pay for working me up so fast."

Embrace the Power

The quirk to his lips melted something inside her heart.

She'd meant it when she'd said she trusted him with her life.

Chapter Ten

Stone went to work on Rosamunde's clothes and he wasn't gentle, something she didn't seem to mind since she kept laughing. He flipped her to one side and worked her arm out of her leather vest, then did the same to the other. Seeing her large breasts, nipples peaked, stopped him for a moment. He wanted his mouth on them right now doing to her what she'd done to him.

He leaned over her and using one hand, shaped her breast into a peak then licked around the outside of her nipple. Her breath came in several odd gasps, which made him smile. He continued licking the tip over and over and when she was cooing and her back kept arching he finally took her nipple in his mouth. He suckled greedily which had her crying out and gripping the back of his neck. When he was sure she couldn't take much more, he added a vibration to his tongue.

"Sweet Goddess, you could make me come like this."

He rose up to look down at her. "Good. Now you know exactly how you made me feel."

Her fairly wild expression softened and she grinned, but tears touched her eyes. "I think you're amazing."

He stalled out as he stared back at her, at the admiration shining in her eyes. His heart kept feeling as though it was expanding with every second he spent with her. Was this truly Rosamunde?

He said the only thing that made sense. "I love doing this with you."

She nodded.

Since she still wasn't completely undressed, he moved down her body. He worked on her boots next, unzipping them and tugging them off as gently as he could.

"I love your shoulders and arms. Stone, you're built as hell."

Her voice had deepened, a sexy sound that made his cock twitch a couple of times. But he stayed focused on his task.

Once he had her boots off, he spent the next couple of minutes tugging her snug leathers down. Her skin looked beautifully pale next to the black leather and as he eased her pants over her hips, a reddish landing strip appeared, making his mouth water.

He knew exactly what he wanted to do next, but he had to get her pants off first. He worked them down her legs and once they lay on the floor, he met her gaze. "My turn."

She cried out in surprise as he caught her thighs in hand and dragged her quickly to the edge of the bed. Dropping to his knees on the floor, he spread her thighs and heard her pleasurable moans, very deep and throaty, as he began to kiss down the short length of her groomed pubic hair.

He slid his arms under her legs and when he reached the seam of her clitoris he began to deepen each kiss, adding more pressure and nipping at her. When he licked her, the groan she uttered went on and on so of course he began to lick in earnest. He wanted those sounds to reach a feverish pitch.

Her woodsy, herbal scent hardened him as he continued to lick. Rosamunde smelled and tasted like Aralynn. They really were the same woman.

When he took as much of her in his mouth as he could and began to suck, she cried out and her fingers landed on his head. She caressed him moving her hands down until he could reach her fingers with his lips.

He switched to lick her fingers, then lifted up enough to take one of her hands and press her palm to her sex. He licked the tops of her hands and she began to massage. He held her gaze as her hands went to work. She was gasping and panting.

He licked harder then pushed her hands away. Sliding his arms beneath her thighs, he found her well and drove his tongue inside. Her back arched as she cried out. He held onto her legs and went vampire fast, then added a vibration to his pummeling tongue.

She writhed as she came screaming. Her body jerked in his hands, but he held on and kept up the quick pace of his tongue, until her shouts lessened and her body grew lax.

He glanced down at his cock, weeping at the tip, needing to be inside Rosamunde.

Rosamunde.

He rose up over her, settling his hands on the bed so that he could look at her. She was breathing hard with a soft blush to her cheeks. He leaned down and kissed her throat.

His nostrils quivered as he caught the scent of her blood. It would taste better because she'd come, different, richer and he couldn't wait.

But just as he began to get serious, she caught his neck and pushed him back a little so that she could look at him. "There's something I want to do for you."

A shiver went over his shoulders. "What's that?"

"I want to be both women for you. Would you like that?"

Another shiver raced down his body and had his erection jumping all over again. His lips parted but no words came out, so he nodded.

Her lips curved. He felt the vibration first then he watched as her features blurred then suddenly Aralynn was beneath him. He groaned. Two women. A fantasy he'd never imagined before.

He'd loved Aralynn first. That's what went through his head. Her brown eyes glinted with desire as she slung an arm around her neck. He kissed her hard. She grabbed his ass with both hands and with her shifter strength rolled him onto his back.

She didn't wait. She didn't ask for permission. Instead, she climbed up on his hips, took his cock in hand and guided him to her well.

Slowly, she eased down on him, her back arching slightly, a wicked smiled on her lips. "Hey," she said. "You feel damn good, Stone."

"Aralynn." The wolf in this woman was much more demanding and in control.

She began riding him, up and down. She settled her hands beside his head and worked her hips. He gripped her bottom wanting to help, but she shoved his hands away. "Let's keep this slow because I'm going to change back."

He barely had time to register what she meant when she rose up and he felt the vibration begin.

Staring at Rosamunde, his eyes were drawn naturally to her

larger breasts, but there was something more. He loved Aralynn's take charge attitude, but Rosamunde's sensuality got to him.

Her lip were parted and her eyes closed. She moved her body in a slow undulation so that she worked his cock. At the same time, her hands glided down her breasts. Pinching her nipples, she moaned softly.

He shivered and his balls tightened. Rosamunde was much more sensual. Yet he loved the qualities of both women.

Aralynn.

Rosamunde.

When she opened her eyes, she slid a finger in her mouth and sucked. *Now if only I could ride you and suck you at the same time.*

His eyes rolled back in his head at the image she'd just created for him.

Then another vibration and Aralynn's more muscular shifter body was on him again, her hips moving fast. She leaned over him and went wolf fast.

His neck arched. "I can't hold back."

"Then don't."

Another vibration and Rosamunde was on him. She had the same power, so her hips never stopped. "I want you to see me as you come." Her violet eyes turned silver. Sweet Goddess, she was adding a fae thrall and it felt amazing. "Come for me, Stone. Come now and come hard."

With her sex all but fisting his cock, he began to release. He shouted as each pulse of pleasure barreled through his cock.

But when she began to slow her movements and the last of his semen poured into her body, he could tell she hadn't come.

He slid his hand through her hair, cupping the back of her

neck. He dragged her down to him and kissed her, plying her mouth with his tongue.

And still he felt the elf-lord power moving through him, a residual amount but enough to make him firm again.

"My turn to take care of you," he said. "But I want you to stay as Rosamunde now. Okay?"

She nodded.

He didn't give her time to think. Instead, with a swift levitating trick and a hand on her ass to hold her in place, he flipped her midair so that she landed on her back, his cock still buried inside her.

"Oh. That was fantastic." He felt her internal muscles glide over him hungrily. He began to drive into her, letting her feel him.

"I'm going to feed from you now."

He slowed the movement of his hips and began to lick above the vein in her throat.

Her breaths grew ragged. "I want this, Stone. I want it so bad, just as we are right now."

His fangs descended fully and he tilted his head for the right angle. As soon as he had it, he pathed, *You ready?*

I am. Do it. Please.

He struck quickly, retracted his fangs and formed a seal around the wound. This time, her blood in his mouth was like a series of powerful fireworks that flew down his throat. He groaned heavily and put his hips back to work.

She released a series of profound cries. The taking of blood always brought pleasure.

He heard the growing ecstasy in her voice. *I want you to come while I'm drinking from you, Rosamunde. Can you do that?*

Yes. One single, breathless, telepathic word. She was tight around him. He wouldn't last long either.

At the same time, his mating frequency lit up. He didn't ask permission about this either but pushed inside her body and found her frequency. As his mating vibration rolled over hers, Rosamunde shouted at the ceiling.

"Stone, that's heaven. Oh, what you're doing to me."

With her blood now firing up his veins, and his mating frequency swirling all over hers, he left her throat and swiped the wounds to seal them, then lifted up. He had to look at her as she came.

She slid her arms around his back, her hands anxious and moving. "I'm going to come."

"Me, too. But let's make this special."

The next moment, he levitated them both above the bed. They remained locked in the same thrusting and receiving movement. As she surrounded his hips with her legs, his movements became lightning quick.

She cried out over and over.

Ecstasy built like a massive wave in the distance and what was about to flow had him grunting ferociously. A soft keening sound left her mouth. *Stone ... Stone ... Stone ...* came from her mind in a series of repetitions that sent a thrill straight up his groin and through his cock.

I'm coming, he pathed.

I'm with you. He felt how tight she was as her back arched.

Pleasure like a rocket shot through his body as he released into her again. He shouted as he came and as he watched ecstasy roll over her beautiful face. She writhed in the air with him, her body grasping at his cock, pulling on him.

Stone! Came one last time from her mind to his.

The pleasure seemed to roll longer than usual, sustained by the elf-lord power and squeezing every single drop from his cock. His mating frequency had formed a solid shield around hers. He saw how easy it would be to forge the blood rose bond with her, but they hadn't agreed to it, so he held back.

As his hips settled down, he floated them to the bed until she lay beneath him. He stayed connected to her and she held her legs locked around him for the longest time. Her beautiful violet eyes held an expression of gratitude. Somehow he hadn't expected that.

"Thank you," she murmured softly. She caressed his face.

"Can you feel our mating frequencies?" he asked.

"I'm prone inside yours in the same way I'm lying beneath you now. With a word, we could bond. Do you think we should?"

The question took him aback. "I don't know, but something inside me resists it. Is this what you want?"

"Not my rational mind, but every other part of me seems to be shouting at me to go the distance. Yet we barely know each other and we have a war going on."

"I'm thinking the same thing. I'm tempted because I know from the other ruling mastyrs that their powers increased once they bonded with their blood roses. But it doesn't seem right to me. I'm just getting used to you as Rosamunde and Aralynn."

She petted his shoulders and caressed his arms. "You are so magnificently muscled, Stone. I'm overwhelmed."

He loved that she'd praised his body. Like all the mastyrs, he worked out and he battled. Both kept him fit, something he had to be. But it pleased him to know that Rosamunde liked what she saw. He was struck all over again by just how much he'd gotten her wrong.

He withdrew from her body slowly and reached for tissues on the nightstand. Handing them to her, he shifted on his side and watched as she tucked them between her legs. Strange to think how satisfied he felt that she needed the tissues. He liked that he'd left something of himself behind in her. With every other woman, he used condoms, but not with Rosamunde. Or Aralynn.

She turned on her side to face him her wild hair covering her shoulders and arms then sliding down to shade her breasts. He settled his hand on her waist and caressed her hip.

"I can't believe this happened." She stroked his arm. "Never in my wildest dreams. And I loved that we did that while levitating. We were high up in the air, too, much farther than a foot above your bed."

"It was amazing. And my mating vibration is still covering yours, almost protectively."

"I like it. I'm sure you could disengage, but please, don't, not yet. It feels comforting to me in a way I've never experienced. And for this moment, I don't feel alone or even so burdened with the rule of Ferrenden Peace."

"I'm glad." And he meant it.

He felt her sigh. He didn't say anything further in response, he just caressed her and slowly rubbed her back. Her body began to relax and she scooted closer. She even nuzzled him, pushing her head into his shoulder.

He held her for a long time. He didn't quite understand all that was happening, but he found himself grateful that she'd shared the terrible guilt she lived with because of her mother's death.

Stone knew about guilt. He carried his own damn weight on his shoulders.

His thoughts were drawn back to Charborne. The village and farms were situated at the foothills of the Dauphaire Mountains, in view of the tall, mist-shrouded peaks.

The village had shown him so much love. He'd been raised on a nearby farm, in the predominantly troll community.

The villagers had been nothing but supportive when he'd finally joined the Tannisford Vampire Guard. They'd thrown him a farewell bash that had lasted for hours. He was pretty sure the ale he'd drunk hadn't left his system until at least two nights later.

If only better provisions had been made for a possible future attack.

But who could have predicted the arrival of twelve wraith-pairs that went through the village and surrounding farms, slaughtering anyone they could find.

Half the villagers had perished by the time three squads of Guardsmen had arrived to take on the Invictus. Two of those good men had died as well because of the overwhelming numbers.

It had happened centuries ago, but like the aftermath of so many tragic events, he still felt the pain of it. His parents had been two of so many who had died that night. Grief had been a constant companion since, a reminder of the necessity of staying focused on his Guardsman duties.

Rosamunde stirred in his arms and he pulled her closer. He realized he could relate to her. He knew what it was to lose family to Margetta's depredations and now that she'd shared more of her life experience with him, he'd begun to understand her.

Still, he smiled. Rosamunde, both Aralynn and a blood rose. His blood rose. It seemed impossible.

And the sex had been fantastic.

~ ~ ~

Rosamunde had never felt so satisfied, so content in her entire life. Lying in Stone's bed, with his arms around her felt like she'd come home after a long difficult journey. She wanted to stay there forever.

She still couldn't believe he'd made love to her.

After a few minutes, she drew back so that she could look at him. She even shifted to lay her head on the pillow and meet his gaze. "You know what I'd love to know. When did you first meet Davido?"

He chuckled softly.

"What?" she asked.

"Just wasn't what I was expecting."

"I guess I want to know more about you and your life. I mean, we're here, together, and this might be a good time to exchange histories. Davido and Vojalie have been part of my life for a long time and they've been such a huge support. I don't know what I would have done without them." Especially when it came to the horrendous Margetta visions, but this she didn't share with Stone. She honestly hoped she'd never have to.

Stone shifted onto his back. "I know both Davido and Vojalie really well. As for the first time I met Davido, well that's hard to say. He took an interest in me early in my life. I've never told anyone this but he used to sneak into my room during the day when I was a little one. My earliest memory is of him sitting on the floor, near my cradle and talking to me. Or rather, *pathing* with me."

"Do you know why he used to do this? Didn't it seem odd?"

"I asked him about it later on. He said he knew I'd be a mastyr one day and he wanted to be sure I was protected."

"Davido is a good man and one of the best husbands I've ever known."

"He's very devoted to his wife."

"That he is."

The conversation continued in this vein for a good long while. He asked her about castle life and she asked him his favorite swimming spots. He preferred his lake, but he also enjoyed the chain of grottos at the Sea of Vermed. She confessed to swimming naked in a small spring at the western edge of Ferrenden Peace. Teleporting made it possible. If anyone ever came near the spring while she was paddling around, she simply took herself with a thought back to the castle.

No, she'd never driven a car.

Yes, he'd owned several Harleys over the years. One of them had been stolen, maybe Joseph's devilment.

The hours moved swiftly by and their sharing of stories was steady except for the occasional hourly contact Stone made with Harris. Throughout the night, Tannisford remained quiet, a circumstance that continued to trouble Rosamunde. Her fae instincts told her Margetta was up to no good.

After Stone's final conversation with Harris, he made love to her again, only this time she remained solely as Rosamunde.

When dawn arrived shortly after, she fell asleep in his arms.

When she woke up the next night, she lay on her right side, in a bed that didn't feel familiar to her. Yet it was comfortable and warm and she was naked and she didn't want to move. The hour was late, almost full-dark. She'd slept through the day, again, which seemed incredible. She was always up at least two hours before the sun disappeared in the west.

Yet as sleep began to roll away from her, memories surged of having made love with Stone, of all men, on the night before. He'd come to accept her as Rosamunde.

She could smell coffee and the wonderful aroma caused her to roll on her back, flopping her arms to either side. This was heaven, nothing less. She could even forget about Ferrenden Peace, especially knowing that Vojalie and Davido were keeping watch over the veil of mist.

She could also recall falling asleep in Stone's arms.

But at this thought, she frowned. She knew something about Stone's birth parents that she wished he knew. She hated having carried around so many significant and difficult secrets all these centuries. She might need to talk to Davido about finally removing the silence-ban on who Stone's biological parents had been. She was pretty sure most adopted kids, no matter their age, wanted to know their roots or at least to be given the opportunity to say 'No, thank you. I don't need to know'.

She stared up at the natural wood rafters of the bedroom ceiling and sighed deeply. Was this really happening? Was she a blood rose? Had she fed Mastyr Stone while in her Rosamunde form? Had Stone truly accepted her?

It all seemed so impossible, yet wonderful in an amazing way. From the time she'd battled beside him as Aralynn, she'd come to discover that she and the Mastyr of Tannisford actually shared some things in common. He was as devoted to his realm as she was to serving the people of Ferrenden Peace. She might have been given the job under extremely difficult circumstances, but never once had she questioned the value of serving as queen. She'd loved being a protector and so had Stone. Neither, it seemed, had looked back once the journey for each had begun.

Stone arrived in the doorway, wearing jeans but no shirt. He must have showered since his long black hair was damp and he wore a towel beneath to cover his shoulders. He carried two cups of coffee.

Without thinking, she sat up and stretched out her hands, ready to receive one of the cups. But the comforter fell away.

Stone started for the bed, then stopped as his gaze dropped to her breasts.

"Oops." She lifted the comforter and caught it up under her arms to cover herself.

He put his feet back in motion. "Don't do that on my account."

But she felt heat on her cheeks again. She had such a terrible tendency to blush around Stone. As Aralynn, not so much.

He handed her a cup and she drew it in a swift motion to her lips. In part, she wanted to cover her embarrassment but also nothing was quite as good to her as coffee first thing at night.

She loved the unique flavor. "So this is cardamom."

"It's served in one of the shops near the Com Center. They import a lot of spices from the States."

"Well, I love it." She continued to sip while sitting up in Stone's bed, still feeling very naked though she had the comforter wrapped around her.

He sat down in a wood and leather chair angled across from the bed, which meant it faced the windows and the emerging night sky. He leaned back and with his elbows on the dark wood armrests and the cup in both hands, he sipped along with her. He didn't seem inclined to talk but fixed his gaze out on the lake.

With the low, wrought iron headboard positioned against the wall of windows, her view was of wood paneling, nice in its way but not the view she preferred. She craned her neck and saw that the protective day-shutters were already half raised, and the sky was filled with a beautiful lavender sunset.

She appreciated that she could look at this level of light, as could Stone, without suffering. She wouldn't be able to tolerate but a few seconds standing in such light, but now that the sun was behind the hills, she could marvel at the beauty of the sunset.

"Why do you have the bed facing away from the lake?" She took another sip, the mug still in both hands. The warmth felt good against her fingers.

"It seemed right to me because this chair suits me better for viewing when evening comes. Once I'm done batting for the night, I'm usually dead asleep about two seconds after my head hits the pillow. But when I wake up, I like to sit right here."

She wanted to see the lake at this hour as well, with the sun behind distant tree-studded hills and soft wispy clouds catching the last of the color. So, she made the decision to let her embarrassment go.

She rose up then turned around on her knees, careful to keep her coffee from spilling. She gasped softly since the entire lake was lavender. She knew her backside was fully exposed, but she didn't care. This was worth it. "Oh, it's so beautiful."

"It certainly is." She glanced back at him and saw that he was looking at her tush, his brows raised as he brought his cup to his lips. She was pretty sure she saw the tip of his tongue emerge before he sipped.

She chuckled softly. So, this was what she had missed through the years.

He waved her in his direction. "Come sit on my lap. Or better yet—" She watched him set his cup on a nearby table, then levitate. He moved toward the bed, caught up a knit gray afghan, cast it over her shoulders then picked her up in his arms.

She chuckled as she held her cup steady, looking up at him as he maneuvered her slowly through the air and back to his seat. He had her covered up and situated on his lap as though he'd done it a thousand times. And not once had her coffee sloshed in the cup.

Rosamunde leaned her head against his shoulder and couldn't keep the tears from touching her cheeks. She'd never known this kind of relationship before.

As surreptitiously as possible, she wiped at her face. She was completely overcome. Maybe it was the sky full of a deepening lavender light, now graying at the edges.

Or maybe it was being cradled in Stone's arms and so thoughtfully covered with the soft knit afghan.

Or maybe the cardamom flavored coffee.

She didn't know, except that somewhere in her memories she could recall sitting on her father's lap in a similar way as a very young child. This felt like family to her, the way a family was meant to be.

But her father had been killed while protecting the Fae Council in her kingdom.

A thousand years was a long time to be without kin of any kind. She had Lorelei, of course, though she rarely got to see her. Maybe she'd make a greater connection once Margetta was defeated.

"I can feel you thinking very hard."

She smiled and sighed. "I suppose I am. Your kindness, Stone, has undone me. I want you to know that straight out. I've been alone for a very long time and I forgot what this could be like."

"But you had boyfriends occasionally?"

"Only a few times. My rank made long-term relationships very difficult."

When she finished her coffee, she extended her arm across him to set the empty cup on the side table. Leaning back once more, she looked up at him. "I love that you brought me to your chair so I could see the sunset. This has meant a great deal to me, more than you can know."

He looked very serious. "I can guess. And I'm sorry I held such harsh opinions of you."

"But how could you have known the truth?"

"I would have never guessed, especially that you were Aralynn."

"Now you know us both."

"That I do." He kissed her forehead. "By the way, I contacted Vojalie when I got up an hour ago. She very kindly brought you some clothes and toiletries from both the castle and the cottage."

She leaned her head against Stone's shoulder once more, but her thoughts took an entirely different direction. "You're coordinating the Combined Forces with Mastyr Ian and Mastyr Zane. Am I right?"

"Yup. They're my two right-hands."

"Have you spoken with them this evening?"

"Of course."

"How fares the war? What's been happening since last night?"

He chuckled softly.

"What?" She sat up a little and craned her neck to meet his gaze.

"War talk. I like it, but you've surprised me again."

She dipped her chin. "You have to remember that my life has been dedicated to preserving Ferrenden Peace and keeping Margetta out. I've followed all the Realm newspapers from the time they were invented. So, what's the latest?"

"There's good news and bad. The good news is that the realms are quiet. Also, Delia says we're all set for the gala later tonight."

"She's worked hard on the event."

"She has. I'm sure it will be, um, eventful."

She chuckled. "Not exactly your thing, is it?"

"Not quite. But I know it's a necessary celebration for all the realms, so I'm happy to do my part."

She thought for a moment. "So what's the bad news?"

He cleared his throat. "Well, the same as the good news: All the realms are quiet. There is no Invictus sign. Anywhere."

At that, Rosamunde sat up and shifted her bottom just enough to face him. She had to grab the edges of the afghan to keep from exposing her breasts again. "What? Not even a few rogue wraith-pairs? Oh, no."

"We figure the Ancient Fae is rounding up her troops."

"So, we really are building to a final battle."

"Yes, that's what we believe. Though, given events of last night, we're all in agreement that she's still after me. Any thoughts on why?"

She loved that he asked her opinion. "It has to be about your ability to channel the elf-lord power. Margetta must know this about you, maybe through her fae prescience, and she wants you in her arsenal."

She slid off his lap, tugging the afghan around her. "If Margetta's winding up for a showdown, then I want to be ready, because who knows what she has planned for tonight." She glanced around. "So, where are the clothes Vojalie brought for me?"

He gestured to the opening to the left of the bed. The entire wall was made of a beautiful gray stone. "I have a small dressing room off the bathroom. I've laid out some of your clothes and the rest I hung up on the far side of the closet. You can arrange things as you like."

"Thank you."

Rosamunde tugged the afghan tight around her as she made her way into the bathroom. Once she passed through the opening, there was only one way to turn, which of course was away from the lake. Every room of Stone's house faced the lake. There weren't even windows on the non-lake side.

She saw the natural wood-framed entrance to the dressing room. As she passed through, she was struck with the smell of leather, which made sense since Stone had a large collection of Guardsmen gear off to the right.

She let the afghan slide off her shoulders then folded it up. Seeing which clothes Vojalie had brought, she retraced her steps and made her way to the walk-in, stone-lined shower. She didn't hesitate to turn on the two opposing heads and it didn't take long for the hot water to arrive. Adjusting the temp, she stepped beneath both sprays then turned in a slow circle. The water felt wonderful, a kind of massage after two harried nights of battling wraith-pairs, then tussling with Stone.

Now they were lovers and she served as his blood rose.

As she washed her hair, she knew it would take so little to bond with him. She would barely have to say the word 'yes' and the deed would be done. She could still feel her mating vibration deep within her body and how it seemed to be on a constant hunt for Stone as though this part of her recognized him as her mate and was missing him.

After she rinsed the soap from her hair, she pressed a hand to her chest. She could also feel that she was slowly building a new supply for Stone, even though she could tell that for the present he was satiated. The whole thing was as intriguing as it was unsettling.

She wondered why the blood rose phenomenon had come into existence in the first place? Even as she mentally posed the question, her fae instincts already seemed to know the answer. The increase in essential power as a result of the bond aided each couple in defeating whatever enemy was present at the time.

In this case, her Aunt Margetta.

She found Stone's crème rinse and applied it liberally. They shared the managing of long hair in common. She loved Stone's thick wavy black hair.

She loved his tattoos and his lean muscled body.

His eyes.

His shoulders.

His tight ass.

And she'd loved looking into his mossy-green eyes last night when he'd brought her to the peak and beyond.

Her body warmed up and set to tingling all over again. She'd truly never dreamed sex could be this amazing.

Through the years, she'd had an occasional lover, but she'd always pretended to be someone else. When the man discovered her identity, he usually found an excuse to disappear.

She didn't blame any of them and the truth was, she'd never fallen in love.

Now she was with Stone and part of her knew it all made sense.

Yet, as she stepped under the spray once more, she also knew she couldn't complete the bond with him since she had more than one difficulty still standing in the way.

She pondered the secret of his birth parents. The compulsion to tell him what she knew became a powerful force within her. Given his hot bloodedness and his strong beliefs in the right way of doing things, he would see it as a betrayal that she hadn't told him.

But how could she have done so? When she'd learned the truth herself, Davido had sworn her to secrecy.

Finally clean and with all the crème rinse out of her hair, she shut the water off. She'd long accepted the curse of the occasional entrapment vision that Margetta would set for her and she'd learned to settle those horror-filled visions into a locked-up place deep within her mind.

Each vision had meant the death of beloved realm-folk. Without jeopardizing the lives of the entire population of the Nine Realms, she'd had to live with the terrible foreknowledge of those acts Margetta had planned to inflict on innocent people.

The first few times it had happened, she'd nearly lost her mind. Only a series of counseling sessions with Davido, and later Vojalie, had kept her sane. They'd each helped her to build a personal, if painful, vault in which these visions lived. She'd had to separate herself from the terrorist that was her aunt, to keep the blame firmly on Margetta's shoulders, rather than be consumed by her own guilt.

She had no intention of telling Stone about these visions, at least not if she could possibly help it. He wouldn't understand, especially since one of those visions had been of Charborne and the subsequent slaughter of half the villagers and outlying farmers, including his adopted troll parents.

She'd long since forgiven herself for what she had been unable to control and hoped she'd never have to confess her foreknowledge to Stone. The man was a warrior vampire. How could he possibly understand her need for complete restraint?

He wouldn't. He would have believed he could have done something, which meant if he ever learned this secret, he'd never forgive her for holding back.

She felt weighed down again with the cost of being Queen of Ferrenden Peace and a conduit for the elf-lord power. Sometimes she wondered who she would have been if she'd never ventured with her baby goats into the mist and her mother had lived. Of course that was a fool's game and she quickly set it aside.

This was her life. She must deal with it as it was.

~ ~ ~

The moment full-dark arrived and his fragile vampire sensitivity to light was no longer at risk, Stone stripped out of his jeans, grabbed a swim towel from a stock he kept near the sliding glass doors, then headed outside to the end of the dock.

By then, he'd heard his hair-dryer whirring and knew it would take some time for Rosamunde's long and very curly hair to dry.

So, a swim it was.

He made for the far shore and swam in long easy strokes, swinging his head from the water every now and then to drag in some air. As he drew close to the far end of the lake and his fingertips touched the mossy rocks, he flipped in the water and headed back.

It wasn't long before a very fine euphoria began moving through his veins. He loved to swim, especially when things got chaotic and tough. Ploughing water always helped.

Halfway back on his second full lap, he began to slow down. He wanted his breathing almost normal by the time he reached the dock.

When he finally pulled himself from the water, he saw that Rosamunde was busy in the kitchen, the woman who never cooked.

Uh-oh.

He grabbed the towel he'd left for himself, dried off then wrapped it around his hips.

When he entered the house, she was pulling bread and ham from the fridge. "I hope you don't mind. I thought I'd make a couple of sandwiches. I can at least do that."

Sandwiches. He breathed a sigh of relief. "Good idea."

He smiled, aware of the strange amount of affection floating around in his chest for the woman who had so recently been on his shit-list.

He took a moment to really look at her. Her violet eyes were large and extraordinary, her brows softly arched and her lips full.

She was a beautiful woman. She'd managed to tame her hair with two braids then secured the mass in a Guardsman-type woven clasp, the design intended to keep long warrior hair in place during battle.

She was dressed for war as well in what he recognized as Aralynn's battle gear, down to the oh-so-sexy snug boots she wore.

As she set the ham and bread down on the cutting board, she glanced at him. "Is anything wrong?"

He moved toward her quickly and took her chin in hand then kissed her on the lips. "Not a thing. I contacted Harris and got the latest. The realms are still without incident. Okay that I shower now?"

"Of course. Would you like a sandwich? I mean maybe you'd prefer something else."

At that, his brows rose. He almost teased her with a comment about her soft life in the castle and didn't she wish she had her chef with her, then thought the better of it. From what she'd told him, her life had been anything but, more like a prisoner of war.

"I'd love a sandwich." He then headed in the direction of the bathroom. Before showering, he went into his dressing room and checked his tux. He'd had it specially made for tonight's gala. His Italian leather shoes were ready, his cuff links, everything was in order.

He smiled as he thought about taking Rosamunde as his date. He knew she was going. At the time, he'd felt obligated to invite her. Now, he was beyond grateful he had and he'd ask her before the night got too busy.

A few minutes later, he'd just finished toweling off, when he heard Rosamunde call to him. "Stone?"

At first, he thought maybe the meal was ready. But something in her tone made him grow very still.

"What's wrong?" He called back.

"The elf-lord power is rumbling again."

Chapter Eleven

Rosamunde stood on the end of the dock staring out into the night sky. She felt Stone behind her, levitating swiftly. The elf-lord power rumbled deep in the lake and was heading right toward her. She prepared herself to feel the painful cramps in her legs.

Instead, just as the elf-lord power began to flow, Stone caught her hand and directed all that power into himself.

She squeezed his hand hard. "A vision." She lifted their joined hands. "And thank you."

"You're welcome. The second I felt that rumble, I got my ass over here."

She nodded and the power flowed, her back arched suddenly. A powerful stream of images began to roll through her mind. *Are you getting this Stone?*

I am.

In the vision, the forested hills that surrounded the lake became filled with a golden mist.

Margetta was coming for Stone.

On the vision rolled, showing the sky filling with golden light, as well as with dozens, even hundreds of wraith-pairs. Worse, at least seven of the pairs had mastyr vampires as bonded mates.

Rosamunde shuddered and gripped Stone's hand even harder. "Mastyrs bonded to wraiths. That's bad, isn't it?"

"It doesn't get much worse."

She saw Margetta's form begin to emerge in the heavy mist, then just like that, the vision dissipated.

Rosamunde's hand vibrated heavily where she was connected to Stone, but she couldn't let go. "I'm frightened."

He released her hand and drew her into his arms, holding her tightly against him. "From what I get, we've got ten minutes and I can do a helluva lot in that time."

She pulled back, looking up at him. "The Combined Forces?"

He nodded. "Exactly." He pivoted away from her slightly. She could feel him access his telepathy and knew he was talking to Ian, then Zane.

She stepped away from him, letting him do his job. The elf-lord power was still on him, and he had a silver glow, but with faint bits of lightning shooting everywhere.

He wore the heavy black leather Guardsman coat, braided at the shoulders, sleeveless and hanging to mid-calf. He wore no shirt, which meant his muscular arms and the knife-points of his tattoos sent a clear warning not to mess with him.

She glanced down at her hands. She'd broken the connection with him and the elf-lord power continued to flow, but the channel remained steady even though she stood several feet away from him.

He turned to her, his eyes lit up. He switched to telepathy. *You're covered in a violet glow. It's beautiful.*

Look at your arms.

He glanced the length all the way to his fingers. *Holy shit. I've got a glow as well.* He gave himself a shake. *All right. I'm taking it to mean that we've got access to the elf-lord power right now.*

I'm thinking the same thing.

Good. Because we need to move troops into position immediately.

It took her a moment to process what he meant. *You mean the way Margetta does?*

Exactly.

But that's not something I can do. Had Stone just lost his mind?

He drew close and took both her hands. He held her gaze, locking onto her firmly. *We can do this together. Feel the power. Really feel it, because I know we can teleport a portion of the Combined Forces straight into the forest all the way around the lake.*

Her first thought was that she wasn't like him and she had serious limitations. But when he squeezed her hands and reiterated, *Feel it, Rosamunde,* suddenly it was there, what the elf-lord power could be for them as a unit, as his mastyr status to her blood rose.

What she lacked as an individual, her connection to Stone made up for.

I'm getting it now. Her heartrate soared. With the ability to bring the forces into the area, they might even have a chance to defeat Margetta. *So, where are the troops?*

He smiled. *I'm bringing you in on the group telepathy. Everyone, the queen is with us.* A series of quick greetings followed and that's when she realized all eight ruling mastyrs were with Stone.

He launched into the process that would be required as together, they worked to bring half the Vampire Guards in from each realm. He even relayed the locations where he wanted each mastyr's force. *Think of the lake as a clock and my house is 6 PM. Gerrod, if you're ready, your regiment will be at 12 midnight.*

Understood. Gerrod's voice sounded formal within her mind.

You'll arrive just above the forest canopy, then drop into the trees to take cover. Ready?

Ready.

With that, Stone stared at Rosamunde and spoke a private, *You can do this.*

Rosamunde closed her eyes and focused on channeling the elf-lord power and moving a hundred of Gerrod's vampire warriors into position. The vibrations became a roar in her ears.

She felt the movement of troops all the way from Merhaine Realm to the opposite side of the lake.

She opened her eyes and followed Stone's gaze. She could see at least a hundred vampire Guardsmen floating down into the forest.

Stone didn't hesitate. He addressed the second mastyr. *Ethan, are your men gathered at the training center?*

Damn straight. Teleport our sorry asses at will.

Stone even smiled.

Again Rosamunde repeated the process until she saw his men land at about two o'clock, once more descending into the forest as a well-trained unit.

The rest followed swiftly, with Mastyr Quinlan and Seth's troops to the right of Stone and Jude, Malik and Zane's to the left. Ian's were last, arriving at eleven o'clock next to Gerrod's troops.

Once in place, the ruling mastyrs checked back in, one after the other. Each had arrived with his force, the warriors hunkering down and remaining hidden in the trees. The lake vibrated with the energy of so many powerful men ready to do battle.

Embrace the Power

How we doin', Ian?

Ian's deep voice returned. *Holding steady. I'm moving my men as close to the water as I can get them without exposing our presence.*

The rest of the mastyrs reported the same.

Rosamunde contacted Stone privately. *What about your Guardsmen?*

They'll remain on duty in Tannisford to watch for any activity outside the perimeter of the lake. A hundred of my men are already en route, with half of them having arrived to hold the area behind the lake. I'm using them to protect our flank, or in this case, the area well behind the hills that surrounds my lake. Harris is in charge of them.

Rosamunde squeezed his hands. *So we won't be caught off-guard.*

Exactly.

A moment later, the sky filled with Margetta's golden light.

Stone snorted. *The bitch is back, men.*

Rosamunde had a sudden recollection of Margetta a thousand years ago. The same glow, a result of her power and energy, had taken her mother's life. Anger boiled up within Rosamunde. How many lives had Margetta's ambitions taken?

Let me distract her, Stone. If I can lead her on a chase again, maybe it would help. Only this time, I think I want to go as Aralynn.

When Stone didn't immediately respond, she wondered if she'd erred. *Did I say the wrong thing?*

No, not at all. For now though, I think you should stay put because look up there, Rosamunde. Does this look different to you?

Rosamunde drew closer to stand right next Stone, following the line of his gaze. *Thicker.*

That's what I thought. Will she show even herself?

I saw her at the very end of the vision.

You're right. She was there.

A few beats passed, then Rosamunde saw Margetta and felt the woman's battle energy revving up. The mastyr vampire wraith-pairs surrounded her, the best and most powerful of her creations.

Rosamunde's fae prescience kicked in again. *She's testing us, Stone.*

She didn't wait to tell him the rest. Instead, she grabbed Stone's arm, reached for an extra punch of elf-lord power, then took him into the forest canopy, above his house, so that she could see the dock. A split-second later, a bolt of Margetta's power exploded the exact spot where they'd been standing. Fire began to consume the wood planks.

Shit. That would have been us. Your prescience?

Yes.

I don't get it. I thought she was after a bond with me.

She still is. But right now, she wants to see what we're made of. My prescience is lit up like I'm reading her every intention. Right now, she's searching for me. We're in trouble again. She's locked onto me.

Not both of us?

No. This is about me tonight and I want to try something, what I'd mentioned earlier.

What do you have in mind?

To see if she's tracking me or Aralynn or both. You okay with this?

Go for it.

Rosamunde left Stone, teleporting to the top of the house but letting him know her destination so he could watch her as well as Margetta.

She could see Margetta pivot precisely in her direction and as soon as she did, Rosamunde teleported again to the tops of the trees to the east of the lake. Margetta appeared to move as Rosamunde moved. She felt the charge of her aunt's battle power rev up yet again.

Rosamunde needed to understand everything and transformed into Aralynn then created her violet wind and protective shield.

As swiftly, Margetta's energy diminished so that she didn't fire off a strike.

So, here was something she could work with. She pathed to Stone. *Margetta can track me easily as Rosamunde, but not as Aralynn. I'm the latter right now. I'm going to harass Margetta if I can.*

Stay with it.

For additional protection, Rosamunde wrapped herself up in the same violet shield she'd created in the cave. She rose high into the air. At the very least, she could get a different view of Margetta's troops.

When she was two hundred feet above the Ancient Fae, she saw the thick golden veil of mist that surrounded the entire outer perimeter of the forest. Margetta had locked down the battlefield.

She relayed the information to Stone. *I'm well above Margetta. She's centered herself over the lake, but she's also set a veil of her gold mist all around the forested hills, probably for the purpose of keeping your Vampire Guard out. But we already have our troops in position, so they're not affected. But Stone, I think Margetta has added a new layer to her power. I just don't know what it is or what it can do.*

Okay. Got it. Now, tell me what you're seeing. Give me the lay-out and the number of the wraith-pairs she's brought in.

She did a quick estimate. *I see at least a hundred pairs and they appear to be in equal distances spread out around her.*

That's what I'm able to see as well. I'll let the ruling mastyrs know.

While he pathed with the mastyrs, she moved closer to Margetta. An unusual vibration was flowing directly above her aunt, something that felt laden with power, as though designed for a very specific purpose. In fact, it felt like a weapon.

Stone! She shouted telepathically.

Give, was his succinct response.

Rosamunde could now see that the strange power, with both gold and black smoke, had begun to boil in the air. *She's got something new in her arsenal, a weapon of some kind. Tell your troops to be careful.*

~ ~ ~

For about two seconds, Stone marveled at how much he trusted Rosamunde, the woman he'd once despised. Another second and he was back to the coming battle.

He pathed to the mastyrs, letting them know what Rosamunde had seen. Through carefully rehearsed lines of telepathy, he could feel the information being dispersed from mastyr to warrior, all around the lake. He realized how much the elf-lord power was enhancing his abilities that he could actually sense the communication of all the Guardsmen.

As Rosamunde had predicted, Margetta's golden glow began to darken and change shape. Dark smoke had started streaming up and out and forming a new kind of mist. When it began to swirl and move, he alerted the ruling mastyrs, pathing with them all at once. *Margetta's got some new trick to show us tonight, a mist or a shield of some kind. Be ready. Rosamunde, are you there?*

I'm here.

Tell us what you see. I've got the mastyrs with me.

Rosamunde's voice broke in. *I'm still above Margetta. Her army is getting ready, fanning out and moving into position all at the perimeter of the lake. It's clear she knows she's in for a fight. It appears to me that her army is moving with the dark mist toward the edges of the forest.*

Silence reigned for about a quarter of a minute, then the Invictus wraiths began to shriek.

Damn that's loud. Stone covered his ears.

Through the trees, he saw that the boiling gold and smoky-black mist continued to move closer to shore. It was just thin enough that he could make out the shapes of the wraith-pairs moving with it.

Rosamunde once more reported in. *Margetta is still in the air centered above the lake and her mastyr vampire pairs appear to be her protection. But her army has almost reached the shoreline. They've dipped down to just above the water and are levitating slowly. The Ancient Fae seems to have complete control over her wraith-pairs.*

Stone had to agree. *Mastyrs, you can break silence now and let the troops know what's going on. But no advancing until ordered.*

He heard Malik and Zane, the mastyrs nearest him, repeat Stone's orders to stay tight and to wait for the command to engage the enemy.

When he felt the intensity of the enemy's battling vibration rise in strength, he pathed, *Arm up,* and almost instantly heard the order repeated.

When a red wind appeared near the black and gold mist, all around the edge of the lake, he shouted and pathed at the same time, *"Fire at will!"*

Stone swept forward to the lake's edge, his focus narrowed on the Invictus pairs right in front of him. They didn't move beyond the thin swirling mist that now contained red, gold and black. It almost looked spidery the closer it came.

Suddenly, he saw streaks of red coming at him. He used his own wall of blue battle energy, typical of mastyr level power, to keep the enemy's killing vibrations from reaching him. Red and blue sparks struck the air where his shield held.

When he started hearing cries of distress and occasionally a scream up and down the Combined Forces ranks, he kept his shield tight and glanced at the shoreline. Dozens of men had fallen. He heard Seth next to him calling for his men to fall behind his shield.

He watched as any attempt by Seth's men to pierce Margetta's battle shield failed to penetrate the mist, leaving them open to attack.

He didn't hesitate to call out the order for retreat, pathing it at the same time to those mastyrs hundreds of yards down the shoreline. His order spread quickly through the ranks and the troops nearest him disappeared into the forest. He'd trained the Combined Forces well, but the number of wounded and dead at the edge of the water hit him hard.

He moved back as well until the trees gave him cover.

Rosamunde come back to me now. Margetta's created some

kind of mass shield and you and I have to break it or the war will be lost right here on this lake.

A second later, she appeared beside him. *I've been watching and I agree. I thought the gold-black mist would create a weapon. Instead, she's using it to shield her troops, protecting them while they fire on your men.*

He turned toward her, startled to find she was Aralynn, with her brown eyes and stronger features, and not Rosamunde.

She settled her hand on his shoulder. *I should have reminded you that I'm in my wolf-form. The thing is, when I'm Rosamunde I have a significantly better connection to the elf-lord power, which means I'll need to change back. But Margetta can track me as Rosamunde, so once I return to her form, we'll have to move fast.*

He nodded. *Got it.*

Movement toward the lake caught his eye. Those Invictus still shielded in black and gold were moving in fast.

I'll let the mastyrs know what's happening.

As he pathed to the ruling mastyrs, he felt the earth rumble as it never had before. When he'd let his team know what was going on, he pulled Rosamunde into his arms. The elf-lord power surged through her and into him. There was no way Margetta wouldn't know they were up to something.

He levitated swiftly, taking her into the air above the trees. *Keep channeling, but we'll need a surge and I mean a big one. Can you manage it?*

As long as you're with me, I can.

As the black and gold mist reached the shoreline, he said, *Do it now.*

Rosamunde was as good as her word. Power bolted through

her, then into him and he sent it away from his body and straight toward Margetta's shielding mist. It was a stream of energy similar to Rosamunde's violet wind so that he could watch its progress and his troops could as well. The color was a blend of green and violet, impossible to ignore.

The point of initial impact sent their stream into the black and gold shield, causing an eruption to blast high into the air. A roll of explosions followed, breaking apart the black and gold mist and exposing the Invictus pairs. The troops didn't need to be told to go after them and a few seconds later, a deadly battle ensued with his men engaging the wraith-pairs in close combat on and near the shore.

Stone held Rosamunde elevated in the air, his gaze moving constantly between Margetta, a hundred yards away surrounded by her mastyr vampire wraith-pairs, and the battle below. He watched as Quinlan and Seth took care of business on the west nearest him and Jude and Malik on the east.

He couldn't see much beyond their troops, the lake being as large as it was. But he saw the clash of red and blue battle energies everywhere.

Stone, Margetta's coming closer.

He shot his attention back to the golden glow. He was still heavily charged with the elf-lord power and without giving it a second thought, he revved up his battle energy again. The moment his elf-lord power connected with it, he sent it in the Ancient Fae's direction.

Margetta met the attack with a blast of her gold power and the two streams met in the center. Violet-green and black-gold exploded once more in the air, rising higher and higher.

Keep it coming, Rosamunde.

With pleasure. But if only we could take her right now—

I'm thinking the same thing.

He still held her pressed against him and the power flowed steadily. He had no idea what it looked like from the ground, but violet-green hitting black-gold was strangely beautiful.

He sensed a shift at Margetta's end, but he couldn't tell in what direction. *Hold tight, Rosamunde. Something's happening.*

I can feel it, too. What's going on?

I don't know.

Should we try another boost? I mean, maybe this is it?

Give it a sec.

Suddenly, Margetta's battle energy gave way and their violet-green stream of power flowed through the night sky stronger than ever.

For a moment, he thought they'd broken through, that they'd destroyed Margetta, and he was ready to give a shout of triumph. But when he slowly drew the elf-lord power back, nothing remained of the Ancient Fae or her mastyr wraith-pairs.

She left. Rosamunde's stunned voice was quiet in his mind.

Glancing below, he watched as on the shoreline the Combined Forces overran Margetta's wraith-pairs. It was clear that though Margetta had retreated with the most powerful element of her force, she'd left the Invictus to battle on their own, without her further support.

Stone immediately pathed to the mastyrs to take as many prisoners as possible. *Margetta quit the field and left her wraith-pairs behind to fend for themselves.*

Despite the men he'd lost, if he could save some of the wraith-pairs and get them to Ethan's realm for rehabilitation, he would.

He flew Rosamunde slowly around the perimeter of the lake. Bodies floated in the water or lay close to the shoreline, some Invictus, some Guardsmen.

He rose high into the air, an arm around Rosamunde's waist checking for any sign that Margetta was still in the vicinity. But once he saw that Margetta's gold mist was completely gone from the forest as well, he immediately contacted Harris. He wanted the Tannisford Guard to move in and help with the last of the fighting and to gather up as many prisoners as possible.

It wasn't long before his Guardsmen were pouring over the hills in support of the rest of the Combined Forces. Shortly after, he pathed to Cole, whom he'd left in charge of the Com Center for the duration. He let him know what had happened and asked him to send troll clean-up support.

The whole time he held Rosamunde tight against his side. She kept the elf-lord power humming through him in a steady, though much less powerful stream. He hadn't asked her to continue, but right now he knew they were of the same mind, that they both wanted to be ready in case Margetta returned unexpectedly.

~ ~ ~

Later, when the last of the wraith-pairs had been subdued, Rosamunde stayed quietly out of the way. A sober spirit had run through the ranks as the mastyrs of each of the Nine Realms cared for their wounded and their dead. A solemnity had fallen over the lake, the forest and the night air. A breeze carried the last of the smoke out of the area and the fire on the dock was extinguished.

She sat in a chair on the lake house deck just outside the living room. The end of the dock was now burned and unusable. Several of the trolls had worked to put out the fire and to make sure the rest of the wood didn't have even the smallest ember that could ignite later.

She had to admit she was exhausted from the stress of the battle and from the grief of seeing how many strong vampire Guardsmen had died this night because of her aunt. Even the amount of elf-lord power she'd channeled had taken a toll.

She saw Stone now as he levitated with Harris and a group of trolls. They had a vampire on the stretcher, severely wounded but alive, the last of the Tannisford Guard being carried out.

Stone stopped at the forest line, but the rest continued on. She watched him, the drag of his lips and cheeks. He looked haunted but with good reason. Too many men had died tonight.

Each of the mastyrs had thanked her for her part in turning the tide of battle. More than one of them had mentioned their amazement at seeing her as both Rosamunde and Aralynn and expressed appreciation for her long service. It was therefore no longer a secret that the Queen of Ferrenden Peace was not only a blood rose, but could transform into a second woman entirely.

Once each had assembled his troops, as well as the dead and the wounded, she and Stone together had used the elf-lord power to send them to their respective realms.

At last, the lake was quiet. Stone's hidden retreat was no longer hidden, though eventually, and with the right fae spells, it could be returned to a completely private, unknowable location. But not for a while.

Stone at last flew in her direction.

She rose from her chair, wanting to be fully present for him. Ferrenden Peace didn't have a Vampire Guard, so in that sense tonight's battle hadn't touched her personally, not in the way it had for Stone and his fellow mastyrs.

She knew his Vampire Guard had moved in once Margetta's mist had disappeared. "How did the Tannisford Guard fare?"

He touched down and nodded solemnly. "We lost one of our own, but it was nothing compared to the other Guards. There will be mourning in each of the Realms tonight. But the end must near now."

"Do you think the Gala should be postponed?"

"I discussed it with the ruling mastyrs. Though we lost good men here tonight, none of us wants to set aside our event because of Margetta's attack. We've built a federation and tonight we've proved that we can work together against the Ancient Fae."

She didn't care that he was battle-stained. She could feel his need as though it was her own. Without giving it too much thought, she went to him and slid her arms around his waist, settling her head on his shoulder. *It was amazing tonight, start to finish. Men died here tonight and I don't want to diminish the loss this is to the Nine Realms. But Stone, we took Margetta out at the knees. You and me.*

He held her tight. *We did that together, didn't we?*

I would have been crippled to have had that much power flowing through me. But it was so easy because of you. She drew back. "Did you see how the power we built stood up to hers?"

His lips curved slightly. "It was a thrill."

She smiled. "It was. When the battle first started and I saw her golden light, I was taken back to being a child of nine and an awareness that the same light had killed my mother. Tonight has made up for a lot of the anger I've felt toward Margetta. We may not have ended her takeover attempt for good, but I'm sure we're on our way."

Some of the drawn look left his face. "We are. I know we are. It's only a matter of time now."

When he kissed her again, and she felt his urgency, she knew how this would end. But she had another idea so she drew back. "I want to be with you, but not until the gala is over. I hope that's all right with you. Wait. Why are you smiling?"

"I was thinking about something Delia suggested. She thought I should take Aralynn to the ball, but I think I'd rather have the Queen of Ferrenden Peace beside me. Will you be my date?"

She couldn't help herself. She landed on his chest and hugged him hard. She laughed at herself and how silly she felt.

"What is it?"

When she pulled back she shook her head. "I don't know. I just haven't felt this way in so long, like a girl. It's nice. You have no idea." She'd always planned on attending the gala, of course. She'd even had a gown made for the occasion. But she'd never thought she'd go with Stone. It all seemed so miraculous.

"How about I pick you up at the castle in about an hour."

"That would be perfect." She kissed him again on the lips then without another word, teleported back to the castle.

Once in her bedroom, she unlocked the doors and summoned her maids, grateful for the full hour to get ready. She wanted to look her best for Stone.

But as she pulled out the silk gown that she'd had made for the occasion weeks ago, she realized to her surprise that the fabric was a beautiful mossy-green and very nearly the color of Stone's eyes.

She fingered the fabric gently. How far they'd come in just three short nights.

A decision came to her suddenly. There were still two large roadblocks to continuing her relationship with Stone, and she wanted at least one of them resolved tonight.

She pathed Vojalie and asked her and Davido to come to her private living room for cocktails before the gala. When Vojalie agreed readily, Rosamunde added that the time had come for Davido to give up his secret because she wasn't keeping it a moment longer.

You've changed. Vojalie sounded awestruck. At least she didn't try to argue with Rosamunde. *Never fear, I'll tell Davido and we'll both be there. It's time that Davido made his confession. I feel it as well.*

With this next hurdle ready to be crossed, she called down to her butler and ordered drinks and appetizers to be served in her private parlor. She didn't want a breath of what would be said tonight anywhere near her staff.

She hopped in the shower and gave herself to the pleasure of getting clean and having hot water beat into her muscles.

~ ~ ~

The tuxedo, ordered from the U.S., fit Stone like a glove. It had cost a small fortune. But as he tugged on his cuffs, the only thought in his head was whether or not Rosamunde would like him in this get up.

The clothes felt odd since he rarely wore shirts of any kind. Now he had on a couple of additional layers and he found it irritating. Yet it seemed like a very small price to pay for the event that had been inciting interest throughout the Nine Realms, and especially Tannisford, for over two months now.

Delia had booked a room for him at the Sterling Arms. After Rosamunde had returned to Ferrenden Peace, he'd flown to Sandismare with his tuxedo and shoes in a bag over his arm. A shower had followed.

The Sterling Arms was the swankiest hotel in Tannisford's main city and the rooms had been fully booked in the skyscraper within hours of the gala announcement.

Fortunately, Sandismare had several conference level hotels so that the prominent officials from most of the towns and cities of the Nine Reams had been able to get accommodations.

The local merchants were over the moon.

Several smaller events were being held around the downtown area, but the main gala was in the premier ballroom of the Sterling Arms.

After a good hour had passed since he'd last seen Rosamunde and with his long hair secured in a silver facsimile of the Guardsman clasp, he contacted her and learned she'd made special plans of her own.

He was pleased that she wanted to have drinks with Vojalie and Davido. The latter was already at the castle and happily teleported Stone straight to Rosamunde's private parlor.

Davido, as ugly as he was, beamed with his usual charisma and seemed like the most striking person in the room. And that was saying a lot since Vojalie's beauty outshone most of the women of their world and Rosamunde tonight gave her some serious competition.

Her unruly red hair had been tamed into a soft fall of curls over her bare shoulders. Her olive green strapless gown showed off her beautiful creamy skin as well as a line of cleavage that had him wishing they were alone. Her violet eyes held him entranced for a long moment broken only when she turned and reached for a martini for him.

"Davido made them for us."

He took a sip. "Gin and vodka and nicely chilled. Perfect."

Davido smiled. "Thank you, Mastyr."

But as the drink eased down his throat and sent the usual warmth flowing through his veins, he was struck by an undercurrent in the room.

He saw that Rosamunde's lips were in an odd tight line and that Vojalie kept taking deep breaths. Even Davido cleared his throat a couple of times.

Stone set his martini down on the nearest table. "What's going on?"

He watched Rosamunde grab for some air as well, which set up a racket inside his chest. He wasn't fae, so he didn't get hints about the future. But the tension in the room was enough to set his jaw-muscles to flexing.

Rosamunde lifted her chin. "Davido has something to tell you, something I've known for a long time. It's about your birth parents. I was sworn to secrecy, but given the events of the past few nights, I felt it was time that you knew the truth."

He stared at her for a long moment, digesting each word. He didn't know which aspect of her statement to address first, but finally decided on her complicity. "So this is something you've known for how long?"

"Decades."

"And you didn't tell me?" He had a hollowed out feeling that she'd betrayed him yet again.

She straightened her spine a little more. "This wasn't my secret to tell, Stone. But given our growing level of intimacy, I've forced the telling. As to the details, they belong to Davido." She gestured with her hand in the old troll's direction.

He glanced at Davido. "Am I to deduce that you've known who my birth parents were all this time?"

Vojalie tilted her head. "I've known as well, Stone. But let Davido tell you everything, then you'll understand. And we both hope you won't blame Rosamunde for keeping the secret. It was no small thing that we'd asked her to do so."

He'd weigh in on that subject later, after he knew what this was all about.

For now, he shifted to face Davido, "So, tell me, old man, did you know my birth parents? If so, I'd sure as hell like to know why you kept the information from me all these centuries." He wished his damn heart would settle down since he felt like it was about to jump from his chest.

Davido also set his martini glass on a nearby table. He then turned and sat down on a leather ottoman in front of a chair by the fireplace. Like most short trolls, his feet didn't touch the floor.

He was half bent over, his lips turned down. Stone had the worst feeling about what he was going to hear. Davido rarely lost his confident composure.

Davido spread his hands wide. "It's odd, after all this time, that I find it hard to begin. But, I knew your mother well. Her name was Inez and she was an elegant, black-haired, green-eyed woman, the most beautiful vampire I'd ever beheld and you are very much in her mold. She was loving and had the sweetest temperament.

"When she became pregnant, I'd never seen a woman so devoted to a child before it was ever born. She talked to you all the time and rarely had her hands away from her swollen belly. But, for reasons I'll never understand, she didn't survive your birth. She had a rare, untreatable condition in our world." He lifted shimmering blue eyes. "These things you need to know, how much you were loved."

The ridges of Davido's forehead were in tense tight rolls. Tears trickled down his cheeks. "And there's no other way to tell you the rest, except that I'm your father."

Stone had heard about the phenomenon of 'spinning rooms', but until this moment he'd never experienced one before. He felt Rosamunde slam into him and grab him around the waist. He fell backwards with her onto her sofa. He tried to right himself, but couldn't. The room shifted about like it was moving on heavy seas.

He covered his face with his hands and wondered who was firing a gun in the room then realized it was his heart beating against his eardrums.

Davido the Wise was his father?

What. The. Fuck.

He'd always wanted to know where he'd come from, who his birth parents were, why they'd given him up. These were natural questions. But knowing that Davido was his father, whom he'd always considered to be an excellent friend and mentor, made no sense.

When he could open his eyes and all the objects in the room

finally remained in place, he realized he was leaning hard against Rosamunde's arm, keeping her pinned to the back of the couch.

"I'm sorry. I must be hurting you." He moved so that she could slide out from under him. Her dress was slightly askew and she had to tug the bodice back in place.

He shifted to sit forward on the couch which put him directly opposite Davido and a little more eye-to-eye. "So I'm vampire and troll, then?"

"Yes. But you're something else as well. You're part elf."

"Elf?"

"Yes. It's not generally known that I'm both elf and troll."

Rosamunde interjected. "I didn't know that. I always thought you were pure troll."

He shifted his gaze toward her, his lips curving slightly. "Mostly, I am."

Stone knew something else was in play here and he wanted the whole picture. "Then all your children are elven."

"Yes. But not an elf like you, Stone. And that's the rub, that's why after Inez died, and I saw what you were, I gave you to a wonderful troll family to be raised."

Vojalie took a step forward, drawing Stone's attention to her. "You were the reason Davido and I met and the reason I persuaded him to find adoptive parents for you."

"You talked him into giving me up?"

"Let me explain. Please. Will you permit me to do that?"

He knew and trusted Vojalie, but she'd all but stated she was the reason he hadn't grown up knowing his birth father. Anger swelled as it always did. He was too quick-tempered, so for once he worked at tamping it all down. "Yes. Please go on."

She breathed a sigh of relief. "Stone, I'd had a horrific vision of you and of Davido, that if you'd stayed with him when you were born, you would both have been slain early in your life. You wouldn't have made it through your childhood."

"Why?" But even as he asked the question, the pieces began fitting together. Kaden came sharply to mind and how familiar he'd been with Vojalie to the point Stone had told him to back off. Kaden. The elf-lord. Davido. Part elf. "Holy fuck."

Davido inclined his head. "You never lacked for intelligence."

A long string of invectives left Stone's mouth. "Sweet Goddess, this can't be happening."

Rosamunde shook her head. "What am I missing?"

But Davido didn't answer her. Instead, he kept staring at Stone.

Stone grimaced. "Prove to me right now that everything I'm thinking is true. Show me. Now, old man. Or by the Goddess, I'll pick you up and throw you against the wall." He wanted no mistakes in understanding, not tonight. And he needed 'his father' to know how serious he was.

He wanted the whole truth.

Davido slid off the chair and stood upright. As he'd seen Rosamunde transform into Aralynn, a vibration ran through the room and Davido emerged as Kaden. He even wore a tuxedo that fit his large frame.

More invectives followed coupled with a kind of pacing across Rosamunde's fairly small parlor that did not give him enough space. He shoved his hands through his hair which dislodged the silver clasp.

An elf-lord.

Embrace the Power

Davido, his birth father, was an elf-lord, or as near to it as he could be. Stone wasn't sure of the difference. Maybe it was about capacity.

He moved to stand in front of Rosamunde again, his anger surging. She needed to know he didn't approve of her part in this at all.

But she rose to her feet as well, pressed her lips together for a moment then narrowed her eyes. She shoved a finger into his chest. "I swear to the Goddess that if you blame me for this, I'll belt you one, Stone. I swear it! This was your father's secret. Not mine! And I really didn't know about Kaden or the whole elf-lord thing. That's all new to me as well."

Her cheeks were bright red and for a moment her anger sidetracked him. He kind of liked this side of the very controlled Queen of Ferrenden Peace.

But the other reality, all the elf-lord shit, grabbed him by the nuts again. He whirled on Davido or Kaden or whoever the hell he was. He even saw some resemblance though not much.

Kaden continued. "Yes, you take after Inez. I loved your mother so much and you were all that I had left of her. It's so rare for any of our kind to perish that I couldn't believe she'd died giving birth to you."

Stone watched tears form in Kaden's eyes. "I didn't want to give you up and if Vojalie's vision hadn't been so grave, I wouldn't have. But Vojalie talked me through it. She even helped me choose the family."

Stone glanced at Vojalie. He wanted to hate her for separating him from his birth father, but he knew the woman's power and he knew her heart. "So this vision was bad?"

"I wept for days, it was so bad. I'd never met Davido before and though I knew of him, I'd had no idea until this vision that he was an elf-lord."

Stone shifted his gaze back to Kaden abruptly. "Why are you still alive? I thought they killed off the last of the elf-lords thousands of years ago."

Kaden's expression grew solemn. "I assassinated the very last one myself."

"What does that mean?"

"That I'm not a true elf-lord. I never gave myself fully to the power as the others did, though I managed to sustain the ruse. Becoming an elf-lord, in other words embracing the power fully, is always a decision and I chose against it."

Vojalie moved close to Kaden and took his hand. It was so hard to think that this ugly troll was probably one of the handsomest elves Stone had ever seen. Kaden swallowed hard and Vojalie covered their joined hands with her free one.

Vojalie met Stone's gaze once more. "Davido led the resistance movement against the elf-lords, even though as Kaden he was part of their number. He was basically a spy and helped isolate each of the elf-lords one at a time until there were only two left."

"I had to kill the last one," Kaden said. "By then, he knew what I'd done. After that, I disappeared for a long time, hundreds of years until the elf-lords fell into historical renderings and eventually mythology.

"Even then, I only transformed into Kaden when I knew I was alone and safe."

Stone felt as though he'd just been beaten into the ground. He returned to sit on the sofa. He was oddly numb. Rosamunde sat down next to him, more on the edge of the cushion, though she angled her body toward him. She settled her hand on his shoulder and nothing had felt so comforting in a long time. He felt her faeness flowing into him, a warmth and love that stunned him.

He covered her hand, much in the same way Vojalie had covered Kaden's.

He glanced once more in Kaden's direction, who now sat on the ottoman as he had before in his troll form. "Does the Sidhe Council know about you?"

Kaden nodded. "Vojalie insisted that I come clean. It took five years of the council's deliberation, of interview after interview, of reading the historical documents before I was allowed to live."

"It was that bad?" Rosamunde asked.

Vojalie had never appeared more serious. "I almost lost him. I'd found the right man for me then the Council almost took him away. It was the hardest time in my life."

"Do you mind if I transform back?" Kaden asked.

Stone shook his head. "I guess you don't want to be seen in your elf-lord form."

"No. I don't."

In the same way he'd watched Rosamunde become Aralynn, Kaden blurred through the movement, his power changing his clothes as well, until he was once more an ancient, charismatic troll. Vojalie drew a ladder-back chair close to Davido and sat down next to him.

"You know one thing that bothered me all this time?" Vojalie asked.

Stone shrugged. "I can imagine there were a lot of things."

"There were. But what troubled me the most was that *you* never got to know your half-brothers and sisters."

"But you brought them round." His gaze moved back to Davido. "That's why you were always there, from the time I could remember."

"Yes, my son. Exactly. But it was paramount that you never learn of my true identity." He paused, his lips turning down. "Or of yours."

"You mean as the son of the last living elf-lord."

But Davido's eyes once more filled up. "No. As an elf-lord yourself. That's what Vojalie saw in her vision. If we'd remained in the same house, you would have one day chosen to become an elf-lord and I would have been forced to slay you."

Stone leaned forward and buried his face in his hands. He understood so much in this moment that he could barely contain all the overwhelming feelings. That he had such potential explained why he could easily receive and make use of the elf-lord power through Rosamunde.

Unfortunately, it also confirmed why Margetta was after him. Not only could he channel the elf-lord power, but he could become the real thing. What kind of mate would that make for an extremely powerful woman like the Ancient Fae?

Vojalie was suddenly on her feet, her hands clasped together. "Stone, please listen to me. I know this has been a lot to take in, but it's imperative that you bond with Rosamunde as soon as possible."

He looked up at her. He'd never seen the lovely fae so tense, almost overwrought. For that reason alone, he knew how serious she was. But it was all too much. "Just tell me why?"

She crimped her lips together the same way Rosamunde had earlier. "I can't. It's a fae thing, a *knowing* without being able to give you a *why*."

"Did you have a vision?"

"That's just it, no, I didn't. If I had, I'd be able to give you my reasons. But if you could trust me a little in this, I think everything might be okay. Though I think it may have something to do with her blood rose abilities. They might serve to protect you from the seductive nature of the elf-lord power."

He shook his head. "You're not inspiring confidence, even as much as I value your counsel."

Davido left his seat and took one of Vojalie's hands. "My love, you can't control this. I know you want to, but you can't."

Vojalie, to Stone's great surprise burst into tears. Davido levitated and embraced her, holding her close.

He didn't realize Rosamunde had shifted to sit right next to him, her hip and leg cemented against his, until she grabbed his hand and held on tight. Rosamunde was trembling.

He didn't understand what was happening as he pathed to her. *What's going on here?*

I'm not sure. In fact I have no idea, but I'm frightened.

Because Vojalie's crying?

She squeezed his hand hard. *No, that's not it. I'm feeling it too, that if we don't bond soon, something terrible, something uncontrollable will happen.*

Stone slowly rose to his feet, lifting Rosamunde with him. "Vojalie, please look at me."

She lifted her tear-stained face to him. "I'm so sorry. I didn't mean to lose it."

"It's okay. I'll make this right, however I need to do it. From the beginning, I wanted to bond with Aralynn. I had no doubts about that. And yes, it was difficult when I learned that she was really Rosamunde," he tucked her arm around his, "but I know now that I seriously misjudged this good woman who has sacrificed so much to keep the Nine Realms safe.

"I will be very open to the bond, but for now, let's enjoy the gala which will give me some time to get used to all that Davido has told me. Afterward, Rosamunde and I can discuss the future privately. But it would help me a lot if you would dry your tears because in case you didn't know, we men can hardly stand it since we never know what to do."

Vojalie chuckled and wiped at her nose. Rosamunde tugged her arm away from Stone then moved quickly across the room to grab a box of tissues.

Vojalie plucked several from the opening then blew her nose. Afterward, she turned to kiss her husband. "We'll have to go home for a moment so I can repair my make-up."

"Of course, my love." Davido glanced at Stone. "We'll see you later, son. And in case you don't know, it gives me the greatest pleasure to say that to you."

When Vojalie burst into tears again, Davido rolled his eyes and the couple vanished.

It took Stone a moment to gain his bearings. They were a true power couple, because even though they no longer occupied the space, he could feel the vibrations of their shared energy radiating in the space where they'd just been.

Rosamunde dabbed at her cheeks as well. "I feel as though I was just caught in a cyclone and couldn't get out."

He turned to her. "That's it exactly. Sweet Goddess, this was too much fucking information."

Her lips quirked. "How about I make you a fresh martini?"

"How about a Scotch, a double."

She moved toward the decanter and picked up a tumbler. "Triple, maybe?"

"Hell, yeah."

"And I'll have one myself."

Chapter Twelve

"There's nothing worse than deception. Secrets. Lies."

Rosamunde heard the harsh tone in Stone's voice and she shuddered. "It's no wonder then you were so angry when you learned my true identity."

"Deception is evil and keeping this secret from me? I know I shouldn't blame you, but part of me wonders if I'll ever be able to trust you."

"I'll say this again: It wasn't my secret to tell. I only learned of it by accident and Davido begged me never to say anything to you. What would you have had me do, especially when Davido and Vojalie had a reason for their restraint given the disastrous nature of the vision?"

He turned to face her fully and caught her arm. "You should have told me."

"No. Davido should have. And in my defense, I was the one who forced the matter tonight. I've come to know you better and because of the difficult decision we have to make about the bond, I was unwilling to proceed without you knowing the truth. You have to at least give me credit for that."

She grabbed her black silk gloves from the mantel of the fireplace and began pulling them on. She was shaking, but not because of his anger over his father's identity, but because she was still holding back one last secret.

She pretended to be having difficulty working her fingers into the gloves, but the truth was she didn't want to meet Stone's gaze.

Her cheeks were warm and her heart, especially laden with the extra supply that had grown since cocktails, had started pounding in her chest. Until now, she'd rationalized her silence on the subject of the terrible visions Margetta would send her. Yet, given Stone's reaction to the current situation, she had a strong premonition she needed to tell him about the visions.

The trouble was, she wasn't certain Stone would be able to comprehend or appreciate the hopeless situation the visions had placed her in.

"I'm angry," Stone said.

She finally turned in his direction, ready to face him. He'd replaced his silver clasp but a few strands hung near his face and looked ridiculously sexy. "Can you forgive me for keeping this secret, Stone? If not, I don't see how we can move forward?"

He held her gaze. "I don't see that we have much of a choice. Both you and Vojalie are adamant that we bond, that we must."

"I'm not adamant about any of this." Her voice grew in strength. "I know there will be a serious problem if we don't bond, but that doesn't matter. We have to be of one mind and right now, you're definitely too angry to even think about sharing the blood rose bond."

He huffed a sigh. "You're right. I need time to process. At least the realm is quiet. I've checked in with both Harris and Cole and everything remains as it's been all night: No Invictus attacks in any of the other realms, either. Which has made me uneasy as hell."

"Me, too." Rosamunde had felt Vojalie's fear and her own prescience had confirmed that Margetta would soon bring matters to a head.

She felt as well a profound need to bond with Stone for his sake as well as for the future of the Nine Realms. But for now, he needed time to let some of this new information settle into his soul. He'd just learned that the most ancient man in the Nine Realms was not only his father but the last living elf-lord. On top of that, even Rosamunde now sensed exactly what Stone was, that he could, with a simple decision of his will, become an elf-lord himself.

And therein lay the greatest danger of all. If for whatever reason, Stone ever gave himself fully to the elf-lord power, Davido would be forced to kill his own son. She also knew, as Vojalie had suggested, that somehow the blood rose bond would protect Stone.

She didn't say as much. She chose, instead, to let everything rest for now.

Donning her black silk wrap, she took Stone's arm. Once he was ready to leave, she moved them with a thought to the red carpet entrance of the Sterling Arms Hotel.

The Nine Realms wasn't all that different from the U.S. and an event like a gala to celebrate the Federation of the Nine Realms was covered by every news outlet in each of the realms. Light bulbs flashed and reporters shouted questions.

"Queen Rosamunde, are you dating the Mastyr of Tannisford?" Since she was holding his arm she could hardly deny the connection, but she merely smiled and waved in response.

"Queen Rosamunde, why won't you give an interview and tell us what you've been doing for a thousand years?"

This time she shrugged and smiled.

"Queen Rosamunde, why haven't you helped the Nine Realms battle the Ancient Fae?"

She'd intended to keep going, but Stone stopped her and turned to face the reporter. "The queen has sacrificed her entire life, a full thousand years, to do everything in her power to protect our world. She's served in ways that I can't share with you at this time, but I promise you that without her, the Nine Realms would have fallen to the Ancient Fae a long time ago. So, I won't hear a bad word spoken against her. Do you understand?"

He didn't wait for an answer, but she felt his ire. He was a man with a quick temper. She supposed it made for a good warrior, but it was sometimes tough to deal with moment to moment.

On the other hand, she loved that he'd defended her especially on an issue, which until recently, he would have normally agreed with the reporter.

He ushered her into the foyer where hotel staff took her wrap.

But as she looked up at him, doubts swamped her all over again. She didn't know what would happen once she related the vile nature of Margetta's visions. If he had trouble forgiving her for keeping a secret, how would he ever be able to forgive her for what happened at Charborne three centuries ago?

As he guided her toward the ballroom, however, she set aside her fears and doubts. Soon enough, she'd be forced to deal with these issues.

For now, with Stone looking unbelievably sexy in his tux, she chose to give herself to the gala. She might be Queen of Ferrenden Peace, but tonight she felt like a real princess.

As she moved into the ballroom, the first sight that greeted her was all the ruling mastyrs dressed in their finest, each hovering near his woman. Each was a blood rose, a sister of sorts to Rosamunde because of their shared experience.

Those nearest turned in their direction, then offered a spattering of applause that caught on and began to grow until the ballroom thundered. She couldn't believe the outpouring of gratitude for Stone. Her heart melted and tears touched her eyes.

She squeezed Stone's arm and he smiled as he looked down at her. His deep voice touched her mind, *I forgot how much we have to celebrate tonight. I didn't mean to be a bear and ruin things.*

Her heart melted a little more but for a different reason this time. This was the flip side of the man, that when he calmed down, he was very tender and even kind.

He removed his arm and took a step away from her, then turned in her direction and stated in a loud voice. "For Rosamunde and her part in vanquishing Margetta at the lake." He applauded her as well and the guests joined in with a second thunderous round.

She was stunned and grew very still. Her fingers clung to the sides of her gown. She didn't know what to think or even what to do. Naturally, her cheeks warmed up. She hadn't expected to be honored by Stone's peers, by anyone really. She'd gone it alone for so long, she wasn't used to being praised on any level.

By now, her part in the battle at the lake as well as the nature of the protective veil of mist around Ferrenden Peace must have become widely known. Appreciation for her efforts swelled from all corners.

Like Vojalie earlier, Rosamunde was very close to bursting into tears. A couple of the women must have understood because they rushed forward and supported her by taking an arm each.

Abigail, Mastyr Gerrod's blood rose, kissed her on the cheek. "You haven't met us yet, we're your sisters of the blood rose. Come with me."

"Thank you," she whispered. "I didn't know what to do."

"I know," Abigail whispered back.

On her other side, Samantha, Ethan's woman said, "It's all overwhelming, isn't it? Then we have to make it worse by making a fuss. But you deserve this, Rosamunde. So suck it up!"

Something in Samantha's manner made Rosamunde smile then laugh. She soon found herself in the middle of a group of women she could relate to. Abigail was right. They were a sisterhood and each would continue to do her part to make the Nine Realms safe again.

When the band struck a jazzy rock tune with a lively beat, Mastyr Malik, his brown hair loose past his shoulders and sexy as anything, took Willow away to dance. Jude, whose massive shoulders practically pushed everyone out of the way, grabbed Hannah and took her twirling into the crowd. He had rhythm and a certain amount of grace he enhanced with levitation.

Lorelei drew close. Rosamunde remembered healing her mortal wounds, delivered while Lorelei had been in her wolf form. She embraced her cousin, a hug that lasted a long time.

Lorelei was Margetta's estranged daughter. Raised by a lovely troll woman, who had been enslaved to serve as Lorelei's nanny, Lorelei had gained her fine character from the love and values the nanny had given her. "We have a lot to talk about, don't we? And now that you're free to leave Ferrenden Peace, we'll get together soon."

Rosamunde had a sudden prescience of being close to not just Lorelei but all the women. Mastyr Seth came for Lorelei and kissed Rosamunde on the cheek. She had a bond with the mastyr because she'd saved his woman. She always thought fondly of the sensitive vampire.

Olivia, Zane's blood rose, came up to her next. She had a very direct way of looking at anyone and didn't hold back now. "Heard you kicked ass out at the lake. Well done, Rosamunde, and welcome to hell." She laughed, which made Rosamunde smile in response.

But Olivia wasn't all brass and kissed her cheek. *It will all work out, you'll see.*

She wondered how Olivia could tell what she was suffering but the compassion in her eyes told Rosamunde she'd been in her shoes. All the women had. Zane greeted Rosamunde but Olivia quickly took him onto the dance floor. "Let's party!" she shouted. Olivia was all wolf.

Regan moved close to her, with Ian beside her. Ian thanked her for her service in sustaining the veil of mist and for her part in defeating Margetta at the lake. "It was my pleasure. It felt so good to be doing something."

"I get that," Regan said. Regan led a fae retreat in which for centuries she'd trained young fae in wisdom and skill. "Once I learned of your existence in Ferrenden Peace, I often imagined that your isolation had been extremely tough to bear. Knowing how important community support is, I hope that you'll think of me, and of your blood rose sisters, as your community. We have a loop, for one thing, and we deal with a lot of very specific blood rose issues. You're welcome to join us any time."

"I'd love to."

Batya came to her last with Quinlan at her side. Rosamunde smiled. "And how is your daughter?"

Batya dipped her chin. "Viola is beautiful, the light of my life and my heart."

Rosamunde felt a swell of *knowing* pass through her, a strong fae response. "She'll be the new queen, soon."

Batya glanced at Quinlan. "We know. Vojalie was with me at her birth and confirmed what I'd known nearly the whole time I carried her."

"She'll be wonderful, especially with the both of you as parents."

Batya's eyes glowed. "Thank you so much."

Quinlan took her hand and kissed her gloved fingers respectfully. "You've served the Nine Realms extremely well, and I want to thank you for your service." Quinlan's voice, deeper than even Stone's, eased something inside Rosamunde.

"And I appreciate you saying as much."

He smiled. "You're welcome. And now, I'm hearing a slow song and I want to dance with my woman."

Rosamunde pressed a hand to her chest as the couple moved away. All the mastyrs were dancing now as well as at least two hundred of the most exalted personages in the Nine Realms. Even Davido levitated Vojalie around the floor. When the couple passed by, he winked at her.

Stone was answering questions from several men who looked

like a variety of puffed up city officials. She could see his choler rising and decided she'd had enough drama for one night.

She went to him and caught his eye. The look of relief that spread over his face nearly made her laugh. He wasn't a politician at all.

She kept her composure and pulled her queenly rank on the men who each bowed to her in turn.

"Sorry to take Mastyr Stone away, but he promised me this dance."

Stone excused himself then drew her into a wonderful swirl of movement that was half-levitation. She followed his lead and for the next several minutes allowed herself the pleasure of just being with Stone, moving to the music and being held in his arms.

She felt young and happy and gave herself to the unusual delights of the gala.

Later, dinner was served in an adjoining banquet room and all the ruling mastyrs and their women sat at a long head table. Dozens of toasts followed. The trolls present often leaped on the tables and did a jig, their feet being an active reflection of emotion.

After desert and coffee were served, Stone rose to make the final toast of the evening. He spoke for a couple of minutes about the Federation and what it meant for the ruling mastyrs to at last be able to work together against a foe as powerful and dangerous as the Ancient Fae. "Please rise and lift your glasses." When everyone had gained their feet, he finished with, "To the Federation of the Nine Realms."

'Here! Here!' resounded through the room.

After a fourth glass of champagne, and perhaps because it followed on the heels of her own glass of Scotch as well as a

Embrace the Power

martini, Rosamunde was giddy. She kept encouraging the nearby
trolls to outdo each other on the tables and so they did. She couldn't
remember laughing so much in her entire life.

More dancing followed until one by one, the various ruling
mastyrs took their women back to their rooms. Because Stone was
the guest host of the festivities, she knew he felt obligated to stay
to the end. Though he finally drew the line at remaining to watch
several drunken trolls playing craps.

Rosamunde walked with him back to the foyer where a hotel
maid stood with her wrap, waiting for her. Rosamunde thanked
her and Stone placed it over her shoulders.

As she moved with him to the front walk, the street was quiet.
Gone were the news crews. In their place, several hotel employees
canvased the sidewalk, picking up any debris that had been left
behind.

The air was cool at three in the morning. "I thought we'd go
back to my house. It's not far."

She looked up at him, loving the feel of his hand on her waist.
"I remember. I can teleport us there or would you prefer to fly?"

He smiled, dipped down and picked her up in his arms,
cradling her. "Let's fly." He took off almost at the same moment so
that she gave a soft yelp.

He nuzzled her neck. *You smell so good. I've been meaning to
tell you that all night.*

Thank you, but I'm not wearing perfume.

*And I'm not talking about anything that comes from a bottle.
I'm smelling your skin, your blood and your sex.* He growled softly.

She wasn't used to this kind of intimacy and her cheeks warmed
up again. At the same time, his words made her tingle all over.

As he flew higher into the sky, he kissed her neck. *I've been smelling your blood for the past hour. You've made an extra supply for me, haven't you?*

As he moved slightly to keep his eye on his trajectory, she drew close and nipped his skin at his throat, just below his jawline. *All night, the heaviness in my chest has grown. Each time it increased, I'd look at you and think about yours fangs.* She kissed him repeatedly, adding a little more pressure each time.

He groaned softly, the sound from his throat vibrating against her lips. But she needed more. She needed to be Aralynn.

Without warning him, she transformed in his arms.

What the fuck?

She didn't respond with words. Instead, making use of her wolfish abilities, though still in her womanly form, she opened her mouth wide and took hold of his throat.

He lost control and they started to spin.

~ ~ ~

As Stone righted himself, he slowed and levitated in place not far from his house in the hills. He'd never had such a strong, instantaneous reaction as he'd experienced just now. Rosamunde had not only changed into Aralynn but she'd bit him hard and his mating vibration as well as his cock had lit up and sent him into a spin.

Thank the Goddess he'd been a few hundred feet above the tree canopy or he could have crashed into something and killed them both. He suspected, though, that Rosamunde knew exactly what she was doing.

She still held onto his throat. Very wolf.

He eased her slowly from the cradling position so that he could pull her against him. She slung an arm around his neck then began sucking at his throat.

He groaned so loud he was sure he'd sent shock-waves into the starry night sky above.

You'd better stop. Even his telepathic voice sounded hoarse.

Why? She writhed against him, shifting her hips back and forth. He could tell she was working to feel his arousal.

Because I'm about to lose control again and I won't make any promises about what could happen this time.

He felt her shudder head-to-toe though not in fear. He wasn't surprised when she shifted in his arms into a large beautiful, reddish wolf then vanished.

His entire body was on high alert, his keen vampire senses honed as he leveled out like an eagle, staring down into the forest that surrounded his house.

He smiled when he saw her racing through the forest just as she'd done the night before. His arm muscles flexed. Battle power flooded him as he dove through the trees, flying head-first and moving with rocket speed. With tremendous ease, he made the subtlest adjustments to avoid contact with the pine trees. Even if he hadn't known the winding path as well as he did, he was in warrior mode and it was time to bring the wolf down.

She ran like lightning on all fours and he could feel her joy as well as her intensity.

I'm behind you, Rosamunde. He used her fae name easily now, though she was very wolf in this moment. Somehow, it felt right. *Is this all you've got?*

She picked up her speed so that he had to work to keep up

with her. He drove her now, though, because he knew the place in the path at the eastern end, where he wanted to bring her down. It was the most private place on his estate, because for what was going to happen next, he'd need privacy.

You ready for my fangs, Rosamunde?

Yes. Even telepathically, the sound of her voice was wolf-like, almost a yelp.

Good. You've got three seconds. Three...

When she bounded he kept up with her. *Two...*

Before he reached 'one', he leaped on her and brought the wolf to the ground, hard. Together they tumbled until they came to a stop. He had his hands in her fur and his legs wrapped around her hindquarters. He pinned her to the earth.

She was laughing as she shifted to leave her wolf behind and become Aralynn.

He bit down hard on the back of her neck.

Ah, Stone. You have no idea how good that feels. Harder.

He gnawed on her and she kept gasping. He could feel her pleasure.

He pulled up her gown and when the mounds of her ass were exposed, he unzipped. Both feats he performed as fast as he could then tore at her thong until it fell away. He grabbed her hips, hauling her to her knees.

Grinding his teeth into the back of her neck a little more, he felt her back arch and her pelvis tilt so that her spine swayed and her head rose as much as he would let it. He wasn't surprised when a howl left her throat.

Taking his cock in hand, he found her streaming entrance and pushed inside. He groaned heavily, then began to stroke her in long deep thrusts. Rosamunde let a series of soft howls flow from her mouth.

I have to do something, Stone.

What? He had her where he wanted her and he knew she wasn't about to change position. He wasn't even sure she could, not with the wolf-hold he had on her.

Then he felt the earth rumble.

Holy shit, she'd accessed the elf-lord power. What did she have in mind? As connected as they were, he felt the power hit her then channel easily through him. And as the power flowed, her violet mist began flooding the nearby trees. Within seconds, he could no longer hear the distant sounds of the city, which in turn meant no one could hear them.

He understood and ground his teeth on the back of her neck a little more. *You can let loose now. I'll fuck you hard and you can howl your head off.*

Fuck me, Stone.

He used a combination of his physical strength and levitation to hold her in place, then thrust faster and faster, pistoning inside her.

She arched her back more and more. He could feel he would need to release her throat for her to really howl. But he waited for the exact moment when she was close to orgasm.

He pummeled her, going vampire fast.

She jerked slightly from her chin, a sure sign she was ready.

He let go of her neck but grabbed her hips and let her have it, slamming into her and making her come.

The howls that erupted were magnificent and grabbed him by the balls. His release came like the rush of a wind. He pulsed hard and shouted as the exquisite pleasure of ecstasy rocked him to the core.

But to his surprise, and maybe because of the elf-lord power flowing through him, the moment didn't end.

Rosamunde was full of surprises as she transformed back to her fae self and at the same time whirled to face him. His cock slipped out of her, but damn if he wasn't still hard and ready for a second go.

He fell on her, kissing her and as she parted her lips, he drove his tongue into her mouth. His hand was on her hair and he stroked her head, her arms, then went low to feel her thighs.

But the damn dress was in the way.

He rose up and using both hands, he gripped the top of the bodice.

"Do it!" she cried.

He used his bare strength to rip through what had to be several layers of fabric. He kept going until he'd rendered the garment in two and it fell away from her body.

She wore no bra and her large breasts lay in an inviting milky landscape. He contorted himself to suckle her.

She began working his tie off as he nursed on her.

But he had to pull back to get the rest of the job done.

He disengaged and in a flurry of movement got rid of his jacket, shoes, and pants. Rosamunde was already helping and in the same way he'd destroyed her dress, she ripped his shirt apart, tearing it off his body.

As he leaned in to kiss her again, she caught his face with both hands. "Stone, you've got to feed from me. Now. I'm on fire with need and your hunger is stroking me between my legs." In proof, she rolled her hips and groaned heavily.

She swept her hair away from her throat which caused his fangs to descend like a pair of rockets. 'Hunger' was too small a word for what he was feeling.

He angled his shoulders and head and licked a line up her throat, teasing the vein to rise to the surface.

Her voice pierced his mind.

Be inside me, Stone.

He was so consumed with the sudden awareness of his blood hunger that he'd forgotten his cock. How in the Goddess's name was that possible?

He groaned as he took his cock in hand again and pressed himself into her, pushing in fits and starts because he was coming unglued with need on every front. Even his mating vibration had started to buck.

He wanted to calm down, but then again, he didn't.

Once inside her, she cooed and groaned and fondled his back muscles, then his ass. It felt so good.

He licked her throat again, his lips dripping saliva. He popped his head back in a quick jerk, struck with his fangs to the right depth, and her blood poured into his waiting mouth.

Sweet Goddess who rules us all, you taste of heaven. He formed a seal around the wounds and began to suck. The earth rumbled again and the elf-lord power flowed.

Stone continued to move his hips into her, staying seated deep so that he could piston evenly and hit her sweet spot over and over. But as the elf-lord power flooded his body, for the first time he felt the seductive nature of it, that it was something he wanted moving through him forever.

He felt stronger than he ever had with Rosamunde's blood

flowing into down his throat. But the elf-lord power was doing something to him. He broke the flow and licked the wounds to seal them. He then lifted up so he could look at her, though he continued to thrust into her.

She met his gaze but her violet eyes shifted to brown and back repeatedly. Her features altered as well in a way that made her more beautiful than ever. She was both Rosamunde and Aralynn. His mind became filled with an array of images, from the center of his world and expanding through the universe in brilliant waves of light and heat and every color imaginable.

His cock fueled the images and for Rosamunde he added the vibration she loved so well. She cried out, her back arching. She dug her nails into his arms, then squeezed her eyes shut. Pleasure flowed over every lovely feature.

His muscles expanded and he rolled heavily into her now, waves of movement that had her writhing beneath him.

Rosamunde, open your eyes and look at me.

She obeyed and as he made this connection with her, his mating vibration dove into her body and covered her. She cried out repeatedly. *So close. So close.*

Yes. He began to thrust faster, vampire fast.

She threw her arms back and screamed, her pelvis arching against him, her body writhing. His release came for the second time like a wave of pleasurable fire pulsing through his cock. He shouted and groaned. The images in his mind exploded into a mountain of light. He saw stars, the birth of the heavens, the seat of the angels.

He was light and heat and man and vampire. He was of elven and troll stock, and the son of Inez and Davido. He was

Rosamunde's man and the receptor of her blood rose power. He was everything he was always meant to become.

He hovered between two worlds as the reality of his elf nature came to the fore. As the elf-lord power hurtled through him, he could feel the call to become what Davido had warned him against. An elf-lord.

But he held back. Somehow, especially buried inside Rosamunde, it didn't feel right, so he let the desire go.

~ ~ ~

Rosamunde was breathing hard but she wasn't sure where she was or who she was. She'd been both her fae and wolf self in alternating fits, while Stone had fed from her and made love to her. He was still thick inside her and she was loose, relaxed and deeply satisfied.

She felt so much in this moment that it was hard to separate the different strands of thought and emotion. For one, Stone looked like a god as he stayed in an almost statue-like position. He was still connected to her, but his arms were fully flexed and his body bowed away from her. His face was glowing, his lips parted, his eyes closed.

As she looked at him, her throat tightened. Her gaze searched his face, the strength of his cheekbones, the muscular line of his neck. His chin and nose. His brows were thick and arched giving him a regal look. The knife-like tattoos along his upper chest stood out like warrior blades and the glow of the elf-lord power made him appear invincible.

She could feel that he was in this moment almost an elf-lord. She didn't know whether to be awestruck or deeply afraid. She understood Vojalie's biggest concern, that Stone would surrender to his elf-lord potential and take on a mantle that would require his execution.

Yet, the way he looked was incredible. She wasn't sure what all was involved, but it was a lot more than merely channeling the power. In a burst of fae insight, she saw that a decision of the will would bring the elf-lord power permanently into his body, changing him forever.

A terrible prescience came to her that soon he'd be faced with the decision.

Slowly, he came back to himself. The arch of his back decreased and his head leveled out so that he could look down at her. "I swear I saw the heart of the universe just now."

She stroked his arms and shoulders deciding then and there that she would do everything she could to help him keep from following the deadly path. "You're glowing."

He lowered himself onto his forearms and kissed her. "And you're beautiful." He glanced around. "The mist you made was exactly what we needed."

She smiled and pushed back some of his thick hair with her fingers, dragging it over his shoulder and down his back. "And I definitely needed to howl."

"And so you did. It was hot as hell."

She nodded. "Everything about this was amazing. And the vibration you can send through your cock." A shiver went straight through her at the memory.

He used his thumb to stroke her cheek. "I love being able to give you pleasure like that. I also love that our mating vibrations are so fully joined. Not quite a bond."

"No, not quite, but the nearest thing." She smiled. "I don't want to let you go."

"And I don't want to leave your body." He shifted his hips so that she felt him. He was in that beautiful half-state of arousal.

"I never thought I would feel this way," she said. "Ever. Or even have the chance to experience this kind of closeness. And now, I'm here with you. It's beyond imagining for me."

He kissed her again and again. They were on the ground in the forest surrounding his estate and she didn't want to leave.

"How about we go to my bed and talk a bit more." He reached down and stroked her breast, fondling the tip. "What we did here was great, but it was so quick. I'd love to slow things down. How does that sound?"

This time she leaned up and kissed him. "We could make sandwiches, have some beer, then find out how strong your bed is. I'm still feeling very 'Aralynn' right now."

He smiled and it was such a look of joy that she gasped softly as her heart made a swooshing sensation. "I love you, Stone."

He kissed her in response. "I never expected love. I was committed to the Nine Realms especially after the slaughter at Charborne when my parents died. I dated a lot over the centuries but this," he pressed a hand to his chest, "was made of flint.

"Yet here you are, beneath me and I'm inside you and your blood is in me and you've allowed me this amazing gift of channeling the elf-lord power. I'm so grateful for it all and for you and your steadfastness as queen and for the part you played in the battle earlier tonight. I love you, too, Rosamunde."

The words caused her heart to soar so high, she was sure she would start levitating, then rise to the moon and keep on going.

When he finally released himself from her body, he grabbed the remnants of his shirt and tucked it between her legs. "Thank you," she said. "I appreciate it."

He then tried to draw her dress around her, perhaps with the intention of flying her to the house. But she stopped him. "Grab your clothes. We'll teleport."

He looked relieved. "Good plan."

It took a moment for each of them to pick up the shoes and torn clothing. But once everything was in hand, she hooked his arm. "I think I'd like a shower right now. What do you think? Care to join me?"

His lips curved. "Love to."

She thought-the-thought and with a blink, she took them both right next to the large shower. She dropped her clothes to the side, then turned to set the heads running and the water to warming up. There were several, including an overhead rain shower.

After removing the pins in her hair, she stepped in. Stone joined her and the next half hour became a playful time of soapy body parts, a lot of massaging and at last finding her back pressed up against the tile as he entered her again.

Being in the shower was genius because afterward clean-up was really simple.

Sandwiches followed, as well as a very nice amber ale.

When he took her to bed sometime around dawn, he was as good as his word and this time, he slowed everything down. She was pretty sure he'd kissed every part of her body before easing his cock between her legs.

He told her he loved her many times and she reciprocated. It all seemed so beautiful and easy that she wondered for a moment whether they should heed Vojalie's advice and complete the bond. Maybe, in this way, she could help keep him from being seduced by the elf-lord power.

But his loving attitude pleased her so much that in the end she chose not to disrupt the moment with the difficult idea of completing a bond which neither of them had fully accepted.

By the time he took her all the way for about the tenth time, Rosamunde was in a state of blissful contentment and afterward fell fast asleep.

When she woke up that evening, with the sun just setting, she rolled onto her back and a wonderful feeling of euphoria flowed through her. She could hear the shower running and the sounds of Stone washing his long hair.

What a night!

She knew the troublesome bonding issue sat just offshore, but right now she took a few minutes to savor all that had happened between herself and Stone. In addition to several rounds of amazing sex, vows of love had been exchanged. Her mating vibration, though now separated from Stone, still hummed from the number of times his frequency had covered hers.

All. Amazing.

She sighed and smiled as she stared up at the ceiling. She was completely naked beneath Stone's comforter and content beyond words.

Except…

She pressed a hand to her lips. She felt young right now, unversed in relationships and especially timing.

Her fae senses warned her that she'd erred, but in what way?

She sought about in her mind. Stone now knew who his father was and he had begun to enjoy her two separate identities.

Her lips curved slowly. She'd loved transforming into Aralynn several times, especially when she wanted Stone to be extra physical with her.

She sighed contentedly.

Just as she started to relax, there it was again, a fae sensation, growing more and more intense that she'd left something undone.

Of course, there was the issue with the Margetta visions.

And there it was, the one issue she'd refused to touch.

Her heart began to thud in her chest.

She had to tell Stone about the nature of the visions and Margetta's purpose in sending them to her each time. More specifically, she needed him to know that she'd seen the attack on Charborne before it happened.

She shook her head. Surely by now, Stone would trust her judgment. But would he understand the terrible position that Margetta's visions had put her in and that it had taken enormous courage for her *not* to take action? The Nine Realms would have fallen if she'd even once given into the horror of the visions and tried to contact someone.

Yet as a man of action, she knew in her gut he wasn't going to get this.

She recalled that when he'd learned Davido was his father, he'd cursed a very long line of words. A similar collection passed over her lips.

She'd forgotten one thing: Vampire hearing.

Stone appeared in the bathroom doorway. "Anything wrong?" He was laughing.

He'd just shaved and showered and had a towel wrapped around his hips. She had to blink several times to make her brain stop moving in the wrong direction.

Dear sweet Goddess. She now knew she'd screwed up royally and had no way to soften the truth or to make him understand. "Is there coffee?"

He nodded. "Can I get you some?"

She shook her head, for a moment uncertain how to proceed.

Then it suddenly seemed that the only thing she could do was say it straight out. "I knew of the attack at Charborne before it happened."

He cocked his head. "I know you did. You went to the mine to protect Elias."

"Not the recent attack, Stone. The one that occurred shortly after you joined the Tannisford Vampire Guard."

She drew her knees up and wrapped her arms around them. She tried to gauge his reactions, then had to look away.

From her peripheral vision she watched him draw close to the bed. She bolstered her courage because she had to face him, had to make him understand it all.

She shifted slightly in his direction, lowering her knees, but pulled the comforter up to cover her breasts.

He was frowning. "I don't understand. You had foreknowledge of the attack that nearly destroyed the village, the same attack that took the lives of my parents?"

She nodded very slowly. She became lightheaded and forced herself to take a breath. "It wasn't the usual fae vision, not the kind you and I have used to battle side-by-side for the past several weeks. It wasn't even like Vojalie's fae visions, *not at all*. And that's what I need you to understand. These visions were delivered to me, by Margetta, for a specific reason."

"You're saying Margetta warned you what she intended to do?"

"Yes. They originated from her."

"They? You mean that over the centuries there have been several visions."

She looked away from him, remembering. "Dozens. Each one a painful nightmare."

"What did you do about them? Who did you tell? I don't understand. I don't recall any warning about the attack that killed my parents."

"That's what I'm trying to say. I couldn't tell a single person about the visions, not while they were in progress. Stone, try to understand. Margetta laid them over my mind with the hope that I would reach out to someone, to anyone. But if I'd done so, she would have locked onto my physical location and teleported into Ferrenden Peace. The moment she succeeded, she would have channeled the elf-lord power and the Nine Realms would have been lost."

The color drained from his face. "But if you'd let anyone in Tannisford know about the attack on Charborne, so many lives could have been saved. My parents would still be alive."

"Margetta would have acquired the elf-lord power and who knows what would have happened that night at Charborne. But every fae ability I have tells me that she would have used the resulting power to take over our world. Think how many realm-folk would have died then?"

His nostrils flared. She felt his temper in hard, bitter waves, rolling off his skin. "All I'm hearing is that you've confirmed my original take on your character. You've always lacked the courage to act, to do what's right. You should have contacted the ruling mastyr and given him a chance, given all the mastyrs a chance."

She shook her head. "You're not seeing the bigger, much more horrible picture. Try to envision what it would have been like if Margetta had gained control of the elf-lord power? If I'd reached out to anyone, and I mean *anyone*, Margetta would have used my position to get inside Ferrenden Peace."

Stone closed his eyes. She watched him swallow hard as he shook his head back-and-forth several times. "I need to understand everything here." He opened his eyes once more, but his complexion remained pale, almost gray. "In the visions that Margetta sent you, did realm-folk die?"

Her throat closed up and tears sprang to her eyes. Of all the things she'd suffered through the years, including the painful solitude of her castle life, the visions had been the most difficult to endure, even worse than the physical pain of receiving the elf-lord power each time. Having knowledge of the death of hundreds of realm-folk over the years, possibly thousands, yet being unable to act on that information, had required a great deal of prayer, of fortitude and of self-forgiveness.

Vojalie and Davido knew of the visions and had counseled her as well. But she'd still had to live with the results.

In response to his question about whether or not realm-folk died with each vision, she could only nod solemnly.

His nostrils flared and he bent over at the waist to plant his fists on the bed. His arms were spread wide, so that he could dip low enough to look her in the eye. He wasn't but a few inches from her face.

She felt his growing anger. "How do you know for sure that

Margetta, even if she'd made it inside Ferrenden Peace, would have been able to access the elf-lord power? How, Rosamunde? Because I'm telling you right now that the deaths of all these people are on your head. Every vision you received and failed to report to the ruling mastyr who could have taken action, placed a dagger in your hand that might as well have slit each throat."

He breathed heavily through his nose, raspy, fiery sounds that set her heart to pounding once more. "What's more, you've confirmed my original belief that you're a coward. For what realm-person could have done this who had the smallest shred of either a conscience or a heart? You disgust me. You always have."

He drew back full of so much righteous fury that when his color returned, his golden skin had a reddish hue over every visible surface his body.

"You don't believe me, then, because I want to be clear on that point. You don't trust that my fae instincts were and are strong enough to warn me not to act on her visions."

"That's what I'm saying exactly."

Rosamunde straightened her shoulders. "Then I think it a very good thing that we didn't bond last night."

"If we'd bonded, and you'd revealed all of this afterward, I swear I would have killed you, or myself if need be, in order to be free of such a despicable connection. Now get out of my sight before I do something I'm sure at some point I'll regret."

Rosamunde stared at him for a long moment. "If you need me, Stone, I'm here for you. I know you don't believe me, but you're wrong about this."

"Get out!" He shouted so loud that her ears rang.

Chapter Thirteen

Stone stared at the empty bed for a long, long moment.

His entire body vibrated with rage.

Sweet Goddess, he couldn't believe how many different ways he'd made love to Rosamunde last night and right now he regretted it all. He felt as though he'd slept with a demoness, a woman who had tricked him with one set of seductive behaviors, yet all the while she'd been the real reason his adopted troll parents had died.

He should have stuck with his initial instincts about Rosamunde as a woman lacking courage and action. Her life might have been uncomfortably secluded, but it had been a soft existence. She hadn't learned how to really do battle in a world constantly harassed by wraith-pairs.

And her story about Margetta forcing these visions on her yet making it impossible for her to act rang false to his warrior ears. If she'd really cared about all the realm-folk who'd died, she would have alerted the ruling mastyrs. She would have done something. A failure to act was as damning as anything else in this situation.

He dressed for the night in battle gear, as usual. Though like Ian, he'd left off wearing the woven shirts. He liked seeing his tattoos in the mirror as he wrestled his black mane into the woven clasp. Each time a major catastrophe had happened, he'd added a tattoo so that every single ink blade point on his body reminded him why he fought as he did.

He pulled the leather Guardsman coat aside and touched the point nearest his heart. He'd gotten it a year after the death of his parents, a reminder of why he would always serve as a Guardsman. He would battle for the safety of the Nine Realms until the day he died.

Grief swelled over him suddenly and so profound that he had to catch himself with both hands on the edge of the sink or he would have fallen forward and crashed into the mirror.

Sweat beaded up on his forehead.

He could recall the night he learned of the attack on Charborne as though it was yesterday and not three hundred years ago. He'd been as far from the village and the family farm as he could have been in Tannisford. He'd flown faster than ever before, but it had still taken him twenty minutes to get there.

By the time he arrived at Charborne, several Vampire Guard squads were in play taking care of business. Dozens of wraith-pairs lay dead on the cobbled streets of the village and the rest were being run to earth.

He'd sped the remaining distance to the family farm, but the house was on fire as were the haystacks scattered through the pasture. He found his parents already dead and lying in a ditch near their vegetable garden along with two female dairy workers and three field hands. The wraith-pairs had been in such a frenzy, they'd slaughtered forty head of cattle as well.

He'd carried his mother to a quiet, untouched place in their peach orchard, then gone back for his father and the others. He'd spent the rest of the night preparing funeral pyres. Relatives of the dead had come from miles around to mourn the loss.

His best friends, Harris and Cole, had stayed with him until dawn. He'd wept unceasingly. He'd always known that he'd been a shield of protection for Charborne. Wraith-pairs had attacked the village at least once-a-year and because of his ability, he'd fought them off from the time he'd learned to ply his battle frequency.

Though he'd had the current ruling mastyr of Tannisford drill the village in security maneuvers and some of the Guard had even trained the more stalwart trolls, elves and fae how to fight, no one could have predicted such a large number of wraith-pairs descending all at once on Charborne.

Except … Rosamunde.

Unbidden tears fell from his eyes, only what he felt wasn't just the grief of having lost his family three centuries ago or even that their deaths could have been prevented. But in this moment, he'd also lost a woman he'd come to love.

Earlier, while making coffee and preparing ingredients for a frittata, he'd come to a decision to bond with her. He'd even taken a few minutes to mentally lay in all the arguments he would use to persuade her.

He'd shaved and showered, wishing she'd wake up so they could discuss the immediate future.

Now, he felt as though her revelations about Margetta's visions had set his whole life on fire, burning it down to embers, and there was nothing he could do about it.

He could only return to the Communication Center and get back to work.

~ ~ ~

As Rosamunde showered in her castle bathroom, she felt numb from head to foot. She'd been a fool not to address the issue of Margetta's visions much earlier in her relationship with Stone. In fact, the best time would have been when she'd served cocktails before the gala and both Vojalie and Davido had been present. They could have supported her claims.

But when she thought back to the scope of Davido's revelations, she recalled the state of shock Stone had been in. He'd learned Davido wasn't just his biological father, but an elf-lord as well. She couldn't have layered yet another explosive piece of news on top of his parentage. It had seemed way too much at the time.

Yet without Davido's support of her position, all Stone saw was her supposed weakness.

She realized she was emotionally worn out from the last three nights. Leaning her forearm against the tile and as the warm water beat down on her, she gave herself to the tears that had tightened her throat.

When she'd wept long enough and felt more at peace, she shut off the shower and took her time drying herself. She spent the next twenty minutes using her blow dryer in an almost haphazard manner. She didn't even care that her disinterest resulted in a huge, frizzy mass.

When she went to her closet, however, and saw the long row of beautifully wrought gowns, each one specially designed and hand-stitched for the Queen, she grew very still. They were all elegant, a few in silk or velvet, but most in the woven fabrics common to the Nine Realms, though heavily hand-embroidered.

Much to her surprise, she realized she couldn't put any of them on, not anymore. They no longer suited her and she closed the closet door.

Once she'd become Aralynn, she'd started down this path, good or bad, right or wrong. She'd loved the freedom of embracing her wolf side, whether running through the forest in fur and four paws or battling beside Stone with her hair held back by a woven clasp, but essentially set free from the Queen's intricate braids.

She turned to face into the room, to the large, heavily carved, four-poster bed, to the ornate dresser and overly tall, upholstered chairs. The drapes by the window were velvet. The carpet on the floor was an expensive antique Turkish rug imported from the U.S. The hardwood floors had been recently refinished so that they gleamed.

Paintings by the most famous elven artists of the past several centuries adorned each wall. The frames alone cost a fortune. The room was … *opulent*.

She wasn't. She never had been.

She fingered her frizzed-out hair.

As a child, she was happiest when she was outside playing with her goats.

The decision that came to her was so simple, she hardly knew what to make of it. She decided in that moment she would abdicate as queen and leave the castle for good. Her extensive staff governed Ferrenden Peace as it was. She'd truly been a figurehead and little better than a prisoner all these years.

Aralynn's life, on the other hand, was one of action and doing. Rosamunde's nature leaned to these qualities. She'd loved the weeks she'd served as Stone's battle partner well before they'd become lovers.

Bottom line, she couldn't go back. She couldn't live in the castle any longer.

A new path opened up suddenly, one that Stone would fight her on, but she didn't care. And, she had nothing to lose.

She teleported to the cottage then transformed into Aralynn. By now, it was no doubt well known that she was both the queen and Aralynn. She didn't even care about that, not really. It was time to move on, to be who she was meant to really be, no matter which woman she brought to the fore.

She dressed in battle gear, but focused on her faeness and channeling the elf-lord power. When the earth began to rumble, she didn't wait but teleported just outside the Tannisford Communication Center.

She took a deep breath and pushed open the glass door of the building then moved to the end of the hall to the room where Stone had his main display of screens.

The moment she crossed the threshold, her hand on her sheathed dagger for support, Stone's deep voice boomed. "What the fuck are you doing here?"

All the screens began to crackle and every head turned first in Stone's direction, then in hers.

The room fell deathly quiet.

Delia levitated to face Stone at eye-level. "Ease down, Mastyr! You're going to explode the electronics!"

Stone, however, clearly couldn't hear Delia. He levitated swiftly through the room, heading toward her. As he flew over the heads of his Com Center operators, several leaned or ducked to keep from getting clipped.

Rosamunde had enough sense to back into the hall.

Once he reached her, he shut the door to the center, then grabbed her arm, his mossy-green eyes lit up like a bonfire. "You are not welcome here and don't ever come back." He glanced down at his feet no doubt feeling the earth rumbling as well. "Shit. You're kidding me. The elf-lord power? What's going on?"

She offered him a wry smile. "It's time to rock-and-roll, Stone. You with me? Because I'm not giving up serving Tannisford as Aralynn. I'm sorry for the way things fell out—"

"Fell out? You call that kind of deception and indifference to the plight of your fellow realm-folk a simple 'falling out'. Fuck you, Rosamunde."

She flared her own nostrils. "And fuck you right back because I know in my powerful fae heart that you're wrong about how you've interpreted the Margetta visions." This time she glanced down at her feet then grabbed Stone's arm to channel the power into him. Whether he liked it nor, he was going to participate. She was tired of his temper and his rage. He needed to get with the program no matter what he thought about her.

Stone started to protest, but the vision rolled so fast that she watched him clamp his lips shut. His eyes widened as he stared back at her, so she knew he was receiving the vision at the same time.

Stone summed it up. "A bunch of wraith-pairs have got several troll teens trapped out at the grotto." He blinked a few times as the vision faded then met her gaze.

He narrowed his eyes and remained silent for several potent seconds. "Fine. This once, then we're going to set some boundaries because I can't function like this. We'll get Vojalie to help us out if we have to."

She lifted her chin and one strongly arched brow. "Fine. You ready, Mastyr?"

"You don't have to be sarcastic."

"Oh, yes, I think I do." She didn't wait for him to argue further, but gripped his arm tighter and teleported him to the far southern edge of the realm where the Tannisford fir forest met the Sea of Vermed. The constant force of the waves had created a string of caves filled with white sand and blue water. It was a favorite place for swimming and for troll teens at night, a place to let romance take its course.

~ ~ ~

Rage still had hold of Stone, but he took a few seconds to channel all that frustration and anger into the sight of three wraith-pairs circling above the wide hole that led down into the most central grotto. The wraiths were up to their usual scare-the-shit-out-of-the-enemy with their loud, piercing shrieks.

What's the strategy? Do you want me to teleport as many of the trolls out as I can?

He turned to her, frowning. *That's right. You can do that now. Good. We've got new options.*

Her brown eyes glittered, a sure sign she was ready to take on the mission. He could at least appreciate this part of her.

Tell you what, he said. *Teleport to different locations around the edge of the forest first. See if we've got any other wraith-pairs in the area. We don't want to be outflanked.*

Got it. She vanished instantly.

He remained in the shadows of the coastal firs. While she searched the area, he pathed with Harris letting him know the location and the nature of the attack. Harris happened to be checking out a rogue attack a few miles to the east with a team of three and he knew of another squad only ten minutes away.

Harris pathed, *A sighting of three rogue wraith-pairs came in about twenty minutes ago. But they left the area. Looks like they've headed to the grotto.*

Sounds like it. Aralynn's on recon, scouting the area, but I've got a visual on the Invictus. Shit. One of the pairs just dropped down into the grotto.

Go get 'em, Mastyr. We'll be there shortly.

Rosamunde returned quickly with a frightened troll kid in tow.

Stone spoke in a low voice. "Son, listen. I know you're scared, but I need you to hold it together. My Guardsmen are on the way. But Mistress Aralynn and I have to know the lay-out. How many of you kids are down in the grotto and did you see more than just these three wraith-pairs?"

The troll was shaking. "We shouldn't have come here tonight. My parents will kill me when they find out."

Rosamunde put her hand on his shoulder and Stone felt her fae vibrations kick in. "Calm down, Sweetheart. Mastyr Stone and I can get everyone out safely, if you'll tell us what we need to know. Look at me."

As soon as the boy met her gaze, Stone watched him fall under Rosamunde's fae thrall. The kid dragged in a deep breath, visibly relaxed and in a few words detailed the situation: Only three wraith-pairs, but there were nine troll teens below, ten in all counting the boy. Several swam to the farthest caves but would end up trapped once the Invictus got into the grotto.

Rosamunde told him to sit down and to stay put.

The troll dropped to his ass, his three forehead ridge rolls tight. He had tears in his eyes. "I will. I promise."

Rosamunde had calmed him with her faeness and Stone felt certain he wouldn't have to worry about this kid doing anything stupid.

Rosamunde turned toward him. She even smiled. *How do you want to do this, Mastyr?*

For a split second, he thought she might be flirting. Then he realized she was as she'd always been: Game for battle, as was he.

He repressed the urge to smile in response. *You got your dagger?*

She drew it from its sheath in a soft rasp. *Let's go.*

Follow me. Stone levitated just a few inches above the forest floor. It was an unusual stretch of land, a narrow isthmus not more than thirty yards wide with the Sea of Vermed crashing against both fairly short cliffs. That trees had grown in the narrow space indicated the density of the land above what had to be a solid stone base below.

When he reached the edge of the forest, he pathed to Aralynn. *I want you to come out above the uppermost pair and take out the wraith. She's bonded to a troll which will make it easier to disable this pair. I'll swing around then come in from the north. And remember, if you're in danger—*

I know: Get the hell out of there.

Good. Let's roll.

He felt her vanish and when she did, he levitated straight up then shot forward. By the time Rosamunde had cut the wraith's hamstrings, Stone had reached the bonded troll. He caught him around the neck, squeezing to render him unconscious.

The second pair turned to do battle, the wraith screeching.

He watched Rosamunde appeared suddenly behind the second wraith and cut her wiry legs as well. The wraith fell screaming to the rocky ground near the upper cave entrance. Her companion elf wasn't far behind.

Four down.

Stone dove into the cave, flying swiftly.

The bonded vampire, a vicious-looking woman, already had a female troll in her arms. The latter was screaming and thrashing, which only incited the vampire, who dragged her onto the nearby sandy beach ready to feed. For Stone, this was a good thing since the Invictus vampire would stay focused on her prey and not what was coming at her.

I've got the male wraith. Rosamunde's telepathic words were exactly what he wanted to hear.

Knowing the vampire's wraith-mate would be taken care of, Stone flew swiftly to land in front of the female. "Let her go. Now."

The vampire hissed and for a moment held onto the troll. But as Stone lifted his arm, his blue battle energy sparked in the humid air. The vampire released her victim then levitated, hissing again and ready to do battle.

But Stone didn't move against her right away. In the distance, Rosamunde appeared behind the woman's bonded wraith-mate. Using her dagger, she quickly incapacitated the male wraith by slicing the backs of his thighs and he fell hard to the sandy beach. His ensuing pain caused the bonded female vampire to list in the air.

Stone lifted his arm and let his battle energy fly, though not at full-bore because he wanted her alive for rehabilitation. When his power struck, she flew backward and landed unconscious, about five feet from her mate. Both remained inert.

Rosamunde pathed, *I'm going back for the kid in the forest.*

Good idea.

He called out to the troll kids. *This is Mastyr Stone. We've got the enemy in hand, but I want you to stay put until my Guardsmen arrive. They'll come and retrieve each of you. We want to make sure the grotto is completely safe first.*

A few called back to him, letting him know he'd been heard and would be obeyed.

A moment later, Harris tapped on his telepathy. Stone opened up and Harris gave his report. *I've got my team up here and we'll be able to send these two wraith-pairs for rehab. How you doin' down below?*

The last pair is unconscious and I've told the kids to stay where they are until our Guardsmen come for them. Rosamunde is in the forest with one of the kids who wasn't in the grotto when the wraith-pairs attacked. But I'd like you to take charge.

Will do. I'm heading down to your position now.

Stone lifted his gaze to the central opening some thirty feet in the air and watched as Harris levitated down into the cave followed by one of his Guardsmen.

When they drew close, Stone pointed in both directions. "We've got teens hiding out in several adjoining caves."

Harris gestured to the second Guard squad now descending into the grotto. "I've got this, Stone. Head out, if you want. I'm bringing in another four Guardsmen as well, so we're good." Harris glanced at the wounded couple on the sandy beach. "From the look of this crew, they weren't part of the Ancient Fae's main force, that's for sure."

"I agree." Their clothing was in a bad state for one thing. In recent months, Margetta had transformed her army, outfitting them in decent uniforms. She'd built not just a battling force, but a support machine for keeping them fed, trained and clothed.

He instructed Harris to call for him as needed then levitated back up through the central circular opening. He passed the additional Guardsmen arriving to help find all the teens and get them back to their parents. Two of Harris's initial squad were tending to the wounded wraith-pairs. One of the men was on his phone arranging transport.

He found Rosamunde, still in her Aralynn form, back in the forest with the troll boy. She was sitting on the ground beside him, her arm around his shoulders. He had his knees drawn up and his arms around boney legs. He kept curling his toes into the balls of his feet. He was weeping. "We just wanted to have some fun." He wiped at his cheeks but kept his head down.

Stone glanced at Rosamunde. She met his gaze. *He's only thirteen.*

Stone nodded. "Hey, what's your name?"

The boy looked up at him. "Todd."

"Listen, Todd, I was doing the same thing at your age. I was into spelunking like you wouldn't believe. I got in trouble a few times and my dad loved to double my nightly chores. He used to joke that he wished I'd get in trouble more often."

At that Todd's eyes went wide. "You used to cave dive?"

"I was pretty hopeless. Besides, I take it there were a few girls with you tonight."

Todd grinned then pursed his lips. "Is everyone okay?"

"Everyone's fine. My men are searching the caves for your friends now. I only care about one thing, making sure you each get back home safely."

Todd gained his feet and swallowed hard. "Is there anything I can do?"

Stone loved the courage of his people. He settled a hand on the boy's shoulder. "My Guardsmen are bringing out your friends now. Why don't you join them so they know you're safe as well and make sure the girls get home first, okay? We protect our women."

Todd puffed out his chest. "I will."

Stone moved aside and watched as the kid headed to the central hole, shoulders back, spine straight. Rosamunde rose to her feet to stand next to him. "He'd climbed up to this level to jump through the hole into the water. He'd barely escaped being seen. Poor kid."

"He's a brave one, though. I'm impressed."

"Is everything taken care of in the grotto?"

"Harris is in charge."

"Well, then." Her sudden smile made something inside his chest ache. She continued, "He'll have the grotto scoured in a trice." Her hand crept to her chest which of course drew his eye to her cleavage.

His heartbeat suddenly thudded in his ears.

He might not be able to forgive her for Charborne and all the other events she'd failed to report, but he couldn't deny his profound attraction to her.

Lifting his gaze to her face, he saw she was frowning. Something was bothering her. "What is it? I can tell you're distressed."

She shifted her gaze to him. "You won't like this, Stone, but not only can I feel your blood hunger beginning to rise but I've built a supply for you. You need to feed and I need to get rid of all this extra."

Her cheeks were a rosy color. She drew a deep breath as she let her hand fall away from her chest.

Stone didn't know what to do. "We can't keep this up. You know that, right?"

She held his gaze for a long moment. "But you understand this means I'll need to find another Mastyr. Rez, maybe."

At the mere mention of Rez's name, Stone's temper about shot through his skull. He put his hands to his head and turned in a slow circle. "Don't ever mention that man's name again."

"Fine, I won't. But you might as well get used to the rest of the reality. Either I feed you or I find someone else to take the extra supply I keep building."

"Fine. Then for now, you feed me." He growled. He was pissed. He was being forced down this rabbit hole by the demanding nature of her blood rose abilities and he didn't like it one bit. "But we're too close to other people right now. Come with me."

He didn't wait for her to acquiesce. He grabbed her and slung her easily into a cradled hold. He flew northwest away from the site.

You could have warned me, she pathed, *that you meant to rocket me into the sky.*

We just need to get this done. He kept his gaze focused on the forest below and when he saw a small clearing, he dropped down. Once on the ground he released her then turned in a slow circle to listen to the forest.

Caris Roane

When he was satisfied they were alone and safe, he turned back to her. But damn if he wasn't pissed all over again.

She drew her shoulders back. "Listen, Stone, I have an idea. I know that drinking from my wrist would take way too long, so how about if we do it this way." She pushed her mane over her shoulder then turned her back to him. "Come at me from behind. You won't have to look at me. That should help."

Now that the scent of her blood was in his nostrils, desire for her began to rage all over again. Her choice of words about coming at her from behind didn't help at all.

But the deed had to be done.

He set aside his anger and disgust for her centuries-long decisions, and focused on the line of her neck.

His fangs descended swiftly as he drew close.

He slid an arm around her waist, drawing her tight against him, her back to his front. He heard her gasp and moan at the same time.

He wasn't surprised. He was fully erect and just to punish her, he ground into her letting her feel him.

You'd better stop. My wolf loves this.

Then maybe you should get rid of Aralynn, at least for now.

Probably a good idea.

~ ~ ~

Rosamunde didn't want to transform out of her Aralynn state. All her wolf senses loved what she was feeling and not just Stone's arousal. His arm around the front of her waist was doing something to her.

But he was right. They had to make this work somehow. "I'll

do it now." She whirled through her transformation, but remained in the same position. He'd loosened his grip on her slightly, but now that she was Rosamunde again, he drew her tight against him once more. Vampires liked to have full control when they fed.

It was an odd sensation to have two separate reactions to Stone. Aralynn loved that he was behind her. For a wolf, anything at the back of the neck gave rise to all kinds of reactions and pleasures. Yet as Rosamunde, the spooning embrace felt so warm and comforting that she never wanted to leave.

As he began to lick her neck in long swipes of his tongue, shivers chased up and down her shoulders and back, her sides and even all the way to her toes.

She closed her eyes, savoring everything, his tongue, his body, his arousal, his maleness, the strong virile scent of him. Oh, sweet Goddess, the way he smelled, like a flowing stream over mossy rocks.

She ached now deep between her legs and her mating vibration was leaping around as though not understanding why Stone's frequency hadn't joined hers.

I'm going to bite you. His voice in her head made her gasp. His fangs struck and she cried out.

If she'd thought she was feeling sexual before, the feel of him sucking heavily on her neck had her knees turning to water. She could hardly hold herself upright.

Fortunately, he had an iron grip around her and kept her from falling. His free hand slowly moved to her breasts and began to massage. She wasn't even sure he was aware of what he was doing.

But it felt so good.

She covered her hand with his and helped him so that soon she was arching her back and pressing her bottom into his erection.

His hips began to rock. She couldn't help the veil of violet mist that she began to release to create even more privacy. She wasn't sure if they'd take things all the way, but she wanted to be ready.

You think I'm going to fuck you, Rosamunde?

I don't know. This feels beyond us both right now.

Like hell. He suddenly drew back and licked the wounds on her neck, then pulled away from her. He even turned his back on her.

She felt his anger and disgust all over again. Her mist evaporated and a cold sensation began to flow down her body. She didn't recognize it at first but soon thought it felt like grief again, her friend from childhood, her torment.

She still seemed to be paying for what Margetta had done to her all those centuries ago, meeting her at the edge of the veil of mist in order to force Evelyn into the open. No doubt Margetta had used her fae abilities to mesmerize her and therefore to make it impossible for Evelyn to do anything else but to leave Ferrenden Peace and battle her sister to save Rosamunde's life.

Now, Stone had shut her down completely because of Margetta's torturous visions. Would she never be free of her aunt?

She was about to tell Stone that she would return to the castle to await the usual prescience that would define their next mission. But just as she opened her mouth to speak, Vojalie appeared in front of them and she looked frightened. "You both have to return to the castle now. If we're to save the Nine Realms, you must both be there."

Stone turned toward Rosamunde and even moved closer to her as he addressed Vojalie. "You've had a vision?"

"A definitive one."

Rosamunde grabbed for Stone's hand and he didn't reject it. "What's the nature of the vision?" She asked.

"Margetta somehow finds the castle and attacks it. You've got to be there, both of you, to stop it. And clear the castle as soon as you arrive. I'm returning to Davido at Joseph's. We're struggling tonight. For reasons I can't explain, holding the veil of mist intact is proving extremely difficult."

Rosamunde felt dizzy. "Then Margetta is getting closer to breaking through to Ferrenden Peace."

"It appears she is." As quickly as Vojalie had come, she vanished.

~ ~ ~

Rosamunde, still holding Stone's hand, looked up at him. "Will you come to the castle with me?"

"Yes. Of course. I trust Vojalie implicitly."

Rosamunde felt the cutting nature of his words, designed no doubt to remind her of his opinion of her. But she didn't care about that at all right now. She trusted Vojalie as well and knew that whatever was about to happen in Ferrenden Peace or how Margetta would be able to attack the castle had to be addressed right now.

"Ready?" she asked.

He nodded solemnly. "Let's go."

She teleported him to the castle grounds on the southeast side of the royal property.

To Rosamunde's surprise, Vojalie joined them at nearly the same time then quickly took Rosamunde in her arms. She held her close and pathed, *What happens this night will determine the fate of the Nine Realms. You'll need to be very brave. Tell me you understand.*

Rosamunde drew back. She'd never seen Vojalie this distressed. She didn't understand either why she couldn't have said these things to Stone as well. *Of course.*

Vojalie pivoted slightly to address Stone. "Davido and I will be at Joseph's and will do everything we can to keep the veil of mist in one piece. Stone, I ask only one thing of you, to remember that the power of love is much greater than any other force in our world, than any seductive, exalted vibration could ever be. Remember that!"

Stone appeared as though he wanted to answer Vojalie, but the lovely fae woman vanished once more.

Just as Stone had done earlier, Rosamunde turned in a slow circle extending her fae senses in order to see if she could detect any intruders. But the garden felt very safe to her. She immediately pathed with the head of her Castle Guard, and had him start evacuating the castle. Her staff would make use of escape tunnels that led a mile distant to the west.

The royal lands were a noisy place at night as the Nine Realms night birds swooped here and there, fighting for territory and the best nesting sites.

Yet a moment later, a wave of silence suddenly swept over the garden.

Stone pathed, *Rosamunde, what's happening? Why have the birds stopped chattering?*

Rosamunde knew now why Vojalie had come to her and why she'd insisted that Stone be with her. She turned to face him as the first dagger-like strikes of pain pierced her mind. *Stone, this is a Margetta vision.*

You mean, like the one you had about Charborne just before my parents were slaughtered.

She nodded solemnly.

Stone glanced down at his feet. *But the earth is rumbling as well. Is that normal?*

No. She shook her head. *I think, in fact, I know this is about you. Margetta has come for you. The vision that will arrive is meant to tempt you.*

He glanced around. *Is she here? I thought you told me that with these visions, she could only get here if you communicated during the vision.*

No she's not here and yes, it's my belief that a single telepathic thought directed anywhere beyond either of us right now will allow her to enter Ferrenden Peace.

She grabbed the sides of her head. Tears rolled down her face as the pain grew in strength. When the elf-lord power hit at the same time cramping her legs, she threw her head back and screamed.

Stone grabbed her and when he did, the elf-lord power began to channel away from her and at least part of what she was suffering dissipated quickly.

Though she was in agony as though her skull was about to explode, she could sense just how much Stone was savoring the elf-lord power.

This was very much about Stone and Vojalie's words now made sense.

Margetta's voice suddenly penetrated her mind. *This is your last chance, Rosamunde, the last vision I'll ever send you. I know of your love for the Mastyr of Tannisford, so it seems only fitting that I destroy what he loves most.*

The vision was suddenly on her and in it she watched

a series of images as Margetta's army swept down on Stone's Communication Center. She watched as bombs exploded and the building collapsed completely. Margetta had never used explosives before, but it appeared she would tonight.

Rosamunde trembled. She heard the screams of the women and the terrified shouts of the men as they failed to evacuate the building.

Through her pain, she lifted her gaze to Stone. What she saw there frightened her beyond words. His eyes were wide and his skin glowed with the elf-lord power. "Stone, you're seeing the vision."

He nodded. "All of it."

Rosamunde squeezed his arms hard. "Don't do it! Please, don't contact your people. Can't you feel that Margetta is focused on us right now, because of the vision? She's doing this to get a fix on our location."

He sneered. "You keep forgetting that I'm not like you. I can't let these people die. I won't and now I can prove to you how wrong you've been all these centuries."

She tried one last time. "If you contact your center or any of your men, Margetta will come straight here, to us. Then she'll have the two things she covets above everything else: She'll have you and she'll have access at last to the source of the elf-lord power."

He gripped her arms in return as though locking her in battle. His hair began to writhe as the elf-lord power moved through him stronger than ever.

"You're a coward, Rosamunde, and now you're going to see what you've really done to the Nine Realms all this time."

"Stone, please. Don't do this!"

But Stone only smiled.

Chapter Fourteen

Stone felt … exultant. Victorious. He could now prove how wrong Rosamunde had been all these years then she could live in shame the rest of her life.

He didn't know what it was, maybe being so close to the castle and to the elf-lord power, but he could feel the heavy vibrations all around him now. He knew then he could become a true conduit.

His muscles flexed and un-flexed. He moved slowly around the garden, savoring the feel of the elf-lord vibrations.

And Rosamunde was right. Margetta was with them; here, yet not here, like a sticky syrup clinging to the onslaught of the terrifying visions.

"It doesn't matter if she's intent on coming for me tonight. The only thing that matters is the safety of my people. I'll battle the Ancient Fae to the death, if I have to."

"Stone, it's not that simple. I'm telling you, once she gets in, she'll attach to the elf-lord power and we'll lose the Nine Realms. Why won't you believe me?"

He lifted a hand to her. "Enough! I'm not letting Margetta destroy my Communication Center."

He closed his eyes and opened his telepathy. At the same moment, he brought Rosamunde into the pathing stream as he contacted Harris. *Get all of our people out of the Com Center. Margetta intends to reduce it to rubble. Harris do you hear me?*

But nothing returned and his heart rate doubled.

Harris. Talk to me.

Rosamunde remained silent, but she was trembling and tears flowed down her cheeks.

Harris?

But that's as far as the communication got because the next moment, a golden light filled the entire garden and suddenly Margetta was right in front of him. Her stench filled the otherwise fragrant space, but she was beautiful in a scarlet velvet gown with her blond hair arranged in immaculate ringlets that hung to her waist.

He drew Rosamunde close to his side and kept moving her backward away from the Ancient Fae.

Once more, he tried to reach Harris. *Are you there? Evacuate the Communication Center. Now!*

Margetta's violet eyes were enormous as she glanced between him and Rosamunde, then downward toward the earth.

Her eyes glittered like diamonds. He felt her begin to draw in the elf-lord power. She spread her arms wide and arched her neck. She gave a cry of sheer ecstasy. "The power of the elf-lords is everything I knew it would be. Isn't it amazing, Mastyr Stone?"

When the first wave of power passed through her, she drew in a deep breath then focused all her attention on him, extending her arms in his direction. "I knew I could count on you to finally reveal the location of Ferrenden Peace. Rosamunde has been ridiculously stubborn for the past millennium. She was always such a good girl. But you and me, Stone, we're alike and it's time to join forces.

"I've felt it for several weeks now, who you really are in this world: One of the last two remaining elf-lords and together, we'll rule the Nine Realms because tonight, you'll be mine."

Now that Margetta had attached to the elf-lord power, her golden light began to pulse. *Look at me, Stone. Come to me. Join with me. Taste for yourself what it is to fully be an elf-lord. For I have the power to deliver it to you as my niece never could. Come to me and feel what your father, Kaden, has experienced all his life.*

Stone began to move in her direction. In some part of his mind, he knew Margetta was enthralling him, yet he couldn't stop his feet. Power flowed from her, tasting of both her incredible abilities and what she now streamed from Ferrenden Peace. She was as much a conduit as Rosamunde yet so much more.

"Stone!" When Rosamunde grabbed at him, he pushed her hands away from his arms. Still, she clung to him, yelling things that he couldn't quite hear. He wanted no part of such a weak woman. She wasn't a fit mate for an elf-lord.

When she continued to shout at him and grabbed both of his arms hard, he turned and shoved her with all his might. She didn't just fall backward, she flew into the air, then vanished.

Good riddance. He was done with her for so many reasons.

You did the right thing. My niece was a weight around your neck, holding you back. This is your moment, Stone, and yours alone. She lifted her arms in a dramatic gesture then moved close enough to touch him lightly on both shoulders. *Let the elf-lord power flow.*

The same power that Rosamunde had channeled tripled in

strength. This time his back and neck arched and he shouted. What he felt was an extraordinary rush of power, a vibration like none other. Ecstasy flooded his mind and he could see into the future. He sat on a throne much grander than Rosamunde's, with the beautiful Margetta beside him. She was right; he would rule beside her. Together, they'd conquer the Nine Realms.

Suddenly, Rosamunde's voice entered his mind. *This isn't the future, Stone. Margetta has overlaid your mind with her own vision. Think this through. She'll bond her mating vibration to yours, she'll have continual access to the elf-lord power because of you, then she'll do as she pleases. Remember, that she killed her own sister. Think! And rumor has it, she killed her husband, Gustave. She's been planning this for a long time.*

His mind cleared just enough that he knew what Rosamunde said was true. He backed away from Margetta, breaking contact with her, but another wave of her channeled elf-lord power engulfed him.

The power took him into the air, spinning him slowly and filling him with a lust he'd never known before. He craved to hold each of the realms in the palms of his hands, to set the ruling mastyrs beneath him in a way that they'd never doubt his dominance. He experienced a profound need to rule everything in his realm, in all the realms; the industry, the arts, commerce, the news outlets, everything.

He knew what he could accomplish, the elaborate mansion and estate he would build in his own honor. He'd set the trolls and elves to laboring for centuries. And they'd do it for love. They would worship him as their ruler.

These thoughts spun in his mind the way the power kept him

moving slowly through the air. He emitted a glow like Margetta, only his was silver.

Stone, hear me! Rosamunde again. He wanted to cut her off, but there was an odd part of him that refused. She continued, *The elf-lord power is a seduction, like Davido said, and it must be fought, it must be conquered.*

He needed her to understand. *Rosamunde. I see everything now as it should be. It's my destiny to rule the Nine Realms. Try to imagine the beauty and order I could create.*

But think what you're saying, Stone. You never cared about such things. You only wanted to serve and protect your people, to help them be safe enough in their lives so that in turn they could live as free realm-folk, to order their own lives. Remember what Margetta did at Charborne?

"*What's going on, Mastyr Stone?*" Margetta's voice coupled with telepathy took him away from Rosamunde.

He found he'd stopped spinning. He looked down at her from his elevated position. He was thirty feet in the air and she hovered just above the garden lawn.

His mind flew back to Charborne, remembering that Margetta had ordered a massive attack on the village and surrounding farms. Margetta had killed his parents.

But Margetta hit him with another wave of the elf-lord power and his mind exploded with pleasure all over again and he wanted more of it. She rose in the air to levitate beside him.

"*Look and see what we'll be able to do.*" She pivoted to face the castle. He could hear the earth rumbling as she channeled more of the elf-lord frequency. It grew louder and louder.

She held up both hands and her battle frequency flew from

her hands in lightning bolts of gold. Each streaked toward the top ramparts of the castle and exploded the thick gray stone blocks. She kept firing and the explosions continued. Fire engulfed the wooden ceilings and floor supports.

His brain was drenched with chemicals now that felt too good to be denied. He wanted this kind of power that could tear apart enormous blocks of stone as though they were nothing.

"How do I access the elf-lord power myself because I want it?"

Margetta smiled. "You've earned this, Stone. You've sacrificed for centuries and now you'll receive your reward. Come."

She beckoned him forward then planted a hand on his shoulder. With her touch, the elf-lord power flowed into him in an even greater way. He was consumed by the power as he took it in, drank it in, soaked it in into every pore of his being. This was what he was always meant to be: An elf-lord.

Something hard struck his back.

Rosamunde. Again.

What the fuck?

She wrapped her arms around his neck and her legs around his waist. She held on forcefully, then pathed and spoke aloud as Margetta had. *"Don't do this, Stone! Think who you are in this world, who you really are! You're the man who helped shape the Federation of the Nine Realms. You've fought against Margetta for centuries. She's the one who killed your parents and tens possibly hundreds of thousands of realm-folk. For the love of the Goddess, think! Come back to yourself!"*

"Leave him alone, Rosamunde! The vampire is mine."

Stone's mind cleared just enough to feel Margetta's battle power strike Rosamunde, while she clung to his back. She had to be in enormous pain, but still she held on. *Don't do this, Stone.* Her telepathic voice sounded weak and she no longer spoke aloud at the same time.

Please, Stone. I love you so much and I want you to be the man, the vampire, you've always been, a man of service and honor. Margetta will use you and cast you aside.

He felt Margetta siphon a new stream of elf-lord power then ramp up her battle energy again.

When she fired, Rosamunde screamed then slid off his back, tumbling to the ground. He whirled and found her face down, burned all along one side of her body where Margetta's power had struck.

The sight of her did something to him and the pleasure that clouded his mind began to dissipate. He dropped to his knees and touched her shoulder. He let his own healing energy flow, but even amplified by the elf-lord power, it wouldn't be enough to restore her.

What was he doing here?

He saw the silver glow coming off his arms. Margetta was with him. She was flooding him with the elf-lord energy so that his mind had begun transforming and not in a good way. He was in severe danger of becoming an elf-lord.

He looked back at the Ancient Fae. "She'll die if she doesn't get help."

Rosamunde didn't have to come back to the garden, to throw herself on him, to try to stop him from this madness. Rosamunde was the one who had sacrificed for a thousand years, not Stone. He'd served, but she'd lived in Ferrenden Peace, a life so solitary he didn't know why she hadn't lost her mind centuries ago.

"Let her be, Stone. She's nothing to us."

"She doesn't deserve to die."

"There are many tragedies in a war. My niece has always chosen the wrong side. Your parents didn't need to die. If Rosamunde had just contacted anyone in your realm, I would have aborted the mission. She's the cause of your parents' deaths, not me. You need to remember that."

He felt the Ancient Fae's hand on his shoulder once more and again, the elf-lord power flowed. He understood now why the original elf-lords had succumbed. Worse, he didn't know how to resist the pleasure that flooded his mind.

But what had Vojalie said to him? Embrace the power of love.

Though the seductive nature of the elf-lord power worked in every part of his being, he forced himself to remember all the evil Margetta had spread throughout the Nine Realms for the past millennium. For as long as he could remember, the Invictus – her creation – had terrorized his world. Had his people ever known a moment's peace because this woman was intent on conquering the Nine Realms?

Margetta had killed Rosamunde's mother, which in turn forced Rosamunde to spend centuries sustaining a veil of mist that would prevent the very thing Stone had just brought down on the Nine Realms. And he'd done it because he was stubborn, arrogant and impulsive.

Margetta now had her own, permanent access to the elf-lord power. She'd created a path to Ferrenden Peace through which she'd be able to return at will and take from the infinite source. She might even, as Rosamunde could, access the power from all other parts of the Nine Realms now that she'd established the connection.

Embrace the Power

Despite how strongly the elf-lord power called to him, he chose in that moment to follow Vojalie's path.

He reached deep inside himself and found love, a very deep permanent love that Margetta could never understand. He loved the Nine Realms. He loved his world. He loved the realm-folk that he'd served from the time he could remember, even long before he joined the Tannisford Vampire Guard.

He also loved the woman lying at his feet, barely conscious, but shaking and moaning. She'd thrown herself on his back, knowing what she risked, to help him return to himself.

He turned toward Margetta. "I won't go with you. I won't embrace this horrendous power. I won't become an elf-lord, or rule beside you. I'm staying here, with Rosamunde." He drew in a deep breath and squared his shoulders, ready to fall when she struck him down with her deadly battle energy. Enhanced as it was, he was no match for her.

Margetta's beauty suddenly distorted as rage took her over. Her violet eyes turned black, her gold hair flew around in twisted writhing strands. She lifted both her hands, forming them into claws as she drew in the elf-lord power. Black and gold sparks flew from her fingertips.

Tonight, he would die.

His life rolled through his mind like a deck of cards flipped in his hands. He saw Davido sneaking into his room at night, talking to him, when he was very young. Davido had always been there. He saw his wonderful troll parents who had loved him like their own and who had rebuilt their house at least three times to accommodate his enormous size compared to their five-three heights. He saw the first wraith-pair he ever fought. He'd only been fifteen, but he'd had all this ability from the time he could remember. He saw his first few weeks in the Vampire Guard and how much he loved being among a band of warriors, of like spirits and minds.

On the brisk memories flowed, of the various women he'd loved at times, though his heart had always remained with the Guard and to his commitment to fight for his fellow realm-folk.

Images of his parent's funeral pyre came next, of the depth and longevity of his grief. Then his rise to mastyr status came and he knew it wouldn't be long before he surpassed the then ruling Mastyr of Tannisford. He'd spent the next several months searching out every corner of the realm to learn its geography. He visited every village in his spare hours, every town, every outlying farm.

He recalled the agony of the crippling stomach pain that accompanied mastyr level blood hunger, then most recently the arrival of Aralynn and the discovery she could ease that suffering because she was a blood rose.

Now he was here, with Aralynn as Rosamunde, lying on the ground behind him, moaning softly in her own dying pain.

Death would come from those black and gold sparks flying around Margetta's hands and there was nothing he could do. Even if he revved up his own battle energy, Margetta would slay him. He knew it in the same way Rosamunde had always known that Margetta's visions had been a heinous burden intended to open a pathway into Ferrenden Peace.

But it was better to die than to spend even a second bonded to Margetta.

Margetta suddenly began to spin, creating a gold whirlwind and he wondered how painful his death would be.

Before Stone knew what had happened, he was spinning as well and rising into the air with her. He tried to stop, to return to the garden and Rosamunde, but he was caught up in Margetta's fury and her newly acquired elf-lord power and there was nothing he could do.

~ ~ ~

Rosamunde lay shivering on the lawn, the flames from the burning castle flickering oddly on the nearby shrubs. Through her pain, her fingers clutched at the grass. Tears trickled but not because of her suffering. Instead, she knew tremendous relief that in the end, Stone had rejected Margetta's offer. He'd even thought he would die.

So had Rosamunde.

But Margetta had taken him away in a whirlwind of black and gold light.

She took shallow breaths, the best she could do.

Her thoughts became fixed on Stone. Because Margetta hadn't killed him, she no doubt had other plans which probably meant enthrallment or torture or a combination of both to bend Stone to her will.

But where she'd taken him, Rosamunde didn't know.

She had to find out and she had to help him, though she had no idea how she could possibly counter Margetta now that the Ancient Fae had channeled elf-lord power. Rosamunde couldn't imagine just how much stronger Margetta had become.

But before she could do anything to change the situation, she had to survive the agonizing burns.

She knew one man who could help her. She teleported just

as she was, smoking clothes and all, to Joseph's front yard. If she'd been able to land inside she would have done so. But Joseph had his no-special-powers rule protecting his house.

She then reached telepathically for Davido. *I need Kaden's healing power. I'm outside.*

Just as Davido, in Kaden's form, appeared beside her, the small door to Joseph's underground abode banged open. "You can't bring her inside, unless she pays a toll."

"Joseph, you'd better get your trolley or I will ring your fucking neck."

Joseph levitated just above Kaden's shoulder to stare down at her. She was shaking badly and looked up at him. "Sweet Goddess, you look like a fried turnip. What happened?"

She could barely talk, but she managed anyway. "I was cooking and caught on fire. What do you think?"

Joseph made a fat raspberry sound. "No need to be sarcastic. Besides, I hear you can't cook so maybe it makes sense."

Kaden gripped Joseph by his reedy neck and shook him twice. "Stop it. Let us both in, or I'll finish you off for good and I'll auction every last bit of your stolen wares so that your wife won't get a cent."

"As if you ever would." He offered a crooked smile. "Fine. But I'm only doing this for my wife's sake."

The corner of Kaden's lips twitched. "Now who's being sarcastic?"

Joseph waved an arm and Rosamunde felt the spell break. She was then moving through his home at lightning speed. Kaden had control of her now and she began to relax. Help was at hand.

She ended up on the same marble slab as Stone before her,

though it had a motor oil smell to it this time. Whatever else forest gremlins were, they were a busy, restless sort, always doing. Maybe he'd been working on something he'd stolen recently.

But the shaking returned, harder than ever. Kaden placed both hands on the top of her head and a cool flow of healing eased the burns. She cried out from the relief of it.

After a moment, she said, "Kaden?"

"Yes, Sweetheart?"

Tears trickled once more. "Margetta has him. She took Stone away after he refused to become an elf-lord."

"I know. Vojalie saw it in a vision."

"I should speak with her."

When she tried to get up, he pressed her back down. "Let me get you healed up. Now, I'm going to do something, but don't worry about it." She almost asked, 'Worry about what', but she felt a pressure on her head, then a stream of something that felt like the best wine she'd ever drunk in her life. She began to float, then she disappeared into a deep sleep.

~ ~ ~

Stone was colder than he'd ever been in his life. Margetta had him stripped down to his leathers and shackled to the wall of an ice cave. He was barefoot as well and his extremities had frost-bite. Though he was grateful he still had on his pants, he swore his cock had crawled up into his body to keep from freezing straight off.

She sat on a lounge about fifteen feet away, wrapped up head-to-toe in silver fur. Near her, several slaves kept a brazier heated up with white-hot coals. In the bed of coals was a single branding iron.

He'd never been this close to the Ancient Fae before. Some of her beauty seemed to have faded. In fact, she looked old, something very unusual in their world unless a realm-person was approaching the final years of life. Was it possible?

She sat up slightly, pulling her furs closer around her neck. "I see you're noticing the wrinkles. It's a waste, isn't it? That we live such a long life then succumb to old-age just like a human. I feel like I've barely gotten started and now it looks as though I've only got a couple of years left. Ah, well, I intend that you and I will make the most of it." She rose to her feet and drew the poker from the fire. The tip had a figure eight on it, the symbol of infinity, and it was red hot.

She moved slowly, her lips pursed. Her violet eyes were now a muddy color, almost brown-gray, and not pretty at all. Her lips turned down as she got closer. Getting within inches of him, she glared. "Did I tell you Gustave is dead? I killed him a week ago in anticipation of bonding with you. Now, of course, having awakened with my aging issue, I wish I'd kept him alive. He was the one who created the Invictus bond in the first place. He was a great scientist. He might have been able to discover a serum or something to correct my growing disfigurement. Ah, well. I will simply have to make the most of what I have left."

She looked him up and down. "And I definitely intend to make the most of your body. You're built, Stone. A masterpiece among the male species."

If there'd been any way he could have killed himself in this moment, Stone vowed he would have done it. "I'll never bond with you, Margetta. It's that simple."

She smiled then lifted the poker to eye-level so that he could see the heated end. She then jammed it into his cheek and held it there. He felt the burn over his entire face and deep into his bones. But he gritted his teeth, refusing to utter a sound.

She tossed the poker on the floor and he heard her minions scramble for it. They no doubt knew to keep the poker ready at all times. Margetta wouldn't hold back on punishing any of her servants, if she felt the need.

Margetta remained close to him and stroked the uninjured side of his face. "You're mine, Stone. No one will find you here, ever. And I have a thousand ways to make you take back your words. But let me give you another taste, only this one will be sweet."

With his face throbbing, he steeled himself.

He felt the earth rumble and her troll minions screamed in fear. But he knew what it was. She drew the elf-lord power into herself then it flowed into Stone's mind. Everything he'd felt earlier in the castle garden he experienced again. It was as though for a man with elf-lord capacity, the power hit every pleasure center his brain possessed, and then some.

Even the agony of the branding disappeared with so much feel-good coursing through his body that he moaned.

"You like that, don't you?" Margetta leaned in and sniffed his skin then licked a line up his cheek. "Be with me, Stone. Take what belongs to you. We can make the Nine Realms anything you want it to be. Just join with me, accept your birthright, and let's fly to the heavens together."

Despite the seductive nature of the power, he forced his mind to focus on Rosamunde and what it had been like to be with her, to fight beside her when she was Aralynn and later as Rosamunde. He loved her spirit and her willingness to battle for what she believed. He knew now that learning to transform had given her freedom. Davido had been at the heart of it, helping her through the process. Davido, the wisest of the trolls and an elf-lord who had killed off all the cruel ruling elf-lords.

He understood now why it had been necessary for him to do so. The elf-lord power corrupted all who gave themselves fully to it.

The pain in his cheek slowly began to return, as well as the agony of hanging in shackles, and the freezing cold against his skin.

He shook his head. "Margetta, I will never join you. I can't. I love another."

Her aging features twisted in derision. "My niece? She's as weak as her mother, Evelyn. And you're a fool to give two thoughts to her, never mind your heart. But don't you understand, if you don't join me, I'll have to kill you."

At that, he lifted his chin and met her gaze full on. "Then have at it."

~ ~ ~

Rosamunde sat on the edge of the marble slab, just as Stone had three nights ago. He would have died if she hadn't brought him here. She would have died as well, if Kaden hadn't used his healing arts to restore her burned skin.

She held a change of clothing in her hands that Joseph had brought to her. Not surprising, they were Aralynn's clothes, pilfered from her cottage. But all she could do was laugh as she slid off the slab, removed her ruined clothes and put on battle gear once more.

Joseph had even provided her with one of her first daggers, the one she'd 'lost' the first week she'd moved into the cottage.

When she headed back to the front rooms, she found Davido seated in the chair by the window with Joseph perched on his shoulder. They were doing a crossword puzzle together. "You can't use proper names, not in this puzzle. It says so at the top."

"Where?"

Davido pointed and Joseph leaned forward. "No Proper Names. Oh, so that's what that means." He blew a raspberry and for good measure added a gurgle from his throat as well.

It was strange thinking that Davido had been in his Kaden form just a few minutes ago and that he'd healed her. He looked up from the paper. "Your color is much better."

"I feel perfect. Thank you." She glanced around. "I thought Vojalie would be here."

Davido frowned. "She is, but she's deep in meditation for Stone's sake as well as for the fate of the Nine Realms."

He pinched his lips together and tears touched his eyes.

Rosamunde could see he feared for his son.

He rose to his feet and folded up the paper, which caused Joseph to spit and sputter. "I wasn't done."

He handed Joseph the paper who then levitated near the window where he remained. From the outside, the sill was at ground level, giving the home a basement feel. He opened the paper and continued studying.

Davido crossed the room to her and took her hands in his. "What are you going to do, my dear?"

Tears burned her eyes. "I don't know. I want to go after Stone, to find him, to bring him home, but how? Margetta probably took him to her base camp. And even if she didn't, I have no way of locating him. I was hoping you and Vojalie would be able to help me."

Davido squeezed her hands. "I'm afraid what happens next is on you. I have no way of looking into the future and Vojalie is doing her best. But she says she's blocked. We've suspected that Margetta has been interfering for some time. Rosamunde, you need to dig deep right now."

She shook her head, fear encasing her heart. "I don't know what to do, where to begin."

"Remember that Stone has your blood in him and that the blood rose power has unusual capacities for each couple. Maybe you should dwell on that."

With his three forehead ridges in tight rolls, Rosamunde realized how desperate Davido really was. And why wouldn't he be? He had no way of helping the man who was his son.

"So there's nothing you can do as one who channels the elf-lord power?"

Davido shook his head. "I'm not a fully realized elf-lord, which is one given completely to the power. And I've taken vows never to become one, not even for the sake of one of my children. Without that vow, I would have been executed a long time ago."

Rosamunde knew then that any hope she had of finding Stone truly was on her. "I'll leave you now. But I promise you that I'll do everything I can to bring Stone home. Okay?"

Two fat tears rolled down his cheeks. He levitated suddenly so that he could wrap his arms around her. He hugged her for a long moment. "I know you will."

She didn't wait for further conversation or good-byes, but

teleported straight to the cottage. She sat down on the end of the bed, moving her dagger sheath slightly so it didn't pinch her leg.

She focused all her attention on Stone and on what they'd shared together. It was hard to calm her pounding heart, to reach a place of serenity that would allow her to properly meditate and to consider the problem.

After several minutes, however, she reached a place of peace and to her surprise her fae instincts drew her suddenly to her mating vibration. Chills raced up and down her spine because she knew, *she knew*, that somehow the same stream of energy, so personal and sexual in nature, was the key. But how was she to engage with Stone if she couldn't locate him?

She rose to her feet and with her eyes closed, she extended her arms as though in supplication to the Goddess. She gave herself to the love she felt for Stone and let it fill her heart and mind. In doing so, her telepathic vibration began to hum, softly at first then growing stronger.

Without thinking, she turned toward the northwest, a direction facing a portion of Tannisford Realm, the part high in the Dauphaire Mountain Range. So high in fact that no matter the time of year, the peaks were always capped with snow.

She could feel him now though what she sensed was that he was close to death.

Her heart ached as she let the stream of her telepathy flow in his direction. On and on she sent what felt like a fragile string of hope toward the mountains and the snow.

She also knew the exact moment she reached him because a flow of energy returned in her direction that felt like Stone.

But it was so weak, too weak.

She didn't know what else to do except to try to talk to him. *Stone, I'm here and I'm doing everything in my power to locate you. My telepathy has found you, but Margetta's blocks are too strong and I can't pinpoint your location. Stone, please hear me.*

She stayed fixed in position, holding her mating energy open and repeating her plea.

But nothing returned to her.

No matter what, she'd keep trying. However, she broke her meditation long enough to contact Mastyrs Ian and Zane. She wanted them on call, as well as Davido, if she was finally able to determine Stone's exact location.

The men responded as she expected. Each would await her telepathic call to arms.

But was she too late?

~ ~ ~

Stone had branding burns over a large part of his upper body and the temperature seemed to be dropping. He'd thrown up several times and now shook all over. He felt death creeping up on him.

Margetta was looking more and more shriveled as she sank into her furs and waited as her minions continued to press the heated branding iron against his skin. Her eyes were closed. He realized she'd fallen asleep.

The three troll slaves who kept the fire burning and the iron hot, were miserable creatures, beaten into submission by their mistress. Each had mouthed their apologies to Stone when they'd seared his skin. He didn't blame them. He knew exactly what would happen to them if they disobeyed. He wished like hell that he could do something to save them.

He was weak now and at times confused. He kept hallucinating Rosamunde's voice in his head, *Stone, can you hear me? Please respond. If we work together, I'll be able to find you. Then I'll bring an army to get you away from Margetta.*

Death couldn't be far away, not if he was hearing things that couldn't possibly exist.

One of the minions had just finished sinking the brand into his flesh. The smell alone was hard to bear. But at least he'd have a few minutes before it would be hot enough to do its job again.

Stone! Please hear me! Stone, are you there? I want to bring you home. Please, talk to me. Tell me you're okay.

Though he hung forward in the shackles and his joints ached, though his feet were frozen and his blood sluggish, he realized it was an odd hallucination to invent a series of repeated urgings. Either that, or he was closer to death than he thought?

Besides, Rosamunde had a lot of power. Maybe she'd found a way to reach him?

Is that you, Rosamunde?

He really didn't expect a response. Yet Rosamunde's voice came through with startling clarity. *I'm here! Stone, I've been meditating and hoping we could reach each other.*

You're not dead? But you were burned so badly when Margetta took me away.

Kaden healed me.

Kaden. Davido. His birth father, his mentor. *Thank the Goddess.*

The unexpected connection to Rosamunde filled him with

hope and his energy began to rise. Yet at the same time, his heart hurt and he was filled with remorse. He'd been so harsh with Rosamunde, judging her badly because she'd refused to act on Margetta's visions. But here he was, shackled to a wall in an ice cave because he'd been so sure he could make a difference when she couldn't.

He'd been arrogant beyond words and so willing to believe the worst of her.

Yet, if he was truly honest with himself, he knew now that Davido was right, that he'd been using his bad-opinion of her to keep her at a distance. Beneath everything was his fear he'd lose someone again that he loved. His parents' deaths had strangled his heart, closing him off from meaningful relationships.

He'd thrown himself into his Guardsman missions because the harder he worked, the less energy he had to either feel his grief or to try to have a real relationship with a woman.

Well, what he had with Rosamunde was very real and they shared their love of the Nine Realms and an equal passion to keep their world free of tyrants. And he no longer wanted to hide from potential grief.

He wanted Rosamunde.

Can you forgive me? He asked.

For what?

He would have laughed if his cheeks weren't frostbitten and his lips frozen together. *For everything. I've been an arrogant ass.*

Stone, you are so forgiven. How could you have known what Margetta was truly capable of?

Is the Communication Center intact?

It's fine. You were what Margetta was after.

Then I was duped.

Yes, you were.

Rosamunde?

Yes? Her feminine, telepathic voice was like a balm on his soul.

I think I feared being close to anyone after my parents died. I kept telling myself that I had to make Tannisford safe first. That's why I was so willing to think the worst of you. It kept me from getting too close.

I know.

You do? He was surprised.

I'm not so different. On some level, it was easier to stay in the castle, to do my job, to not think about engaging in a relationship when at any moment Margetta could inflict another of her visions on me. I've born so much guilt, I didn't think I was worthy.

Margetta made you feel that way.

So many people died.

I know. We've born the same guilt. But I'm here now, Rosamunde.

Do you know where you are? Because even though we've made contact, I still can't determine your location.

He looked out the cave opening into the dark night sky. *I could be anywhere. I'm in an ice cave, but the location is beyond me. However, I have an idea. I don't know if it can work, but I want to try.*

Anything!

Stone loved her response. He realized she'd been this way from the beginning, always game whether in her Aralynn form or just Rosamunde. *How about we try to bond?*

You mean now? At this distance?

Well, we're not a couple of slugs, we have some power between us, and I have your blood in my veins.

Stone. I love you so much. I'd try anything right now and I mean it. The minute I can locate you, I'm bringing you home.

Margetta was still dozing by the brazier, her minions shivering and huddling together. Stone closed his weary eyes and focused on his mating vibration. It came to life easily despite his intense suffering. He reached for Rosamunde and at first it was as though he was trying to penetrate a dense fog and his frequency didn't know which way to go. *I've accessed my mating vibration, but it seems lost, maybe blocked. Have you engaged yours?*

I have, but like you, it can't reach very far.

He drew a deep breath. *What if you accessed the elf-lord power? I know it will hurt—*

Yes! And the pain won't matter, but I'm giving it a shot. Just be ready. Okay?

He watched Margetta stir, but she heaved a sigh and fell back into her slumbers. He felt certain that the moment she woke up, she would know what was going on and would disrupt the process. *Go for it. I'm with you. All the way.*

He waited and everything fell so silent he wasn't sure if Rosamunde was still there. But after a full minute, his own mating vibration began to hum with greater strength.

His gaze was glued to Margetta. She shifted her shoulders, but her eyes stayed closed. Even more lines had appeared on her cheeks.

Suddenly, his back arched as Rosamunde's mating vibration, full of the elf-lord power, headed straight for him. He could also feel her pain, so he immediately channeled the power. He could tell her relief was instantaneous.

Embrace the Power

When his mating vibration reached hers it felt like two waves crashing into each other for a brief moment then a full-on embrace. Nothing held back. The elf-lord power covered their vibrations. He went straight to the issue. *I bond myself to you, Rosamunde.*

And I, to you.

With complete acquiescence, it was as though the two frequencies melted into each other and became one.

He opened his eyes and saw everything as though it had been made new.

Dear Sweet Goddess! Stone, I've got a fix on you! And I'm not alone. I've got both Zane and Ian with me as well as Kaden. Your father has his hand on my head and he's sending healing through me. Can you feel it?

The stream hit him suddenly and his back arched again as warmth flooded him, protecting him from the frigid air. He felt his branding burns and frostbite start to heal. *Yes, it's working.*

But it was then that Margetta woke up with a start and leaped from her chair. "What have you done?"

He didn't answer the Ancient Fae. Instead, he pathed with Rosamunde. *The beast is awake, but I'm almost healed. Still in shackles, though.*

We're teleporting together, though I've created a protective mist. Be ready.

I am.

The ice cave filled suddenly with a violet glow and Margetta shrieked as she transformed into her wraith state. Rosamunde covered his body with hers. The cave was small so that the massive physical presence of Kaden, Ian and Zane took up a huge portion.

Each was lit with battle power, their hands outstretched

toward Margetta. She didn't hesitate to rev her energy up and the next moment her black-and-gold power sang through the air. But it was met with Kaden's, Ian's and Zane's in quick, hard response.

The result in the small space was an explosion that blew apart the ice cave and sent everyone within tumbling through the air.

The explosion freed Stone from his shackles. He righted himself quickly and caught one of the flailing trolls in his arms. He encompassed the group in telepathy. *Save the slaves.*

He watched Ian dive for another and Zane for the last one. They'd been held against their will for a long time, but Stone knew they could be rehabilitated.

Margetta, however, was gone.

Rosamunde levitated close to him and settled her hand on his shoulder. He spoke quietly to the troll, reassuring the slave that she was safe. He'd half-expected a battle, instead the woman wept against his shoulder. "Mastyr, I was taken from Tannisford three decades ago. Thank you for saving me."

"You're safe now."

He glanced at Rosamunde, who shivered in the cold air. He began descending swiftly to a lower altitude and Rosamunde tracked with him.

Both Ian and Zane, with their troll-slaves well in hand, flew close to Rosamunde as well.

As the group continued descending, Kaden drew up on his other side. *Glad you made it son.*

Me, too. And thank you.

This was Rosamunde's doing, Kaden pathed.

I want you to know that you were right, father. I'd used her supposed sins to keep my distance from Rosamunde.

Kaden nodded slowly. *And now you've bonded with her.*

I have.

He pinched his lips together and clapped Stone on the shoulder. *I'm glad for you. Rosamunde's a good woman and you'll be very happy. Now let's get these trolls to safety.*

Kaden then shouted at Zane and Ian. "Come over here and I'll get us back to Ferrenden Peace."

They flew toward him and once within a few feet, Kaden raised his arm and moved the entire group to the front walk of Aralynn's cottage. Stone set his shaking troll on her feet. "Stay here. We'll take care of you."

"Thank you, mastyr." But the slave dropped to her knees and embraced Stone's ankles then started sobbing.

Rosamunde drew close and dipped down to place her hand on the slave's head. Stone could feel her fae healing, something that touched the troll's mind and eased her. A moment later, the troll stood up and wiped her cheeks.

Kaden drew close. "Let me take care of the mastyrs and these trolls. I sense you need time with Rosamunde."

He held his hand out to his woman and she took it, drawing close. "I do." He smiled at her, his heart full of love, then turned to Kaden. "If you can take everyone to the Com Center and turn the trolls over to Harris, he'll know what to do."

He felt the elf-lord power begin to rumble, which meant a vision was coming. Both Ian and Zane, still cradling their trolls, glanced at Stone.

Ian shook his head. "What's going on? Why is the earth shaking?"

He explained in brief terms all that had happened with

the power that originated in Ferrenden Peace. He also had Kaden explain who he was. Each of the ruling mastyrs appeared dumbfounded, as they should be.

When the vision drew close, Rosamunde squeezed his fingers. *Shall we let it roll?*

He nodded and the moment she began channeling the elf-lord power, he let it flow through him. It was a milder version of the onslaught Margetta had delivered, almost tempered as though Rosamunde was a necessary filter. Maybe she was. Maybe her blood rose gift was the means by which he'd never fall victim to the seductive side of the elf-lord power.

Whatever the case, the vision began to move through his mind. He spelled it out for Ian and Zane. "In an hour's time, Margetta will bring her full army to the Plains of Tannisford, at the southern end near the Sea of Vermed."

Zane whistled.

Ian nodded solemnly. "What are your orders, Commander?"

Stone felt humbled by the appellation, a very different experience in contrast to the out-of-control ambitions that Margetta had delivered through the elf-lord power.

First, he shifted slightly to address Kaden. "Will you serve with us this time? We'll need help moving the full complement of the Combined Forces to the plains."

Kaden nodded. "I will."

He turned to Ian and Zane. "Go with Kaden to my Com Center and prepare each of the mastyrs, along with their Vampire Guards and Shifter and Troll Brigades for a final battle here in Tannisford. Kaden will help teleport the various units onto the field of battle."

He turned to Rosamunde. "Does this agree with what you're getting?"

She smiled. "One hundred percent."

Stone had one more act to perform before he dismissed the mastyrs. "And you, Kaden."

"Yes, son?"

Stone released Rosamunde's hand and embraced the tall elf. He hugged his father hard. "Thank you."

After a long moment, and a serious tightening of his throat, he drew back. Kaden smiled at him, his eyes brimming with tears. "Proud of you."

"And I'm proud that you're my father." He nodded briskly, then shifted his attention to the mastyrs. "This is it, men. Margetta will come at us full-bore. Let's get ready to take the bitch down."

Ian and Zane gave a shout. Even the trolls each added their whoops and raised fists. Kaden picked up the female troll that Stone had carried to the cottage.

Then just like that, Kaden spirited them back to Tannisford and he was alone once more with Rosamunde.

Chapter Fifteen

Rosamunde turned to face Stone. He extended his other hand to her and she took it so that now he held both. The elf-lord power still flowed, but it seemed to be a steadier, softer version than before. The bond of their mating frequencies was in place and more powerful than she could have believed possible. But more needed to be accomplished to cement the full Blood Rose bond.

Her fae instincts told her they would need to join physically and he would need to drink her blood. She knew it wasn't the same for every couple, but these elements had to be in place for the rest to happen for her and Stone. The forged bond would make it impossible for Margetta to ever get that close to Stone again.

"I'm glad we're here, in Aralynn's cottage. For me, my path to you began in this place."

"I'm sorry Margetta destroyed your castle."

She shook her head slowly "It was never mine. Not truly. I was a place holder as you know. From this night forward, you're my future. I served Ferrenden Peace to the best of my ability and now all I want is to be your woman, your blood rose, and to work alongside you to make the Nine Realms safe."

He nodded, releasing her hands but only so he could pull her into his arms. "I'm so sorry, Rosamunde. I used you badly because I was caught up in my grief. I know you've said you forgive me, but I want to be clear on this. I was at fault."

She put her hand on his lips. "All is forgiven, now and forever. You're the man who saved that busload of troll kids, remember? Everything else pales, including how you viewed me."

"It doesn't seem like enough."

She saw the deep remorse in his mossy-green eyes and sought for the right words to convey what she meant. "I was hurt that you thought so little of me. But I understood because you'd never walked in my shoes. You're a man of action in the truest sense. You chart a course; you go for it. How could you understand my horribly passive role in Ferrenden Peace? Or believe how much it hurt each time Margetta brought a vision to me?

"I'm trying to say that I understand who you are and now that I was finally given a more active role in the war as Aralynn I've come to understand who I am."

Stone stroked her cheek. "But a thousand years of living this life. How did you bear it?"

"The same way you bore the deaths of your parents: One tough day at a time."

He frowned and shook his head. "Sometimes I got so drunk I had to be carried home unconscious."

She thought her own confession wouldn't hurt. "And at times, I drank too much wine. But we're here now."

"Yes. We most definitely are."

~ ~ ~

Stone slid his hand behind Rosamunde's neck and kissed her. She moaned softly, leaning into him and when she parted her lips, he slid his tongue inside. A soft vibration enveloped him, one that felt all Rosamunde.

His mating vibration was now uniformly linked with hers. It was almost impossible to tell where one began and the other ended.

After a moment, he drew back. "Will you complete the bond with me, Rosamunde, as mastyr to your blood rose, as my vampire mate, as my woman, now and forever?"

Her lovely violet eyes were misty, full of love and something else. It took him a moment to recognize the emotion, but he felt it, too. It was joy, pure and without restraint.

"I will." She smiled suddenly. "Now take me to bed."

He chuckled, loving that the Aralynn part of her got straight to the point.

He lifted her into his arms, cradling her as he moved to the cottage door. The smallish dwelling, however, made it impossible for him to carry her over the threshold. He snorted as he set her on her feet, which made her chuckle.

"The cottage belonged to a troll."

"Thought as much."

She took his hand and he followed her inside, loving the feel of her palm against his as well as the sight of her mass of red hair flowing behind her.

Once within, he shut the door. When she started to strip, he saw no point in pretending there was anything else they needed to do right now. Of course his task was much simpler since he only wore his leathers.

By the time she was free of her clothes, he picked her up and tossed her on the bed. She laughed as she landed on her back.

As Rosamunde, she had a beautiful shape with an abundance of curves. His mating vibration, joined to hers as it was, sent thrills through his body, tightening his thigh and arm muscles.

He was already aroused as he stretched out on top of her. "You are so beautiful, my love."

She gasped softly. "Oh, you said that the same way Davido speaks to Vojalie. I love it."

He smiled. "I guess I did, didn't I? But I love you, Rosamunde, with all my heart."

She slid her hand into his hair, something he knew she loved to do. She leaned up and he met her with his lips, guiding her back down with the kiss.

This would be different, that's what he knew. He loved her and he was secure in her love for him. Rosamunde was *all in*. And he was too. There would be no holding back or recriminations because he feared losing her. He was fully present. Committed.

And *hungry*.

Facing death and hours of torture would do that to a man.

He drew back, sniffing her neck then licking. She writhed beneath him then grabbed at his shoulders, pulling him closer.

Do you want me, Rosamunde? He kept licking her neck.

As though I haven't been with you in decades. And my heart is heavy. I have what you need, Stone. Take it!

Stone reached low, took his rigid cock in hand and found her opening. Seating himself, he pushed inside her beautiful warm wetness. He was already on the verge and had to take a couple of quick breaths to keep from coming.

"I love you so much."

"I love you, too." She petted his hair, his shoulders, his arms. She rocked her hips slowly, pulling him deeper inside.

He was one with all his movements, the way his mating vibration pulsed through hers, the way he began to drive into her steadily, and the descending of his fangs, two sharp points, ready to pierce her.

Do it. She was panting, her body very still. *I want to feel you breach the vein and take what belongs only to you.*

Stone drew his head back slightly and opened his mouth wide. He struck to the right depth and felt the first pulse of blood flow into his mouth, warm and tasting woodsy and full of an herbal undertone. He groaned as he formed a seal around the small wounds. He began to suck, timing each thrust of his cock with the pull of his lips. He added the vibration she loved.

She cooed and moaned, then cooed some more. A warmth enveloped him. He opened his eyes to discover that her violet mist had wrapped them both up in a cocoon of privacy and pleasure. Everywhere the mist touched his naked body, shivers chased over his skin, adding sensation on sensation.

All the pieces of their bonding puzzle were now in place: Sex, the taking of her incredible blood, and the joining of their mating frequencies. They'd each acknowledged a desire to bond, and even the elf-lord power was still humming through them both.

He wasn't sure what was supposed to happen, but he almost didn't care, only that the bond formed as it should. Being this close to Rosamunde, and giving her pleasure, was enough for him.

When his thirst was slaked, he drew back slowly and licked the wounds. She was in a euphoric state, her brows high on her forehead, her violet eyes glowing softly.

She stroked his cheek with the palm of her hand. "Are you satisfied?"

"I am. More than I can say." He was stroking her low, sustaining the level of pleasure pervading the moment. The pinnacle hadn't yet been reached, but there was something very magical between them.

"I've never felt like this as though I'm floating in water and you're rocking me."

"I am rocking you." He smiled down at her as he pushed into her more firmly.

She smiled up at him. He saw love in her eyes.

"I want to go to the grotto."

"What? You mean, now?"

"I want to be in the central pool as we make love. I've seen something there for us. Are you willing, because I can take us with a thought, but we'll be in the water. And my mist will still cover us and warm us, in case you're concerned."

He didn't know why, but he knew it was the right thing to do. Rosamunde was fae and much more connected to the hidden magical elements of the Nine Realms than he was. "What if there's someone there?"

Her lips curved. "There won't be. And remember, this time is for us. We've been granted this hour."

He inclined his head. "Take us there."

He felt himself move, yet not move and in the blink of an eye, she was floating on her back, holding herself in the water through levitation and he was still connected to her. The violet haze of her mist covered and warmed them but he could still smell the sea and feel the push-pull of the waves. But even the sea was calm for them.

The grotto had been the last place they'd worked a mission together.

"The elf-lord power is rich here. Can you feel it, Stone?" She extended her arms in the water. He lifted her up so that she stayed connected to his cock. She wrapped her legs around his waist, holding him securely then balanced her arms on his shoulders. Her hair streamed water.

Because he was essentially standing, with Rosamunde riding him, he very slowly turned in a circle. "I can sense the elf-lord power all around us."

He could feel the layers of rock below the water start to rumble and the elf-lord power begin to flow. Only this time, it entered him as well as Rosamunde at the same time.

Her eyes went wide. "This is different. I always received it first. Now, it's together. Have we bonded?"

He nodded. "We're in the process of the bond, but I can feel something coming."

"Stone?" Her voice, very soft and sensual, drew his attention back to her. Her eyes were at half-mast. "I think you should kiss me."

Everything he felt for her coalesced in that moment. He desired her, he needed her, he wanted her.

His hips began moving on their own, driving into her well, making her his woman.

But the elf-lord power seemed to have a mind of its own

because suddenly, they were caught up in a cyclone of fast moving water, spinning yet safe in the vortex. The green stone of the grotto blended with her violet mist, coloring the cyclone.

He held her close, his heart swelling with ecstasy. He spoke aloud and pathed at the same time. *"Rosamunde, my love."*

"Stone, you're everything to me. I'm yours now and forever."

He kissed her and moved his hips swiftly, driving in and out. Their mating vibrations tightened. Ecstasy became a swift, mad rush.

"I'm coming, Stone."

"I'm with you, my darling." His hips slammed into her now and she held him tight around his waist with her legs.

She arched her head and began to cry out in long streams of pleasure. He could feel her pulsing around his cock.

He drove faster and suddenly his own release came. Intense pleasure shot through him, in heavy powerful waves. He shouted, then roared. The cyclone kept him moving fast as he gave Rosamunde everything he had.

Just as he began to come down from the high, he felt the bond lock into place like a latch turning.

She'd been fully arched away from him, her eyes closed, caught in ecstasy. But at the sensation, she lifted up to meet his gaze. "Did you feel that?"

"I did. Something like a dead bolt."

She began to laugh. "I expected the heavens to part, the angels to sing. Not the sound of a lock clicking in place."

She was so beautiful to him in that moment, precious in his eyes, the woman he loved. But how to tell her what he was truly feeling. "Well, I've had a different experience because I'm hearing the angels sing right now. I hear them in your voice. And the heavens have parted that they allowed me to know you and to love you as I do. Heaven is here, in your love for me and with the privilege of loving you."

"Oh, Stone, you are such a beautiful man in every possible way."

She threw her arms around his neck and kissed him. Nothing had felt more wonderful in his life.

~ ~ ~

When Rosamunde drew back, she held Stone's gaze for a long moment, savoring the rich, mossy color of his eyes and the profound glimmer of emotion that radiated from him. She could feel his love in the same way the water flowed around her. She'd felt her mother's love in this way as something that moved around her, comforting her, encouraging her.

Now she had Stone and not just in the normal way, but through a blood rose bond. She searched his face, then closed her eyes and traveled her mating frequency, loving the feel of how they were joined.

She went deeper. *Stone, are you with m? Can you see what I'm doing?*

I can.

She felt her way along the bond and found the location at the base of Stone's heart, a second pulse. She moved swiftly back into her own body and found the same thing, a steady, ruby-like pulse of love and joining, of mystery and magic, of everything she could ever want.

When the earth rumbled beneath the water and a second

wave of elf-lord power began to flow, she stayed within her fae abilities. Stone wrapped his arms arounds her securely.

It won't hurt anymore, she pathed. *That much I know. Because you and I are bonded, I'll be able to channel like you. And I suspect when the visions come, you'll always see them at the same time.*

His voice penetrated her telepathy. *We're sharing our powers now.*

Yes, we are.

But I feel something else, Rosamunde, that our joined powers have increased.

As the second wave of elf-lord power struck, she opened her eyes and met his. Her heart began hammering out a level of excitement she could hardly contain. "Stone, I think together you and I might be able to defeat Margetta."

His lips curved. "I think this was what she was after. She wanted to bond with me because of this level of power."

As the elf-lord power flowed through each of them, Rosamunde knew it was true. She could feel the difference in her bones, that what had been so difficult for her to achieve for the past thousand years, now seemed simple. "This was what I couldn't help you understand, how deeply I understood that I couldn't have battled Margetta on my own. But now, I know we have a chance to defeat her."

He kissed her again and once more she melted against his body, drinking in the pleasure of being loved by him.

But as she drew back, the elf-lord power began to create very specific images in her head of the Tannisford Plains. "Are you seeing this?"

"I am. The final battle."

"Yes."

Stone grinned. "Then I think we should get some clothes on."

She laughed and hugged him hard. She started to teleport him to her cottage, but he was before her and she landed with a surprising jolt at the foot of her bed.

"Stone, you took us here! This was you, not me."

"I know. Yup, we're definitely sharing abilities."

"I'm going to grab a shower."

He gestured west, toward Tannisford. "And I'm going to take a quick hop to my lake and pick up some clothes. I'll be back here before you know it." He kissed her once on the lips, then with a smile, vanished.

She went into the bathroom, turned on the shower, then took a few minutes to rinse the sea water off. Afterward, she didn't bother to use her hair dryer; there wasn't enough time. Instead, she towel-dried as best she could then arranged her damp hair in a single braid down her back.

When she was ready, she found Stone standing very still near the foot of the bed but clothed in fresh battle gear. She sensed he was communicating with the ruling mastyrs. He waved for her to come close and when she did, he slid his arm around her waist then pulled her into the telepathic conversation.

Rosamunde is with us. Ian, say again about Margetta's army.

She's been moving her wraith-pairs in large groups to the east foothills at the top of the plain.

Rosamunde knew the location well. Massive rocks formed a shelf that stretched for three miles in both directions. Margetta couldn't have chosen better. Her army could scramble back through the hundreds of pathways that led through the rocks and into the nearby cave-riddled hills.

Ian continued. *We have the Combined Forces still arriving in waves from every Realm. Davido and Vojalie have gone from realm-to-realm and have moved all the Vampire Guards and Shifter and Troll Brigades to the plains. I doubt Margetta expected that.*

Rosamunde agreed. She gripped Stone's waist tight. He met her gaze and nodded.

This was it.

The final battle.

Whatever happened here tonight would determine the next thousand years for the Nine Realms.

Rosamunde and I will be at the promontory near the Sea of Vermed.

Ian's voice strengthened. *All the mastyrs are assembled there, Commander. We're awaiting your orders.*

At these words, Rosamunde felt Stone's shoulders lift slightly and his spine straighten a bit more. She was proud of him, of what he'd achieved in bringing all the ruling mastyrs together. It was always believed that a unified Nine Realms would be impossible given the fiery nature of the mastyr vampire.

But the blood roses had come, tempering each man, while adding power on power. Rosamunde thought it a beautiful juxtaposition, even a paradox that while the men gained power through their women, they also developed an ability for a kind of collaboration that had never happened before.

We'll head your direction shortly.

Yes, Mastyr. The latter was a group response, a flow of

masculine telepathic voices that filled Rosamunde's heart with pride and hope.

Rosamunde felt Stone shut the telepathy down. He turned toward her and kissed her again. "I want you safe."

She loved the level of his concern, but her lips curved. "To hell with that, my darling. I will do whatever needs to be done to rid the Nine Realms of Margetta forever."

His eyes glowed with a like spirit. He nodded several times in a row. "Then let's do this."

She let him teleport them both to the raised section of rocks at the base of the plain. The sea cliff wall, just forty yards behind them, was tall enough that the sound of the crashing waves was distant and muted.

As Stone released her waist and moved to the highest point, Rosamunde put a hand to her lips. She couldn't believe the massive size of the gathered armies.

In the far distance, toward the rocks, Margetta's wraith-pairs had already started making their usual racket, clanging their axes and swords together. The wraiths shrieked.

She noted that because of the discipline inherent in the Guard and Brigade ranks, Stone's Combined Forces remained still and steadfast against the growing noise. She sensed a profound determination emanating from the thousands of vampires, wolves and trolls that stood against the Ancient Fae's army this night.

Rosamunde had foreseen these elements in the vision. But her gaze continued to shift toward the southeast and an open area of the plain from which Margetta's golden wind had appeared in the prescient images.

With her gaze fixed in that direction, a sudden restlessness moved through the thousands of realm warriors of the Combined Forces.

Rosamunde knew the cause since a moment later Margetta arrived in a swirl of her gold wind. Not everyone would be able to see her, but Rosamunde could. The Ancient Fae was surrounded by at least a dozen mastyr vampire wraith-pairs, the cream of her army.

Stone, do you see them?

I do. The solemn response reflected his frame of mind more than anything else could have. Mastyr vampire wraith-pairs were impossible for a single ruling mastyr to defeat and here were a dozen, as well as Margetta, and all heading for their east flank.

Rosamunde became fixed on her aunt, the woman who had killed her own sister. Hatred wasn't quite what she felt for the Ancient Fae. The feeling was much broader and deeper. She despised the woman, who had all this amazing power and ability, but no heart or conscience. She'd killed countless realm-folk and enslaved thousands more.

She'd built an army by kidnapping unwilling realm-folk and turning them into monsters, ready to obey her will no matter what.

Maybe it was the sharing of Stone's powers, but as she watched Margetta, she knew what needed to be done. But would Stone agree to it?

You and I need to take Margetta on. What do you say?

~ ~ ~

Yes.

Stone felt Rosamunde's focus as though it was his own. His gaze, like hers, had become fixed on Margetta. A profound need to stay close to Rosamunde came over him, a sensation that felt more fae than vampire, elf or troll, another indication he was bonded to Rosamunde.

He drew close, though he didn't touch her. Instead, he felt the elf-lord power begin to rumble around the promontory.

So, we're doing this then, you and me?

We are. She smiled up at him. There wasn't a hint of doubt in her telepathic voice.

He switched mental paths and turned the reins of the army over to Ian.

What's your plan? Ian asked.

Stone brought Rosamunde into the telepathy. *Rosamunde and I are going after the Ancient Fae and her band of mastyr vampire wraith-pairs.*

Silence returned for a hard moment. He could almost feel Ian's vampire determination rising strong. *The ruling mastyrs will join you, including me. I've trained my seconds to handle our force and we've drilled as you've taught us to for months now.*

Stone needed another opinion. *Rosamunde, thoughts?*

Ian's right. We need all the ruling mastyrs involved. But there's something more.

What's that? Yet even as he asked the question, he knew the answer and his heart started thumping in his chest. *Holy fuck. Then as a group, all nine ruling mastyrs will share the elf-lord power.*

That's it.

Then nothing can stop us now.

The air boiled with excitement. Ian delivered Stone's orders and within seconds all eight mastyrs flanked Stone and Rosamunde, four on one side, four on the other. Stone explained what was about to happen, including a brief sketch of the elf-lord power that originated in Ferrenden Peace.

All the mastyrs levitated in a line at the promontory and he let the elf-lord power flow.

He sensed the thrill that each vampire experienced as the power hit. At the same time, he felt his bond with Rosamunde grow stronger, so much so that the elf-lord power sparked violet and green hues all around them. The world that was a place of energies and frequencies had united in this moment to form a formidable array against the most dangerous entity in the Nine Realms.

Margetta kept her mastyr vampire wraith-pairs circling around her. Stone knew it was more than just for protection. He could see things now he'd never seen before.

Margetta's power streamed in long rivers, reaching each of the pairs but also flying in heavy constant waves toward her army. It was no wonder she'd been after Stone. With what he'd experienced with Rosamunde, Margetta's abilities would have put them, as a couple, into the stratosphere.

Stone remained levitating with Rosamunde thirty yards away from Margetta. At half that distance, her mastyr vampire wraith-pairs waited. Margetta paid no heed to her Invictus security force, but continued to gather her power. She wasn't beautiful anymore now that her face was lined with deepening crags.

Rosamunde pathed, *She looks like a haggard witch. What happened?*

I'm not sure, but it started in the ice cave. The more she used the elf-lord power, the worse she became.

It's fitting somehow.

I would agree.

Though Margetta also now streamed the elf-lord power, he and Rosamunde were a match for her. They also had an advantage that Margetta didn't. He sensed that all the ruling mastyrs knew what was about to happen and each was ready. The blood rose bond they'd each achieved with the women given to them by the fates, had taught each man to be open, to trust, and to embrace the powers that came to him.

Power was what Stone summoned in bountiful waves. The elf-lord power might not have a mind, but their world had created a force by which the Ancient Fae could be defeated.

One with Rosamunde, together they continued to channel the elf-lord energy, dispersing it down the line both directions. The ruling mastyrs began to shout and raise their fists as each experienced the boost.

Margetta responded by revving up her power, which started flashing in brilliant gold and black streaks.

He gave the order to have the ruling mastyrs surround Margetta and her wraith-pairs. The mastyrs took up the same array as at Stone's private lake so that Gerrod was on the other side of Margetta, directly opposite Stone.

When the elf-lord power reached its pinnacle, Stone gave the order to commence fighting. Each man chose his target and the battle was on. Red and blue energies clashed midair and rose high in the dark night sky.

Stone let his battle power build in his hands and Rosamunde, now sharing his power, did the same. The time for taking Margetta on approached quickly.

A wave of pure gold energy streamed in the direction of

Margetta's army. He heard her army's battle cry and the Combined Forces almost at the same time.

Harris, tell me what's going on. I can't see the battlefield from my position.

Harris's voice came back strong. *We're advancing, most levitating in swift flight. The two forces will clash in three ... two ... one.*

Stone felt the mass collision as though he was in the mix himself.

The ruling mastyrs fought hard against the mastyr vampire wraith-pairs. Margetta fed those pairs with more power. Stone opened wider to the elf-lord power and channeled more and more of the powerful frequency to the ruling mastyrs. With that power, each mastyr was more than a match for the Invictus pairs.

Stone stayed close to Rosamunde and felt her level of concentration. She channeled the power as well, only she kept her full attention on Margetta.

Then he understood. This was for Rosamunde, to avenge her mother's death.

Take her, Stone commanded.

~ ~ ~

Rosamunde had never used her battle power before, but it felt as natural to her as if she'd been wielding the powerful frequency for centuries. She sensed Stone was feeding power to the ruling mastyrs, which gave her permission to focus on the woman who had caused so much trouble in the Nine Realms for as long as she'd lived in their world.

All her life, she'd known she was inferior to Margetta in power and even in the capacity to gain power. Now, because of her bond with Stone, she was her aunt's equal.

She lifted her arms and let her violet power flow. The moment it did, Margetta's eyes widened in alarm and she returned fire with massive waves of her black-and-gold frequency. The battling energies met in the middle, a colliding of vibrations that sent sparks rising hundreds of feet into the air.

Rosamunde couldn't believe the difference in her ability. She pathed to Stone. *I can hold Margetta like this indefinitely. Want to take advantage of it?*

Hell, yeah.

She felt Stone encompass the ruling mastyrs in group telepathy once more, while including her at the same time. *Rosamunde is holding Margetta in battle. Now's the time to finish off these pairs.*

The sudden resulting shift as the eight mastyrs doubled their efforts, began a cascade of failing mastyr vampire wraith-pairs. The elf-lord power was helping them to win the night.

Rosamunde never flagged, but kept her focus. Yet she could tell by the shrieking of the wraiths that the tide of battle had turned. From her periphery, she watched as the dying pairs began falling one after the other to the ground. It was a long way down, at least a hundred feet, so not much would remain of these deadly Invictus.

Margetta, part wraith, began to shriek as well, a sound that practically split the night sky in two. It was designed to disable a weaker opponent. But Rosamunde's time running missions with Stone, as well as a thousand years of waiting, had made her strong and she held her ground.

As each of the ruling mastyrs slayed a wraith-pair, soon the Ancient Fae lost her security team and was now surrounded by nine powerful mastyrs.

Rosamunde's arms sang with the power she wielded and still the sparks rose into the dark like an extraordinary stream of violet, gold and black fireworks.

She felt Stone shift his telepathy to Harris, though he included Rosamunde as well. *What's happening on the ground?*

Margetta's army is in disarray. We're not sure what's going on, but at least half her force has no will to fight and they've laid down arms. But we're pressing on, taking prisoners of those who've given up and continuing to battle against those who are still actively engaged in the fight. Whatever you're doing up there, keep doing it!

Stay after the army. Don't let up.

Yes, Commander.

Rosamunde finally understood the reality of Margetta's army, and why she'd pursued Stone as hard as she had: Margetta controlled her entire force through her own power. But having to use a portion of her energy to keep from being submerged by Rosamunde's battle power, she'd severed her connected to both the now defunct mastyr vampire wraith-pairs and a large portion of her army.

They were so close to taking her out for good.

As Rosamunde continued to fire at Margetta, the ruling mastyrs began moving in. Stone put his hand on her back and physically urged her forward. She moved with him and as she did, her battle energy increased.

Her arms shook with the level of the vibration that her battle energy created. Stone slid behind her and surrounded her with his body. The vibrations settled down quickly and her violet stream continued to grow in strength.

Stone's telepathic voice hit her mind in a group contact. *Ruling mastyrs, move low to use an upward angle to prevent crossfire, then release your battle power at will.*

She watched from her peripheral vision as all the ruling mastyrs levitated to lower positions so that each would utilize his battle energy in an upward trajectory. In that way, friendly fire could be avoided.

When the barrage began, Margetta tried to create a gold shield around herself, but each effort diminished the energy she could stream toward Rosamunde. She shrieked harder still as Rosamunde's battle energy hit her dead on.

It wasn't long before Rosamunde felt a breach in Margetta's power. The Ancient Fae was weakening. Rosamunde held her stream steady as did all the mastyrs.

Suddenly, Margetta's power gave way completely. And as all the battle streams hit her, she bucked in the air several times, screaming in agony. After a full minute, and no one relenting, the Ancient Fae floated in the air unconscious. With no counter-stream of power emanating from her, Rosamunde finally began to ease back and at last drew in her battle power.

Her body hummed from having had so much elf-lord power rolling through her. At last, she broke the connection and drew a deep sigh of relief.

I think we did it, she pathed to Stone privately.

He was still holding her from behind and he hugged her. "I believe we did."

Embrace the Power

~ ~ ~

Stone didn't want to let Rosamunde go. He loved that together they'd made this moment possible, that Margetta hung in the air, her velvet gown smoking from the terrible array of battle power she'd taken directly to her person. That she still levitated, though unconscious, indicated she wasn't yet dead. But even he could sense how close she was.

At last, the war was over.

Ian took charge and soon had a net that covered Margetta's body. With Margetta being towed down to the Tannisford Plain, Stone headed in the direction of the two armies. Rosamunde followed in Margetta's wake.

Stone could both see and hear that some of Margetta's army were still fighting. He called on Zane and Malik to join him in running the last few rebellious wraith-pairs to earth. From the beginning, he knew that there were some realm-folk who had joined Margetta willingly, including a large number of wraiths. Those that had fully embraced the Invictus bond were no doubt resistant to the idea of the war finally being at an end.

He hadn't gotten thirty yards away from Rosamunde, however, when a terrible explosion ripped the air behind him.

Whirling, he caught sight of Margetta burning the net off and releasing a black-gold stream of her power like nothing he'd seen before. Ian and the other ruling mastyrs who hadn't been touched by the stream, began firing on her ruthlessly.

But it was the other sight, of Rosamunde caught in Margetta's battle power that turned his blood to ice.

With the mastyrs directing Margetta's last streaks of power in their direction, he teleported straight to Rosamunde. He caught her burning body in his arms, then moved her quickly to the grotto, where he'd felt the strength of the elf-lord power. He submerged her in water, except for her head. She'd been writhing. Now she grew still. Too still.

The damage to her hair, her face, her body, took his breath and wouldn't bring it back. He made weird gasping sounds until he could finally shout his anguish.

She wasn't dead, but he didn't see how she could ever recover from these wounds.

His mind flew to his father, to Davido and to Kaden.

Kaden had healed her before when Margetta had burned her.

Kaden! He shouted telepathically. *Rosamunde is dying. Help me, father. Please help me.*

Though only a couple of seconds passed, it felt like an eternity before he heard Kaden's voice. *I'm coming, my son.*

Then Kaden was there, in the water beside him.

Kaden took her from Stone and held her close. He stood, as Stone did, waist deep in the water. He held Rosamunde to his chest.

Stone lifted his hands in supplication. He could do nothing else. The woman he loved was close to death and there was nothing he could do for her. He called on the Goddess and begged for her help, her love, her mercy.

Then he grew very still, very quiet.

If she died right now, he wasn't certain he wanted to live.

Kaden's eyes were closed and healing warmth emanated from his body, pouring into Rosamunde.

Even so, he could feel that her spirit hung between two worlds as though she longed to move on, uncertain if she should return.

Kaden opened his eyes. "You must call her back, Stone. Come closer and touch her very gently on the shoulder and call her back. I'm healing her, but her spirit refuses to re-enter her body."

~ ~ ~

Rosamunde stood behind a beautiful but very thin veil of familiar teal mist. She watched a woman playing with young goats. The woman's voice entered her mind, *I always loved how much you enjoyed your baby goats, my sweetheart daughter.*

Rosamunde didn't at first understand what she was seeing, then she knew. *Mama?*

The woman turned in her direction but made no move toward the veil that separated them. *You've become a beautiful woman, Rosamunde, and I'm so proud of you. My only regret was leaving you when I did, knowing you would have such a hard road ahead of you. But how well you've done on every front. You protected the Nine Realms for a thousand years. And now you've bonded with Mastyr Stone, a good, trustworthy man.*

Rosamunde reached toward the veil ready to touch it. Instinctively, she knew that all she had to do was whisk it aside, take several smallish steps, and she could be with her mother. Forever.

But she'd never be able to go back.

She held her fingers inches away from the mist veil.

Stone would be lost to her until his own death sometime in the future. She'd barely begun her life with him, a life apart from Ferrenden Peace.

Yet, she'd missed her mother so very much and this afterworld called to her soul as nothing else could. *I've missed you, Mama.*

Her mother tilted her head slightly. *And I missed getting to see you grow up.*

I'm so sorry that I disobeyed you and found my way through the mist. I know it was my fault you died that night.

Evelyn moved several steps toward the veil. *Oh, Sweetheart, you were never responsible for what my sister did. You were being adventurous and I loved that about you.*

But it got you killed.

Evelyn shrugged. *You'll find that once beyond the veil, at least this veil, such things don't matter. Time becomes a very fluid thing and letting go is the most important thing to do. I never blamed you for what happened. My sister had a bad heart and I sacrificed my own life to make sure you had a future. But I must know, did Margetta finally succeed in her schemes?*

Rosamunde shook her head. *We trapped her on the plains of Tannisford just a few minutes ago, the ruling mastyrs and I. It was an amazing experience to be part of a community and to work to save the Nine Realms. But, she killed me in the process. At the last minute, she used a stunning wave of elf-lord power and well, here I am, ready to join you.*

Rosamunde, listen to me. You're not dead, my darling girl, though, you're close. But you need to work very hard and return to the Nine Realms.

Rosamunde didn't understand. She felt very disconnected from her body, even from Stone. Besides, she felt the pull of the afterlife like nothing she'd ever experienced before. Her fingers trembled as she lifted her hand to the mist veil, closing within an inch.

She had no real connection to the physical realm any longer. The tug to take the next step was enormous, yet something held her back, a different kind of pull.

For a moment, she didn't know what it was, until in a very distant part of her telepathy she heard Stone's voice, *Come back to me, my love. Come back to me. I can't live without you. I won't want to. You're everything to me. Please, Rosamunde, come back. Please.*

Stone.

Her spirit shuddered. He sounded despairing and she didn't want him to feel that way. But she was so close to reuniting with her mother and to moving on. She should move on.

Except…

Stone's voice once more flowed through her mind. *I love you, Rosamunde. You're the sun, moon and stars to me, the reason the tides come and go and the planets fly through the night.*

Be with me, my love. Live with me as my blood rose and as my wife. I want children with you, to raise them with you, to create our own family. And we would have a small farm with goats, lots of goats, of all sizes. Your children will love them. Come back to me.

She responded at last by pathing his name. *Stone.*

~ ~ ~

When Stone heard his name telepathically, he doubled his efforts at winning Rosamunde away from the pull of death. *I love you, Rosamunde, with all my heart. I want you by my side. And I meant what I said, I want babies with you. You'd be a wonderful mother, only come back to me. Please.*

The whole time, tears rolled down his cheeks.

Kaden had one hand on Rosamunde's head and another on

Stone's shoulder. Most of her beautiful red hair was gone and the burns on her face and body were healing more slowly than they should have been; she was that close to death.

And the only reason he'd been able to reach her was Kaden's flow of elf-lord power that he'd added to Stone's channel.

But he'd heard her. She'd said his name.

Rosamunde, please come back. Please.

The moment of decision had come. Even through the distant path of death, he could feel that she had to decide. He needed to say one last thing to her, something that would turn her spirit in his direction. But what?

He recalled the look in her eye when she would transform into Aralynn and how, as Aralynn, she loved running on all four wolf paws. Then he knew what he needed to say to her. *Hundreds of wraith-pairs escaped into the Dauphaire Mountains. I need you to run missions with me ... as Aralynn. You've got to come back. Help me protect the innocent of our realm. We still have work to do here in the Nine Realms.*

~ ~ ~

Rosamunde heard his plea, but it was the word 'innocent' that struck her the hardest. She didn't want one more realm-person to die because of the Invictus scourge.

She met her mother's gaze and searched each beloved feature. Her mother nodded in understanding as though she didn't need words to know that the decision had been made.

I will always love you, daughter.

And I, you, Mama.

With that, she directed her spirit away from the afterworld.

However, the moment she returned to her body, she opened her mouth and screamed. The pain of the burns was like having her flesh scraped with a sharp blade.

She felt a second hand on her head and an increased healing warmth flow through her, easing every nerve ending. She felt the elf-lord power surround her. She was back in the water at the grotto, only this time both Stone and his father were with her.

She was back, she was safe and Kaden was healing her.

With that, she let go of consciousness and fell into a blissful dream state.

Sometime later, she woke up in a strange bed with a very low ceiling and walls that looked like shellacked dirt.

Ah, Joseph's lair.

Even thinking about the forest gremlin made her smile.

She heard voices in the hallway. "I made it for her, so I'll take it in." Joseph was complaining about something. Typical.

The she heard Davido whisper angrily, "Joseph, you give that tray to Stone, or by the Goddess I'll smack the back of your head so hard, all your teeth will pop out."

"Hunh. Fine." A fat raspberry followed.

Stone's voice came next. "There's a ruby in it for you, Joseph."

"Damn, but you were always a right one."

Davido again. "No, Joseph you're not going in there. In fact, you and I are leaving. I wish to pay compliments to your lovely wife."

"That woman is an avaricious she-devil, but her hips. Dear, Sweet Goddess, her hips. Did I ever tell you she has these delightful rolls that I hold onto when I'm pumping like a diesel engine on crack?"

"Stubble it, you lecherous forest vermin."

Their voices disappeared at the same time Stone appeared with a tea tray in the doorway of the bedroom. "You are awake. Davido said you were, but I had a hard time believing it."

She stretched. Her back ached in a few places as did her shoulders and knees. "How long have I been asleep?"

"Four nights, my love."

"That long? Oh, well that explains my thirst, my hunger and all these unusual pains." As he rounded the side of the bed, she sat up then arranged two pillows behind her. She was wearing a soft cotton nightgown, though she had no idea whose it was. All 'the Queen's' clothes would have been destroyed in the fire and she didn't keep sleeping gear at the cottage.

She realized suddenly that her head felt very cold. She reached up to touch her hair, but there was little left of her thick red mane, just a short couple of curly inches. "Oh, my."

He smiled. "Kaden assured me it will grow back."

She stared at him for a moment. She didn't care about her hair, not really. She did, however, have a critical question. "Stone, please tell me, did Margetta escape the net?"

His lips formed a grim line as he shook his head. "Seth, Quinlan and Ian burned her to a crisp, literally. She's nothing but ashes now. We saw to it, I promise you."

She put a hand to her chest as tears burned her eyes. "Oh, thank the Goddess. She's gone."

"She is. And there's been nothing be celebrating for the past several nights, though Harris tells me his Guardsmen have made more drunken arrests during this time than in the past century."

She smiled as he settled the tray over her lap. He poured the tea and she took in the aroma. "Joseph makes the best tea."

"That he does. He almost refused to let me bring the tray into you, though."

"I heard." She chuckled softly.

"You did?"

"I did. And what a pretty little silver dome covering the plate. In fact, it looks like something we used to have at the castle." She gasped. "That damn gremlin! He must have taken it. Well, no surprise there." She lifted the lid, but instead of a couple of slices of toast, sitting on a small black velvet pillow was a ring of Joseph's she'd once admired, with a row of small green Peridot stones. The band was in antique silver. "What's this?"

"Joseph said you liked this one, so I bought it for you."

She glanced up at him, her throat tight with tears. "Did he tell you why I liked it?"

Stone shook his head. The room was very small, especially for a man of Stone's proportions. He was already bent over to keep from hitting the ceiling. He looked around and reached for a broad stool that he pulled close to the bed.

He sat down and took her hand in his. "No, Joseph never told me anything, only that he thought you would want this one."

"It was a few weeks ago and I was only Aralynn to you then, but the moment I saw these stones I thought they looked like your eyes. That's why I admired the ring. I mean your eyes have a deeper, richer color, but the shade was very similar."

He took their joined hands and covered it with his free one then leaned down and kissed her fingers. "We were meant to be together, Rosamunde. That's what I believe."

"Me, too."

He appeared to search her face. "Thank you for coming back."

She had to think for a moment to understand what he meant. Then she remembered her mother behind the teal veil. "Mama was there."

"Then it was no wonder you wanted to stay."

"It wasn't that. Yes, it was amazing to see her and I longed to be with her. But, the pull of death is a profound force. Stone, I was so close to leaving the Nine Realms forever."

"I know."

"But now I feel bad, because of why I returned. It should have been for my love for you. Instead, the moment you spoke of more innocent people dying, that's when I made the decision. How will you ever forgive me for not loving you enough?"

He squeezed her hand. "Rosamunde, I love you even more for returning because other innocents will die without your help." He leaned close and kissed her on the lips. Nothing could have felt more perfect.

When he drew back, he wore a soft, affectionate smile. "Will you marry me, Rosamunde?"

She loved that he wanted it all, the blood rose bond and a marriage that would involve a riotous ceremony. With any luck, she would be pregnant on the day of her wedding, a sign of good fortune and blessings among the fae.

She was overcome as tears spilled from her eyes.

He picked up the ring and slid it on her left ring finger. "Marry me, my love. And let the wearing of this ring be a token of our pledge to each other. So what do you say?"

The ring fit as though made for her, but she suspected Joseph had something to do with it, the finagler that he was. "I will marry you, Stone, with all my heart."

Embrace the Power

~ ~ ~

The wedding a month later, which Delia organized to perfection, turned out to be one of the largest events in Nine Realms' history and lasted three days. Stone took his bride from realm-to-realm and danced with her at immense balls that celebrated the end of Margetta's terror-filled assault on their world and the beginning of what Rosamunde had said more than once would be a thousand years of peace.

Now that he was married, he wanted a family, something he'd never allowed himself to desire before. With the Vampire Guards in each realm hunting down the last of the wraith-pairs and much of Margetta's army in a state of rehabilitation through the efforts of Samantha and Ethan, he could finally start to think like an ordinary man.

When he'd drunk the last of the champagne at the final Tannisford welcoming-home ball, he took Rosamunde to the lake house, now made private and secure once more.

She shed her full-skirted green satin gown, green diamonds in an elegant piece around her neck, and kicked off her high heels.

Since she now stood in only a thong, he stripped down as fast as he could as well, caught her around the waist in a slick levitating move then carried her to bed.

He made love to her for hours and more than once played with her short red hair. He told her at least a hundred times how much he loved her.

When she lay in his arms exhausted, she twirled a finger through his long hair. "How many children do you want?" Her voice sounded lazy, a very satisfied woman.

"Davido once told me he has eighty-eight children and more progeny than he can number. I'd like to best his goal."

At that, she rose up from his arms and stared down at him. "I beg to remind you that the man had more than one wife, and that over a period of millennia."

Because she was naked, her posture put her breasts very close to his mouth. He did what any normal male would do, and suckled his way to pushing her back into the pillows.

She laughed, but was soon cooing her need for him and he obliged her.

~ ~ ~

Rosamunde awoke that evening to the smell of coffee with cardamom. How long ago it all seemed that she was alone in her castle, removed from a normal life, stuck supporting the veil of mist by herself.

Now she lay in bed aware that this was one of her most favorite times of the night: The beginning. Stone always rose before her and made the coffee. And once the sun set fully, he would have a swim in the lake.

She wasn't sure if he checked on her to see if she was finally opening her eyes or if the blood rose bond told him the state she was in. She suspected the latter, though he often told her he liked to watch her when she slept.

He was the most surprising man, so tender and loving with her, yet a commander in the field.

Her heart was full for two reasons. She'd built an extra supply for him and she was so in love with the vampire.

She sighed contentedly and a moment later he appeared in

the doorway with two mugs in hand. He wore only jeans, a great look for him, which meant that his gorgeous, tattoo-laden chest was on display.

She didn't stay in bed, though, because she knew what he wanted and she wanted it, too.

She dragged the gray afghan from the foot of the bed and pulled it around her. He set both mugs on the small table next to the large chair, then sat down and held his arms out to her.

She climbed into his lap and he adjusted her until she was nestled against his chest and feeling as though life could never be sweeter. He then handed her cup to her and afterward picked up his own.

As she sipped her coffee, she watched the sky grow darker and the stars twinkle. With her realm-vision, she could adjust from night to a warm afternoon glow.

She loved her world and her husband.

Suddenly, she felt a quickening deep in her body. She gasped softly and tears sprouted to her eyes as awareness dawned.

"What's wrong?" he asked.

"Nothing. It's wonderful."

"The view?"

"The view inside." She leaned toward the table and put her mug next to his then took his hand and settled it low on her abdomen.

He frowned as he glanced at her stomach, then met her gaze. "Why are you—" His eyes widened suddenly. "Sweet Goddess, we've created life."

"We have. Can you feel her as well?"

"I can. And she's a girl. I know that as well. She'll have violet eyes but my black hair. What a miracle this has become." He kissed her after that, then took her to bed once more.

Rosamunde got lost in the beauty of her relationship with Stone. He took her to the heights, he fed from her, he communed with her as together they channeled the elf-lord power.

He told her he loved her. Again and again.

She hugged him hard and thanked him for their daughter.

He said he wanted to name her Evelyn Inez.

She wept again, and embraced him harder still.

Love had come to her and the sweet joy of giving her love so fully to Stone.

Together, they would build a life in Tannisford Realm, serving the people they both loved, no longer fearing what was beyond the veil, in this life, or the next.

The End

A Note From Caris

I hope you enjoyed reading EMBRACE THE POWER! And remember, you can claim a free e-Book right now by signing up for my mailing list on my home page: www.carisroane.com/

If you enjoyed EMBRACE THE POWER, I'd love it if you took a minute to leave a short review – two or three sentences only -- at your favorite online retailer. And you don't have to be a blogger to do this, just a reader who loves books!

Coming Up Next

REVEALED, Book #3 of the Rapture's Edge Saga: As the third story of the Rapture's Edge Saga and set in the world of the Guardians of Ascension, REVEALED is the culmination story for Rachel and Duncan. Revealed also prepares the stage for more to come with the Warriors of the Blood. Both Luken and Endelle are featured in REVEALED. Read more about the Rapture's Edge Saga: **www.carisroane.com/raptures-edge/**

EMERALD FLAME: The next story set in the world of Five Bridges will be the fifth book of the Flame Series and features Alpha Wolf Warren. Read more about the Flame Series: **www. carisroane.com/flame-series/**

About the Author

Caris Roane is the New York Times bestselling author of thirty-five paranormal romance books. Writing as Valerie King, she has published fifty novels and novellas in Regency Romance. Caris lives in Phoenix, Arizona, loves gardening, enjoys the birds and lizards in her yard, but really doesn't like scorpions!

Find out more about Caris on her website!

www.carisroane.com

Author of

Guardians of Ascension Series – Warriors of the Blood crave the *breh-hedden*

Dawn of Ascension Series – Militia Warriors battle to save Second Earth

Rapture's Edge Series – Militia Warriors, Luken and Endelle battle to save Third Earth

Blood Rose Series – Only a blood rose can fulfill a mastyr vampire's deepest needs

Blood Rose Tales – Short tales of mastyr vampires who hunger to be satisfied

Men in Chains Series – Vampires struggle to get free of their chains and save the world

The Flame Series – Hunky 'Alter' warriors battle for control of their world

CPSIA information can be obtained
at www.ICGtesting.com
Printed in the USA
FSOW02n1104090217
30618FS